The Diar

Brother Prious

Cornwall 106s

The Tale of
The Brother, The Father, And The Knight.

Ray Tyrrell

Published by New Generation Publishing in 2021

First Edition

ISBN
Paperback	978-1-80031-179-4
Hardback	978-1-80031-178-7
Ebook	978-1-80031-177-0

www.newgeneration-publishing.com

New Generation Publishing

Prologue

189 AD

Lucius Artoris Castus stood on the watchtower beside the western gate and gazed across the gently undulating moorland beyond the river.

The sun was rising in the east, but he couldn't feel its heat on his back. It was masked by the low ceiling of grey clouds which threatened rain and held a mist low across the moors in the dawn light. The warmth he felt came from the woollen shirt he wore beneath his heavy leather tabard, and the hooded fur cloak that was fastened at his throat and tied at his waist. He wore no body armour that day, but his unique cavalry sword parted the front of his cloak and raised it behind his knees.

The fort of Nemetostatio stood high on a ridge and looked down on the ford below, the lowest crossing point of the River Taw. From there, the river flowed north, tumbling down its steep-sided valley. It was joined by many streams, all adding to its power, until it widened into its estuary on the north coast, where the waters of the Torr from the west, and the Yeo from the east, helped it battle with the tides at its mouth.

Pushing a stray lock of long, dark hair back into his hood, he looked to his left, to the south. His hair was too long for a Roman officer, but then he was not a typical Roman.

Within three thousand paces, the land thrust up into high moorland hills, which were still capped with recent snow. Even in the summer months the high moors were impassable, and to their south, the River Tamar was a barrier to travel, from the moor to Tamaris on the southern sea. No-one could enter or leave the south-west peninsular without being seen from the fort.

Smiling to himself, his eyes turned to the camp. It marked the boundary of Roman rule in the south-west. The paved road from Isca Dumnoniorum rose steadily for some twelve hundred feet over seventeen miles before it ended at the ford. These roads allowed the 20th Legion of Rome, Valeria Victrix, to march rapidly across the province, to wherever they were needed, keeping the peace or putting down rebellion.

The Romans had been in Britain for almost two hundred and fifty years now, but they had ceased their conquest at borders where the cost of controlling the tribes, in both men and resources, became greater than the benefits.

Hadrian had built a wall in the north, to keep the Picts and Scots at bay. Tribune Artoris had fought many years in the north. It had not been an easy time.

They had ceased their advance too along the rivers and forests of the west, keeping the Welsh in their hills. He had fought there too, for a short time, before being ordered south. Here, on the edge of Little Wales, Nemetostatio was the fort from which the Romans kept the Dumnonii, and the far Cornovii, at bay. Tribes all over Britain had stories to tell of the Roman Horse Warrior, and of how he looked in his Roman Armour on horseback, so very distinctive.

The fort had been deliberately built on the Sacred Groves, the Nemeton, of the Dumnonii. It was a display of Roman power that infuriated the native Dumnonii and had led to much bloodshed at the time. To the native Celts of the Cornovii, the Sacred Groves were named Celliwig, but were just as sacred nonetheless.

Artoris had been in command at Nemetostatio, Road Fort of the Sacred Groves, for six years now. His Vexillatio had diminished in strength over the twenty years it had served in Britain. Originally it had been two cohorts in strength, almost a thousand strong, four hundred and eighty cavalry and four hundred and eighty supporting infantry, all auxiliary volunteers, fighting for their Roman conquerors.

Artoris had brought the cavalry from lands far to the north and east of Rome where the tribes seemed to live their entire lives on horseback, and where he had been born and had grown to manhood, the son of the Roman Governor. The infantry came from northern Gaul, where Artoris had blooded his newly trained cavalry, and he had gained a healthy respect for the fighting men of that region.

Although their leaders liked to ride at their head, the Roman Army hated cavalry. They hated fighting them, and they hated fighting with them. To be made an officer of cavalry was to have your career ended. Artoris was not an ordinary Roman officer however. He had grown up with horses, understood their strengths, and he knew what cavalry could do best. His men fought for him, not for Rome. If they survived twenty years in service they would become citizens of Rome. Very few did, but in the meantime they enjoyed relatively comfortable lives, if they fought well and stayed alive.

The Fort held the two hundred and seventy cavalry, and the one hundred and fifty infantry that remained. There had been a few replacements in the early years, of infantry only. Once a cavalryman was down he was lost to the cohort.

Some had died in battle, some of disease, but their reputation had grown amongst the tribes of Britain. These did not like cavalry either, but in their case it was because they knew what it was to fight them, especially when led by Artoris. He had become a legend to those he fought, and he had even won encounters without a fight, his enemy backing away when his helmet and breastplate were seen at the head of his cavalry.

His sword had become a legend too, as famous as he. It had been forged by Arab craftsmen in the far east of Roman control. It had been a gift to Artoris' father, who in turn had given it to Artoris as a leaving present when he left to take up his command.

It was an unusual shape compared to western swords. It was of comparable length to a single-handed war sword, far longer than a Roman gladius. The blade was of comparable width too, but it curved gently away from the strike blade and had a full cupped hand guard. It was beautifully balanced and ideal for fighting on horseback.

It also had engraving in Arabic on each side of the blade, near the handle. It was spindly scratching to most, but Artoris knew its meaning. One side said 'take me up'; the other said 'cast me away'.

Instantly recognisable to his Celtic foes over the last six years, they had given it a name, 'Calesvol', meaning 'battle-hardened'. Hearing the name, his men had Romanised it into 'Calivo'. With no clear translation, it became 'Out of Calivo', 'Excalivo'.

Artoris heard movement below, then the heavy creak of the ladder.

"May I join you, Sir?"

The voice was that of his closest friend, his Second in Command, Centurion Castor Locro, the only other Roman in the Vexillatio.

"Of course Castor, my friend, but it is no warmer up here!" Castor laughed as he climbed into the tower's open-sided watch platform. He too had a fur cloak pulled around him. He had removed his armour, and having no hood on his cloak, was bare headed. His hair was a mid-brown and close cropped; far more Roman. He lent on the rail beside Artoris.

"I am damp and cold to the bone after last night's ride, but I'm glad we pressed on and got back before this storm brews properly. Those two wagons would have bogged down, they're cursed heavy. I'll be glad when the summer comes."

It had been the clamour of the Century's return that had woken Artoris a little earlier than normal that day. He had walked to the watch tower chewing on some cold lamb, climbed up and given the two guards a break. He wanted a few moments peace before Castor came to report. He knew his Centurion would seek him out and find him there.

Apart from guarding the narrows, their main role was to keep the track open and secure between Nemetostatio and the small Fort at Deventiasteno, or Nanstallon to the Celts, about forty-five miles further south-west.

Like Nemetostatio, Deventiasteno stood above a ford, this one crossing the River Camel. A small signal station on a beacon just five miles to its south, above the River Fowey, meant that the Romans controlled movement in this area too.

The small garrison was out on quite a limb however, and had often had to hold out desperately from native attacks, awaiting the next regular column from Nemetostatio, and regular they were. It wasn't just the safety of the garrison that meant most to Artoris, it was the tin they escorted back that was both his and Rome's main concern.

The Celts had panned for tin and sold it to ship-borne merchants for very many years, but on a fairly small scale, even finding a little silver, and more often a little gold. The Romans brought their mining knowhow with them, and they had opened two tin mines close to Deventiasteno, near the Cornovii villages of Carnanton and Treloy.

"Your breastplate and helm are back in your quarters. Your man is drying them off."

Artoris grinned broadly at him, his dark skin crinkling around his eyes and giving away his age. He was just forty. Many didn't live that long, let alone after years as a soldier.

"You had no trouble then?" he asked. Castor turned and gazed into the same distance as Artoris.

"None Sir, your armour sees to that. It has saved many lives"

"It has my friend, but it has cost many lives to have such a reputation, including Roman ones."

Castor didn't answer. His head nodded slightly. They had fought together for the last twelve years; he didn't need to say anything.

Castor had been a replacement officer, and one that had lived, mainly because he was comfortable fighting on horseback. Artoris had established a reputation for getting through Second Officers. More importantly, Castor had won the respect of the men, not an easy task for a new officer amongst veterans.

When they had first arrived in the south-west, Artoris had led every column himself, and soon became an instantly recognisable figure to both Dumnonii and Cornovii warriors. They learnt to fear his presence. He never attacked first, always allowing his enemy a chance not to fight, but if they did he was merciless in victory. It took little time for the tribes to realise that if Artoris was there, rebellion and attacks on Romans meant death.

One of the first columns Artoris did not lead himself was badly mauled by Cornovii, led by Celtic priests who were still angry at the Roman desecration of so many of their holy sites. It was Castor who first suggested that whoever led the column should wear Artoris' body armour and helm. Artoris readily agreed, retaining Excalivo however, which was already a legend but was not recognisable from a distance.

It worked well. The legend of the man, the sight of his armour, kept the tribes at bay.

Artoris broke the silence.

"I'm going to stay here, Castor."

"What do you mean, Sir?"

"In the spring, when my twenty years are up. You will take command of the Vexillatio, and I'm going to stay. I'm going to make a home here, here in Dumnonia."

"You're not going back to Rome?" The surprise was clear in Castor's voice. It made Artoris smile.

"Rome is hardly home to me. It never was, and my boyhood home holds nothing for me now."

"Have you thought where, exactly?"

"Under your protection, my friend. Over there." He pointed northwards. "Beyond the marching camp, about another mile."

Just to the north of Nemetostatio was the outline of the ditched surrounds of a marching camp that once held four cohorts, a relic of the early troubled years in the south-west. It was still used occasionally, but didn't have the wooden buildings that their permanent road station did.

"It's a perfect spot for a small settlement. Most importantly, Guineve loves it." He looked directly at Castor for a moment, and Castor could see instantly that he was absolutely serious. Legionnaires were not allowed to marry in service, but his were auxiliaries and he was Artoris.

"I have learnt to love this land, and it is Guineve's land. There are over sixty who finish their twenty years in the spring and wish to remain here. They were all with me in Gaul at the start of all this." He paused. "You won't get replacements, you know?"

"I know."

"If you want me to get you transferred, I will try." Castor shook his head slowly.

"Once a cavalry man, Artoris, always a cavalry man. You told me that when we first met." He only called him by name in their closest moments, when like most Romans, they spoke in Greek.

"Yes, there is that, but Vexillatio life has not been so bad has it?" There was almost a real moment of doubt in the question.

"No Artoris, it's not been too bad." He chuckled and smiled as he said it, "and I'll be proud to lead what's left."

Artoris slapped a hand down on his shoulder.

"I should have told you sooner, but I wanted to see if some of the men would stay with me. Most of the married ones wish to stay. I'll show you the place later, you'll know it, the Celts call it Tawetona, but we'll call it Celliwig, after the Sacred Groves that stood here. It overlooks the river, on a stream, defensible. It's perfect. With wives and children it will be a sound settlement."

"Well, leave room for me. I may retire earlier than you think!"

"Not you Castor, I need you to wear my armour and protect us."

Castor's reply remained unspoken as the ladder creaked below them. The two guards were returning, so he just nodded.

Howel, King of Cornwall, had cursed the name of King Arthur many times in the last few weeks, but now he, and the bedraggled remnants of his once proud army, owed him their lives.

It was over seven hundred years since Artoris had settled in Celliwig, Tawetona. Within two years his Vexillatio was disbanded, the cavalry reassigned to the 20th Legion and the infantry spread around new outposts on the Peninsular.

Castor never wore Artoris' armour once Artoris had retired, and when the Vexillatio broke up, he left the Legion and joined Artoris, bringing the armour with him. Artoris still bore Excalivo.

For over two hundred years, Artoris' and Castor's descendants lived at Celliwig under Roman rule. The Romans had changed tactics in West Wales, expanding the number of small stations and trading with the native Dumnonii and Cornovii. Most importantly, they built a port at Ictis Insula, a small island in a large bay on the south coast, and traded tin with the Cornovii.

Occasionally, Celliwig was threatened and the head of the village would don Artoris' armour, take up Excalivo, and lead the defence of the village, or indeed, the area, uniting with anyone else so threatened, but they were always led by the legend that was Artoris.

The Romans left West Wales in the late three hundreds, and left Britain altogether in the early four hundreds, leaving the country exposed to many threats for hundreds of years.

Celliwig, Tawentona, became too difficult to defend without new ditches and ramparts. British tribes were being pushed west by the slow but steady Saxon advance. They all needed land so badly that they would fight for it. Artoris was busy. Still an instantly recognisable figure, whoever wore his armour. He was still held in awe by those he fought, but as the British tongue mixed with Celtic and Dumnonium, Artoris was corrupted to Arthur, and Excalivo to Excalibur.

Eventually, in 620 AD, Artoris' descendants left Tawetona and moved further west. They took a long time to find the right home. It was only because of the famous Roman body armour of Arthur, that Perdred, the head of the family at that time, was granted title to the remarkable natural fortress of Tintagel, by King Mark of Cornwall.

They renamed their new home Celliwig, of course, and continued to document the history of the family. A history which they had kept since Artoris' death: a promise to him on his death bed by his friend Castor.

For more than three hundred years they lived in their fortress home. They were visited by Kings and envoys from across the land and still, when threatened, Arthur led their defence. Attacks came from Viking raids and

Irish pirates, and later from Danes. Occasionally Bretons would attack the south coast, but when Arthur was there he was always victorious. His legend grew to the point that the Kings of Cornwall and Devon, tribal leaders, every one, would unquestioningly serve under Arthur's banner. When it was unfurled and he was there, in his polished breastplate, greaves and red-crested helm, all would follow. To give him the authority to command Kings he inevitably became King Arthur, and Excalibur became his legendary source of power.

By 930 AD, the Saxons had conquered most of Britain, halting along the same natural boundaries as the Romans had done almost a thousand years before. Although they had pushed further into Devon, Cornwall remained an independent Kingdom. England however had finally become one Kingdom, united under the banner of its first King, Athelstan.

King Howel visited Celliwig in an aggressive frame of mind. He had been greeted and feasted by Bardrel, bearer of Excalibur, in his fortress home. It was now a stone castle, unassailable on its mount, joined to the shore by a track that crossed a solid rock bridge from the shoreline. One day, the sea that had formed the natural fortress would eat away the connecting rock, making it an island. Then, however, the castle gates at the end of the bridge made it impregnable.

Howel felt confident; encouraged by the wine for which Bardrel was renowned.

They had eaten in the Great Hall, but now it had been cleared, leaving only Bardrel and his Steward, Randfel, to talk with Howel and his son Howerd. They sat at a table before a large fireplace, taller than a man and twice as wide. The table was round with arm chairs surrounding it. Twenty four, Howerd noted. Bardrel spoke first.

"So my King, what really brings you to our table?"

"Athelstan. Did you doubt it, Bardrel?"

"No, Sire. I hear he has kicked the Danes out of the North and pushed the Welsh back across the border. Given your recent moves, I imagine we are next."

"He calls himself King of all England, with all the ancient boundaries once more under single rule, but he won't stop at the old boundaries unless we stop him. He has ruled for twelve years now and he's forty-one years old. We just have to keep him at bay a few more years. When he dies his Kingdom will crumble. The new King will have greater difficulties than us."

"And so you chose this time to cause him problems? It seems a strange strategy!"

Howel visibly stiffened, holding back his anger. He wasn't used to being questioned and few would have had the confidence to do so.

"If I just waited for him to come he could choose the time to suit himself. He still has troubles in the north. He can't concentrate all his forces against us. I have united the Peninsular against him. Cornishmen, Devonians, all the British that fled here. I have Irish and Danish mercenaries." He paused and looked directly into Bardrel's eyes. What did he have to say to this man?

"I have come here from Exeter. We have taken all of Devon. The Bishop cowers in his Cathedral in Crediton. I have shown Athelstan strength. He will respect me." Bardrel shook his head looking at the table top in front of him. He looked up.

"You have shown him he must deal with you first before you become a greater threat." Howel slammed the table with his fist.

"Damn you Bardrel, I need Arthur to lead my army against Athelstan. With you at the head we will be invincible. They squabble and vie for reward under me. It is another battle just keeping the army together, but they would all rally to Arthur's banner and with belief of victory."

There was a long pause as Bardrel sat back and looked at Randfel, who was trying to keep any emotion from showing in his face. Howerd was mesmerised, he had never heard anyone debate with his father before.

"I cannot do that. I will not have Arthur fight an aggressive battle of conquest." The silence was tangible.

"You will lose my friendship, Bardrel. We may even become enemies."

"I fear, my King, that I doubt you will live long enough for that to be a problem to me, or my family. However, Arthur will do one thing for you." He could see Howel's knuckles white as he gripped the table's edge in an effort to control his anger. "Arthur will gather his forces and march to Tawton, our old home. We will occupy the old fortress above the ford and hold it should Athelstan reach there, in defence of our homeland. Let us pray it will be a wasted trip!"

It wasn't wasted however. An extremely angry King Howel returned to Exeter to discover that Athelstan and an army almost the size of his, was marching through Dorset towards him.

Part of him was cautious and told him to prepare Exeter for a siege, but he did not have the solid support of the city, and he feared treachery. As the English army closed from the east, he marched south a few miles and took up position on Haldon Hill. The English would have to attack up a very steep slope.

He could not lose, but lose he did, and badly. His army was ill-disciplined and untried. The English were battle-hardened from fighting Danes in the north and Welsh in the west. They were simply tougher and experienced. It was slaughter.

King Howel led the survivors along the old Roman road north of the moors. Athelstan rested his army before pursuing. He sent a Company south to clear out any rebels south of the moors. They were to swing west below the moors and halt at the Tamar. No rebel should remain alive on what he deemed the English side. He would lead the rest of his force north of the moors and drive the Cornish the length of Cornwall and into the sea. He wanted the Cornish in their place for once and for all.

About one thousand Cornish and Devonians reached the ford near Tawton, as Tawetona was now called. Its name had changed in 905 AD when the Synod of Canterbury created the See of Devon. Werstan became the first Bishop of Devon and built his first wooden Cathedral in Tawton. He died two years later, replaced by Bishop Putta, who himself died on a trip to meet King Edward in Crediton some years later. He was buried in Crediton and King Edward ordered the See to be moved there out of respect for Putta.

Bardrel was at Tawton as he had promised. He led almost one hundred mounted men. They were well equipped with swords and light spears, but also each man carried a short bow and a quiver of crafted arrows, true and fletched.

His second son, Remband, wore Arthur's armour that day. It simply wouldn't fit Bardrel. He hadn't worn it for a number of years now, but he bore Excalibur, as was his right. They rode a sweep behind Howel's retreating rabble. They were all encouraged by the sight of Arthur leading the column of cavalry as it raced across the van' of the English.

The English had heard of King Arthur, he was timeless, a legend they told stories to their children about. They sent word urgently back to their King. Athelstan broke camp immediately he heard the rumours and rushed his army in pursuit.

All that day, Arthur harried the English advance, a volley of arrows from the cover of trees, a pass with lances across the advance skirmishers, but the English came on steadily.

As night fell the harriers returned to the old Roman fort, the smaller of the two. The larger camp, slightly to the south, was too big, even if the ditches and banks had been in better condition. With the numbers they had, the small one was more defendable. The ditch was still deep and the bank still steep and high, even without the wooden rampart that had once stood around it. The wooden buildings had long gone too as had, most importantly, the eastern gate.

The numbers in the fort had grown however, since they had left. To Bardrel's delight, and surprise, many of the retreating Irish and Danish mercenaries had joined those preparing the camp. They had nowhere else to go. The boats that had brought them had long gone.

The old Roman road ran between the camps before descending to the ford. The land to the east was fairly flat open moorland that sloped gently down. It was the same to the south until the hills rose into the high moors. The English could advance a shield wall and wrap it around them with ease, trapping defenders into a fight to the death. It would cost them lives, but they would win easily by pure weight of numbers.

Across the ford the land was a little more rugged. It undulated gently for a few miles before becoming real moorland, but not high moors. All Bardrel could hope to do was delay the English enough to give King Howel a chance to gain some ground to the south-west towards Cornwall, before leading his men on the forty mile dash due west to Tintagel. They would be safe there; besieged for a time perhaps, but safe.

It would be death for the Danes and Irish though. With no mounts, they would be hounded down by their foe. The English had no cavalry to speak of but they had purpose.

Bardrel called a council of his older men and the Irish and Danish leaders. They sat in the centre of the old fort around a good fire. There was nothing to hide. In fact he wanted the English to know he was there.

They talked for over an hour, examining possibilities, teasing out ideas. The Danes and Irish numbered about forty each, eighty foot warriors. Almost everything suggested meant the certain death of those on foot. Bardrel wouldn't agree to anything that didn't give them some chance, and his men agreed.

A conclusion reached, they broke up to wait for the dawn. They had a small screen of scouts out just in case the English came in the night, but he was sure they would not, and they did not, so everyone was in place at dawn.

Their plan relied on the English acting as one would expect them to, so it could go wrong from the outset. Every hour past dawn that they did not come would mean Howel was further west, but the English did not keep them long.

They knew the camp was defended, but not by how many. The camp fires were all in the small camp and they did not expect the Cornish to sacrifice many men in a hopeless stand.

Athelstan deployed his army a mile to the east, in good sight up the gentle slope to the forts. To commit too many men would make it hard to manoeuvre, so he sent forward two companies in a fighting line. Two ranks in the centre, a single line on each flank; two hundred and fifty men aligned on the small fort. When their centre reached the ramparts, the wings would fold around encircling the defenders.

They marched forward singing and banging their brightly painted round wood and leather shields with the hilts of their swords. It was a daunting sound to the unbloodied, a noisy mass of colour and death moving steadily towards them.

They were expecting flights of arrows but none came. Instead the Irish came, over the east rampart and ditch and charging down the slope, making nearly as much noise as the English; just forty men in a headlong charge at the English line, slightly to the left of its centre. It was the last thing the English expected.

Before the Irish reached the English, the Danes rose from hiding behind the banks of the larger fort, and shouting loudly, charged at the English left. As the Irish hit the centre with a clash of wood and steel the Danes drove into the English left. Inevitably, hit in the centre and from their left, the English right began to pivot around the Irish to envelop them. At that moment the figure of Arthur, mounted in full body armour, led almost a hundred cavalrymen over the brow of the river course and into view. They thundered at the rear of the English right, exposed by trying to surround the Irish.

The English were in a panic. Those in the centre and on the left were fighting man to man with hardened professionals, and although they were veterans too, it was not the easy fight they had expected. Their confidence was shaken. Their right was shattered by the cavalry charge. Hit from behind as they turned, they were in no way prepared for the raw power and weight of the horses.

Arthur's cavalry cut them down as they ran. Many dropped their weapons as they tried to avoid both swords and hooves. Arthur screamed to his men. Those who heard him broke right and began to sweep around behind the English line that was beginning to give ground in their uncertainty. The sight of the cavalry manoeuvring to get behind them and cut off any retreat was too much, even for the strongest minded. They turned and ran.

Arthur's men hit them once from the side as they fled. More companies of English advanced towards them. Athelstan had watched the debacle develop, but they were too far back to do anything about it in time to affect the outcome.

Arthur's horsemen disengaged and rode back towards the Irish and Danes who were cheering and shouting obscenities after the English. It was now that Bardrel's plan became a risk. The horsemen steadied their mounts and sheathed their weapons. Bending forward with an arm outstretched, many helped an Irishman or Dane climb up behind them, where they hung on grimly.

The Irish and Danes had lost about eighteen as far as Bardrel could see. He didn't think he had lost any cavalrymen. No there was one empty horse. With an Irishman behind him, he headed for the ford and waded his horse across, climbing the far bank.

"Away Father, we will hold the ford a while." It was Arthur commanding him, his son Remband. He raised a hand and rode on, his burden clinging to his waist.

There were over thirty left at the ford. They grouped in fours, three handing the reins of their mounts to the fourth as they jumped down from their saddles. Those dismounted freed their bows from their bundles and untied their quivers. They would not stay long, just long enough to loose a dozen arrows each at the English as they neared the opposite bank, and enough time to give those double mounted a good start to ensure they could not be caught.

The English line reached the forts and split around them. The air hissed as arrows arced over the ford and tore into their centre. Those on the road between the forts crouched behind their shields as the arrows struck. Many were wounded, some were killed.

Far on the English left, upstream of the ford, it was possible, if awkward, to wade across the river, but the company of flanking English archers did just that. Soaked from the chest down, they formed up loosely and sent a volley of arrows into Arthur's men before drawing swords and charging along the bank towards them.

Their arrows struck from long range, arcing down from above unexpectedly. Eight were hit, including Arthur. The arrow sliced into his neck, just inside the edge of his breastplate, just below the collar of his helm. It penetrated downwards into his chest. He staggered, calling to his men to mount and leave the ford until blood filled his mouth. His hand held the arrow but it didn't help. He reached his horse before his legs gave from under him and he slid into darkness.

Twenty one rode from the ford to catch their twin-mounted comrades, accompanied by fourteen riderless horses. Two days later they were all within the castle walls at Tintagel.

Bardrel was distraught. He had lost a son, and he had lost Arthur's body armour. He stood alone on the keep tower staring out to sea. His left hand gripped Excalibur's leather bound hilt as tears began to run down his cheeks and into his beard.

King Athelstan of England was standing on the bank of the large fort above the ford, where the watchtower had once stood. At his feet lay the polished greaves, breast plate and red feather crested galea of Lucius Artoris Castus. They were piled on top of his leather tabard which was laced with iron platelets. All had been stripped from the body of Remband, son of Bardrel of Celliwig.

"Even a legend can die, Sire."

"Indeed, my Lord Egbert, but I'm not sure he is quite dead yet. What of this sword he is supposed to have carried?" Athelstan turned his gaze to his War Lord.

"Of that there is no sign, Sire. It was not near the body, although he was wearing a sword, a very ordinary sword."

"Well, at least the army is in good spirits now. A victory at Halden, the death of the legend Arthur, we will not stop now. On into Cornwall, my Lord, we'll put these Celts down once and for all." He looked down again. "Get all this moved to the Church in Tawton. Tell them to take it to Bishop

Aethelgar at Crediton. He is to keep it safe until I come for it. He is to let no-one have it but me, I do not want this legend reborn."

"Do we follow Howel's army, Sire, or the horsemen? The army went south-west, the horsemen west."

"The army, my Lord, most definitely," then he added, "West to where though?"

"The wounded horseman died before we could get much from him, Sire, but it would appear they come from a place on the north Cornish coast called Tintagel, a place they call Celliwig in Celtic."

"Celliwig?" Athelstan formed the sounds carefully.

"Yes, Sire. It means Sacred Groves in Celtic: Camelot in Saxon."

2010 AD

I slowed as the bright yellow reflecting boards of the thirty limit signs glared in my headlights from each side of the road. They had a semi-circle at the top, containing the top half of the thirty limit sign, with a rectangular name board at the bottom. They announced our arrival at Tregony. Gone were the old roundels on poles and the large white wrought iron name sign that I remembered so well. They had stood a hundred yards or more nearer the town. The new signs struck me as far less subtle. I had to slow further as the road swung right and began the run of 'traffic calming' obstacles that spanned the entrance to the Roseland School, before a left took me past the old vet's practice on the straight towards the main street.

I could have gone beyond Bodmin to Fraddon and cut down to St Cornelly Church without having to come through St Austell, or Tregony, but somehow, driving through Tregony let me say sorry to the town for what I was about to do.

There was no traffic about in Cornwall at three in the morning, particularly at this time of year, so driving through the town added to the risk of being noticed, but I had swept that thought aside. My vehicle had distinctive plates and I was known in the area. It was a risk.

The main street widened and I passed the pub, the King's Head. I'd not drunk there for a long while, and then the strange little clock tower that I had driven past for years and always meant to look and see what it was. The road began to drop steeply down to the river.

I stopped at the T-junction at the bottom. The signs opposite told me this was the A3078. St Mawes was eleven miles to the left, Truro nine to the right. I would have bet good money that I was nearer to St Mawes than Truro.

I turned right and drove across the old stone bridge. It was almost a hundred yards long and, at places, too narrow for cars to pass easily. The

River Fal flowed beneath the bridge. The river was just a few yards wide now, and on the Tregony side of the valley. The rest of the bridge crossed soft grassy mud flats. It was hard to believe that this had once been a thriving port.

The river had once filled the valley, as wide as the bridge was long. In the twelve hundreds, when a bridge had first been built, the river here was still tidal and deep. The Fal had flowed far more strongly down to the Carrick and the sea. The sunken valleys formed deep waterways far inland. One would have thought the river Allen or the Kenwyn, that both flowed through Truro, or the Tresillian that joined them, had always been the larger. However, the town on the Carrick is Falmouth, which alone displays the importance the Fal once had.

There had been a busy dockside at Tregony and the Norman Church of St James had stood beside it. By the middle fifteen hundreds, the bridge and its foundations had caused the river to silt up badly, and the Church had collapsed into the soft mud. The parish moved up the hill to St Cuby at the top of Tregony, but long before there was a bridge the tiny Church of St Cornelly, the patron saint of animals in the times before St Francis of Assisi, ministered to the needs of those who lived north of the Fal.

Penny stirred beside me. She had slept for nearly two hours, since about Taunton, after we had stopped for a coffee at the M5 services there.

"We're almost there. You shouldn't have let me sleep."

"You needed it. I've been fine."

She smiled and reached a hand across, resting it on my thigh.

The road swung left after the bridge, but I turned right, up the tight winding lane that was cut deep into the rock and climbed steeply away from the river. As it levelled, a turning appeared on left. It was easy to miss, but the small white sign was clear in my lights, St Cornelly Church.

It was a tight turn in and a new house had just been completed on the corner. The sort of house I would have given my eye teeth for and never would have got planning permission to build. I had to negotiate some large flat stones which were spilled into the lane from the piles that were being used to build a dry stone wall along the front of the new house. The stone wall and bank on the right bordered the top of the graveyard.

The lane sloped gently down for fifty yards until I swung right, nose first into the lay-by outside the church. I turned off the engine and we both looked around. My whole body was tingling, my heart racing. Dilated cardiomyopathy and adrenalin are never a good combination. I was panting. Penny spoke softly.

"There are no lights on up there that I can see, nor down at the farms." The lane led on down to a house and a farm below, I didn't correct her.

"Good, let's sit here a bit to be certain." I looked up the steps to the gate at the top, a new gate, modern, but of wrought iron. From there, the path was only yards long to the south porch of the tiny church. "Are you sure you want to do this?"

"God, yes!" I smiled to myself; an interesting choice of words for an unreligious lady at a time like this. I hoped He would forgive us.

I had known Penny since my college days. She was fifty-nine now, two years younger than me. She had been the girlfriend of one of my closest friends at the Poly. She married him young and for nineteen years they had been happy. They divorced and she married again. That had lasted sixteen years, and she had been single since. She had survived, found herself a new home and settled into a routine that kept her sane, just.

I had known her as a sociology student but she had been a classics scholar, and she had a gift for languages generally. Wasted on classics I had always thought, until now. I had always wondered what might have happened if I had talked to her that first night all those years before. I doubt I would have lasted nineteen years but it had always been an interesting thought. I still had a weak spot for her.

When I was given the old manuscripts my meagre 'O' level Latin from the sixties was not nearly good enough to cope. My mind searched for a solution and Penny jumped into it.

Although we had rarely seen each other for thirty-five years, we had always kept in touch. We had enjoyed the odd meal once or twice a year and I had got to know her second husband too. I had quite enjoyed his company whilst he had been around. I dug out her phone number. It was written on the Christmas card she had sent from her new home, and rang her. She was intrigued.

I made weak excuses to my wife. She was not the least interested in my researches, so I travelled to see Penny in her Cotswold home two weekends before Easter. We had a meal and a bottle of wine, a particularly good Chilean Sauvignon Blanc I remember, at her local village pub. We tried polite conversation for a while, catching up on each other's lives, but all we both wanted to talk about was the manuscript. I was also very aware of a certain sexual tension beneath the surface.

The food cleared away and half a bottle still in front of us, I told her the story so far.

My father had been researching the family genealogy before he died. It had taken me six years to pick up the threads. It was not until I retired early that I found the time or motivation to continue his work.

He had done incredibly well. Our branch of the family was from Ireland and he had traced the line back to Sir Richard Tyrrell, the second Baron of Castleknock.

His father, Sir Hugh Tyrrell the Second and the first Baron, had gone there in 1169 with his cousin the Earl of Pembroke, 'Strongbow' as he was known, to occupy Ireland. Sir Hugh had been left in charge and given his

Baronetcy, but he didn't want to stay in Ireland. He left his second son, Richard, to govern. It was he who set up the famous pale.

His grandfather was Sir Hugh Tyrrell, Lord of Poix, Viscompte d'Equennes, Baron de Ribecourt, and son of Sir Walter Tyrrell, who history accuses of killing King William the Second, Rufus, in the New Forest. This was as far as my father had got.

I discovered that this Sir Walter was in fact the third of that name. The first had come ashore with William the Conqueror at Pevensey and fought with him at Senlac, Hastings. He had a chateau in Poix, in Picardy, moving there from Archere.

This Sir Walter was the grandson of the first Tyrrell, Ralf de Tirel, fourth son of Walter, Compte de Vexin. Vexin was a small buffer state between Normandy and France, and much fought over. He was the hereditary Standard Bearer of France, but Vexin was absorbed into Normandy by Robert, Fifth Duke of Normandy.

Sir Ralf built his chateau at Tirel, on the banks of the Seine, and adopted the name. His name became Tyrrell, and much later, the village Triel.

The family became Lords, then Princes of Poix, in Picardy, holding court in Amiens, and for many centuries after, the 'Tyrrell de Moyencourt' family of France fought against the Tyrrells of England, at Poitier, Creci and Agincourt.

Discovering all of this I just had to go and see where it all was. I drove to Dover and bought a cheap return ticket to Dunkirk. I continued my journey south to the edge of Paris and found a small hotel near Triel.

I spent days poking around old ruins, trying to extract any information I could in broken English from the locals. It would have been so much easier if I had spoken good French!

The family had founded many Abbeys and Monasteries; The Abbaye de Larne, the Monastery de St Pierre de Selincourt, the Priory of St Denis de Poix, and I visited them all. One however was to change my life, it was the Abbaye Notre Dame de Fontaine Guerard.

At Archeres, a knowledgeable lady in the library who spoke credibly good English, told me that the first Sir Walter, who had built his chateau there, had three brothers. The youngest, Sir Raoul, had built a small chateau near what was now Pont d'Arche, where the Andelle joined the Seine some miles downstream.

The Andelle flowed through a particularly beautiful valley and his home had been beside the river near Radepont. Eventually, his old home had been granted to some Cistercian monks in the mid eleven hundreds.

The Cistercians enlarged it greatly into a classic Norman Gothic Abbaye, believing the little spring that bubbled at the edge of the trees to have healing qualities. They created a 'healing fountain', Fontaine Guerard.

Later that day, as I walked in the spring sun, past the church of Saint Louis and the outside of the main building, I was stunned by its beauty, its setting. It was squeezed at right angles between the gentle waters of the Andelle and the trees that marked the edge of the wooded valley floor. Lush green lawns spread up and downstream, and, as if the monks had run out of space, the building turned at the trees, a chapel and outhouses running down the valley.

It had deteriorated steadily since it had been taken from the monks and nuns by the Revolution in the late seventeen hundreds. The monks had returned to the valley, but never to the Abbaye. The ruins were magnificent.

I entered the main building and walked its length. To those that appreciate such things, the rig-vaulted chapter house and the dormitory's cradle shaped roof, together, make a visit worthwhile. To me, they were just something else enchanting.

Walking back into the bright sunlight I looked towards the chapel of Saint Michael. Beside it stood an old pine tree and an equally old chestnut, their branches intertwined, their leaves brushing each other and rustling in the breeze. They were planted in memory of Lord Hacqueville and his wife, who he had had executed on that spot, but that is another long story.

For a moment I thought I had seen a ghost and stopped in my tracks, but no, he looked real enough. Just to the side of the gravel path near the chapel stood an old monk. The hand on his stick showed his age, and the fact that he used the stick to steady his slightly stooped stance. The hand that gripped the notched wooded handle was thin, and even at the distance I was, the skin looked pale and stretched.

He wore the white habit of a Cistercian with a black apron, but an enlarged apron that was more a full length tabard tied at the waist. His hood was pulled up against the breeze and I couldn't see his wrinkled features until I came close to him.

"Bonjour Frere, ca va?"

"Bonjour, mon fils. Bien merci. You are English, no?" I laughed and smiled broadly at him.

"Is my French that bad, Brother?"

"Oh, it is the look as much as the accent." His accent was extremely good. "What brings you here, my son?"

"Curiosity I suppose. I believe a relative of mine lived here once." He shuffled forward a little.

"You have come at last! I have been waiting for you these few years now."

"Waiting for me! What on earth do you mean?" I tried to look at his eyes below the rim of his hood. The strong sunlight seemed to reflect brightly from the pure white cloth.

"I have been praying that you would come, and after years in the chapter, I have discovered that the good Lord usually provides eventually. You are a descendant of Sir Raoul Tyrrell?"

"I don't think so, I believe my family descend from Sir Walter of Archere, but this is impossible. How did you know I would be here today?"

"I did not, my son, I have been here every afternoon for six years now. It is at least a beautiful place to have had to wait."

I could see the half smile on his old face as he raised his free hand and pushed back his hood. What little hair he had was white too and surrounded a small, shaved circle on the crown of his head. He was a little shorter than me, which was difficult at my five foot seven, but his fine bone structure meant he still retained his handsome features. I looked him in the eye and asked the obvious question.

"Why, Brother? Why on earth were you waiting for me?"

"Come, there is a seat by the chapel." He turned and shuffled towards the ruined chapel without waiting for any assent from me. I followed until he turned and sat heavily. He tapped the seat beside him and I joined him on the wooden bench.

"OK, so why?"

"Well, my son. This Abbaye is on the site of Sir Raoul Tyrrell's chateau. He left here to join the fight for the Norman conquest of Sicily in 1070. He stayed there when the fighting ended in Sicily and never returned. He left a Monk here called Prious, a Breton. He gathered a few monks and nuns to him and they lived here as a small commune. It endured for almost a hundred years, long after his death, as a shelter for wandering clergy, until eventually those here joined the Cistercians and the land was legally granted to them. Sir Raoul had had no known descendants in Normandy."

"Then you knew I could not be descended from him!" He chuckled with a small shrug, but continued without comment.

"Prious wrote a history, a diary almost, a record of the time he spent with Sir Raoul in England in the spring and early summer of 1068. It was passed down from generation to generation of the monks and nuns here, with many other papers, all long forgotten. They were all saved from the Revolutionaries when the Brothers and Sisters were ejected from here. They were held at my monastery. Once every hundred years since its foundation, the monks of our order would copy every indexed scroll in our possession onto fresh parchment, until the Revolution. Since then they became forgotten, but they have been dry and have kept well. I discovered them ten years or so ago and began to re-catalogue them and copy them again where I could."

He struggled to stand and I jumped up to take his arm. He leant heavily on me until he steadied himself on his stick.

"Merci, mon fils, alors, the story Prious told is one that should be known. It is a story that explains one of the mysteries of English history, but it is up to a Tyrrell to decide what should be told. So I prayed for guidance and you are my answer. Go now, and be here at this time tomorrow, I will bring the scrolls. They are in Latin." The last bit had been almost an afterthought.

"Can I not take you somewhere? Help in some way?"

"No, my son, I have been doing this for years. Go."

I went, returning the next day as told. I had checked out of the hotel, packed the car and was ready to return to England. The old monk was there, standing exactly as he had been the day before but this time with a bundle under his free arm.

He handed me the bundle. It was wrapped in a supermarket plastic bag. That struck me as odd somehow.

"Thank you, Brother."

"Do with it as you will, my son. It is your history."

"How can I get in touch with you?" He smiled warmly.

"We will not meet again, my son. May that bring you what you wish. Farewell."

He turned and shuffled away from me. I took a step after him, trying for the right words. They didn't come, so I walked quickly back to the car and headed for Dunkirk.

Penny reached across the table and put a hand on my arm, then the top of my hand, squeezing gently. I realised I had been staring at the table between us as I had been speaking.

"Then we should drink up and go back to my place and make a start. I'm really quite excited." I raised my eyes to hers. "By the scrolls, stupid!" She withdrew her hand quickly as she said it and sat back sharply.

"What did I say?"

"Nothing. Pay the bill while I go to the ladies."

Within half an hour we were back at her little house, the manuscript scrolls piled flat in front of her, her dictionary to hand. I turned on the tape and she started to read, slowly at first, but then more quickly as the script became more familiar and the Latin began to flow into English more easily.

Thirteen hours later we were still there, empty coffee cups in front of us, as she came to the end. I could not believe what I had heard.

We slept as much as we could, but our minds were full of the story the manuscript told. We ate a hastily prepared sandwich each and left at dusk for the church of St Cornelly. As we drove down the M5, the words of Brother Prious of Breton would not leave me.

The Tale of
The Brother, The Father,
And The Knight.

Cornwall 1068

From the Diary of

Brother Prious

Written between 1069 and 1070

Adapted from the Latin translation

By Ray Tyrrell

The First Scroll

Morwenna eased herself forward a little on the woollen blanket she had laid on the balcony floor and raised her head. The Great Hall of Tintagel Castle was lit by candles mounted on dark iron brackets around its walls and by the large fire burning in the enormous fireplace. She could see quite well through the balustrade that surrounded the gallery, but she had to be very careful her father or brother did not see her.

She had never been so excited in her life but was becoming uncomfortable after lying there for so long. The woollen blanket did little to soften the hard oak floor.

She had heard they were coming at breakfast. Real Princes. She could hardly contain herself. Her father, Jowan, Lord of Tintagel, a direct descendant of Artoris, had announced at breakfast that their ship had arrived off shore just after dawn. It would take a few hours for them to land and travel to Tintagel.

Morwenna had been born the third child of Jowan and Blejan, seventeen years before. Her eldest brother, Myghal, stood beside her father, between the fireplace and the large round table. With twenty-four chairs surrounding it, it dominated the Great Hall.

Her elder sister, Steren, had died of a fever four years before. Her death had left a hole in Morwenna's life. She was close to her sister and was just becoming a woman herself. She was beginning to learn about boys from her, but Steren had died a month before she was to marry a Cornish Lord, a marriage arranged by her father and King Mark.

Her youngest brother, Jorn, had died of the same fever that took Steren just days after her. Her beloved mother Blejan had died within the last year, taken by a winter consumption, so her whole family was there in the Great Hall.

Most young women would have been married by her age and her best friend, Elowen, their ostler's daughter, was married with a second child due soon. They were raised together amongst the few children living within the Castle, aristocratic or not. They quickly became almost inseparable.

Her father, Jowan, had tried to arrange a suitable marriage for Morwenna but it had not been easy. Elowen and Morwenna had always loved the old tales and sagas that told of love, where beautiful maidens were swept off their feet by handsome Princes, and Morwenna was convinced it would happen to her one day. She refused to discuss possible suitors with her father.

Elowen's marriage had brought a new perspective too. Whilst arranged, Elowen liked her husband, not loved, but she was learning to. Elowen introduced Morwenna to the physical side of marriage and this was much discussed with her. Now she could not wait to try for herself. She had learnt a lot from her friend and she knew much about how to please a man, and herself. Now here, in her own home, two Princes were due to arrive at any moment. Her stomach ached with anticipation. Her whole body seemed to tingle.

There was a loud knocking on the large oak doors beneath her. Her father shouted permission to enter as he turned towards them. Daveth, the Castle's Chief Steward, opened the heavy doors and stepped through. Moving to one side, he spoke.

"Your guests, My Lord."

Before Jowan could reply, the doors opened wider and two young men strode through. Unlike her father and brother, who were dressed in the normal woollen and linen clothing of castle life, the newcomers were dressed in black leather leggings and thick studded leather tabards over rough cloth shirts.

Her father greeted them.

"My dear Princes, welcome to my home, welcome to Camelot." He turned slightly, a hand outstretched towards his son. "This is my boy, Myghal. Please introduce yourselves."

It took a few moments for them to walk the length of the room and pass the table. The slightly shorter one, who stood a little nearer than the other, replied in a strong Saxon accent.

"I am Godwine, eldest living son of King Harold, and this is my brother, Edmund."

Her father and brother bowed slightly as her father spoke.

"Please, be seated at the table. There is wine. You must be tired after your journey."

"Indeed we are, My Lord Jowan. The seas were not kind to us, and in such weather, Dublin seems so much further away."

Morwenna watched as wine was poured and they all sat at the table in the chairs nearest to the fireplace. She took in every detail of the two Princes as they began to discuss their business with her father. Her excitement was waning however. She did not know what she had expected but they both seemed so normal. In fact, they both almost seemed a bit grubby. She decided they had been at sea for a few days and had come straight to the castle. She would put it down to that.

She began to listen to what they were all saying. Her Father was speaking and her eyes moved to him.

"King Mark has pledged a thousand Cornishmen and I am quite confident he can produce them. Bishop Leofric has raised five hundred Devon men at Exeter, and there are some three hundred displaced Britons.

With your army of one thousand five hundred arriving from Ireland, we will have a combined army of some three thousand eight hundred men."

Edmund leant towards Jowan.

"Are you absolutely certain Exeter will rise and join us?"

"Oh yes, quite sure. Bishop Leofric is working closely with your grandmother, Gytha Thorkeldottir, who resides in Exeter under his protection, and she is in close touch with Archbishop Stigand."

Godwine spat at the fireplace.

"That man cannot be trusted. He encouraged us to raid Bristol last year. He said they would rally to us, but they fought us, closed the city to us. We had to retreat to our boats."

Edmund joined the condemnation.

"He is a Pope's man, and the Pope gave William the Bastard his Papal flag, made the invasion of our country a Holy fight, even excommunicated our father before the battle at Senlac."

"My Princes, please." Jowan broke Edmund's flow. "The Archbishop is no Pope's man. He has been excommunicated five times by three different Popes. He spent much of last year in Rome with King William to free himself from the latest one."

Jowan realised his mistake as he said it. The Princes had looked at each other, then at their wine goblets, when he had said King William.

"The bastard didn't let Stigand crown him so that no-one could claim he was not crowned legally. That hurt Stigand, and he is no friend of the bastard's either, but he is a survivor, powerful. How he can have been excommunicated five times and survived as Archbishop of Canterbury is beyond me. He is still Bishop of Winchester too, so that he can be close to the Court, a second See, which is not allowed by the Pope. He remains Archbishop because he is too strong for William to oust him. His church network is too strong. The bastard cannot be rid of him until he has a firm hold of the Kingdom and we will stop that happening."

The Princes looked towards him before Godwine spoke.

"Two more things then before we talk timing." He took a slow and deliberate mouthful of wine, replacing the silver goblet on the table in front of him. "Firstly, Stigand has hinted strongly to us that he has a secret that will shake the very ground the bastard walks on. Do you know of what he speaks?"

Jowan looked directly into Godwine's eyes.

"I do not. I too have heard such rumours, but it is a secret known only to the Archbishop and, I suppose, one or two very close to him."

"Secondly then, who will command our combined army."

"In effect, you will."

Godwine sat back in his chair, obviously losing his patience.

"I mean, my Prince, you will give the orders, you will command, but to the army, they will be led by the legendary King Arthur."

"I know the name of course and was told of this by Stigand's envoy, but you had better explain."

"The men of Cornwall, Devon and Britain will not be led by anyone but their own, and I am sure your men will be the same." He pointed at the wall above the fireplace where Excalibur hung majestically. "That is Arthur's sword, Excalibur. It has been in my family for nearly eight hundred years. When Bishop Leofric moved his Cathedral and See from Crediton to Exeter, he found Arthur's armour, which had been lost to our family for over a hundred years. Leofric told Stigand of his discovery, and Stigand saw the opportunity to unite the country against the Normans, behind the legend that is Arthur. He is someone who every man of every corner of England will follow, and once we achieve some success, there is a good chance the men of Wales and Scotland will join us. It is only a matter of time otherwise, before the Normans turn their attention to them too."

Godwine stood and turned towards the fire, looking up at Excalibur.

"And who will wear the armour and bear the sword?"

Jowan rose beside him.

"My family is of Arthur's direct bloodline. Various members of my family have borne the armour and sword over many hundreds of years. The armour will be too small for me, I am certain, so my son Myghal will have the honour. It was the one condition I insisted on when I discussed it all with Archbishop Stigand."

Godwine put a hand on Jowan's shoulder, which looked a little strange to Morwenna, as her father was by far the taller.

"Lord Jowan, my brother and I have only one interest here, and that is to drive William the Bastard and his Normans out of England, avenging the death of the true King, our father, Harold. So we will leave all politics and manoeuvring to you and Stigand and Leofric. We will return to Dublin tomorrow and ready our army and our ships. It is the end of February now, Easter is early in April, so we will sail in the first spell of good weather after Mayday. Now, some rest for us, then some dining and more of this fine wine this evening."

Morwenna was shocked by what she had heard. It was too much for one day, Princes and rebellion.

+ + +

Bishop Leofric of Exeter shrugged off the two Norman guards who had been holding his arms and entered the confessional. He was a prisoner of the Normans in his own Cathedral. Encouraged by Gytha, mother of the defeated King Harold, he had led a rebellion by the people of Exeter, refusing to pay their taxes to the new Norman King William. The King had been away for almost a year since his coronation on Christmas Day 1066. He had gone to Rome to plead his case with the Pope as to why he should retain the English throne and not cede it to the King of France, to whom, as Duke of Normandy, he paid homage. William had won the argument and returned as King to an England where the likes of Bishop Leofric had been trying to take advantage of his absence.

William had not taken the rebellion lightly. He had marched west with two thousand men and took little time taking Exeter back under his control.

Leofric had helped Gytha hatch a plot far beyond Exeter's walls. It involved King Harold's sons who had gathered a small but loyal army in Ireland, and King Mark of Cornwall. Leofric was convinced however that there was even more to the rebellion than he knew. Gytha had been in regular contact with Archbishop Stigand, who he was certain was behind it all.

Leofric was a survivor and knew when to wait. He had become Bishop to the See of Devon in 1046. His Cathedral was at Crediton. When he became Bishop he carried out an inventory of church treasures stored there. The enormous wealth he discovered included armour rumoured to have once belonged to the legendary King Arthur. Leofric began a search for the truth about the armour, but more importantly, he determined that such wealth should not remain in Crediton, as it was not even a walled town and so should not be a Cathedral city. He petitioned his friend King Edward and the Pope in Rome to allow him to move to Exeter and build a new Cathedral there. Both agreed, and King Edward, his wife Queen Edith, and her mother Gytha Thorkeldottir, attended his consecration as Bishop of Exeter. Gytha's son Harold Godwinson was with her. Leofric had made friends in very high places, but none could help him now.

He had asked his custodian, Sir Baldwin de Redvers, a Flemish knight who had fought at Senlac and was now Sheriff of Devon, to allow him as a Bishop to at least go to Confession. It was agreed that he could go under guard.

Leofric sat in the Confessional and closed the door, whispering urgently to the young priest behind the screen.

"Waestan, is that you?"

He heard a tense voice hiss a reply.

"Yes, Your Grace, at your command."

"Good, now hear me well. You must get word most urgently to Archbishop Stigand. He should be in Winchester for the Easter celebrations. Tell him they have the armour and I do not think King Mark of Cornwall will join the rebellion without it. Tell him to stop Godwine sailing from Dublin until we can recover it. Understand?"

"Yes, Your Grace."

"Good, now where is the Lady Gytha?"

27

"She has been taken to the island of Bradanreolice in exile Your Grace."

"I see, and what of our city, Brother, are the people still defiant?"

"Angry, Your Grace, but not defiant. The Normans cleared over forty dwellings on Rougemount and have built a castle. It took them less than two weeks. They had more than two hundred soldiers dig the ditch around it and pile the earth on the hill. Others cut wood outside the city. It was all done so quickly."

"Thank you, Brother. Now get my message to Archbishop Stigand immediately."

"I will, Your Grace."

Leofric opened the Confessional door and stepped out. His two guards held him roughly and led him to his quarters.

Waestan left the Confessional too, but he walked quickly away, leaving the Cathedral through its heavy wooden doors. He turned up the narrow street that led to the new castle, almost breaking into a run.

He had been born on a farm to the south of Exeter, on the far slopes of Halden Hill. He was his family's third child and was both welcomed and a burden to them, another mouth to feed at a difficult time. Three more siblings arrived before he was six years old, so in his early years he became used to a life of hunger and of a damp coldness.

As he grew he became his father's boy. His two older sisters were constantly with his mother. His eldest sister died of a fever when she was just 10, which they all caught to some degree but it only took the one child.

His sister's death meant his first visit to the village church. His parents were religious but the church was too far away for them to attend often. Waestan, however, was filled with awe at the church. Although it was not large and built of wood, it was the biggest building he had seen.

The Priest spoke kindly to him as he left the ceremony and Waestan had made his first step towards the church.

He had taken to the priesthood quickly and easily. From his fourteenth to eighteenth birthday, he had been schooled in a small monastery beside the mouth of the River Exe. He had joined the Cathedral as a cleric two years ago and had learned a lot about church politics as a secretary to Bishop Leofric.

Waestan was ambitious. He saw the Norman invasion as an opportunity to progress. The Normans would not be defeated now, and the Pope himself had blessed their invasion, making it a holy crusade. It was far better therefore to co-operate and befriend them.

He reached the gates and approached a guard. The guard spoke.

"Well now, Brother, what business do you have here?"

"I need to see the Sheriff, most urgently. I have the information he requested."

Brother Prious heard the horses before he saw the knight. The streets of Winchester were narrow and the stone road strewn with rubbish. The street on which he stood had a small stream flowing down its centre so the smell was not quite as bad as it had been. The midday sun was almost overhead, casting deep shadows and forming shafts of bright light between the wood and stone dwellings.

He stepped back into a gap between two houses and studied the horseman that rode towards him, unaware of his presence. The knight was a fighting man; that was certain. He seemed a Norman, but, Prious noted, not a typical Norman.

He rode a fine grey charger, a Norman courser, and led a chestnut palfrey that had linen bags tied to its back. The charger was sweating a little and looked as if he had travelled far that day.

The bright April sun lit the knight, flashing as it reflected off his mail. Prious could just see the dark grey linen of his shirt and the black wool of his breeches, which were loose until they met the tight criss-cross bindings below his knee, which laced up from his light leather ankle boots. He was a nobleman. Only nobles criss-crossed their bindings.

The metal of his chainmail hauberk was bright; it had been polished quite recently. It was split front and back, almost up to his waist, so that it fell across his legs on either side of the charger. It was his sword and scabbard that took Prious' attention though. The fashion that year of 1068 was to wear your scabbard belted under your hauberk, the sword hilt projecting from the mail's front split. It was an affectation though, and made it difficult to draw your sword quickly. This knight wore his sword outside his hauberk, the scabbard hanging loose down his left side under his long shield.

The shield too was typically Norman. Kite shaped, it hung down his left side at an angle, tied to a strap that crossed his chest and back and over his right shoulder. It would protect his left side and his charger's rear flank as he wheeled away from a shield wall in a fight. The shield was pale blue, a man of Poix, famed for their fighting prowess since Sir Walter Tyrrell had led his men against the Saxon left at Senlac two years before. Strangely, however, it was overlaid with a white lower tip and a straight white bar, just off centre down its length; a Breton symbol.

His helmet hung from his saddle, suspended by the leather ties that would attach to his ventail, which itself was permanently attached to the neck of his hauberk and hung in a loose square of mail over his chest. With his helmet on, nose guard down his face, the ventail would tie to the edging of the helmet, looping below his nose but protecting his cheeks and throat. His coif hung down his back. He was definitely a professional soldier, yet he looked very young, twenty one or two at most.

He was clean shaven, but again the fashion was to have short hair, with neck and the back of the head shaved, almost to the crown. This knight had long dark hair that fell raggedly onto his shoulders and down his back.

As he rode up to Prious, the knight saw him and stopped at his side.

"I hope you enjoyed the Easter festivities, Brother." He spoke in Norman French.

Prious was very obviously a monk. He was not tall and wore a black habit that trailed the ground. With the hood thrown back, his cropped fair hair and shaved crown was in clear sight. He looked in his late twenties, possibly thirty. The knight's tone left Prious wondering if it was a genuine hope or a mischievous jibe.

"I'm afraid I was at sea, my son, on my way here, and was only able to celebrate our Lord's resurrection privately, the ship's crew being busy seeing to our safety." He had answered in Norman but his accent gave away his Breton roots. The knight laughed, his face lighting up with a genuine smile. He spoke in Celtic Breton.

"Ah, a Breton I hear, then you will help me I am sure." Prious answered in the same language.

"If I can, my son, of course, what do you need of me?"

"I have ridden as hard as was sensible from the boat that landed me at Portsea, summoned from my home in France by the Duke, uh, King William." He corrected himself. "Having come all this way, I am trying to find the castle in this confused maze they call a city. I have passed the Cathedral three times."

Prious grinned; he was beginning to like this knight.

"Well, I have walked from Portsea, having sailed the coastline from Cornwall. It may have seemed a long ride for you, my son, but it was a longer walk for me, I tell you." He looked straight into the knight's eyes. They twinkled. "But if you follow my path, Sir Knight, you will be delighted to know that the castle is just a few moments away."

"Lead on then, brother, I shall follow the path of righteousness."

"I doubt that, my son, but follow nonetheless."

Prious turned away and walked on up the street, trying to avoid most of the muck. The knight rode behind. Both were grinning to themselves.

+++

The castle at Winchester had been constructed in early 1067, one of the first King William had ordered built, in the heart of Saxon England. Castles were fundamental to William's plans to dominate and rule the English Saxons.

It was less than two hundred years since 886, when Rollo had led his marauding Vikings in their ships, up the Seine, finally laying siege to Paris.

They fought the French constantly until they were eventually beaten in open battle by King Charles the Third in 911.

The French did not know how to fight the Vikings at first and many noblemen built castellans, fortified buildings where they could defend themselves against attack. The Vikings knew well the strength of such defences, and they never forgot it.

Rollo made peace with the French in 911 with the Treaty of St Claire-sur-Epte. He converted to Christianity, and became a vassal to Charles the Third. In return, King Charles granted him lands around Rouen and Rollo, with his new Christian name Robert, became the first Duke of The Nordhommes, the Normans, of Normandy.

Tales from his youth gave William his faith in castles, as did his own experience. He had brought three prefabricated wooden castles in his invasion fleet from Normandy. The first men ashore at Pevensey were engineers to erect the first of these. Once built, in a morning, the cavalry came ashore; two thousand horses and their knights, who rode out from the beaches to cover the landings. Only then did the main force come ashore; their equipment and stores safe within the wooden castle.

The other two were erected at Hastings to cover the rear of his army and to give them a place to retreat to should the invasion go wrong, as it so nearly did.

The castle at Winchester was a simple motte and bailey castle. Three hundred men had taken two weeks to clear the site of buildings right in the middle of Winchester, and to dig the outer ditch around the bailey. They used the earth they dug to raise the motte, a man-made hill in the centre. A wooden defensive wall was then erected around the inside of the ditch and a tall wooden fortress was built on top of the motte, with a wooden staircase leading up to its gates. This fortress, the heart of the castle, had a number of rooms within and it was in the largest of these that King William the First of England, Seventh Duke of Normandy, now stood.

He was quite tall for a Norman, but not over so. His hair was short, his neck and the back of his head shaved up to the crown. His clothes were of heavy but strongly coloured linen, reds and greens that day. They were just as he would have worn under his chain-mail hauberk, but he wore no armour, only a belt and a scabbard, which was home to a fine sword. He stood with a confidence that commanded the room, the charisma of a king.

There were three men in the room with him, gathered around a central table on which stood platters of venison, cheese, bread and flagons of red wine. All of which had been partaken of.

Two of the men were dressed like the King, but in different colours. Standing beside him was his childhood friend, William Fitz Osbern, who had become his most trusted advisor.

Seated casually, leaning back with one leg outstretched along a wooden bench, his elbow on the table, was Robert, Count De Mortain, half-brother to the King.

His other half-brother, Bishop Odo of Bayeux, stood at the far end of the table, still holding a pewter cup of wine. He wore a very plain habit of undyed wool that looked shabby in comparison to the others. His head was covered in short hair, the crown shaved.

They were all looking at an old set of Roman armour that was laid out on the end of the table. It had been cleaned and reflected the sunlight that lit the room. There were greaves, thigh guards, wrist guards, a heavily studded tabard and a simply engraved breast plate, but beside these was a fine Roman helmet, its crest still red, although faded from its original brilliance.

"I am told it is eight hundred years old." It was Odo who was speaking. "I don't think there is any doubt it is Roman."

"They certainly knew how to work metals. It is strong but not too heavy." Robert spoke with the trained eye of a cavalry man, "Ideal for horseback. Where did you find it all?"

"In Exeter," William replied, "Odo will explain all to you both, but Osbern, go and find out where our guests are. They have had plenty of time to rest and we have much to do."

As Osbern turned towards the door it was opened by an Officer of the Guard.

"Your Majesty, Sir Raoul Tyrrell of Radepont, and the monk, Prious."

"Send them in, send them in." The King waved an impatient beckoning hand.

The monk entered first, the knight almost beside him, but they stopped together and each dropped to one knee, head bowed.

"Stand and join us, both, we have much to discuss." King William stepped forward and held out a hand to them both, helping them to their feet and pulling them forward into the heart of the room to the table.

Prious saw Bishop Odo and immediately turned to him, kneeling again, taking Odo's hand and kissing his Bishop's ring.

"Enough of the ceremony," snapped William, as again Prious got to his feet.

"Come, my son, attend the King." Odo smiled as he said it.

"Let us make sure we all know each other." William turned to the newcomers and held out a hand towards Odo. "This is Bishop Odo of Bayeux, my eyes and ears in England. Odo has spent the last year in Dover, gathering knowledge on my new Kingdom whilst I was debating with the Pope. He knows Prious well as Prious is his eyes and ears in the west."

Both men nodded acknowledgement and Odo smiled comfortingly at Prious, who was amazed the King had used his name so casually. The King continued.

"This is my brother, Robert, Count De Mortain, who looks after my army, and this is my dearest and oldest friend, William Fitz Osbern, who looks after me." He laughed as he threw an arm around his friend's shoulders.

"Now, Odo, please introduce us to Prious."

"Certainly, Sire." He waved an arm towards Prious who took an involuntary step forward.

"Prious has been in my service for just over three years. He is Breton by birth and was introduced to me shortly after the King's victory over Count Conan, as a Norman speaking Breton monk. For a few months he was in close service to me as an interpreter, whilst we were getting Brittany under control. During this time I learned he spoke English as well as Celtic and Norman. I persuaded him to move to Cornwall for me. Little Wales is Celtic speaking with a little English and not yet part of the Kingdom of England. We founded a small church for St Cornelly by the river Fal and he has preached there since. He has kept me well informed of the thoughts and opinions of the Cornish and served us well."

"Thank you. Robert summoned Sir Raoul Tyrrell from his home in Radepont at my special request. Knowing him as I do, he is exactly the man we require, and so I will introduce him."

William took a large mouthful of wine.

"Sir Raoul is the youngest brother of my loyal friend Sir Walter Tyrrell, Lord of Poix, who, as you all know, led our opening charge at the battle of Senlac Hill and acted as Viceroy in London whilst I was in Rome. His recent illness and death has been a great loss to us all. However, four years ago we rescued the shipwrecked Harold Godwinson from the Count of Ponthieu. I needed an English interpreter and was offered Raoul Tyrrell, a seventeen year old English speaking French noble. He entered my service and before long he found himself riding into battle with me against Count Conan of Brittany. Ironically, Harold fought with us too that day."

William paused and drank again. He waved to the servant who stood by the main doors.

"Pour wine for everyone," he ordered, "I am forgetting my guests."

There was a brief pause whilst goblets were refilled and new ones given to the recently arrived.

"Now all but my guests and friends, leave us."

The servants and guards left by the main door.

"Now, where was I. Oh yes, it was a bloody fight. I was unhorsed that day, as were many of us, and found myself separated and fighting back to back with some young Knight, or so I thought. It was in fact, Sir Raoul, or so he became as soon as the battle was over. Without him that day I would not have lived through the fight. At my request, he stayed in Brittany with

Robert and learned Breton when I returned to Normandy. As you can see by his hair, I think he became one."

The other laughed at Sir Raoul's discomfort, but he was used to such comments.

"We met next whilst we were waiting for decent weather to cross to England. With the Pope's blessing and his papal flag, many joined our cause. As Sir Walter arrived with his men of Poix, Sir Raoul was there to greet him having led a sizable force of Bretons to join us. When our left broke at Senlac and many English pursued our men down the hill, it was Sir Raoul who rallied the Bretons with their backs to the stream, long enough for me to bring the cavalry across to cut the English down from behind. Senlac too, might have been lost without him."

William Fitz Osbern moved restlessly around the table, standing closer to the King. Robert smiled to himself. Osbern always got restless when the King praised another man too highly for his liking. Robert couldn't contain himself.

"Quite a career for one so young! Don't you think so Osbern?"

Osbern's eyes turned to Robert, who just kept his own on the King, but it was Odo who spoke next.

"So, we have a Monk and a proven soldier, both loyal, and both speak Breton, English and Norman. Neither look Norman however. Once out of his mail and in leathers, Sir Raoul could be a Breton priest's servant and protector."

Prious felt Sir Raoul stiffen beside him. They had both been concerned why they had been summoned to Winchester, and that was the first hint of what was to come. Odo turned his head towards the King.

"Shall I explain, Sire?"

"Please do so."

Odo moved to the table and placed his hands on its edge, encouraging the others towards it. As they stood around it he began.

"This is Roman armour, eight or nine hundred years old. It first belonged to a Roman leader, a cavalryman, called Artoris, or so my scholars tell me. He fought all over England and became legendary. He settled in Little Wales, on the edge near Tawton. His family then moved to what is now Tintagel. Folklore has turned him into the legendary King Arthur; you have probably all heard the name. He is a ghostly king who comes back to fight in this armour whenever the lands in the west are threatened. The last time he fought was at Tawton against King Athelstan. Arthur that day was killed. Stripped of his armour he was a son of the Lord of Tintagel. The armour went to the cathedral in Crediton, but Arthur's famous sword, Excalibur, was not found."

Odo pointed across at Prious.

"Prious here has confirmed it is at Tintagel with the current Lord and family. Still direct descendants of this Arthur." He paused and looked up at the faces watching him, all with different expressions of concentration.

"More importantly, Prious got word of plotting between the previous king's mother, Gytha Thorkeldottir, her grandchildren in Dublin and Bishop Leofric of Devon. Gytha has lived in Exeter since escaping from my grasp. She was a prisoner with Edith Swan's Neck, Harold's Queen, in a monastery near Canterbury. We are certain Archbishop Stigand is the heart of it all but we can prove nothing.

"It all led to Harold's son, Godwine, landing a Saxon force from Ireland near Bristol and attacking it. We were all both delighted, and a little surprised, that Bristol closed its gates to him and repulsed his assaults on the city. He retreated and sailed a little further west, landing in Somerset. Our Master of Horse, Ednoth, met him with two hundred cavalry, and though killed himself, drove Godwine back to his boats, which sailed for Ireland."

Odo turned towards the King.

"Forgive the detail, Sire. I feel it is important that Prious and Sir Raoul know everything."

"Indeed Bishop. Pray continue." He waved a hand at Odo as he spoke.

"We were certain their plotting would develop further, and Prious was ordered to find out all he could in Cornwall, as were all my ears across the west. The King was with the Pope, of course, for most of the year, but when he returned, confirmed King of England by His Holiness, we announced a new tax to raise money to build castles across England. Stone castles. Gytha and Bishop Leofric had become too confident, and Exeter refused to pay its taxes. It was a heaven sent blessing. Led by our King, we marched to Exeter, besieging the city and breaking the gates in just eighteen days. Within two more weeks we had cleared more than forty houses on Rougemount in the heart of the city and built a new wooden castle."

King William interrupted.

"Odo, thank you, I will tell the rest." He had felt a change of voice might help their guests digest so much information.

"I had Gytha and Bishop Leofric arrested. Gytha is an old woman now. I had her imprisoned on the island of Bradanreolice, or Flat Holm, in the Severn estuary. Whilst the castle was being built I questioned Bishop Leofric."

He looked around the faces of all listening. All were attentive.

"Leofric too is an old man now. He has been a Bishop too long and had begun to believe he was untouchable. Well I proved him wrong and he told us all he knew quite quickly. He had found the armour attributed to this 'King Arthur' when he moved to Exeter more than twenty years ago. He kept it safe but told no-one of it until there was talk of rebellion against our rule last year. He told Gytha of it and contacted Stigand, who was in Rome with me, so it all took some months. All agreed, however, that the whole of Britain would rally to a rebellion led by this legendary king. Little Wales did, once support was gained from Harold's sons in Ireland. Stigand organised that. Leofric talked with King Mark of Cornwall. With Leofric's own retained support around Exeter, they had an army that might have a chance of success, and with success, they were confident that the Welsh and Scots tribes, as well as the northern English of Danish descent, would all join Arthur's banner. All this was planned for early May."

The room was silent. Odo broke it.

"From what my people tell, including Prious here, without this armour, West Wales will not rise. They might rally to Arthur's sword, Excalibur, but we expect not. So all we should face is a landing in the West of Harold's sons and a force of less than two thousand infantry. They will be demoralised too, because the support they will be expecting will not be there."

The King continued.

"I will not, however, take the chance of this legendary sword being enough for men to follow. Neither will I stand for this legendary family from Tintagel, or Camelot, whatever it is called, ever being a threat to us again."

There was a very real tension in the Hall. Everyone knew what came next would be why they were all there.

"Bishop Odo here will have his monks purge every library in every abbey, monastery, priory and church across this entire Kingdom for any reference to this 'King Arthur'. I want nothing in writing anywhere to support he ever existed. He may live on in stories told to children for a while, but there must be no written evidence to remain, anywhere. It will also help the Bishop begin to undermine Archbishop Stigand's grip on the church."

"It will be done Sire, you have my oath on it." Odo bowed to King William as he replied.

"Thank you My Lord Bishop. I have complete faith in you."

Robert stiffened as the King's gaze turned to him. Sir Raoul could not help thinking all this formality was for his and Prious' benefit.

"Now, my dear brother Robert. As you know, we left my trusted Baldwin de Redvers in Exeter as Sherriff of Devon with two hundred infantry. He will control Exeter and suppress the surrounding area from rising."

He waved a hand towards Sir Raoul.

"We also left your old friend, Sir Breon of Brittany, with five hundred horse, to support Baldwin should our information be wrong, although I am sure it is not. So now, Robert, I want you to dispatch another five hundred horses to Sir Breon's command. His force of one thousand cavalry will await Sir Raoul and act at his command. You will also arrange for them to take Sir Raoul's horses with them, and all his armour and other belongings, understood?"

"Indeed Sire, I will arrange it all."

"Good, good. That just leaves Brother Prious here and my old companion, Sir Raoul."

They too stood stiffly as the King addressed them. Sir Raoul hid a wry smile at the thought of his being a companion of the King.

"Brother Prious, you are perfectly placed and known in Cornwall as a travelling monk, based at St Cornelly near Tregony, I am told."

"Yes Sire. Across the River Fal from Tregony Sire, or Trerigoni as it is known in Cornwall. The river is wide there, nearly fifty paces, and runs deep."

The King seemed quite taken aback for a moment. He had not expected a reply.

"Fifty paces and deep, yes. Well now, I understand that you have visited Tintagel a number of times as a priest and are known to the family."

"I am, Sire, quite well known. There is Jowan, Lord of Tintagel, his son, Myghal, and daughter, Morwenna." It was all Sir Raoul could do not to laugh.

King William turned his head towards Bishop Odo, an incredulous look on his face. Odo smiled.

"I think, Brother Prious, that your King is not looking for answers, but to instruct you of his desires of you."

"I am so sorry, Your Grace. I am not accustomed to…"

"Prious, just listen."

"Your Grace."

The King smiled. He realised there was no impertinence in Prious.

"It is your job, Brother Prious, to get Sir Raoul in and out of Tintagel Castle, and to assist him in any way he requires in his task. You will do this for me?"

"I will, Sire."

"Very good. Now, Sir Raoul, your part in this is crucial to my desires in ridding us of this legend, 'King Arthur'."

"I am at your service, Sire." Sir Raoul had a hollow feeling in his stomach. He was sure he knew what was coming.

"You will travel with Prious to Cornwall as a Breton sell-sword. These days, many travelling monks and friars hire a mercenary for protection. You look like a Breton, you can speak like one, and you almost are one. This task was made for you."

He stepped forward and put his right hand on Sir Raoul's left shoulder.

"Firstly, there are two items you must find and destroy. Brother Prious has seen them both. There is this sword of his, Excalibur. Destroy it. Do not bring it back to me. Get rid of it. The other is a book they keep at Tintagel. It is the history of the family right back to this Roman, we believe. Take it and destroy it too."

That, Sir Raoul had not suspected.

"Secondly, and vital to this, we must eradicate this threat forever. We must end this bloodline. Never will anybody be able to claim to be a direct descendant of this Arthur. You will kill the Lord of Tintagel, his son and his daughter."

His worst suspicion was correct. He would, of course, do his King's wishes. He had killed many men in battle but this was not the same, and a girl too.

"As you command, Sire."

"Good man, good man."

As he turned away from Sir Raoul there was a commotion outside the hall door. Odo acted immediately, raising a finger to his lips and ushering Prious and Sir Raoul quickly and quite forcefully behind the large screen that hid the urinal pot. The doors burst open and Odo came out from behind the screen as if he had just been making use of the pot. A voice he knew only too well boomed though the room.

"Of course the King will see me, I have urgent business with him."

Archbishop Stigand marched across the Hall towards the King and his advisors.

"What is the meaning of this interruption, My Lord Archbishop?"

"I am indeed Your Lord Archbishop, although more used to being addressed as Your Grace. However, I came to ask you the same question. What is the meaning of this? You have arrested and locked up my Bishop, Leofric of Exeter, a devoted and long serving member of the church, answerable to church law and to the Pope only."

"Not when he admits to treason and rebellion against the throne."

"Well, I will make sure the Pope is informed of your view. Having just received his blessing and acknowledgement as King of England, he might be more than a little disappointed in you."

"Then I must make sure he remembers your pledge to him last year when you made that large benefaction. You pledged to step down as Bishop of Winchester if he would lift your excommunication. I'm sure he would happily issue a sixth!"

Stigand suddenly seemed to notice the armour on the table near the fire, although Odo was sure he had seen it as he crossed the Hall.

"Ah, is this the antiquity you stole from the Cathedral in Exeter. Some relic of Roman occupation I hear. Nearly a thousand years old. You really should return it."

Odo held an arm across King William's chest to stop him stepping forward and addressed the Archbishop.

"Your Grace, as one man of God to another, we were in the midst of a very important discussion when you arrived, one which we would like to finish."

"Yes, I heard you were, but I thought there were more of you in here. Ah well, God willing, I must be away to Canterbury in the morning. Do not let me hear any bad news, like the death of Bishop Leofric, will you. The Pope would certainly not stand for that. God bless you all, even those beyond my sight."

Stigand left the room as dramatically as he had entered.

Odo walked to the screen and beckoned Sir Raoul and Prious to re-join them. The King fought for a few moments to control his temper, hands on the beam across the fireplace, staring into the flames. No-one else spoke. He moved to face the Hall again, and pointing to the door, said,

"Now that, is a very dangerous man indeed, but I just need to be patient. I will see him out of office within two years. He has survived beyond comprehension, but he is becoming overconfident, like Leofric. The Pope would see him in hell without his gold. Gold which should be in the King's vaults, not the church's."

Osbern could contain himself no longer.

"Sire, if he should speak to you like that again, I will….."

"You will keep your mouth firmly closed, my friend. I have said, patience. We will have our day."

Prious looked at Sir Raoul. Their eyes connected briefly. Both were astonished by what they had witnessed. A King spoken to in that manner, it was beyond belief. They had both had a lesson in the power of the church.

Odo stepped towards Prious and took his arm. He steered him towards the door.

"Sir Raoul, come with Prious and get some rest. He has clothes for you. The Count De Mortain will have horses ready for you both at dawn for your ride to Portsea Island. The boat that brought Prious from Cornwall will be waiting for you there to take you back to Cornwall, to Tregony. God speed you both."

Odo turned and strode back into the Hall. The doors closed and a guard led them to their quarters.

+ + +

Archbishop Stigand stormed into his rooms at Winchester Cathedral. If anything his mood had darkened since he had left the King but his mind was still racing, sorting the many possibilities that the situation could create. He snapped at his secretary, a young monk named Aelston who had jumped to his feet as Stigand entered the room.

"Get that Waestan back in here now, and I need an urgent message taken to Dublin, find me someone trustworthy to deliver it."

"Yes, Your Grace."

The monk rushed from the room.

Stigand paced impatiently. He was not used to waiting anymore, but as he reached Aelston's table he stopped and placed his hands on its polished wooded surface. He leant forward, looking down blankly at the woodgrain pattern and took two very deep breaths. He grunted, a choked laugh, and a wry smile creased his cheeks. He must not let this king get him angry. He thought more clearly when he was calmer. He had served five kings before this one. He had fallen from favour before and recovered, and he had outlived and survived four Popes and five excommunications, all by using his mind. He would do it again.

The recent excommunication had been lifted, but because of it, many new Bishops would not be ordained by him, insisting on Archbishop Ealdred of York conducting the service. They had taken the lead from King William who had insisted on Ealdred crowning him on Christmas Day, 1066, so that no-one could claim him crowned by an excommunicated priest.

He heard a noise and looked towards the door, but no-one entered. His left hip hurt terribly so he turned and sat back on the edge of the table rather than renew his pacing. He was in his late sixties now. Most men died before they had half of his years. He wasn't sure of his exact age, but he had become Royal Chaplain and advisor to King Canute in 1020. He had been raised an orphan in a monastery and he had never been able to discover any details of his birth or his parents. Forty-eight years he had been dealing with kings and he was sure he could cope with this one.

This time the noise he heard was the door opening. He stood, biting back a groan. Aelston ushered a young Friar into the room.

"This is Father Erste, Your Grace. He will carry your message to Dublin. Waestan will be with us shortly."

Stigand move towards the Friar.

"Excellent, now Father, listen carefully. You are to travel to Dublin with all possible speed. You will, of course, deliver my felicitations to King Diarmait but you are to tell Prince Godwine that all is in hand and to sail as early as the weather allows. Tell him that should he hear rumours of problems in Exeter he should take no heed. If he hears of the capture of Arthur's armour, tell them it has been recovered and returned to Tintagel. Is that clear?"

"Indeed, Your Grace."

"Be gone then."

The Friar nodded his head and backed away before turning and walking quickly to the door. Stigand smiled at Aelston, who was staring at him with a bewildered look on his face.

"You look troubled, Aelston. You want to know how the armour is to get to Tintagel, correct?"

Stigand was amused by Aelston's discomfort.

"Yes, Your Grace."

"Well it is quite simple. You are going to get it back tonight and Waestan will take it to Tintagel."

"The armour is under guard Your Grace, in the Great Hall."

"Yes, of course, but when the King and his court have retired, there will only be guards. You will be persuasive, you will remind them that the King may take their lives from them, but I can take their souls if they do not do as their God wishes. Just get it done. I want Waestan away well before dawn."

+ + +

Morwenna gazed out of her bedroom window at the long, flat line where the dark sea met the grey of the sky.

Tintagel Castle was unlike most castles. Because it was almost an island, set on sheer, high, unclimbable cliffs, it had only a low wall surrounding it with the main fortifications on its landward side, defending the path across the narrow strip of rock that joined it to the shore. One day, in the years to come, the sea would wear through the strip of granite leaving a natural high arched bridge, which itself would one day collapse leaving Tintagel Castle an island.

There were two towers, one on each side of a stone entrance, with heavy studded oak gates and a portcullis. There was no drawbridge, but the path was only just wide enough to allow a cart to cross it, so any attacking force could never get enough men to the gates to be any real threat to determined defenders.

It meant that behind the main gates the castle was more like a hilltop village. On the seaward end stood the Great Hall with the Lord and his family's dwellings. Morwenna's room faced the sea, and if she leant forward into the window, she could see up and down the coast quite well.

She closed the shutter and pulled the heavy curtain back across the window. A large fire of logs burned brightly in a simple fireplace which did much to light the room. Candles burned on the small table beside her bed and on the table against the far wall, which also held a small mirror and a basin and pitcher of water.

Morwenna sat back in the chair beside the fire. It had been different in the castle in the weeks since the Princes had left. Her father and brother had been tense, and all the menfolk were preparing for war. In the last week, however, it had become almost unbearable. She was not certain of what was happening but a messenger had arrived with bad news from Exeter. Then another arrived from King Mark in Bosvena, to say that if what he heard was true, he would not be marching with them. Other messengers were dispatched to Winchester and all seemed chaos.

Morwenna felt alone and unhappy. It had been difficult to see Elowen for any meaningful time and she had felt disillusioned by the two Princes who had visited. In fact, by the end of that evening's feasting she had felt quite repulsed by them. They were bad mannered and loud, and when Edmund had started pawing her, she slipped away without saying good night to her father. She knew he would have insisted on her staying, but as it was, she did not think he had even noticed she had gone.

Somehow, all her girlish dreams were shattered. These Princes were not like the sagas. Was any Prince? She smiled inwardly to herself. Ironically and luckily, her father had been too busy preparing for war to think about a husband for her. She might have agreed to anyone. If only she could talk to Elowen.

She wondered what her mother would have said, if indeed she could have discussed her womanly desires and feelings with her. She could have with her sister, Steren. She had just started to tell her of them before she died. Just thinking about such things, she felt her breasts tingle and her stomach tighten. Her own instincts and Elowen's guidance had taught her to pleasure herself, but it was not what she yearned for. Then again, she even doubted what she did yearn for anymore. The Princes had ruined her dreams, perhaps all men would.

She undressed quickly in front of the fire and slipped under the woollen blankets and furs of her bed. Whatever her dreams, there was only herself for now.

The Second Scroll

Prious woke slowly. He could hear cockerels and a general bustle of sound outside. He opened his eyes and looked towards the small window beside the door. There was a dull grey light, the first light of dawn. No-one had come to waken him.

He sat upright on the old wooden bed, throwing off its thin blanket. He had slept dressed. Swinging his legs around, he leant forward and reached for his soft leather boots. As he pulled them on he gathered his thoughts.

He had been given a small room in the Castle Bailey in which to sleep. Sir Raoul slept next door. Their rooms were the size of a stable and may have originally been built as such. There was a row of eight, side by side along the outer wooden Castle wall. The roofs provided part of the fighting parapet that ran around the entire Bailey, broken only by the entrance, where it was raised higher over the large wooden gates. Each room held a narrow cot bed and a small square table. Beside the door, which opened into the Bailey, was a window just large enough for a man's head to fit through. It had no shutter or curtain.

Prious picked up his travelling pack. It was a sack with a strap sewn into it so he could hang it around his shoulders as he walked. He hadn't unpacked anything so he opened the door and stepped outside. There was a fine rain in the air, the sort that could get everything damp before you realised. The door of Sir Raoul's room was open and the room empty.

He walked to the kitchens, a large wooden block next to the Mott. There was a lot of activity within the castle, and men were running. There was something wrong. A Company of Cavalry was forming near the gates. Prious quickened his pace.

He entered the small refectory next to the kitchen and Sir Raoul beckoned to him, a broad smile on his face.

"Good day, Brother, you're late about this day."

Prious joined him at the table, stepping over the bench to sit opposite him.

"I was sleeping the sleep of the righteous, you would not understand, and no-one woke me. Not even you."

"Ah well, you see, they woke me, and our departure has been delayed, so I told the guard to let you sleep. We will be summoned soon by Bishop Odo. I believe it has been an interesting night."

Prious leant forward as Sir Raoul took a bite from a piece of beef he had been holding.

"So, are you going to tell me?"

"Of course Brother, but take some breakfast, I think we will be travelling quite fast today, you will need your strength." Sir Raoul pushed some plates across the table, bread, beef and cheese, and filled a mug with ale. "I'm afraid there is no wine at breakfast."

Prious wanted to be angry, but he liked this man. He was obviously a hard fighting man, but he had a soft sense of humour beneath his exterior. As he gathered some food, Sir Raoul told him of the nights events.

"We will get the full story from His Grace I expect."

As he finished speaking, a guard came into the poorly lit room.

"Sir Raoul, Brother Prious. His Grace, Bishop Odo, has asked me to bring you to him."

"Lead on then, we will follow."

Sir Raoul picked up his pack and moved around the table to follow the guard. Prious swivelled around, lifting his legs back over the bench. He reached for his pack as he stood and followed the others out into the Bailey.

The drizzle had stopped but the air was still damp. Prious looked at Sir Raoul as they walked across the Bailey towards the Mott. The knight was only a little taller than himself but was thicker set, a result of many hours of weapon training he felt sure. All his fine mail was gone. He was wearing brown leather leggings which reached his boots. A light brown leather waist jacket covered a greying linen shirt, and over both, he wore a heavy dark leather tabard. It hung front and back to his mid thighs, held to his body by a dull metal chain belt. From the belt on his left hung his sword in its scabbard, almost scraping the ground, on his right hip, his fighting knife hung from a leather hoop. It was narrow and double bladed, the length of a man's forearm. His hair hung loosely over his shoulders, almost halfway down his back. It was held off his face by a thin leather thong that was tied around his head, across his forehead and knotted at the back, the loose ends hanging down amongst his hair. He looked like a hardened mercenary, a Breton sell-sword.

They climbed the wooden steps up the Mott. The guard led them through the oaken gates into the wooden fortress where they had met the King the day before, but this time they were led to a side room where Bishop Odo was awaiting them.

The Bishop was standing in front of a small stone fireplace set into an outside wall. There were no chairs in the room. Prious knelt on one knee and kissed the ring on the hand Odo offered him. Sir Raoul stood respectfully behind him.

Without any formality, Bishop Odo began to speak.

"I am sure you will have heard rumours of what happened here last night, but I will tell you all we know." He looked down into the fireplace, then turned towards them. "Sometime after midnight, the armour that you saw yesterday was stolen from the castle. There were three guards. One is dead, two are missing, deserted we assume. Quite how anybody got to them, or indeed, how they left the castle unobserved, we cannot tell."

He paused and walked towards the window, looking out as he spoke.

"This has to be the work of Archbishop Stigand. We believe, with a mixture of threats and violence, he turned the guards. The dead one probably feared the King more than his God. The fact is, the armour is only valuable to the rebellion at this time. It has to be on its way back to Tintagel. We have sent Cavalry Patrols along all the roads west, but if the church has it, we will not recover it that easily."

His habit flared as he spun on his heel and faced them, his face grave.

"This makes your trip even more important than ever. You must recover and destroy the armour, and you must take and destroy the sword and book too. I hold you, Prious, responsible for that. You, Sir Raoul, will help Prious and ensure none of King Arthur's bloodline are alive at the end of all this."

Both men nodded.

"Go then. You have horses waiting for the journey to Portsea, and a boat waiting there. The same one that brought you, Prious. Two days by sea should take you to Cornwall. If you travel north quickly you should get to Tintagel before anyone can travel there by land. Do not fail your King."

"We will not, Your Grace."

As Sir Raoul's words faded, Prious again knelt and kissed the Bishop's hand. They moved towards the door.

"God Bless you both in your task."

They shut the door behind them and did not hear Odo's last words.

"And God help you. I think you will need his hand."

+++

Morwenna was woken by the door to her bedroom being quietly closed as her maid left the room. Her maid came in every morning with a gentle knock to make up the fire and bring fresh water. Her entry usually woke Morwenna, but normally Morwenna had slept well. That night she had cried most of the night, only falling asleep shortly before dawn.

As she opened her eyes, there was little light in the room. The shutters were closed and the window covered by its heavy embroidered curtain. The fire's embers were struggling to ignite the logs her maid had laid on them, and as she had been asleep, no candles were lit. She became aware of rain and wind beating at the shutters, but then her mind began to clear and her memory return. Her chest seemed to fill with emotion until she let out a muffled wail and the tears began again.

She had been such a fool. A messenger had arrived in the afternoon the day before with news from King Mark. He was a handsome young man and well-groomed for a soldier. Morwenna met him after he had spoken with her father in the Great Hall, and her father had asked her to take him to the refectory. They exchanged a few pleasantries as they walked from the Hall across the courtyard.

Morwenna felt a strange excitement. She was suddenly hugely attracted to the man, yet she did not even know his name. As they reached the refectory door he stopped and turned to her.

"I am boarding in one of the rooms above the stables. I will be in my room from dusk if you would like to talk some more."

Morwenna could not believe a common soldier had just invited her, the daughter of the castle's Lord, to visit his room, but he had pushed open the door and was gone before she could think of what to say. She walked on to the stables. Elowen's cottage was beside them. Above the stables were two rooms for visitors to the castle. They were simple but comfortable. Noblemen were roomed in the Lord's quarters beside the Great Hall. The castle's Master of Horse and the Ostler, who looked after visitors' mounts, both lived in tied cottages beside the stables.

Elowen opened the door to Morwenna's knock. They hugged as best they could. Elowen was due to give birth to her second child within the month. Elowen looked tired but was delighted to welcome Morwenna into her home. Her eldest, a boy just a year old, was asleep on a pallet bed in one corner. They both sat on stools beside the heavy wood table in the centre of the room before the cottage fire.

Morwenna told Elowen what had happened. Should she go? She described the soldier and felt herself tingle as she did so. Elowen laughed.

"So you are asking me should you take up his offer" She paused as Morwenna nodded. "Well, I think, my dear friend, by the look on your face, you are going to go anyway. He is not inviting you to talk, you know that, and if you go, you know what he will expect. You may regret it, but if you do not go, I think you might regret it more. There is a time to become a woman, this may be yours."

Her boy-child grizzled and began to awake. Elowen stood and led Morwenna to the door.

"The sun is going down. Make your choice, go to your room or go to his. Enjoy yourself."

Morwenna kissed her and walked around to the stair at the side of the stables. She looked about but could see no-one watching her. She climbed the stairs to the small landing between two doors. She did not know which room was his. She gathered herself and knocked on one. There was no answer so she opened the door. The room was deserted. She tried the other door. Again no reply, but as she entered the room she saw two saddle bags on the small table, and there was a fire burning in the grate. This was the room.

It was becoming quite dark, so she took an ember from the fire and lit the three candles around the room, dropping the piece of wood back into the fire. She sat on the chair to wait for him. She realised she was trembling, a mixture of excitement and fear, but mainly she felt aroused by the anticipation. She moved in the chair as she heard a noise on the stair outside, suddenly aware how wet she was.

She would tell him it was her first time as they kissed and embraced and he would be gentle with her. She had broken and bled whilst out riding more than three years before.

The door swung open and the soldier stood in the door way. He leant against the frame as he saw her. His eyes were clouded. He had obviously drank a lot of ale. He smiled at her, his face contorting into more of a drunken leer.

"Well, my young lady, I thought you had the look of ripeness about you. I am very pleased to give you what you are after."

He shut the door behind him and half stumbled across the room towards her. He reached down, gripping her wrists and lifting her from the chair. He bundled her backwards towards the bed.

Morwenna tried to speak but no words would come. There was fear in her eyes as he pushed her onto the bed. His hands went to his leggings, unlacing his cod piece. He was ready for her. He held himself in one hand as if showing himself off to her.

"Now my young one, let's be about it."

He bent forward, lifting her gown and skirt and pushing her knees apart. She gave a stifled cry he took to be encouragement and ripped at her drawers. They were of a very light cloth with a string tie. They ripped across her left hip but the string held. He tore the front across her stomach. They were still around her right leg but he pulled them aside and entered her roughly.

This time she did scream, a mixture of pain and fear. He clamped a hand over her mouth as he thrust into her.

"Shush now my dearie, you'll bring someone to the door. Enjoy yourself quietly!"

Morwenna's mind was a tangle of thoughts. This was not how it was supposed to be. Romance was gone. This was animal lust. She pushed her hands upwards against his shoulders and tried to struggle. In his drunken state he took her movement to be enjoyment. She just wanted it to stop. It was awful. For a moment she tried to enjoy it, then she wailed at the thought that she might become with child. She had not really thought about it beforehand. To be with child from what she had dreamt of, romance and love with a Prince, was bearable, but the possibility of being with child from this nightmare was unthinkable.

The soldier slowed his movements. He had drunk a lot, and whilst his passion was high, his mind told him he had to piss. The more he thrust trying to seed, the more he needed to go.

He pushed himself off her. She opened her eyes to see him back away from her, holding himself and turning towards the single screen in the corner.

"Do not move girl. I've got to piss."

But move Morwenna did. As he went behind the embroidered screen, she rose as quickly and quietly from the bed as she could and ran the three paces to the door. She pulled it open and rushed down the stairs. She walked quickly across the courtyard, not wanting to draw attention by running.

The soldier heard the door bang shut but was still filling the piss-pot, slowed by trying to go whilst still half hard. He finished and turned back into the room. He was still holding himself and moving his hand slowly to encourage his hardness to return, which it did. It took him a moment to realise she was gone.

"Strange girl! Tonight it was not to be."

He turned back to the bed and standing over it, he finished himself with his hand, seeding over the blanket. He undressed, lay on the bed, and was quickly asleep.

Morwenna reached the Lord's quarters. The two guards wished her a good night, assuming she was returning from visiting Elowen, as it was not that long after sundown.

She went straight to her room, closing the door behind her and leaning back against it as the tears began. She removed her clothes beside the fire that her maid had built up not long before, leaving them in a bundle on the floor.

She stood naked except for the ripped drawers that hung around her waist from the string tie. She shook as she untied the string, letting them fall down her right leg. They were around her right ankle. She shook them over her foot and flipped them into the fire, where they burnt slowly as the crotch was still damp.

Her chest seemed to overflow with emotion. It was as if she could not cry hard enough. She thought she would burst as she stood before the small table that held a pitcher of water and a large wash bowl. She stood with her feet apart, bent her knees slightly and began to wash herself, as if she could eventually wash away the feeling of him there between her legs, but she could not.

Eventually, she dropped her drying cloth on the floor where she had splashed so much water, and climbed into her bed.

All this she relived again that morning. What would Elowen say? She would tell Elowen everything, of course.

For the first time since she had left the soldier's room, a smile flickered on her face. She knew what Elowen would say.

"Well, at least he did not seed in you. You will not be with child, and I tell you, thinking of that, I'll wager he was left with a hard one and did it himself, if I know men. What really makes me laugh though, you have had your first man enter you, what is his name?"

+ + +

Waestan shivered again. He was uncomfortable, cold, damp and frightened. He pulled the greying and frayed old blanket around him. It was damp too but it was slowly warming him. He was sitting on a wooden bench in the bow section of a large wooden boat on Portsea quay. A large canvas sheet hung over the bow, sheltering him from the rain. At his feet was a rope-bound canvas package and to his left sat his two new travelling companions, once guards from Winchester Castle.

He had been roused shortly after midnight by Aelston and ordered to dress quickly, pack his few belongings and report to Archbishop Stigand. He ran from his room through the heavy drizzle, deeper into the Cathedral outbuildings, arriving at the Archbishop's quarters short of breath. As he entered the hallway, two men were changing out of their uniforms of the Castle guard and into old clothes.

Aelston came out of the door from the Archbishop's rooms at that same moment.

"Ah, Father Waestan, come, the Archbishop is awaiting you."

He bustled Waestan through the door and followed him in. Stigand sat near the fire, beside an old work desk. There was a large package beside him, wrapped in canvas and bound in light rope.

Stigand looked round at Waestan. He appeared tired but his eyes were still bright.

"Waestan my son, I have a very important task for you. Can Your God and I rely on you to perform it?"

Waestan had walked around the table as Stigand spoke and stood before him. He knelt and kissed the ring on the hand the Archbishop offered him.

"Of course, Your Grace, anything you ask."

"This package is of the utmost importance and must be delivered with all haste, and in the greatest secrecy, to my friend Lord Jowan of Tintagel in Cornwall. I understand you know him."

Waestan rose and took a respectful step backwards.

"Yes, Your Grace. As Secretary to His Grace, Bishop Leofric, I have delivered and returned private documents between them."

"Of course, of course, I am forgetting it was you who Leofric sent with the news of the armour's capture. Well you may as well know, that package contains it all. The future of this kingdom is in that bundle. Guard it well and deliver it safely. Take it with all speed."

"I will, Your Grace."

He lifted the package and moved towards the door as Stigand spoke again.

"Father Aelston will give you detailed instructions, listen well."

Waestan bowed.

"I will, Your Grace."

They left the room into the hallway. The guards were now dressed in dark clothes with heavy cloaks around their shoulders. Waestan lowered the package. The contents were awkward to carry and felt heavier than they were.

Aelston beckoned them to him and began to speak.

"Father Waestan, you can acquaint yourself with these men on the road to Portsea."

The two men nodded to Waestan. He acknowledged them and turned back to Aelston who continued to speak.

"They were guards of the King who have more loyalty to their God than to him. The loss of the armour has not yet been discovered. Horses are prepared for you and you must make all speed for the wharf there. I dispatched a rider before midnight with instructions to find you a boat to take you to Cornwall. He will meet you in the church by the dock. As soon as the loss is discovered, it is certain the King will send cavalry along all roads from Winchester, but especially all tracks and paths westward. To ride west and reach Cornwall will become impossible, certainly with any haste. Once you sail from Portsea Island, you will be safe until you arrive in Cornwall. It will take longer for news to arrive there by road."

He looked Waestan directly in the eye.

"These men are under orders from His Grace to guard both you and the package with their very lives. They will take orders from you. You command the group. Do you understand what is expected of you?"

Waestan nodded, his lips pressed firmly together.

"Then be away Father, speed is everything in reaching Portsea."

They had ridden as hard as the horses could manage, resting and walking at times, but knowing that any pursuit would not be able to travel any faster.

They arrived in Portsea just after noon. The church by the dockside was easy to find. The priest was expecting them and watching for their arrival. He had the horses taken to the stables behind the church before they could raise attention. He ushered the travellers into the church. It was empty of people.

He had been a dockside priest a long time and had seen many things. He had learned not to look beyond his instructions.

"I do not know your names, and neither do I wish to. Nor do I know your business, and wish to even less. Along the quay is a trader, a working boat, the Rhosmon. It is commanded by its owner, Edmon of Tregony, who awaits your arrival. He is expecting two other passengers to arrive today for passage to Cornwall. They should be here by late afternoon in time to catch the evening tide."

Waestan tried to speak but the Priest held up a hand.

"I know you will have to wait, but there is no other boat ready to leave, nor able to with the tide as it is. Once at sea the Rhosmon is fast and seaworthy and will get you to Cornwall within two days. Edmon will keep you hidden from inquiring eyes until you sail. Now follow me to the boat."

Waestan was uneasy. If these other passengers were travelling from Winchester too, they might well be aware of the armour's theft. However, if the low tide prevented any boat from sailing, there was nothing to be done. He took the priest's elbow.

"Who are these other passengers? Do you know?"

"Edmon said they are a monk and his traveling companion. That is all he knows, except that he brought the monk here from Cornwall a day or two ago and has been paid to await his return. He is to take him back to Tregony wharf on the river Fal. You will have to travel to wherever you are going in Cornwall from there. I assumed that travelling with another man of the cloth would not be a problem."

Waestan looked at him wearily.

"It depends of whose cloth he wears these days, Father, Stigand's or Odo's."

"I find it wisest, Father, to remain beneath such matters, and to follow God's will, whoever he chooses to inform me of it."

He led them out of the church.

It was a short walk to the boat along the quay. They went in two pairs so as to arouse less curiosity. Waestan and his two companions had been sitting uncomfortably in the damp of the increasing drizzle ever since. It was a light drizzle that the breeze blew under their canvas roof and slowly soaked through whatever they wrapped around themselves.

+ + +

The Rhosmon lifted her bow over the next wave and smashed it down into the trough below, sending spray on the wind the length of her, before remorselessly doing so again.

She was some fifteen paces in length and of a wider beam than many her size. She had a relatively shallow draft though, to cope with the tidal creeks and shallow harbours around her native Cornwall. Her single mast rose tall just forward of her centre and a large block of cut granite lay beneath her decking just aft of it, to act as ballast for when, as now, her cargo was light. Her mainsail was not quite square. One side was attached to rings that ran up the mast as it was hoisted. It was secured to booms top and bottom, the top one shorter than the bottom. Both booms were attached to the mast with heavier rings at one end. The fourth side was free and slightly longer than the mast side so that the top boom was raised slightly as the sail filled. Before the mast, two triangular sails were rigged between mast and bowsprit. All was controlled by a maze of ropes which Edmon and his two crewmen used with easy confidence.

Prious and Sir Raoul had arrived before dusk. They had an escort of four riders who took their mounts and left immediately. They carried only a shoulder bag each. They boarded quickly and Edmon sailed without ceremony.

Raoul was plainly well armed with sword and two fighting knives, one longer than the other, almost a short sword. Prious still wore his black habit, hood raised against the wind.

They were seated in the aft of Rhosmon at some distance from their fellow passengers in the bow, but the boat was not long. They too had a canvas sheet strung across the decking below the mainsail's boom, which swung viciously when the boat changed tack.

Edmon had not introduced them to Waestan when they had boarded. He had just wished to put to sea before it got dark. There would be plenty of time for pleasantries during their passage, but both sets of passengers nodded greetings to each other. They were too close to ignore each other without appearing deliberately rude.

Their boarding however had caused much concern to Garth, one of Waestan's two guards. He had been on duty earlier the previous night and had seen Prious and Sir Raoul being shown into the King's presence.

Waestan hissed at him, trying not to raise his voice.

"Stay quiet man. Did they see you, or you Bardred?"

"I do not think so Father, certainly not Bardred."

"Then we have the upper hand. We know them, King's men, they do not know us."

They were leaving the shelter of the harbour and noise of the wind and waves was increasing. Waestan was trying to speak loud enough to be heard, but not so loud for his voice to carry aft.

"You say nothing to them, nothing. We need not speak until the morning, and then only I talk. Probably through Edmon at first. Understood?"

The two men nodded.

"Good, now get what rest you can, and try to eat some of the bread and cheese you were given. Although goodness knows if we will keep it down."

He sat back and sighed to himself. When he thought about it, if this monk had business in Cornwall, it was an almost inevitable co-incidence that they would end up on the same boat. Aelston was not as clever as he thought himself.

Of course the real irony was that there he was, an agent of the King, being protected by men of the Archbishop. Somehow he must communicate his true loyalty to these King's men, but that would have to wait. He only prayed he would not be murdered in his sleep. God help him if they knew what was in the package at his feet, but then again, maybe they did. He wished he had never got involved, but he was ambitious and Baldwin De Redvers had been so convincing.

In the aft of the boat Edmon and one of his crew stood one either side of the tiller, trying to hold the Rhosmon on a steady course. With the wind and tide from the south-west, Edmond had decided to sail around Wight, giving the Needles a wide berth, and was now on a wide tack into the wind. His senses and experience of the weather told him the wind would drop by the morning, but it was going to be a long night.

At his feet, Prious and Raoul were wrapped in blankets under the brown canvas cover slung across the back of the boat. They talked quietly, barely able to hear each other against the roar of wind and waves.

Sleep came and went all through the night. The boat pitched and rolled making both Prious and Raoul feel unwell, but by staying seated they both managed not to be sick. Prious could not help but smile that their fellow travellers were not so comfortable in the bow.

As dawn approached, the tides turned and the wind blew more from the south. The waves settled, not to a flat calm but subdued enough that the Rhosmon cut through them steadily.

Prious woke suddenly. He had not been asleep long and had not enjoyed the night at all. He felt a weight on his shoulder and realised that Raoul had leaned sideways in his sleep and now his head was resting against him. Prious tried to move a little, he was cold and sore. The decking was hard and his clothes wet.

His movement woke Raoul, who sat up quickly sensing he was lying against Prious.

"I'm sorry Brother, I hope I kept the wind off you." Prious smiled, trying to stand, but his legs were stiff.

"I am not a man of the sea, my son, nor will I ever be."

He looked up at Edmon, alone at the tiller now that the sea had abated. He shouted down to Prious.

"Did you enjoy the night's storm Brother? The Lord has calmed the waters for you."

"And none too soon Edmon. My friend here has been suffering all night."

"With the wind in the south we should arrive by dawn tomorrow. There will be food shortly."

"I'm not sure if that's good or bad! What say you Raoul?"

"I say we watch our friends in the bow." He stood as he said it. His hands checking his weapons, his voice a loud whisper.

Prious turned slowly towards the bow as the dawn light showed the coast away to their right. The three men in the bow were talking in voices too low to hear, but it was clear they were arguing.

Prious and Raoul had talked of them the evening before. It seemed almost inevitable that their fellow travellers were escaping with the stolen armour. It made sense to go by sea, avoiding all the searchers on the roads. They could not have known the boat they had joined had been held for their enemy. Raoul was certain they knew who Prious and he were. The way they looked at them and watched them constantly made him very uneasy, but Prious thought it best to wait and see what developed the next day, and although he was uneasy, Raoul did not object, but now he needed something to fill his stomach.

+++

As dawn broke, Father Erste had already been travelling for more than an hour. He was heading for Dorchester, or so he thought, having stopped in Wimborne for part of the night. He had travelled this way before but it had been some time ago. At Dorchester he would take the road north to Wells. From there he would travel to Bath, then down the Avon to Bristol. In Bristol he would board a boat to Dublin. He had been given funds to do so, coins in a pouch attached to his rope belt that was tied around his waist. He could have travelled the north road from Winchester until he reached the London to Bristol road, but both were well used and he felt safer on the slightly longer but quieter tracks he was on.

He rode a two wheeled cart pulled by an ageing shire that seemed to be enjoying the task. It was an old farm cart, well-used and well-worn but very reliable, and it did not stand out as something a Friar should not possess.

As he rode over a brow he sat upright, his heart suddenly beating in his chest. The track ahead was blocked by a circle of round tents, a larger one in their centre. There were many horses, hundreds, and men were moving purposefully around the camp in the dawn's new light. The camp was coming to life.

He heard hoof beats to his right. Three horsemen were riding towards him, Normans. Camp guards he assumed. The first reined in across the nose of the old shire. He spoke loudly as the other two cavalrymen halted each side of his cart.

"Good-day Father, what business do you have on the road this early in the day?"

"God bless you, Sir. I am travelling from Winchester to Bristol under the orders and protection of Archbishop Stigand, with blessings and messages for the Bishop of Bristol."

"Are you indeed! Well now, you may have the Archbishop's blessing, but do you have King William's?"

"The King is a man of God."

"That's as maybe, but he does not always agree with him." He wheeled his horse, his shield and sword rattling on his chainmail. "Follow me."

The guard walked his mount towards the camp and, with the other two flanking his cart, Erste followed down the slight slope and into the centre of the camp.

They stopped outside the large tent. Erste had looked around him as they had approached. This was a larger camp than it first appeared, some four or five hundred cavalrymen he was sure.

A very well armed knight appeared at the tent's opening.

"What have we here?" His accent was very heavy Norman, a knight certainly. The guard replied emphatically but respectfully.

"A travelling Friar, Sire. Claims to be carrying messages from Archbishop Stigand to the Bishop of Bristol. There are no large packages in the wagon, Sire, and there is nowhere to hide one on the cart, but given he openly admits he is in the service of the Archbishop I thought you would want to see him."

"Exactly right, now return to your duty on the road." The knight waved to some guards.

"Get down, Friar." Erste climbed down from the cart and stood before the knight. Only then did he realise how thick-set the man was. He must have been very strong. He looked into Erste's face.

"I do not imagine, Father, that you would share these messages you carry for the Bishop of Bristol with me?"

Erste tried to stand as tall and confident as he could, but he was trembling slightly as he spoke. He tried not to let it sound in his voice.

"That I cannot do Sire. They are God's secrets between Archbishop Stigand and the Bishop of Bristol, entrusted to me only as a messenger."

"I never thought you would, Father. It is not for me to know them, however I have orders to hold any priest I find travelling west and bring them with us to Exeter. There you will be given to my Lord, Sir Breon. He will, no doubt, pass you on to Sir Baldwin De Redvers, and it is he who will decide whether to persuade you further to tell all. Think well on it as we travel, Father. You will tell us eventually. You may decide it better to tell me before we arrive in Exeter. That way one day you may leave there."

He turned to the four guards who had answered his summons.

"Take him."

Erste had never been so frightened in his life. If they tortured him he knew he would tell them everything.

+++

On board the Rhosmon they had all eaten something. Some more than others. A crewman had given each traveller a wooden platter of bread and cheese and a pewter mug of water.

Raoul and Prious sat against the side rail of the boat, which was now hardly moving as the swell had almost ceased altogether. Waestan still sat between his two companions, the large package at his feet.

One of the two guards moved to the side of the boat, undoing his codpiece as he walked. He glanced towards the back of the boat as he began to urinate over the side.

Waestan leapt to his feet, jumped over his package and ran the length of the boat, his shoulder brushing the mast. Raoul was on his feet, his sword in his hand before Prious could react at all. Waestan held his hands above his head as he saw Raoul's sword and stopping his dash, shouted wildly at them.

"Help me please, I am a King's man, in the service of Sir Baldwin. These men are under orders from The Archbishop."

The two guards were facing them, one each side of the mast, swords in their hands. The one on the right had his unlaced codpiece hanging and a wet stain on his leggings. The other was slightly behind him and half obscured by the boom.

Raoul stepped in front of Prious and Waestan. He would get no help from Waestan and he was not sure about Prious. He reached across his waist with his left hand and drew his fighting knife from his belt, his sword was in his right.

"Well my friends, I hope you can use those swords now you have drawn them. You can sheave them and we can discuss this. I do not wish to kill you, but believe me I will if you do not."

Raoul's voice was calm and menacing. He had learnt over his years as a fighting man that apparent confidence was a great weapon. The guard on the right moved forward half a pace. His sword arm was next to the mast. He could not swing his sword to his right.

Raoul moved towards him, away from the boom and the other. He swung his sword from above his right shoulder. The guard had no shield or fighting knife, he could only parry by reaching across his body. Leaning his weight on his sword as they met, Raoul stepped forward and drove his fighting knife into the guard's stomach, wrenching it upwards as he stepped back to face the other.

"I did warn you."

He had been exposed for a second but the other guard had not moved. Now he looked into Raoul's face, fear in his eyes. He knew he was no match for Raoul. He threw down his sword and backed away. Raoul took a step towards him, over the body at his feet to round the mast. The guard turned and jumped over the side into the sea, swimming clumsily towards the shore as the Rhosmon sailed on away from him. Edmon's voice broke the shocked silence.

"He will not reach the shore, we are too far off. The tide will take him."

"Are you sure?" Raoul asked. Edmon just looked at him and nodded. Raoul nodded back.

"I'm sorry about the mess." Edmon laughed

"My lads will put him over the side. The blood will wash off. That was very impressive for a sell-sword! The story will earn me an ale or two."

Raoul turned to Prious and smiled. Prious was almost expressionless, and for the moment, speechless. He knew that Raoul was a trained fighter but what he had just witnessed was frightening. Waestan was white faced and shaking.

Raoul returned his sword to its scabbard. He bent forward and lifted the hem of Waestan's habit, wiping the blood from his fighting knife. Waestan said nothing as Raoul returned the blade to his belt.

"I should thank you, Raoul. That all seemed a bit sudden and very, uh, efficient."

"I did not want to kill them. The one on the left did not want to fight, his whole body showed it. The other felt he had to. As foot soldiers, any fighting training they had would have been with a shield and he did not have one. He was always vulnerable, but enough, what of this one and his package."

"Brother, Sire," Waestan began, "The package is yours. It contains the Roman armour of King Arthur, stolen from the King by Aelston and those two guards. The Archbishop instructed me to take it to Tintagel and deliver it in person to Lord Jowan."

Prious looked into Waestan's face. His eyes were full of fear.

"Why did the Archbishop trust you with such a valuable delivery?"

"I was clerk to Bishop Leofric in Exeter. He was plotting against King William. I am not stupid. The future is in Norman hands now, so I offered my services secretly to Sir Baldwin de Redvers. He accepted me but told no-one. Bishop Leofric gave me messages for the Archbishop. Of course I told Sir Baldwin immediately and he instructed me to go to Winchester and deliver the messages, then to return to him with anything I learnt. I just happened to be there and the Archbishop was aware I am known to Lord Jowan, as an emissary between him and Bishop Leofric."

He paused for breath and Prious filled the gap.

"Enough. Now let us all rest and calm down. We must decide how to proceed from here, and we have plenty of time to think."

He sat down heavily in the stern of the boat. He smiled to himself as he realised his heart was still beating hard.

He had learnt a lot about Raoul in those short moments.

+++

King William was in the Great Hall of Winchester Castle almost as the dawn broke. He had not slept well. His mind was unsettled, thoughts of the church and this King Arthur. The doors opened and Bishop Odo entered the Hall, closely followed by the Count de Mortain.

"You summoned us, Your Majesty."

"I did indeed Odo, Robert. I have had a bad night. What news of your monk and Sir Raoul?"

"They sailed for Cornwall in the late afternoon the day before last. With kind winds they may almost be there by now. We questioned the priest at the dockside church. It appears that there were three other men travelling with them. Given the circumstances, that might prove interesting."

The King turned to the Count.

"What news from the searches on the roads?"

"One report only, my King. A rider from the cavalry I dispatched to Exeter, at your command. They arrested a travelling friar on his way to Bristol at The Archbishop's command. They are taking him to Exeter."

"Mmm. Thank you both. It would appear that patience is required, not a strength of mine!"

Bishop Odo smiled at his half brother.

"I am sure our fortunes are in good hands. Breakfast and a goblet of wine seem our best course of action for now."

King William nodded.

+++

On the Rhosmon, Raoul awoke having slept surprisingly well. The sea had become almost a flat calm with just a gentle breeze. This filled the sails but had slowed their speed.

Raoul stood up, stretching stiff limbs. He had been in his clothes for two and a half days now and was uncomfortable. He had not felt dry since they boarded the boat.

The dawn light was a rich pink in the eastern sky, and it lit the shoreline to their right. Raoul was surprised how close to the shore they now were. Just a few hundred yards. The coast was of rugged granite cliffs with dark green sloping open fields above them. It looked like parts of the Brittany coast.

Edmon called down to him from the stern, his hands holding the tiller steady with ease now.

"That is the Rhosland, good Sir, my home. The small village on the brow of that hill above the bay is where I was born."

"You are a lucky man, having such a beautiful home. Have we far to sail now?"

"Indeed no, Sir. Our timing is perfect. I did not want to get here before the dawn. I did not want to enter the Fal before daylight. Another half a day and you will be at Trerigoni."

Their voices had woken Prious. He had slept in the stern beside Raoul. Waestan had returned to the bow and slept beside his package. He still seemed to feel responsible for it.

"Good morning Brother," Raoul called as he saw Prious sit up.

"Good morning Sir Raoul." He looked worriedly at him as he realised what he had said.

"I never doubted it for a minute!" laughed Edmon behind him. "It had to be, but your secret is very safe with me."

Prious looked anxiously towards the bow. The two crewmen were emerging from their covered shelter in the bow, only just large enough for them both to fit in. Waestan still appeared not to have stirred but he awoke as the crewmen emerged on deck.

Raoul, Prious and Waestan had talked most of the afternoon the day before. They discussed many options about how to proceed with their missions.

The first and main debate was what to do with the armour in Waestan's package. Raoul and Waestan were both for dropping it into the sea immediately. Raoul was sure that would be what King William would have wanted, and Waestan supported him as all he wished was to be relieved of his burden.

Prious argued strongly against it. He wanted to turn circumstance to their advantage, whilst he appreciated it was a riskier strategy. They should travel to Tintagel with Waestan and the package. Waestan would tell how, on the way from Trerigoni to Tintagel, they were attacked by King's men, or thieves. The two guards had been killed but Raoul, Prious' sell-sword, had saved them. They would give the armour to Johan, but if they were going to kill him and steal Excalibur anyway, why not the armour as well? That way they would be accepted and trusted immediately, giving them more freedom once in Tintagel.

It was a strategy that worried Raoul enormously, but there was a logic to it that might produce the result they intended. It was make or break. If they failed, they would give everything to the rebellion, making it stronger, but the risk could be worth it. Waestan never really had a say. Finally, Raoul decided the debate. He faced Prious.

"You are here for your brain, Brother, I am here for my sword. I'm not sure that I agree with this plan, but we will do as you suggest."

Raoul was still uneasy about the idea that morning but he had chosen to support Prious. He had a strange confidence in the monk, although he was only beginning to know and understand him.

The boat reached the end of the Rhosland. Edmon and his crew changed tack, turning smoothly into the mouth of the Fal.

The sea was rougher as they entered the waters around the headland of Rhos. Edmon called down to them. Waestan had just joined Prious and Raoul.

"It will calm again soon. Here the waters of the Fal, the Truro River and the Tresillian meet the tidal currents. It can get quite rough when the winds are strong. Over to your left is the small fishing port that is used by most of the fishermen here about. It has naturally become known as Falmouth. Over there to our right is a small fishing port of St Mawes. In a while we will pass the Church of St Just to our right. You will know these places Brother, and perhaps you too Father?"

"By name only," Waestan replied. "It is a long way from Exeter. I know much of the north coast road as far as Tintagel, but I have never been this far south before." Edmon nodded as Prious spoke.

"It will take some time to Trerigoni, I imagine?"

"It will Brother. The tide is in our favour but the winds are light. It is about ten miles from here to Trerigoni. It is wide and easy here but when we reach Turnaware the river narrows to fifty yards and less. It becomes more difficult to tack a boat this size in the winding river, but my men have done it many times before. Once we reach Lamorran and Lanihorne, with this wind it will be an easier sail for the last mile or two. Five or six hours I would say."

"Thank you, we shall prepare for our journey then. When we reach Trerigoni we will go to my church at Cornelly. I have some provisions there we must collect for our journey. If there is still light we will make a start for Tintagel. It should be an easy enough journey." Waestan returned to the bow and Raoul slapped his hand on Prious' shoulder.

"An easy enough journey you say! I had better sharpen my sword then."

The Third Scroll

It was an hour or so after noon when Prious, Raoul and Waestan stepped off the Rhosmon and onto the wooden raft that formed the wharf on the bank of the Fal, opposite Tregony. The river was only slightly tidal there, but floating wharfs were the practical solution to the couple of feet the river rose and fell.

Opposite them at the bottom of Tregony hill stood a small stone and wooden church, the Church of St James, Tregony, that ministered to the people of the village. The Church of St Cornelly had been built for those on the west bank of the Fal, who were very few in number.

They thanked Edmon and his crew but, as Raoul and Waestan began to climb the path up the bank, Prious was talking with Edmon.

"Just to be clear, you will wait here for fourteen nights, but be ready to sail any time after the first seven. If I do not get back by then, sail for Portsea and report what has happened until now to Bishop Odo. Do not let me down, nor the King."

"I have been well paid, Brother, to do as you command. I will be here if you return within fourteen days. If not, I will do as you say."

"Good man."

Prious climbed up after the others, his small pack slung from his shoulder. Raoul spoke as he caught up with them.

"There is more to you, Brother, than we know."

"You know all you need to know, Raoul. Follow me."

Prious strode along the track that followed the valley away from the river and around the hill above them. After half a mile, Prious turned up a smaller track to their right and up the hillside. As they reached the tree-line on the hillside and moved onto grassland, they could see the little Church of St Cornelly, almost at the top of the hill. It was no bigger than a small barn, a single room it appeared.

There was a small porch on the south side at the west end. As they reached it they could see a sturdy donkey tied to a rail beside the door. Prious said nothing, but drew a large iron key from behind a beam in the porch and unlocked the church door.

They entered the small church. The altar was at the eastern end covered by a large white cloth, and there were some benches around the outer walls. Otherwise, the only furniture was a large wooden table against the west wall. On one end of the table were some wooden platters of bread, cold meats and cheese. A large pitcher of water was beside them. Along the table were some sack bags, strung at the top and filled with similar foods. Beyond them were some large blankets.

"Someone knew we were coming then?" said Raoul. Prious picked up some cold meat. It had been many hours since they had eaten on the Rhosmon that morning.

"There is plenty for the two of us I expected, so I do not think three of us will go hungry. The rest we will pack on the donkey. It will be three days walk, I imagine, to Tintagel. This was here today. There is a farm just along the hillside. I arranged for it to be left daily for the next few days. The farmer would have collected the donkey and the food each night if they were still here and put them back the next morning."

"You knew what the King would order us to do?"

"I knew what Bishop Odo would advise him strongly to do." He took a large bite of bread. "Waestan, I suggest you use some of the rope there to attach that armour to the donkey's back. I cannot watch you struggle with it any longer. Now eat both of you. We must then load this dear animal and begin our walk."

Raoul shook his head a smiled. He took his fill of food from the table and sat on a bench against the north wall. Prious continued to surprise him.

+++

The donkey had a wooden rack strapped securely to his back. The three men loaded their provisions, blankets and the sacking package that held Arthur's armour onto it. The rack had wooden hooks onto which they hung the cloth bags. When everything was loaded, Prious untied the rope which tethered the donkey and handed it to Waestan.

"Yours is the largest package, Father, the animal is in your charge. St Cornelly will bless you for it."

Waestan took the rope without a word. He was in awe of Prious and Raoul, and frightened. He could still see the speed and ease with which Raoul had killed the guard Bardred, and without any obvious hesitation, nor indeed, remorse.

Prious locked the church door and replaced the key in the beams of the porch roof. He looked at the doors, as if saying goodbye, then turned and led his companions across the grassland to the north-west. There were a few hours of light left and they could manage some miles before dusk.

The path led around the brow of the hill then began downwards into trees. Within a mile they reached the bottom of the slope and joined a slightly wider path, a track almost, that ran along the west bank of the Fal. It was rough however and very muddy in places, slowing their progress.

Prious spoke back over his shoulder.

"We will follow the Fal upstream, almost to its source. We will be climbing slowly all the way, and when we reach the top, we head for Nanstallon, but today, just a few miles, maybe four."

On the far side of the river was a small wooden building.

"Over there is Krid. Around the next two bends we will reach Ponsmeur, in Cornish, Grand Pont in Norman. We must skirt the village on this side of the river. There is a bridge there over the Fal, but I do not wish to cross there. I do not trust the villagers, nor the Manor of Tybesta."

They walked on steadily, passing Ponsmeur with its bridge and wharfs on the opposite bank, before striding quickly onward up the Fal.

The banks on both sides of the Fal began to rise steeply and the path grew narrower and more difficult. Another two sweeping bends through the hillsides and the river split. Nestled into the hillside between the Fal and the tributary were two small cottages. Ropes from these dwellings crossed both rivers and were secured to trees on the opposite banks. A large wooden raft was attached to each, moored against the bank outside the cottages.

Raoul stepped closely behind Prious.

"Do not tell me, Brother, that this was arranged for our benefit."

"No, no, my son, these good folk provide crossings here. They are rarely used and not well known. They use them themselves, mainly for hunting the opposite banks. The left fork is the Fal, the right fork is the Brannel that flows through Brannel Manor."

"You seem to know a great deal about the area."

"Ha, I am in the pay of Bishop Odo, but the Count de Mortain has showed a great interest in Cornwall and I have been learning much on his behalf about the Manors here. I think if Cornwall should come under Norman rule soon the Count sees himself as the Duke of Cornwall. He has always been jealous of his brother being Duke of Normandy, but now he is King of England too, Robert is doubly upset."

Prious moved on to where the rope across the Fal was attached to a tree. A large metal triangle hung there with a metal bar hooked to it. Prious lifted the bar off and rang the triangle loudly a number of times. A man came out of one of the cottages and waved. He went back in and came out again with a youth, Raoul assumed his son.

"The hill behind the cottages is Crow Hill, and on its top is Ressuga Castle, a small ancient fort. It will be a good place to stop for the night. At least it is not raining."

The two men pulled the Fal raft across to them. Waestan amused them with his efforts to get the donkey onto the raft, but he succeeded. They were pulled across to the cottages. Prious found a coin for the ferryman, then spoke with him further and gave him a second. He waved to his companions to follow him and led them up a path behind the cottages into the wooded hillside. The donkey seemed happy to have its feet back on the ground.

Prious spoke over his shoulder to Raoul.

"I have paid the ferryman well, very well. No-one else will cross either river today, and not until midday tomorrow."

"Very good, Brother, you think of everything."

"I hope so, my son."

It was a hard climb through the woods and they were all glad when they reached the top. The trees ended and a steep grass bank rose ahead of them. Prious led them around the edge of it until they reached a gap. They entered the old fort. They were all surprised how small it felt once inside. Here they walked into the south west corner where they were most sheltered from the wind.

Waestan unloaded the donkey whilst the others gathered some wood and kindling. Prious used his flint to light the fire as darkness began to fall.

Raoul was comfortable with their campsite. It felt strangely secure within the high banks. They, and the trees outside them, hid the light of their fire, and the moonless darkness hid any smoke.

They selected a blanket each and sat around the fire. Waestan distributed some food and water, and the donkey grazed happily.

They sat silently for a while, all eating heartily. It had been a long day. Raoul broke the silence.

"Tell us then Waestan. Where are you from? Who are you?"

Before he could say anything Prious spoke for him.

"He was born on a farm near Haldon, close to Exeter. He is the third child of six. His eldest sister and youngest brother died of fever. He was monastery educated, entered the church and, because he could read and write, became secretary to Bishop Leofric. Here he learnt about church politics up to a point. He had the sense to accept Norman rule and offered his services to Sir Baldwin de Redvers, Sheriff of Devon. That I think is all there is to know."

Waestan looked at Prious, tears in his eyes.

"I do not know who you are, Brother, but I will not accept much more of this. You both treat me as if I do not exist. How do you know about my life, who on God's earth are you?"

"I apologise, Father." Prious looked into the flames, then back at Waestan. "It is my job to know such things. You have much to learn about true power. Bishop Odo has spent the last year using people placed around the kingdom, like myself, to know such things. Sometimes I forget, I should be more....., understanding."

"I apologise too, Father." Raoul looked Waestan in the eyes. "I too have been unthinking too, but then I am not here to think more than I need, that is for Brother Prious. You are important to our mission, I did not intend to demean you."

Waestan looked from one to the other.

"You both have experience and skills way beyond mine, but I promise you, you have my complete support in whatever you need from me. I want to learn from you. I want to become like you."

"Like Prious perhaps! Not like me, Father, I am beyond help." Raoul laughed as he spoke.

"What of you, Sir Raoul? I heard Prious call you that on the boat."

"Perhaps Brother Prious would like to tell you about me?"

Prious smiled and looked at them both across the flames.

"No, Sir Raoul is the King's man. I have heard stories but not the truth. Please Sir Knight, pray tell us."

"You know Brother, sometimes I think I know how the Father here feels!"

"Then I do most humbly apologise again. I meant no insult, truly, I know little about you, only that you are the very best our purpose."

Raoul took another bite of the cold beef he held before he spoke.

"I am the fourth son of Geoffrey Tyrrell, Lord of Poix. My family are French, not Norman, they came from Archere in Vexin, on the Seine just north of Paris. Walerean became the hereditary Standard Bearer to the King of France. His fourth son was Sir Ralf, who built a castle some miles north and downstream at Tirel. He became Sir Ralf de Tirel, now in heraldry, Tyrrell. When all the lands to the north and west of Paris were given to the Vikings, the Nord Homme, forming Normandy, the Tyrrells were given lands in Picardy and thus became Lords of Poix.

"I too am a fourth son. My eldest brother was Sir Walter Tyrrell, Lord of Poix. As a fourth son I was trained as a soldier from childhood. With three elder brothers I learned how to fight when young. At sixteen I left home with a courser I had trained since a boy, and chainmail my father gave me. That and my horse were all he ever gave me.

"I found myself in Normandy and at eighteen joined the army of Duke William the Bastard. I had my own horse and mail and was taken into the Cavalry where I trained further. About four years ago I rode with King William to fight King Conan of Brittany. Eventually we defeated him and Duke William became the Conqueror.

"During the battle I found myself unhorsed and beside the Duke. It was pure self-defence and desperation on my part. I fought back to back with the Duke on foot until the Cavalry rallied and relieved us. The Duke knighted me that evening for protecting his back. I could speak Breton, English and French, as well as Norman. William had me stay in Breton to help with his rule there.

"When the Pope blessed his invasion of England I recruited and led a small army of Bretons to join the Duke. I fought at Senlac with my eldest brother Sir Walter Tyrrell, who led the first charge of that day, made by the men of Poix, up the hill against the Saxon right. He was Viceroy for a year whilst the King was in Rome with the Pope, but alas, died in January last. My Bretons too had a key role at Senlac, holding the left when our line nearly broke. The King has always been grateful."

Raoul had been staring into the flames as he spoke. He looked up to see Prious and Waestan both staring at him.

"I'm sorry, I should not have said so much."

"No, no." Prious immediately interrupted, "Thank you. I can see you have had much fighting experience."

"There is a huge amount of luck in surviving a battle. You can be the best swordsman in the land and be cut down from behind by the worst. The main thing in battle is to be ruthless and kill. If you hesitate someone will cut you down. Aggression is key. You have to become an animal and fight like one."

Raoul suddenly realised that Waestan was still staring at him, transfixed almost.

"Father, I am sorry, have I troubled you?"

"No! I am so sorry. Listening to you I just thought of my childhood. My father would tell us stories of brave knights and the battles they fought. I never expected to meet one."

Raoul leant back and clapped his hands. He laughed and shook his head.

"My dear Father Waestan, now at least I hope you will see that a famous knight is just a man, like yourself, who luck has favoured at a good time."

"Not like me! I could not fight, not in a battle, I am too light, too weak. I would be killed before the battle had begun in earnest."

Raoul laughed.

"You do not understand Father. Many foot soldiers are just like you. Their strength is in their numbers, the shield wall, interlinked, a unit. Many battles are little more than a pushing contest with some casualties. If you end up fighting man to man the shield wall is broken and the battle is probably already lost. A knight unseated and on foot is a target however. He attracts men at arms who wish to make a name for themselves, either by killing a knight or capturing one and demanding a ransom from his relatives after the battle, whoever wins."

"That is as maybe, but I still think I could not do it."

"You would do it because your friends and comrades do it. All are as one, none wanting to appear to be scared or to let the others down. It becomes easier to stay with the crowd than to run away. One secret though, I am sure, is not to look different to your fellows. An archer picking his next target, or a knight driving his horse at a man on foot, will often decide he'll aim for the one in the red head band, or the one with the yellow scarf, someone who he can pick out from the crowd. You need to be one of the crowd."

Waestan looked away, towards the fortress entrance.

"Well as a Priest, I hope it is something I never have to experience."

Prious broke the moment's silence.

"Build up the fire, Raoul. I think we should think of sleep now. I want to start our walk with the dawn. We have had a long day."

The fire burning strongly, they settled in their blankets around it. Tomorrow's journey would be long.

For the first time since they had left Winchester Raoul felt relatively warm and dry. The ground was cold and damp but his blanket kept his body heat around him. He shut his mind to his thoughts and prayed it would not rain. Surely the Good Lord would look after his own. He smiled to himself. There were servants of the Lord in both camps and he wondered which side the Lord was on. He was soon asleep.

+++

Baldwin de Revers stood with his back to the newly-lit fire. He had risen with the dawn and had not slept well. The Great Hall of Rougemont Castle was not large, but it was by far the largest room in the castle and it would be some hours before the fire warmed it to any extent.

He had been elated at first when the King had appointed him as Sheriff of Exeter. He had been part of the force that had put down the rebellion there, and it showed the trust the King had in him, or rather the trust Bishop Odo had in him. He had learnt that many of the King's best decisions were at Odo's suggestion. Now, however, he was beginning to feel trapped by his position, away from the centre of things.

He had hoped to be able to travel north. He was convinced the Danes would invade the north again and had warned Odo of the dangers of a planned joint uprising, joint co-ordinated invasions even, the Irish and Saxons in the south and the Danes in the north. Odo was convinced it would not happen. The north might rise but he was convinced the Danes would not invade again for some time. King Harold had defeated them utterly before Senlac at Stamford Bridge and Odo was sure they would not have the strength nor desire to invade again so soon.

Odo did agree, however, that a successful uprising and invasion in the south would be joined by the north, so he was determined that any such must not succeed. He had confidence that Baldwin would not let this happen.

There was a loud knocking, the door opened and Sir Breon of Brittany was ushered in. He bowed to Baldwin and joined him by the fire.

"Good day, Sir Breon. Pour yourself some wine. It will warm you."

"Thank you, my Lord Sheriff, I will." He filled a goblet and drunk from it. "You sent for me?"

"I did Breon. A rider has arrived from Winchester. He has ridden almost without a break for three days and three nights. I sent him for some refreshment whilst I summoned you. I thought it best if you heard his reports too, saving me repeating it all to you."

With perfect timing there was another knock at the large double doors. A young cavalryman of the King's Guard entered the room and bowed low before approaching them. Despite some obvious efforts he still looked tired and dishevelled from his long and hurried ride. He looked at the two noblemen before him. Both were obviously soldiers but one looked more typically Norman. The young man guessed correctly. He spoke as confidently as he could.

"I carry messages from the King for the Sheriff of Exeter. That is you my Lord?"

"It is indeed young man, and this is Sir Breon of Brittany."

"Thank you, my Lord, my messages concern him also, but I was instructed to speak to you personally."

"You may do so then, what is the King's will."

"My Lord, there are a number of things you should know. Firstly, Bishop Odo said you would know of the armour found in Exeter and taken from Bishop Leofric." Baldwin nodded. "It has been stolen from the castle in Winchester. It is thought it is being taken to Lord Jowan in Tintagel."

"That would make sense. Carry on."

"Thank you, my Lord. You are to watch the roads to the south and west for any men of the cloth who may be carrying it." The guardsman paused as he brought the next parts to mind. "Sir Breon has five hundred Cavalry here at his command. On the road behind me, and due here in another day or two, are five hundred more cavalry to join his command."

"Very good." Baldwin interrupted. "What more?"

"My Lord, one of Bishop Odo's men, a monk, Brother Prious by name, is sailing to Cornwall. He should be ashore by now. He is traveling to Tintagel to discover what he can. He travels My Lord, with a man disguised as a sell-sword mercenary, known to you both it is believed, one Sir Raoul Tyrrell."

"Ah!" Sir Breon could not help but interrupt. "We fought on opposite sides years ago in Brittany, "but since have become close friends. I fought under his command at Senlac."

"I know the name. His exploits have not escaped me, but I have never met him."

"He is not a typical Norman my Lord Sheriff." Sir Breon laughed affectionately as he spoke. "In fact he is not actually Norman. He has been adopted as Norman by the King but he is French by birth."

"There is more, my Lord."

"Of course, continue."

"My Lord, when his business in Tintagel is complete, Sir Raoul is ordered to come here. The King orders that you, my Lord, should do everything in your power to support him and do whatever he requires of you, and that Sir Breon and his Cavalry are to come under his immediate command. That I believe is all, my Lord. I am ordered to join Sir Breon's cavalry."

"Indeed, go, I will ensure your excellent conduct will be recorded and reported to the King and to Bishop Odo."

"My Lord." The young guardsman bowed to them both and left the Hall.

"Interesting times, Sir Breon, what think you?"

"Well, my Lord Sheriff, two things are most significant to me. Firstly, a further five hundred cavalry, one thousand in total, means they are expecting serious trouble from someone, but secondly and most significant, is that Bishop Odo has recalled Sir Raoul Tyrrell. After King William's Coronation he returned to his home in France."

"Poix, I believe."

"That is now his family's home. Since his eldest brother, Sir Walter, died recently, his nephew, Sir Walter the Second, has become Lord of Poix. No, Sir Raoul returned to his own chateau in Radepont, on the banks of the Andelle, a few miles upstream from where it joins the Seine. He lives quietly there, but believe me, my Lord, dear friend as he is, he is a ruthless soldier, some would say heartless."

"I think, Breon, you should ready your men to move. I can hold the city walls here with the two hundred men I have. As soon as your new contingent arrive, I suggest you move to Tawton and wait there for Sir Raoul. If he travels from Tintagel he must cross the ford there, and you will be nearer to him if he needs your support."

"Indeed, my Lord Sheriff, I will be about it."

Sir Breon left the Hall, his mind was racing.

+++

Prious was awake before dawn. He damped down the embers of the fire, his moving about wakening his companions. They ate hastily and loaded the donkey before wandering to the edge of the woods to relieve themselves. Prious spoke as Waestan and Raoul returned to the fort.

"Better, Gentlemen?" He did not expect an answer, nor the grunts he got. "A long climb today, I want to reach Nanstallon before nightfall."

"Lead on then Brother. You seem to know the way."

Prious picked up his pack, shouldered it and led them out of the fort. The entrance faced east so he turned to his left and followed a small path that wound through the woods and back down towards the river Fal. Prious took them along the ridge with the Fal flowing down the valley to their left. He did not want to go down to the river bank and then have to climb again. If

69

they followed the edge of the hill the valley floor would slowly rise to meet them.

They walked steadily all the morning and past noon. Waestan felt as tired as the donkey looked. He called to Prious who was walking in front of him.

"Is it time to rest soon, Brother, and perhaps eat?"

Prious laughed and spoke over his shoulder.

"Not yet Father. I want to reach that hill to the north of us." He pointed across the moorland ahead of them. The Fal was still to their left. "That is Boslowsa. We will stop and rest there. We should see Nanstallon from the top."

"The top! Dear Lord give me strength."

"I'm sure that he will, Father." Prious shouted to Raoul who was behind Waestan and the donkey. "All clear behind us? Nobody following?"

"Not that I have seen, Brother. I am sure there is not."

"Good. There should not be. No-one should know we are here but you can never be too careful."

They walked on for almost an hour more, still climbing, until they reached a hilltop from which they could see for miles in every direction. In the distance to the north-west Prious pointed to Nanstallon. It was some four miles away.

"That is where I need us to be by nightfall, or close to it. Nanstallon fortress looks down over the ford across the River Kammel where we must cross. It is a popular resting place though. I do not want to sleep there."

They rested and ate. The donkey grazed a little and was watered but not fully unloaded.

"Let us move on," Prious roused them. "The problem with a beautiful place like this with a wonderful view all around is that we can be seen from a long way off too. We will be back in those trees over there soon and I will feel much safer."

They gathered their belongings and followed him towards Nanstallon.

+++

Morwenna had breakfasted with her father and brother in their private quarters beside the Great Hall. They were so busy with their preparations she hardly saw them except at mealtimes.

Her friend Elowen had helped her settle after her experience with King Mark's messenger and her mind was now far more worried about her family going to war. She had learnt so much more of what was happening in the last few days.

A small boat had arrived from Ireland carrying word from Prince Godwine. There had been rumours reach Dublin of troubles in Exeter but he had gathered sixty-four ships to transport his army and would sail as soon as they had some good weather. They intended landing somewhere on the north Cornwall or north Devon coast, ideally in the estuary at the mouth of the Taw. They would climb the tracks to the west of the Taw. Lord Jowan was to take his small force of mercenary Britons, meet with King Mark's army and march to await them at the Tawton ford.

Her father was desperate however. They did not have Arthur's armour and King Mark would not come without it, he had made that clear, and with King Mark came one thousand Cornishmen. With Exeter fallen, all that was left to join the Saxon army from Ireland were the three hundred displaced Britons camped on the clifftop around the small village of Tintagel. The village had grown over many years at the head of the steep valley that led down to the castle.

Myghal wanted to remain in Tintagel but Jowan would not hear of it. He had given Godwine and Edmund his word, and he still hoped that when the army from Ireland arrived they could retake Exeter and, with that success, King Mark would then join them.

There was little else they could do. Even if they sent a messenger back to Ireland now it would probably be too late. Godwine's ships would most likely have sailed before a message arrived.

Morwenna was not sure whether she wished she was a man so she could join the fight or not. She felt useless as the men in her life prepared for war.

Her father had sent one last message to King Mark, to tell him of the news from Ireland, but he was not hopeful that King Mark would change his mind. He would wait for a reply however.

The weather too had been unsettled. It was dry now but cloudy and windy. He did not think that Godwine would have sailed yet, in fact he was sure of it. They would leave for Tawton in three or four days.

+++

Prious, Waestan and Raoul entered a wood just to the north of Nanstallon. They had been walking steadily since the middle of the day but they had not covered much ground. There was no real path and it had been a difficult walk. There was an hour or more of daylight left when the path they were on reached a small clearing just a few yards across.

"This is where we sleep tonight. There can be no fire here. It could be seen from Nanstallon and I do not wish to attract attention from there."

"An ideal place Brother." Raoul scratched the donkey's ear as he spoke. "Anyone would believe you knew it was here."

"I have been here before. I have been to Tintagel village before but not to the castle, or rather not into the castle."

"I have been into it," said Waestan. "It is a formidable place. Getting in or out, against Lord Jowan's wishes, is impossible."

71

Prious looked at Raoul, whose eyes moved from Waestan to his with a grin.

"Brother Prious here will have it all planned I am sure."

Waestan began to unload their donkey at the edge of the clearing.

"It looks as if it might rain tonight. I think I will sleep under the trees."

"Very wise, Father. Rest is what we all need tonight. We have a similar walk tomorrow, although it is generally flatter. By tomorrow evening I want to reach a round called Castle Goff. From there it is less than a morning's walk down to Tintagel. Tomorrow evening we will discuss our arrival at the castle. So, let us eat, sleep early and rise early."

"I'm becoming accustomed to this, Brother. Next time though, if there ever is a next time, perhaps you could plan for horses. I have not walked this far for longer than I can remember. I did not train as a foot soldier!"

Prious smiled at Raoul. He knew Raoul was perfectly aware of why they were on foot and was just goading him to amuse Waestan.

"Well Raoul, we are more than half way now, but you can always go back. Tintagel is nearer than going back, and of course, you would still have to walk!" Raoul laughed.

"We had better go on then. Food, I think Father, if you would?"

Waestan nodded. Sometimes his companions confused him.

They ate and each wandered into the woods on their own before settling down in their blankets under the edge of the treeline.

Raoul surprised himself by falling asleep quickly. He was lying on his back against the base of a tree. He awoke with a feeling of unease. It was very dark. The sky was full of cloud. It had not rained but the cloud covered the stars and kept the moonlight hidden. He did not move except to open his eyes a little and look around.

Something had disturbed his sleep, a sound or a movement. He looked to his left towards Prious. The monk was still and snoring softly, a quiet snuffling sound. His eyes then moved to his right, towards Waestan. The priest's blanket moved gently, his breathing broken. At first Raoul thought Waestan was crying, but as he concentrated on the sound he realised, beneath the blanket, Waestan was pleasuring himself, quietly and gently.

Raoul was filled with mixed thoughts. At first he was amused. It was not anything unusual in a camp full of soldiers, particularly on the eve of battle. Waestan, however, was a priest. He was supposed to be celibate, but then again, he was only human.

Raoul almost laughed but stopped himself. He did not wish to disturb the priest. His next feeling disturbed himself, however. He could feel his own arousal. He could not believe listening to the priest had hardened him so. It was over three weeks since he had lain with a girl in France. That was the night before his summons to Winchester arrived. It was rare for him to be alone for so long but he had no feelings for men. Many Norman nobles had bedfellows, a best friend with whom they shared a bed when not with their wives, the King included, but it was not a practice he had ever indulged in.

He still did not move. He feared he would not sleep again easily unless he relieved his own desire. He lay still as Waestan's breathing unconsciously quickened and caught as he seeded. The priest moved a little as he settled again and was quickly asleep.

Raoul looked up at the clouds. Their dark grey shapes were just visible as they moved over him towards the east, where they would hide the rising sun from the travellers at dawn. He had no sense of how long he had slept nor when that would be. He did what he had done before at such a time. He held himself through his leather leggings but did not undo the codpiece. He watched the clouds and thought of the days ahead, of what he had to do. This time sleep came.

Prious had them awake with the dawn. As Raoul stood up, stretching himself, Waestan returned from the woods. Raoul called to him.

"Well rested, Father?" Waestan looked towards him suspiciously. Raoul was not usually so cordial.

"Yes, thank you, my son." He replied. "Did you have a good night?"

"Not as good as yours it would seem, Father, not as good as yours." He smiled at Waestan and began to fold his blankets.

Waestan began to prepare what little food they had left.

The Fourth Scroll

The wind began to gust strongly but the rain that threatened did not come. The track was dry and the three men and the donkey made good progress out of the woods below Nanstallon and to the ford on the River Kammel.

Although the rain had held off that morning there had been plenty fall on the moors upstream in the last few days, so the Kammel was not as placid as it might have been. They waded across. Prious and Waestan held their habits up as best they could and Raoul lead their very nervous donkey.

Raoul returned the donkey to Waestan and they climbed the path up the bank. They were each wet to some degree but they had to keep going and let the wet bits dry as they walked.

They had not gone far however when the path ahead entered a copse. As they approached, four men moved out of the shadow of the trees and stood across their path. Prious did not stop and walked towards them as Raoul moved up, past the donkey and Waestan, almost to his side. Two paces before they reached them they stopped and Prious spoke.

"Why do you block our way, my children?"

The men all wore woollen and linen garments of dull undyed colours. None wore any armour, not even any heavy leather. Each held a sword, but none of noticeable quality. They were petty thieves. The slightly taller one, who stood second from the right, answered.

"Well now, Brother is it?" He did not wait for an answer. "We just wondered what two men of the cloth, and this other fellow, might possess that needed to be carried by such a fine young animal."

"What we carry is of no-one's interest but ours'. It is the property, however, of Lord Jowan of Tintagel, who would be hugely upset were you to hinder our passage."

Raoul was deliberately standing very slightly short of Prious, so that the monk would be the centre of the thieves' attention. The taller one was certainly the leader and looked confident. The other three obviously had confidence in him but Raoul read unease in their eyes.

Waestan felt his heart racing. Last time anything like this happened was on the boat. He watched Raoul. The Knight was standing with his feet apart, almost on his toes. His left hand on his sword hilt, his right resting on the hilts of his two fighting knives that were in his belt.

"Would he be? That would mean it must be of some value and worth having. I suggest you hand the donkey to us before there is any trouble. One of you may be armed but we all are."

Raoul looked into the man's eyes, taking half a step forward.

"Listen you bunch of horses' arseholes, if you make one move against us I will kill you all. I really would rather not. It is up to you."

Waestan surprised himself as well as Prious and Raoul. He jumped forward between them holding a hand up to the thieves.

"Please, my sons, hold!" Everyone's eyes were drawn to him. "Please. I have seen my friend here do this before. He will kill you. You have no idea."

Their big one laughed.

"Bollocks to that!" He stepped forward raising his sword. Before the other three could follow his lead, in one smooth movement, Raoul's right hand drew his short fighting knife and threw it underhand. It buried itself in their leader's chest.

He was dead before he collapsed to the ground. His knees bent forward but his body fell backwards. He lay in grotesque heap, his legs buckled under him.

The other three were transfixed. Almost in the same instant Raoul had crossed his body with his arms, drawing his sword and fighting knife. Waestan moved to his right, across Raoul.

"Please, please, please, no more killing. I tried to warn you. Now throw down your swords. No-one else need die."

"You might, you bloody fool." Raoul hissed the words into Waestan's right ear.

Prious' voice boomed out.

"Do as the priest says, my sons. There is no need for anyone else to die this day."

Raoul pulled Waestan out of the way and stepped forward. It was all the thieves needed to see. They threw their swords onto the grass in front of Prious and began to turn away.

"Stand still, my sons. This is not quite over."

The three remaining thieves stopped and turned back towards Prious. They were clearly very afraid.

"Pick up your swords and sheathe them." All three were looking at him, disbelieving what he was saying, expecting Raoul to attack them. "Do as I say!"

Each of them picked up a sword and slid it into their belt. Prious undid the tie on a small purse at his waist. He threw it to the nearest of them.

"Listen well. I do not suppose you will mend your ways after this, perhaps for a short while. Today you were lucky, you should be dead. In that purse are four silver coins, one each and one for this fool's widow. When you are asked what happened here today you will say there was a fight and you killed two of our men. You stole this purse but we escaped into the woods. You will save face and also do me a service. Do you understand?" They all nodded, now totally confused. "Then bury this man and make two false graves beside him."

Prious pushed between them and entered the copse. Waestan followed immediately, the donkey behind him, but Raoul turned to the three men as he left them. He leant over the body of their leader. Putting a foot on the body's chest, Raoul pulled his knife from it, then slowly and carefully wiped the blade clean of blood on the dead man's shirt

"You do exactly as the Brother told you, or believe me, I will come back, and I will kill you all."

He did not wait for a reaction. He walked unhurriedly after the donkey.

+++

Rougemount Castle had not been so busy since it had been built. Earlier that afternoon five hundred Norman cavalry had arrived from Winchester to join Sir Breon and the five hundred already there. With them was their prisoner, Friar Erste.

Sir Baldwin had Erste brought to him for questioning, only to find the friar more helpful than he could have hoped. Erste had had a few days in Norman captivity to imagine what he was going to face at Exeter. He had long since decided to tell all in the hope of surviving the ordeal.

He admitted he carried no communication for the Bishop of Bristol. He was to take a boat from there to Ireland with messages for Prince Godwine. He told Sir Baldwin every detail of them. Sir Baldwin ordered Erste to be held until he decided what use to make of him. He might be turned into a good spy to return to Winchester but he needed to be more frightened first.

Sir Breon joined Sir Baldwin.

"My Lord Sheriff. My men are ready to leave for Tawton, but I think it might be better to wait until dawn tomorrow. We should reach Tawton in one day and I'm not sure what the weather will do. It might be better to stay in camp here than to have to set up camp somewhere on the way."

"Yes, Breon, I agree. Wait until tomorrow. The Friar was taking messages to the dead Saxon King Harold's sons in Ireland, reassuring them that all was well in Cornwall, that they had Arthur's armour and that King Mark of Cornwall would join them. They will not now get that reassurance, of course, so we cannot be certain whether they will still come. I believe we have to assume they will, however."

"Yes, my Lord, we must."

"Good. Then we will progress as planned. There was one other rather interesting message that intrigued me. He had no idea what it meant, but he was to tell Godwine that when he took Exeter there would be news here that would change everything. Nothing else, just that. I will have to ponder on that."

"Could Bishop Leofric know more than he has told us, my Lord?"

"I do not think so. I was there for most of his questioning. I do not think he held anything back. He is not a strong man. No, we do not know whether this news is already here or is to be sent by messenger later. We can only guess for now. So, make ready to leave at dawn. You have Sir Raoul Tyrrell's horses and equipment?"

"Yes, my Lord. Thank you my Lord. Farewell."

"You fare well, Sir Breon, you fare well."

+++

Prious led the way into the round at Castle Goff. They had walked all day without any real break, except to replenish their water at one of the clear moorland streams they had crossed.

Their path followed a moorland ridge with the occasional patch of trees. The ridge ran along between two rivers, one to their right and one to their left. Every now and then they could see one or the other in the distance below them. Many streams ran down to the rivers and they had to wade across one quite large stream during the day.

Hardly a word had passed between them since their experience with the thieves that morning. Prious could sense Raoul's anger but was sure Waestan had no sense of anything he had done wrong.

They had little food left. Three had been sharing provisions planned for two and Prious felt a good meal in the evening would be better than stopping in the day. They had much to discuss that evening to ensure their stories were the same.

They entered the round. It was a little below the hilltop, on a south-east facing slope. It gave good cover however and Prious felt secure enough to allow a fire. He set out with Raoul to gather wood whilst Waestan unloaded the donkey and organised what food was left.

Prious lit a fire and Waestan distributed the little food that remained. They began to eat but no-one had yet spoken. Whatever else Prious thought about Waestan, the priest was not afraid to face a difficulty.

"There seems to be problem with me." He looked up at Raoul, who sighed loudly and shook his head.

"I very nearly killed you this morning. You are fool, and if you ever get in my way again, dear God help me, I damn well will."

"Oh, well, I am sorry. I was simply trying to save lives."

"You could well have cost us all our lives. There were four armed men who would happily have killed us all. Prious is not a fighting man and neither, I fancy, are you. So that just leaves me."

He took a bite of salted beef.

"I had killed the large one and would have cut down the one on the right whilst they were still in shock. Then at least it would have been only two

77

against one. If they had kept coming after you got in my way, I might not have been able to defend Prious against three, and to defend Prious, my stupid Priest, is what I have pledged to do. So help me I should have killed you too and stepped over you, and so help me, if you do anything that stupid again, I will."

Waestan was speechless. He stared at Raoul, there were tears in his eyes. He found some words.

"I am sorry. I thought we had become friends."

"I do not have friends, Father."

"Father Waestan, hear me." Prious leant towards the bewildered priest. "The ways of violence are not for us to understand. The death of the wicked at the hands of someone like Sir Raoul is sometimes a necessary evil we must live with. As things turned out, there was no harm done, but there could have been. In fact, hopefully those men will tell their story and about Raoul saving us whilst the other guards died. Which brings us to tomorrow. Finish eating and we will talk."

No more was said about that morning but Waestan now realised he was most definitely involved with matters far beyond his experience. Matters that he had not known existed.

Prious talked through their story so they were all clear on what their journey from Winchester was supposed to have entailed; and that Prious and Raoul were there at Waestan's invitation having met on the boat.

Nothing was said to Waestan about Raoul's mission. All Prious discussed was the taking of the armour, the sword, Excalibur, and the family history. He then surprised them both.

"There is one thing we must do in the morning before we leave here. I do not wish to risk anything going wrong and losing the armour to the rebellion. We will bury it here. Only we three will know exactly where. We will bring the helmet only, to prove we have it all. We will say we were frightened by its near loss this morning. We will tell Lord Jowan that we thought wherever we are to meet King Mark's forces, we can travel back this way and collect the rest."

Raoul nodded. It made sense to him, but then he had learnt that Prious usually did. Waestan had learnt it was better to say nothing. Prious knew so much more about such things than he did. Strangely then he remembered something Bishop Leofric had once told him; that any decision was only as sound as the facts you know when you make it.

They settled down as the sun set. Prious and Waestan fell asleep quite quickly but that evening Raoul could not settle. His mind kept thinking of what he was tasked with over the next day or two, once they reached Tintagel. He had to kill two men and a young woman, father, son and daughter, to end their family line, and finish almost a thousand years of history.

As an experienced soldier, killing in battle did not trouble him. It was kill or be killed and you could never be sure which it would be. This would be murder, cold and simple. The men he could live with, but a woman who had hardly lived yet. That would be difficult.

He was overcome by a wave of self-revulsion as he felt his arousal. It had happened to him before a fight a few times. He had always assumed it was some sort of aggressive reaction, but he knew this time it was the thought of killing a woman. It frightened him that his body did this to him.

He lay on his back looking up at the dark sky, broken black and grey cloud with a few stars visible between them. He thought of his chateau, his home in France. That usually calmed him, but not this night.

Every time he closed his eyes he saw a young blonde girl beneath him, crying as he lay above her, a knife in his hand. Eventually sleep took him, but he awoke a number of times through the night and every time it was the same. Finally desperation to sleep led his fingers to the laces of his codpiece. He loosened them and took himself in hand. He was so aroused by then he seeded almost before he started. He lay quietly as his body relaxed and his breathing steadied. Although everything had happened so quickly he was hardly breathless. He smiled to himself, hoping Prious and Waestan were asleep. They sounded it, but frankly he did not care. He wiped the leather of his leggings with the edge of his blanket and shut his eyes. Sleep came easily.

+++

Waestan and Raoul were both awake with the dawn as Prious went to rouse them. They packed their blankets onto the donkey and each left the round and entered the woods. Arriving back in the round Raoul had a suggestion.

"Brother Prious, there is a tree just inside the wood over there that has a perfect cradle of branches at about a man's height that would take the bundle of armour. If we tied it securely it would be out of sight and safe for the few days needed."

Prious looked at him sideways.

"Why do you propose such an idea, my son?"

"A purely practical thing, Brother. What do you intend digging a hole with? We have no digging tool and we especially do not wish anywhere to look newly dug. I just thought it might save a lot of time and effort. Probably mine." Prious smiled.

"Very well, my son, let us look. There is no food left so if this tree is suitable, let us secure our bundle in place and make for Tintagel. The sooner we get there the sooner we can eat."

Raoul was both amazed and delighted that Prious agreed with his idea. Two small lengths of rope tied the bundle in place. It was almost invisible to the eye from close to the tree and certainly out of sight from the path at the round entrance.

They set off towards Tintagel. Prious was sure it would only take an hour and a half if the path remained in reasonable condition, which it did.

They reached the rise above Tintagel. The village was away to their right and beside it was the large, rather disorganised camp set up by three hundred or so displaced British soldiers. Prious looked at the camp.

"I was hoping we would avoid them. I am not sure how they will behave towards us, or toward anyone for that matter."

The sound of horses' hooves over turf came from behind and to their left. Turning towards the noise they saw four horsemen in dark leather tabards ride up to them and quite deliberately surround them. Raoul smiled to himself thinking them well trained. He could not see them all at any one moment. The one facing them called to them.

"Who have we here, and what business do you have with Tintagel." Waestan answered him.

"It depends who is asking a man of the Church, good sir. Who is your master I would ask?" The rider steadied his horse. He had not expected to be questioned.

"I, Father, am Officer of the Watch this day for Tintagel Castle Guard. It is my duty to protect the Castle and to control the area around it. With a group such as yourselves it is I who must decide whether you enter the Castle as prisoners to be questioned or as guests. In either case, however, the first business is for this sell-sword, or whatever he purports to be, to throw down his arms."

Raoul stepped forward to stand between Waestan and Prious.

"That will not happen, Officer of the Guard."

The sound of swords being drawn rang around them, but Raoul did not draw his. Waestan held his hands up and spun around, ending where he had started, facing the Officer.

"Stop this nonsense and listen to me, and listen well, because your future depends on it if Lord Jowan hears of this." He paused and lowered his hands. "I am Father Waestan, Clerk to Bishop Leofric of Exeter. I have travelled from Winchester with urgent messages and valued goods for your Lord Jowan from His Grace Stigand, Archbishop of Canterbury. When Lord Jowan hears of how this man saved we men of God from thieves, when two others of our party were killed, and how he defended our goods from harm, your Lord will welcome him with honour into your Castle fully armed. Furthermore, your Lord will be so delighted to receive what we bring, he will be very displeased with anyone who hinders its arrival."

Waestan glared at the officer. Prious added his stare, wondering if this was the same priest that boarded the Rhosmon in Portsea. Raoul wanted to laugh but knew this was not the moment. Waestan continued.

"So, Officer of the Guard," he captured Raoul's demeaning tone perfectly, "have your men sheathe their swords and escort us with all haste to your Lord and Master."

The Officer settled his horse again. It could sense its rider's unease. Raoul watched the Officer's eyes. They were a mixture of anger and uncertainty. Waestan had worried him enough. The Officer slipped his own sword back into its scabbard and his men followed his lead.

"Come."

He turned his horse and led them towards the Castle of Tintagel. The track was the width of a cart and a little more. They walked behind the Officer, a guard riding each side of them and one behind, following their donkey.

The track ran down a small valley beside a stream. As the cliffs began to rise to left and right the castle came more and more into sight before them. They could see over the battlements of the gatehouse and up the slope to the village above. At the far seaward end of what appeared an island, was the Keep that housed the Great Hall and Lord Jowan's family quarters.

The valley ended. The stream fell the rest of the distance down to the rocks below. The cliffs to each side rose above them by as much as the sea was below, but ahead of them a narrow strip of land ran for some thirty paces to the large, studded oak gates. There was a low dry-stone wall on each side above the straight drop to the sea. Set as the gates were into the defences around them, and especially with the portcullis lowered too, the gatehouse was impregnable. The cliffs around the castle were vertical to the sea, which smashed noisily against the rocks at their foot.

The Officer rode up to the gates. Waestan led his fellow travellers onto the approach and sat on the low wall to the left of the gate. The donkey stood beside him, unworried by the drop. Prious calmly patted the donkey's head whilst Raoul stood in the middle of the path. The other three guards remained side by side at the valley end. Their horses were obviously nervous of the drop to each side.

Someone had been watching their approach and one gate swung outward, two guards standing where it had been. The Officer shouted down at them.

"The Priest Waestan, carrying messages and goods from the Archbishop of Canterbury for Lord Jowan, but they refuse to disarm before entering. You will need to speak to Lord Jowan."

The gate swung shut again. The Officer turned his horse towards Raoul and looked down at Waestan.

"Now we will see, Father, whether your goods are valued."

They waited some time, but then they heard the sound of raised voices, one shouting above the others. Both gates swung open and to the Officer's astonishment Lord Jowan himself stood before him, his son Myghal by his side.

"My Lord, Father Waestan and fellow travellers."

"What are you doing, man, making an envoy from the Archbishop wait at my gates? Be gone about your duties before I lose my temper with you, away."

The Officer turned quickly away, steering his horse past Waestan and Prious and brushing heavily past Raoul.

"Now, Father Waestan, you and your friends must join me and my son in the Hall for sustenance. You can tell me your news. Come, come, I must apologise for the way you have been treated thus far. Welcome to my home. Welcome to Camelot."

+++

Morwenna was about to start a late breakfast in the family's private quarters with her father and brother. She could tell her father was agitated. Everything was prepared and there was now nothing to do but wait for any reply from King Mark.

The weather had settled and looked as if it would continue to improve. If it did, he expected Godwine and Edmund to set sail from Dublin in the next day or two, so the day after next he would leave for Tawton, with or without King Mark and his men.

There was suddenly a loud urgent knocking on the refectory doors and she heard Daveth calling.

"My Lord. My Lord."

Her father turned towards the door.

"Enter."

The door opened and Daveth, looking somewhat breathless, gathered himself.

"My Lord, I am sorry to disturb you but the guard from the gates report a messenger. A Father Waestan, has arrived from Winchester, from Archbishop Stigand."

A broad smile appeared on her father's face and he walked to the door.

"I know Waestan. Where is he? Why is he not with you, for goodness sake?"

"He is outside the gates, my Lord. The Officer of the Guard is concerned that his armed escort refuses to remove his weapons and he…."

"Dear God, I am surrounded by fools!" Her father pushed Daveth to one side and left the room, calling back as he went.

"Myghal, come with me, quickly now. We have the most important messenger to arrive here for many a year and my guards leave him waiting at the gates!"

From the refectory window, Morwenna watched them leave the building and walk quickly towards the gates. She knew her father was desperate for

82

news. He had almost felt abandoned and was feeling the strain terribly. Then she felt her own excitement. Visitors to the castle were always exciting. Daveth re-entered the room with two servants.

"Excuse me, my Lady, your father has ordered that breakfast be moved to the Great Hall. You are to join him there, if it pleases you, my Lady."

"Thank you, Daveth, I will." She laughed. "You are so good at giving me my father's orders."

"Yes, my Lady."

Morwenna almost ran along the passage that led to the adjoining door to the Hall. The fire had been lit early that morning but had done little to warm the room yet. She felt the heat from it as she crossed the Hall, moving around the ancient table at its centre, surrounded by its twenty-four ornate wooden chairs.

Daveth and the servants began to lay the breakfast foods on the table near the fire, carrying the plates from the refectory on large wooden trays. As they came back and forth Morwenna rehearsed how she would stand to greet their guests.

Daveth was finally bringing the wine and goblets as her father appeared at the doorway, ushering his guests into the Hall and leading them towards the fireplace. Myghal entered last with Raoul.

When Morwenna saw Raoul she gasped, almost out loud. She caught her breath and tried to listen to her father's voice.

"Gentlemen, this is my daughter, the Lady Morwenna, and Lady of Camelot since her mother's sad death. Morwenna, this is Father Waestan, emissary of Archbishop Stigand of Canterbury; his travelling companion, Brother Prious of the Church of Saint Cornelly; and Raoul, escort to Brother Prious."

All three men bowed acknowledgement and Morwenna curtsied to them.

She glanced at Waestan and Prious. She noticed the blanketed bundle that Waestan carried. He looked to be a priest, as Prious looked a monk, but her eyes could not leave Raoul for more than a moment.

Raoul was everything she had ever dreamed of. He had hardened good looks. He was obviously strong. His long and tousled dark hair fell onto his leather-clad shoulders, very unfashionable but more attractive to her for it. He stood confidently with his thumbs in the front of his heavy leather belt. A long polished sword hung in its scabbard on his left side, two fighting knives through hoops on his right. His leather leggings and soft black leather boots held her eyes.

Her legs felt weak. Her stomach tightened and her breasts tingled. She looked up hoping no-one had noticed her staring. Myghal was watching her but looked away. Her father was speaking.

"Father Waestan, I should offer you refreshment, food and wine, and there is plenty here to enjoy at leisure, but I so wish to have news from the

Archbishop. Perhaps we could hear what you have to tell me and then we can eat whilst you let us know of your journey?"

"Indeed, my Lord Jowan. Well, the Archbishop sends his greetings and good wishes but mainly I am here to deliver you this."

Waestan unwrapped the blanket around his bundle and held the plumed Helm of Arthur's armour, lost to Camelot for more than one hundred years.

Lord Jowan stepped towards him and took the Helm from him.

"I cannot believe this. I have seen old paintings and heard that Bishop Leofric had it. It was promised to us but I was told it was in King William's hands now. Have you the rest?"

"We have, my Lord. It is hidden some miles from here for safe keeping. I will explain as we eat. The only message from His Grace was to tell you that when you have taken Exeter, you must free Queen Gytha Thorkeldottir from her captivity on Bradanreolice. She has momentous news for you that will lift our cause enormously."

Raoul's eyes flashed at Prious. Waestan had never mentioned this before. Prious saw Raoul's look and nodded almost imperceptibly. They were both more than disturbed by this. Did Waestan have more secrets from them?

"This is wonderful news, with Arthur's armour King Mark will join us. Let us eat and talk further before I send a messenger to Bosvena. Now, sit everybody and Daveth will pour wine. Father, tell us of your journey."

Waestan recounted their story in detail, exactly as they had agreed. Prious had guided him with his local knowledge and Raoul had saved them in the fight with the thieves. He did a good job of making it clear that he would not have reached Tintagel without them.

Morwenna was now totally convinced that Raoul was the man of her dreams. She looked at him again only to find his eyes fixed on her. She looked away quickly but her eyes were soon back on him. This time she held his eyes and smiled. He smiled back and she looked down. Her father was speaking.

"I must thank you, Brother Prious and Raoul, for helping Waestan arrive safely here, indeed to have arrived at all. You must all stay as my honoured guests for as long as you need. I would expect to be marching the day after tomorrow to meet King Mark, then to meet Prince Godwine at Tawton. Until then, anything you desire, you just ask me, or if I am not here Daveth will deliver in my stead. Understood Daveth?"

"Yes, my Lord, anything."

"Good, then now we are all fed we will show you your rooms. You must stay with us here in the Keep. We have guest rooms on the first floor, Myghal and Morwenna above them and my suite above them. I suggest we all relax before gathering for a light luncheon then we shall banquet tonight to celebrate your arrival. I shall enjoy that. Daveth, have them shown to their rooms then organise the rest of the day."

"I will, my Lord."

"First, however, I will place Arthur's Helm on the shelf here above the fire, under its old friend Excalibur. Until later my friends."

Daveth held out a guiding hand towards the doors. Waestan, Prious and Raoul stood and followed him from the room. He led them along a hallway to the main staircase which they climbed to the first floor. The stairs turned back on themselves and on upwards. Passageways ran to both sides. To the left the passage was only short as it reached the wall on the Great Hall, but to the right it ran on past four doors. Daveth stopped and open the first one. He turned to Raoul.

"Your pack is in here for you, Sir." He gave a quick bow of the head.

"Thank you, Daveth."

Raoul caught Prious' eye as he said it. His head gave the slightest nod down the passage. Raoul took it to mean he should come to his room so he delayed entering fully until he saw Daveth usher Prious into the next doorway along.

He walked to the window and looked out over the seascape below. He could not get the girl's face and body out of his mind. It was ridiculous. He had bedded women since he had been able to, many better looking than her, but something about her had got to him. It was a pity he would have to kill her.

That thought broke his daydream and he remembered Prious. He returned to the door and opened it a little. There was no sign of Daveth so he opened it wider and stepped out into the passage. He closed his bedroom door and walked quietly along to the next.

He did not want to make a noise by knocking. He gently lifted the latch and entered. Prious saw the door opening and beckoned him in. He was standing on a chair in the middle of the bedroom studying the ceiling. He jumped lightly down and whispered to Raoul.

"Come and sit in the window. I think we are not being listened to but we will be careful anyway. I cannot see any obvious false panels or holes in the ceiling or floor. This side is open air. Your bedroom is that side, Waestan's the other, and through that wall is the passage. Any listening holes would have to be above or below. The floor seems solid enough and that would not appear to be a false ceiling."

Raoul laughed and slapped a hand on Prious' shoulder.

"You are the expert, Father, I am sure you are right. So what now?"

"Well, Excalibur and the Helm are at least together for the next two nights, if as Jowan says, he plans to leave the day after next. We will need to locate this written history if it exists but I am most concerned about our escape. If you do your part tomorrow night, we need to find a way out of the castle later that night or very early morning before any bodies are found. We should spend the rest of today and tomorrow working out how. Any thoughts?"

Raoul shook his head, a broad grin on his face.

"You surprise me, Brother. At every turn so far you have been prepared, you have had everything planned. I entered the castle assuming you knew how we were to leave. Only now do I discover you do not. Can you swim?"

"Why in God's name do you ask that?"

"Because the only way I can see of leaving here is to steal a very long rope, throw it out of a window, climb down it to the sea and swim!"

"Well I do not swim, so that is not an option."

"Then I give up. You are the brain, you better start to use it. What about our other friend?"

"Waestan?"

"Yes, Waestan. He troubled me a little with that message we knew nothing of."

"Indeed. He should have told us before. If he had, I would have found a messenger to send to Exeter before entering the castle."

"Perhaps that is why he kept it to himself."

"Perhaps it is. In either case, we were right not to tell him of your mission. As long as we are agreed, tomorrow night you play your part. We have until then to plan something, but if an opportunity to escape arises we must do what we came for and use it. Waestan will not know of our plans until the last moment."

"Agreed Brother."

"And Raoul," Prious looked into his eyes. "I saw you looking at that girl this morning. Are you going to be able to do what you must?"

"Damn you, Brother, you do your work and I will do mine."

Raoul turned sharply and walked to the door. He opened it angrily and stopped in the doorway. He looked at Prious as if about to say something, then shook his head and stepped out shutting the door heavily behind him.

He returned to his room. There was an urn of water and a bowl on a small table near the window. He stood before it and poured some of the water into the bowl. He cupped his hands and splashed his face with water, drying both with a cloth hanging beside the table.

He walked to the large four poster bed unbuckling his belt. He hung it around a bedpost and removed his leather tabard. Throwing it across a chair against the wall, he sat on the edge of the bed. He swung his feet up and lay back against the pillows stacked at its head.

At first he lay staring up at the linen sheet that formed the bed's curtain top and sides, but then he closed his eyes and there she was. Lady Morwenna, he remembered. He swore out loud and turned on his side. She was only a girl damn it, just a woman perhaps. He felt his arousal.

He turned again and threw his legs off the bed and walked back to the basin, splashing his face again when he got there. Dripping water on the floor he stood in front of the window. The shutters were folded open and he placed a hand on each side of the frame, leaning forward into the sea breeze which blew cold on his wet face. He spoke out loud to himself.

"You get yourself into some bloody foolish corners, you bastard."

He was not sure how long he stood there staring at the waves but there was a knock at his door and a voice shouted from outside.

"There is food and wine in the Great Hall, Sir."

"Thank you. I will find my way down."

In one respect it was a welcome distraction, but then he realised he was actually hoping that she would be there.

He donned his leather tabard and strapped his belt around it, his sword and knives hanging at his sides. He sighed deeply and walked to the door. He just wanted to talk to her.

He left his bedroom and retraced his steps down the stairs. The passage seemed shorter walking back. The Great Hall doors were open so he entered and walked towards the fireplace.

He was last to arrive and she was there, standing to one side near her father. Raoul walked around that side of the table. Lord Jowan welcomed him.

"Ah, Raoul is it not? Please, take some wine and a plate of meats, some bread perhaps?"

"Thank you, my Lord, I will."

He lifted a goblet of red wine but did not take a plate. It did not seem long to him since they had eaten. He would eat something shortly. He turned towards Morwenna and smiled. She returned his smile and spoke.

"Forgive my father, he is not good with names. You are Raoul, I know."

"Thank you, my Lady, I am honoured you remember."

She laughed and took a sip of her wine.

"It is not often we are visited by such a handsome and gallant gentleman."

"You embarrass me, my Lady. You are the rose among the thorns in this room."

"Now it is I who am embarrassed. We do not get many visitors. It can get lonely, even in such a beautiful place."

"Surely you have some friends close by?"

Morwenna tossed her hair back and smiled.

"Yes, I have one very dear friend, Elowen. We grew up together and have been the best of friends from childhood. She is the daughter of our Ostler and her husband works for him in our stables."

"Oh, you have horses here, do you?"

"Yes indeed. We have stables next to the house here where Elowen lives with her husband and children. There are usually eight horses stabled there, my father's, my brother's, mine, and some for guests. We keep a few empty stalls for visitors' horses if needed. There is another stable at the landward end of the village next to the guard houses, at the top of the hill above the gates. You would have passed them as you climbed the hill from the gates, at the top on your left. There are usually about twenty horses of our guard there."

"Do you enjoy riding, my Lady?"

"I have ridden since a child. I love it, but it is not easy to go riding outside the castle as much as I would wish."

Raoul felt a hand on his shoulder. It was Lord Jowan's. He spoke as Raoul turned towards him.

"Come my man, do not let my daughter bore you with lady's talk. Have some more wine. This is quite good but tonight we will open some of my very best."

"Thank you my Lord, I will and I look forward to this evening."

Raoul looked at Prious and Waestan who were standing beyond Lord Jowan with Myghal beside them. All held wine goblets and were smiling, except Myghal who was staring at Raoul. It was not a friendly look. Raoul suspected he was protective of his sister. Prious continued their conversation.

"It must be wonderful, my Lord, to live somewhere that has been home to your family for many hundreds of years."

"In many ways it is, Brother, but it has its responsibilities too, as I am sure you would appreciate."

"Oh yes, my Lord, I meant more that you must have so much family history to look back on."

Lord Jowan was enjoying having company and had drunk a little too much wine for the middle of the day. Prious was relying on it and continued.

"I mean, your family call the castle here, Camelot. Is it part of Tintagel?"

Lord Jowan took a mouthful of wine and smiled.

"Well Brother, now you have asked I will explain. The castle and the village are both part of Tintagel, which is the Saxon name that has become common usage in these times. The Cornish name was Trevena, and such was it called when my family were granted the land by the Cornish King some hundreds of years ago. Our ancestor Artoris settled in Devon at Nemeton, which in Cornish is translated to Celliwig. Both mean Sacred Groves in their languages, but Artoris chose Celliwig to name his home. Our ancestors moved here to Cornwall and called our new home Celliwig too. Over the years the name changed to the Saxon for Sacred Groves, Camelot."

"It is astonishing, my Lord," Prious prompted him, "That you can remember all of this. You must spend hours, each generation handing on all the family stories to the next generation."

"Ha, we do, of course, but we have some help which each generation updates. Let me show you something."

"Father?" Myghal called to Lord Jowan.

"Do not fuss, my boy, we are among friends."

The wall above the fireplace was stone but on each side of the fireplace it was clad with dark wood. Jowan walked to the right hand side and pressed a panel. Prious was careful to note which. A door swung out of the wood cladding exposing a large cupboard. A shelf ran around it and on it were four bound piles of parchment manuscript. Jowan turned and proudly pointed to them

"Over eight hundred years of our family history, my friends."

Raoul's eyes met Prious' for a moment of acknowledgement before moving to Myghal. He was frowning disapprovingly at his father. Prious broke the silence.

"You are a fortunate family, my Lord, to have all that history recorded. What language is it in?"

"Just in Latin. We pay a local church whenever we need to update it. The last update was when we first met Father Waestan as he moved papers between here and Exeter, and first introduced us to Bishop Leofric."

Again Prious' and Raoul's eyes met briefly. They were both thinking the same thing. Waestan had never mentioned that before either.

Lord Jowan left the door ajar and returned to the table, the fire and his wine. They continued talking for a while longer before Morwenna excused herself and retired.

The men broke up, all looking forward to the evening ahead. Prious, Waestan and Raoul returned to their rooms before Raoul joined Prious in his.

"Well, Brother, we know where the histories are but they will be heavy to carry. Cleverly done though, my friend. I was amused to watch you draw him out."

"It was easier than I expected, but then I thought the boy was going to stop him."

"Wine and pride will so often overcome sense."

"Indeed, but Raoul, I do not think the boy is fond of you. He was very upset when you were talking to his sister, almost as upset as you were enjoying it."

"Well, if that brain of yours is any closer to finding a way out of here for us, I know where the horses are. Eight or so just outside the keep and twenty or so above the gates."

"Good. Now I think we should rest before this evening's celebrations. They may go on a while and I have thinking to do tomorrow if we are ever to leave this place."

"I have faith in you, Brother."

"You would be better to have faith in the Lord Almighty."

"Same thing to me, Brother."

Raoul left the room and returned to his own.

+++

Morwenna walked as fast as she could without running towards the stable cottage. She knocked urgently, but not too loudly in case the children were asleep. Elowen opened the door and stepped back to let Morwenna enter.

"Oh Elowen, are you alone?"

"Except for the children, but they are asleep. Come and sit. What is wrong?"

They sat opposite each other on the small table in front of the fire. Morwenna leant forward and reached across the table taking Elowen's hands in hers.

"He's here, Elowen, my Prince. Well he's not a prince, he's a soldier of some sort, but he is wonderful, everything I have ever imagined, and he's staying in the castle tonight."

Elowen smiled widely and squeezed Morwenna's hands.

"Now calm down, my lovely, and tell me what is happening."

Morwenna told her of Raoul and his companions' arrival, of the story of their journey and of Raoul's heroics. She described Raoul in detail, his looks, his clothes. Elowen listened attentively.

"He talked to me, Elowen. His voice is so soft. He has a Breton, Celtic accent, almost French. They said he was Breton. He is guarding a Breton monk from the south coast, but that is not important. Oh Elowen, he is my dream. He will be eating again with us this evening. I must talk with him again."

"Now you know what happened last time you fell for a passing soldier."

"No, no, I did not fall for him, that was a desperate curiosity. This is totally different, this is love at first sight."

"Love, my, my. Do you intend to lie with him tonight?"

"Lie with him! No, I want him to love me, possess me. I want him to hold me, feel him inside me. I have to make him love enough to take me with him when he leaves."

"Now Morwenna, my dearest friend, slow down. I do not wish to see you unhappy again. He can lie with you tonight and then leave without a thought. How will you feel then, and besides, what am I going to do if you leave so quickly?"

"Oh, Elowen, I am sorry, but if I do not try, if I do not lie with him then never see him again, I will never forgive myself. If he leaves without me I will be heart broken, but at least I will have a beautiful memory."

"Listen, my lovely, I fear for you, but if you are set on this course you have my blessing and my very best wishes, you know that. You must use some of your rose-scented water and wear that plain long woollen dress of yours, and very little else. It will cling to you and show your curves at their best. The others tonight are family or men of God so you should be safe from other advances. Oh, and try not to be too obvious or you might upset your father, or Myghal more likely."

"Thank you so much. I must go and prepare myself." Morwenna stood up from the table.

Elowen laughed again and spoke as Morwenna moved to the door.

"Yes, you must, but listen, one last bit of advice. If he has been well raised you will need to go to his room. As a guest, if he is caught in your room he is at fault and it can lead to duels and all sorts, so he would not go to your room. If you are caught in his room, it is your reputation that is marred not his. You are best to go to his room."

"Yes, yes, sound advice as always, my dear one."

"Come and see me in the morning. I probably will not sleep now, thinking of you and your man. Good night, my lovely."

"Good night."

Morwenna closed the door behind her and walked the few paces back to the keep then climbed the stairs to her room. Her maid was preparing a bath for her, heating water on the fire to mix with cold water she had already poured into the bath. Morwenna looked at her and smiled.

"You see my thoughts before I have them, Demlah."

"Yes, my Lady, with guests in the castle I thought you would like a warm bath, and I can add some rose water, if you would wish."

"I do wish, Demlah, I do wish. Bless you."

+++

Raoul was lying on his bed. He had slept for a while but now he was awake letting thoughts come and go in his head, mainly thoughts of the Lady Morwenna. There was a knocking at his door and a voice called out.

"Lord Jowan requests your company in the Great Hall, Sir." Raoul replied.

"Thank you."

He sat up on the edge of the large four poster. His toes only just reached the floor if he pointed them downwards. He was fully dressed as his room was not very warm, even with the fire that had now become a bed of glowing embers. No doubt a servant would build it back up and leave more firewood for the late evening.

He had the shutters closed but he walked to the window and pulled the heavy curtain across it on the wooden pole that spanned the shutters. It would help keep any heat in the room. It was cool for a spring evening.

He lifted his belt from the chair beside the bed and buckled his weapons around him. He felt more comfortable with them at his sides. He left his room and knocked on Prious' door.

"Are you ready, Brother?"

"I will be with you now. Give Waestan a call."

Raoul moved on to Waestan's door and knocked.

"Father Waestan, are you ready to join us?"

There was no reply to Raoul's call, and he could not hear any movement in the room.

"Father, are you there?"

There was still no reply so Raoul gently opened the door and stepped inside. The room was very like his own and was empty. The fire had been built up and had a pile of cut logs beside it. It had been attended to since Waestan had left the room. Raoul's eyes cast around rest of the room. The bed had been tidied, or had not been used. The water jug was full and the bowl empty and dry, the cloth was neatly hung beside it. Raoul heard a noise behind him and spun around. Prious had entered the bedroom.

"Waestan is not here."

"Indeed not, Brother. If I had not seen him enter earlier I might even believe he had not been here at all. At the least, the room has been attended to since he left, so he has not been here for some while. I am getting a little uneasy about the Father."

"Yes, well, as we have said, at least he does not know our plans."

Raoul laughed and walked towards the door.

"Brother, I do not know our plans!"

"I will let you know when I have one. Lead on." They walked back past their rooms, down the stairs and along to the Great Hall. Again the doors were open and they entered. Lord Jowan, Myghal, the Lady Morwenna and Waestan stood in a circle before the fireplace, talking.

The side of the round table nearest the fire was laid with six platters, a knife beside each. A wonderful spread of food was laid in front of them with jugs of wine. Silver candelabras lit it all. The candles mounted around the walls were all alight too, and with the light from the large fire, that end of the Hall had a warm comfortable glow. Lord Jowan saw their approach.

"Ah, Brother Prious, Raoul, welcome. Come, join us in a glass of wine before we eat."

He picked two goblets from the table that were already poured and handed them to his guests.

"There, now we all have a drink. A toast, my friends, to our success."

Everyone raised their goblets and repeated, "To our success."

Raoul was suddenly aware that the Lady Morwenna had manoeuvred herself to his side. She smiled broadly at him. He returned her smile, trying to lift his eyes from her breasts. The light woollen dress she wore hugged them tightly.

"Good evening, my Lady. You look very lovely this evening."

"Thank you, Raoul. I was looking forward to seeing you again."

"And I you, my Lady."

"Excuse me."

Myghal stepped between them and reached for a jug of wine. He filled his goblet and turned to Raoul.

"Wine for you, soldier boy?"

"No, thank you. I have hardly had time to drink any yet."

Myghal replaced the jug on the table.

"Not for you, sister dear, you must not drink too much. It might put silly ideas into your sweet little head."

"It sounds to me that you are the one who is drinking too much. Have you stopped at all since noon?"

Before more could be said Lord Jowan's voice rose above any conversation.

"Now, everyone, let us sit and eat, and I have some very special wine to celebrate our visitors' arrival. I will sit here, Morwenna, as Lady of the house, will sit beside me. Father Waestan, please sit next to her and Myghal sit next to our special guest. On this side, Brother Prious, please sit next to me, and Raoul beside the Brother."

They all sat as directed and two servants poured the new wine into clean goblets set at their places.

"Now, Father, pray say Grace before we eat."

"Thank you, I will. We thank you, my Lord God, for your bounty on the table before us, and beg your blessing for the days ahead. Amen."

"Very good. Now please all help yourselves."

They all ate well, making small talk and enjoying the fine wine. Myghal was becoming noticeably louder. In an attempt to engage Lord Jowan, Waestan turned the conversation to the family history and some of the famous battles Artoris had fought.

After some stories of early times of Artoris himself fighting in Cornwall, Myghal was getting bored and irritated that every time he looked at his sister she was staring adoringly at Raoul. At a break in his father's stories he called across the table.

"You're supposed to be a soldier are you not, Raoul? What battles have you fought in?"

Raoul looked sideways at Prious, almost asking permission to reply. Prious began for him.

"I met Raoul in Brittany where he had lived for a number of years. He was a famed fighter then, so when, in these difficult times, I felt I needed protection I sought him out."

"So your master has to answer for you, does he?"

"Myghal, please, do not talk to a guest so."

Raoul leant forward.

"My Lord, forgive Brother Prious. He fears you may not like what you hear, but I would rather the truth be known and you may judge for yourselves."

"I see. Well, pray tell."

"My Lord, I am not Breton by birth, I am French. I was born in Picardy. At sixteen I left home and joined the Norman army. There was not a French army."

There was a sudden absolute silence in the room. Prious wondered for a moment what Raoul was doing.

"I fought with the Normans against King Conan when William the Bastard beat them and took Brittany, and I stayed there after the battle. It was during this time I met Brother Prious."

Prious smiled inwardly. At least Raoul had not called him the Conqueror. Raoul continued.

"You must remember that when the Bastard invaded England he had the support of the Pope. The Pope declared it a holy crusade, even excommunicating King Harold. God-fearing soldiers from France and Brittany, indeed from all the lands of Christendom, joined the Bastard's Norman army, under the Papal Standard. I found myself caught up in a small army of Bretons who did exactly that. It was a Godly thing. We had no love of Normans."

Raoul paused and drank from his goblet of wine. Myghal moved as if to speak but his father quickly raised a hand at him.

"So eventually, after waiting for months to sail, we arrived in England and I fought at Senlac. I fought on the Norman left. The battle began on the right, but on our first assault up the hill at the Saxons, their shield wall held firm and we were pushed back. Many foolish Saxons left the wall and drove us back down the hill, but the slope on that side ended in a stream with a bog beyond. There was nowhere to go so we rallied with our backs to the stream and held the Saxons long enough for the Bastard to hit them from behind with his cavalry and slaughter them. That was in the morning. We fought like that all day."

Raoul looked directly at Myghal.

"So, yes young Sir, I have fought in two major battles and many a skirmish. It is an ugly business, killing, so having returned to Brittany, I was happy to sell my sword to Brother Prious when he needed me. I thought, foolishly, it might lead to a quieter life."

Raoul's gaze returned to Lord Jowan.

"So you see, my Lord, Brother Prious here was worried that you would be upset or misunderstand that I had fought with Normans. I am no Norman, nor have any affinity with them. They either paid me well or I was doing God's work. If it offends you I will leave your castle in the morning and your table now."

"No, no need, no need at all. I admire your truthfulness. You are indeed a very experienced soldier, and an honourable one. It is you who must forgive my son's curiosity."

Lord Jowan waved a hand at the servants standing at the far side of the table. He laughed as he spoke.

"Come, more wine for all. Thank God I brought out the best. I have never had a Frenchman at my table."

"The honour is mine, my Lord."

Raoul looked across at Myghal. He was drinking and leaning into Waestan, his lips close to Waestan's ear. The Lady Morwenna, however, was staring at him and broke into a wide smile. Raoul smiled back warmly. Prious leaned towards him.

"An interesting ploy, my friend. It might have gone awry."

"Well, the way I looked at it, Brother, it would have been my way out of here if it had."

Prious turned back to Lord Jowan.

"This really is a very fine wine, my Lord. Is it from France?"

"From Aquitaine, Father. From an area called Bordeaux. It is one of my favourites. Tell me, how long have you known Raoul? The more I learn about him and speak to him, he seems to have an air of nobility about him. Does he have a sire's name?"

"If he does I have never heard it. I have always felt the same as yourself. I think perhaps if he carried colours they might carry a bar sinister."

"My instinct was the same, Brother. He may be a common soldier but he has the bearing of a noble. He was not raised a commoner."

"Perhaps not, my Lord. I have never asked him. I respect his privacy."

"Indeed, Brother."

Prious hoped that was enough to stop Jowan probing further.

With the food almost cleared from the table Lord Jowan raised his glass.

"My dear guests, my son and daughter, God bless you all and this fine meal we have eaten. There is more wine if you would enjoy it, but I have a special treat for you all, something rare and unusual. My agent discovered it whilst purchasing the wine from Aquitaine. It is a wine spirit, made by monks in Cognac, a region of Aquitaine, you must try it. They make it only for themselves but we managed to obtain many jars a short while ago. You must try some, it is called brandy."

They all rose from the table and formed a group before the fire. A servant arrived and took their wine goblets, replacing them with smaller ones filled with the wine spirit. Lord Jowan raised his goblet. He was enjoying himself.

"To health and good fortune." The group echoed his call.

"To health and good fortune."

They all drank. All caught their breath. Some coughed. Jowan smiled, enjoying himself.

"You see, my friends, it is very special, and as a grape spirit, it mixes well with the wine. Come, more wine all."

The evening progressed with more small talk. Prious questioned Lord Jowan about his contacts in Aquitaine and Raoul manoeuvred himself next to Morwenna.

"Are you enjoying the evening, my Lady?"

"I am, good Sir. I only regret I have not spent enough time in your company."

"A regret of mine also my Lady. One I would wish to redress."

"You are in our guest rooms?"

"Indeed, my Lady. The first room along the passage."

"A pleasant room if I remember. They all are I believe."

Myghal stumbled towards them. The grape spirit had had its affect after all the wine he had drunk through the day.

"Enough, soldier boy. A famous fighter you may be but you will never be man enough to talk to my sister."

Morwenna stepped between them.

"Who I chose to talk to is none of your business, Myghal."

She pushed Myghal away and he took a step backwards. Stepping immediately forward again he slapped Morwenna hard across the face.

Raoul moved like a cat. In one movement his small knife was in his hand and Myghal was on his back on the table, the knife point against his throat.

"Forgive me, my Lord, but I think your son has had too much of your fine wine and spirit. I would not harm him but he cannot do that in my company."

As Myghal lay back across the table a wet stain spread across his leggings. Lord Jowan moved forward.

"Thank you, Raoul. He did not deserve your mercy, although as my guest I would have expected it. You have my humblest apologies."

"It is the Lady Morwenna that should have those, my Lord. I was only defending her honour."

Raoul sheathed his knife and stepped away from the table as Myghal sat up, water dripping from his crotch.

"Indeed, my man. You have honour beyond your station, and I am indebted to you."

Lord Jowan turned to a servant.

"Where is Daveth?"

"He is close, my Lord"

"Then fetch him, in haste."

Daveth arrived almost as Lord Jowan sent for him.

"You sent for me, my Lord."

"Indeed Daveth. See this embarrassment that is my son to his room and put him to bed. He has disgraced both myself and my family's hospitality."

"Yes, my Lord, as you wish."

"And my dear Morwenna, I think you should retire now and leave us men to end our evening."

"Yes, Father, I will retire now, with every best wish to our guests. I would offer particular good wishes to Raoul for protecting my honour. Good night to all."

She turned and left the hall, closely following Daveth and a servant who were supporting Myghal.

"My dear guests, how do I apologise except by offering more wine or spirit."

Prious held out his wine goblet.

"My Lord, the spirit is excellent, but the wine is superb. One more goblet and I think even I will succumb to your hospitality."

Jowan found a jug on the table. Waestan and Raoul took a goblet each too. Jowan stood beside Raoul.

"You are unique in my memory, my man. I can read most people but you are a mystery to me."

Raoul laughed and took a mouthful of wine.

"I am a simple sell-sword, my Lord. I am loyal to whoever pays me until my commission is ended."

"Well whenever your commission with Prious ends, do come and visit me again. There is always a place here for you."

"Thank you, my Lord, I will."

Raoul gritted his teeth for a moment then drank some wine. He had little left and wanted no more. He looked at Prious who slapped a hand on Lord Jowan's shoulder and began to speak of Aquitaine and of their food and wines.

Waestan had been quiet all evening. Raoul approached him.

"Have you enjoyed your evening, Father?"

"Ah, Raoul, that is hard to know in honesty, but whilst it has to be done, stealing from these lovely people is difficult."

"Yes, Father, but as you say, it has to be done. I am away to my bed now, I suggest you do the same."

"Then let us excuse ourselves and I will come up with you."

They thanked Lord Jowan for his hospitality and left him talking with Prious, leaving the hall and taking the stairs to their rooms. Raoul waited by the door until Waestan reached his, then wished him a good night. They both entered their rooms.

+++

Morwenna followed Daveth and one of the servants who were supporting Myghal up the staircase. They passed the guest floor and up the second flight. Myghal's room was the first they reached. Daveth opened the door and they carried Myghal into his room. Morwenna walked on to her door and entered her room.

Her heart was racing. She felt herself quiver with anticipation. She removed her clothes and put on a light linen gown that reached the floor. Her feet were bare and the wooden boards were cold. She stood at her window which was still open. There was a strong breeze blowing across it. She should close the shutters and pull the curtains, but she was not going to sleep in the room by choice.

She breathed deeply. The fresh night air filled her with confidence. The sea was as dark as the night sky and she could not see where one ended and the other began. The clouds had blown over and the stars were bright, but she could not see the moon.

She was sure Daveth and the servant would have left Myghal asleep on his bed and returned to the Hall by now. It was her time. This was her moment, she was sure.

She opened her door quietly and walked gently to the staircase. She stopped and listened. She could hear nothing but she did not wish to meet anyone climbing the stairs. She crept down the stairs, listening intently as she went. She reached the guest landing and hastily tiptoed along the passage to the first door.

She was sure this was the door to Raoul's room, but she could hear no movement within. She opened the latch and entered. The only light came from the fire that had been made up and was burning brightly. The shutters were closed and the curtain drawn. She took a spill from beside the fire and lit it, moving around the room and lighting the candles that were placed in bronze candelabras on small tables and mounted on the walls. The bedroom had a warm, comfortable glow. She moved to the large four-poster and removed her gown, throwing it across the chair on that side of the bed. She slid beneath the linen sheet and lay back against the pillows. Her stomach tightened. She hoped he would not drink too much before he came to bed.

There were voices outside in the passage. She heard Raoul wishing Waestan a good night and the door opened. For a moment nothing happened.

Raoul had opened the door to find the room was lit by candles. He hesitated before entering, moving slowly and fully alert.

He saw Morwenna in the bed and closed the door behind him. He walked to the bedside opposite her and smiled as he unbuckled his belt, hanging it on a chair with his sword and knives.

"This is a very pleasant surprise, my Lady."

"You said you wanted to see more of me."

As she spoke she lowered the linen sheet exposing her breasts. He laughed and began to remove his heavy leather tabard. She could not believe she had just said something so incredibly childish.

"Are you sure this is what you wish, my Lady?"

"More than anything, believe me."

"Well I shall not deny you. You have captivated me since the moment I saw you. I have thought of little else since then."

As he was speaking he removed the rest of his clothing and climbed into the bed. She smiled at him and opened her arms. He lay beside her, his head on her chest. She wrapped her arms around him, one on his back, the other holding his head against her.

He lifted his head a little and gently kissed her neck, then lifted his head higher and kissed her mouth. He slid an arm behind her head and lay back, pulling her with him. They lay side by side, legs intertwined, and kissed.

Morwenna was in heaven. This was how it was meant to be. With one arm around her, hand holding her to him, Raoul gently caressed her back with the other. He moved his hand down to her hip then, pushing her away a little, raised it to her breast and ran his fingers gently around it.

Morwenna moaned softly, her passion rising. His thigh was between her legs and she moved against it, embarrassed a little by how wet she had become. Raoul pushed her away further and lowered his mouth to her other breast, licking it and kissing her nipple.

Morwenna felt as though her breasts would burst. Her body almost pulsed with pleasure; her mind was lost in him. She was desperate for him to enter her but he did not, kissing and caressing her breasts.

She could feel him against her and reached down to hold him. It was something she had never done before although Elowen had described it well. He groaned as she gripped him. He was so hard.

He could contain himself no longer. He rolled her onto her back and laid gently between her thighs, entering her slowly. Morwenna gasped and moved with him, feeling her pleasure begin to build.

Raoul fought his body, desperately trying to think of anything to stop himself from seeding. He thanked goodness that he had done it himself the night before. Otherwise he was sure he would have seeded before he entered her. Then his mind froze, he was pledged to kill this girl.

He could control himself no longer. He groaned as he seeded, feeling it pulse from him inside her. He raised himself on his arms, still inside her, and looked down at her face. She gazed up at him, her legs hooked around his so he could not leave her.

"I'm so sorry, my love. I tried to......"

"Shush," she whispered, still breathless. She raised a finger to his lips. "Those were the most wonderful moments of my life."

"Yes, but the pleasure has all been mine."

"That does not matter, my dear one. It felt wonderful."

He rolled sideways, leaving her body but holding her close. His hand moved between her thighs and she gasped. She was still so very aroused. His finger entered her briefly. She was warm and wet and inviting, her own juices mixed with his seed. He pressed her onto her back and gently rubbed her, his finger just slipping into her a little. He knew the place that had the most affect.

Morwenna did not know how to react. His fingers were sending waves of pleasure through her stomach. It was just how she touched herself. Her back arched as she felt her passion rising. This was unbelievable. Her whole body was going to burst.

She groaned as her passion grew. Nothing mattered in the world now, except the surge of pleasure that grew and burst as she cried out. It sent pulses across her stomach, into her thighs and seeming to consume her whole body.

Raoul smiled to himself as he felt her contractions against his fingers. Experience had taught him well. He raised himself on one arm and leaning across her, kissed her mouth. He looked down into her eyes.

"Is that better?" he smiled.

She just looked up at him with eyes that were glazed with tears and full of a mixture adoration and amazement.

"Dear God, Raoul, what have you done to me?"

He laughed and lay back beside her, his arm still behind her neck.

"No more than you have done to me."

They lay there without moving until Morwenna rolled sideways and cuddled into Raoul's shoulder, her head on his chest. Only then did he realise her cheeks were wet with silent tears.

"What is wrong, my lovely, have I done something wrong?"

"No, no. You have done everything exactly right. You have answered a lifetime of prayers and fulfilled so many dreams. It is just that tomorrow or the next day you will set off to war and I will probably never see you again. I am not sure I can live with that."

His conscience told him that was not a problem, she would be dead tomorrow or the day after. It was at that moment Raoul knew he could never kill this girl. He loved her. He had never loved a woman in his life, but he loved this one.

"Then we will have to think of something. What you need to understand, my Lady, is that despite my best efforts not to, I have fallen in love with you."

She pushed herself up on one arm and threw the other over him, kissing him fiercely.

"You have made me the happiest woman in the land. I love you too, more than I can express. It is as if I always knew you would come, but I was beginning to doubt myself."

There was a sudden noise at the door and it swung open. Myghal stood there in the opening, still dressed in that evening's clothes but with a sword in his hand. He lurched into the room towards Raoul and shouted at Morwenna.

"I knew you would be here. You are more of a whore than a sister, and you, soldier boy, are going to pay for your pleasure with your life."

Raoul tried to jump up from the bed but at first he was trapped by Morwenna draped over his body. He pushed her off him none too gently and she rolled across the bed. He was on his feet in an instant. He had been distracted when he came to bed and had hung his sword belt on the chair near the far end of the bed, where Myghal now stood.

He cursed himself that his lack of professionalism might now cost him his life. He was totally naked and his weapons were out of reach. He had also always been taught that a man fighting in bare feet against a man wearing boots had little chance of surviving.

He looked desperately for something to use as a weapon but there was nothing to hand. He grabbed a pillow from the bed. That might absorb the first thrust. Myghal moved towards him, raising his sword, which he held firmly in both hands. Raoul hoped Myghal was still as drunk as he had been. Myghal paused to gloat for a moment.

"Not such a brave soldier boy now, are we, hey? Bollock naked and no sword. I shall enjoy this."

He lifted the sword above his right shoulder and stepped towards Raoul, but before Raoul could move there was a dull thud. Myghal's eyes rolled up and he fell sideways, deflected by the bed and crumpling to the floor. He left a splatter of blood on the bedcover and blood slowly spread from his head onto the floor.

Raoul looked beyond the body at Morwenna. She stood there, quite naked too, a bronze candlestick that had been on a table on her side of the bed gripped like a club in her hand. She was shaking.

"Oh God, what have I done?"

Raoul looked down at Myghal. His eyes were wide open looking upward. He was quite dead. Morwenna threw the candlestick aside. It hit the floor with a heavy thump. Raoul stepped over Myghal's body and took Morwenna in his arms as she dissolved into tears. Her voice shook as she spoke.

"He was going to kill you. I couldn't let him do that, I have only just found you. Oh God, I have killed my brother."

"And saved my life."

"But what am I going to do? My father will have you killed and I cannot imagine what he will do to me."

Raoul's mind was racing, different ideas flashing through his mind. He hated himself but this was exactly what he needed. This was something they could take advantage of.

"Do not be afraid, my love. We must leave the castle. You will come with me, please?"

"Oh Raoul, of course."

"You are the Lady Morwenna, the guards will obey you?"

"Well yes, they should, although I rarely need to give them orders, but they should."

"And if you go to your friend in the stables and order her husband to ready some horses, they should do so?"

"They will think it very strange, but yes, if I insist."

"Then we shall be gone shortly, but for their safety we will have to take Prious and Waestan with us. Put on your gown and sit there whilst I dress."

He pulled on his clothes and boots as quickly as he could, his mind still sorting possibilities. Finally he buckled his belt around him, sword and knives at his sides. Morwenna was crying, sitting in the chair on the far side of the bed from Myghal. Raoul went to her and took her hands.

"Now listen, stop those tears. Your brother may be dead but a new life is open to us if you can be brave. You wait here a few moments more whilst I wake Prious."

He kissed her forehead and went to the door. He stepped into the passage and ran to Prious room, opening the door and entering without knocking. Prious was asleep but half awoke as the door opened. He sat up as Raoul entered. Raoul held a hand up and spoke.

"No time to explain. Morwenna has killed her brother. She wants to run away with me. She can get us out, and with horses."

He raised his hand again as Prious was about to interrupt.

"Just trust me. Get up, dressed and packed. Rouse Waestan and be ready here. I have work to do."

He turned and almost ran from the room leaving a bewildered but obedient Prious behind him. He collected Morwenna from his room and led her to the staircase. He whispered to her.

"Will there be servants about at this time?"

"Only if someone has called them, but I doubt it."

He led her upstairs to the passage above then pushed her ahead of him. She opened the door to her bedroom and he followed her in.

"Now, my love, dress yourself in something you can ride in and travel in for a few days. Pack nothing else. I have something I must do. Wait here for me. I will be back very soon, I promise."

He kissed her cheek and left the bedroom, walking quietly along the passage to the stairs. He climbed to the floor above, to Lord Jowan's rooms. He did not know which door along the passage was the bedroom but on the other floors the higher status bedrooms were at the far end furthest from the stairs.

He guessed correctly. He very gently lifted the latch and opened the door a little, looking across the room. The only light came from the fire which was mainly embers now but it was enough for him to see Lord Jowan asleep in his bed. He was almost sitting up against the pillows. After all the wine and brandy spirit he had drunk that day he had fallen asleep sitting on the bed before he could lie down.

Raoul crept across the room, drawing the long fighting knife from his belt. He did not want to do what had to be done but do it he must. He reached the bed. Lord Jowan was wearing a nightshirt, open to the waist. The bed cover reached over his stomach but his chest was exposed.

Raoul lent forward over the bed and held the point of the knife just below Lord Jowan's breastbone. Before he could think too much about it Raoul rammed the point home, pushing down hard on the hilt and forcing the blade upward as he thrust.

Lord Jowan's eyes opened and instantly glazed. He was dead before he could have known what had happened. Raoul wrenched the blade free and started to wipe it on the bedding when he heard the faintest noise behind him. He spun around drawing his shorter knife as he did so.

Daveth was crossing the bedroom towards him, Lord Jowan's sword held over his left shoulder and swinging downwards. He hissed at Raoul.

"You treacherous bastard!"

Raoul caught the sword between the crossed blades of his knives. He pushed the sword away to the right with his long knife and stepped forward, thrusting the shorter one up into Daveth's throat. The blade struck up through his neck into his head. Raoul felt it strike the top of Daveth's skull before he ripped the knife downwards and out. Daveth seemed to stand still for a moment then fell backwards heavily to the floor.

Raoul mumbled to himself.

"Where in God's name did you come from?"

He looked around the bedroom. There was an adjoining door to the next room that stood ajar. He had been lucky for the second time that day. But for that tiny sound he would be dead now and not Daveth. He saw that the door was set into the wooden panelling and was disguised to the eye. He would have seen it if he had looked more carefully.

He sheathed his knives and quickly returned to Morwenna's room. She was dressed and waiting for him.

"Where have you been?"

"It's not important. Come, my love, we must make haste."

He took her hand and led her down the stairs. He stopped at the end of the passage.

"Wait whilst I tell Prious to come to the stables."

He ran to Prious' door and pushed it open. Prious was standing with Waestan in the middle of the room. Raoul spoke before they could.

"Go to the Great Hall. Get the Sword, Helm and books and bundle them in some bedding sheets so they cannot be recognised. Morwenna does not know. Then meet us at the stables. Just do so."

He left before they could say anything and ran back to Morwenna.

"Now, my love, we must rouse your friend and her husband. Are there any guards around the castle at night?"

"Only at the gates. If they are secure there is nothing to guard against."

Raoul led her down the final flight of stairs to the Keep's doors, talking as they went.

"We need five horses, four to ride and one pack horse. Waestan has some things from your father to take for him."

"It is rare for anyone to be leaving the castle at this time. It must be midnight. What do I say if they question me?"

"You are the Lady Morwenna. This is a time of war and we have a mission to carry out for your father. We ride to King Mark. Tell them to question Lord Jowan if they must but be prepared to face his wrath for delaying us."

"Oh, Raoul, I do not know that I can do this."

"If you cannot then I am dead and you a solitary prisoner, if not worse."

She nodded and took a deep breath.

"I am ready then."

They stepped through the large wooden doors and crossed the courtyard, passing the stables on the way to the ostler's cottage. Raoul knocked on the door. It had to be loud enough to wake Garth and Elowen but he did not wish to rouse anyone in the cottages around them. He knocked again then once more before they heard a man's voice from within.

"Enough, I hear you. Who in God's name is knocking at this hour? You will wake the children."

"Open the door, Garth, it is Lady Morwenna."

They heard a bolt draw back, then the latch lifted and the door opened inwards.

"My Lady, I am so sorry. I never imagined it could be you at this hour."

Raoul looked past Garth to see who he assumed was Elowen behind him. Morwenna stepped through the door and pushed past Garth. She embraced Elowen and burst into tears. She knew she would. Raoul stepped through the door and pushed it shut behind him.

"Morwenna, what is wrong?"

Garth looked puzzled and very concerned.

"I am sorry, this is so unexpected. I have to leave now on my father's business, urgent unexpected business, and I may not see you again for a long time."

She stepped back away from Elowen. Raoul was surprised how well she lied. Morwenna turned to Elowen's husband.

"Garth, we need five horses, in some haste. We must reach Bosvena by dawn to warn King Mark. My horse, of course, Myghal's horse for Raoul at my father's command, and two guest horses, all saddled. Then I need a pack-horse to carry some goods of my father's for King Mark."

"Do I not need an order from your father, through Daveth perhaps?"

"Garth, I am the Lady Morwenna on my father's business, now please do as I request. My father will be very upset if we are delayed on his business."

"Yes, my Lady. Who else travels with you?"

Raoul's sharp tones answered him.

"Father Waestan and Brother Prious. They will meet us at the stables with the goods for King Mark. We were hoping the horses would be ready before they arrived but unless you get a few garments on, they will be waiting for us. Lord Jowan may be with them, he may not, but let us not tarry."

Garth moved to the corner of the room and pulled on some leggings that were beside the bed. He lifted his nightshirt off over his head and replaced it with a linen shirt that was hanging beside the bed. He pulled on a light leather waistcoat as he moved to the door.

"Come with me then, I will ready the horses."

Raoul moved to the door, opening it and standing back to let Garth pass him. He held it open for Morwenna but she did not move.

"Go on with Garth, I will follow in a moment. I must say goodbye to Elowen."

"Do not take too long."

He stared at her. She nodded. He had to trust her. He stepped out of the door and walked after Garth to the stables.

"Now Morwenna, are you sure all is well?"

"My dearest friend, this has been the best and the worst day of my life. I cannot explain. It is all to do with rebellion against the Normans. A battle is coming, I am sure."

"And with Raoul? He looks marvellous."

"He is. He was the best part, he is a wonderful lover."

Elowen hugged her.

"I am so happy for you."

"Yes, but I fear I may never see you again. If he returns to his home in France, I will go with him. I will miss you so."

"Bah! Get you gone. Be happy. Enjoy your life, make him happy."

She kissed Morwenna and pushed her to the door.

"Go, go now and do not look back. I will always remember our friendship. Be gone."

Elowen shut the door and began to cry. She knew something was very wrong but she was not going to betray their friendship. She prayed Garth would do nothing foolish.

Morwenna walked around the cottage to the stable doors, which were wide open. Garth had saddled her horse and was working on Myghal's. Raoul was saddling the other two.

Garth unhitched the final guest horse and took a rack from the wall. He had removed it from the donkey they had brought with them. By lengthening the straps it fitted a horse just as well. Once secure, he hung some loops of rope from it.

As he finished Prious and Waestan arrived at the stables. Prious was carrying two bundles wrapped in linen, one long, one rounded. Waestan struggled with two heavy squared bundles.

They tied their bundles with rope loops and began to hook them onto the pack horse. Garth held it still. Waestan's bundles were attached, one on each side of the rack. Prious had attached his rounded bundle and was tying the long one in place when it slipped from his grasp. The end he was tying was secured but the other end swung down. The hilt of Excalibur slid out and hit the ground. Prious bent quickly down grabbing the hilt and pushing it back into the bundle, but Garth had seen it.

He let go of the rein and stepped back, looking at Morwenna.

"But My Lady, Excalibur, his Lordship would not let that leave the castle without him!"

Raoul was around the horse with his sword drawn before Garth could move any further. He held the sword against Garth's chest and pushed him back into the stables.

"It is a shame you saw that."

Morwenna ran across the stable and gripped Raoul's arm.

"No, do not kill him." She yanked at Raoul's arm, tears streaming down her face. Raoul called over his shoulder.

"Prious, bring rope. Tie him and gag him."

Raoul raised his sword and struck Garth hard across his face with the hilt. Garth fell to the ground with blood running from a wound on his forehead and cheek.

"I should kill him and his wife. Waestan, go with Morwenna and bind his wife. Tell her to say in the morning we forced them to help us. Tell them I threatened Garth here that I would kill his children and wife if he refused. Do it quickly."

Prious tied Garth's wrists and ankles, then tightened a saddle strap across his mouth between his teeth. He was talking to Garth as he did it but Raoul could not hear what was said.

Raoul led the horses out of the stable and looked up to see Morwenna and Waestan returning from the cottage. Waestan took his mount from Raoul.

"She is tied loosely. She has promised Morwenna she will not leave the cottage before dawn. She has children and…"

"Just get mounted. Morwenna, here."

He handed her horse's reins to her.

"I am sorry about your friends."

He gave the reins of Prious' horse to him as Prious approached.

"All done. Give me your reins and the pack horse. Help the Lady."

Raoul did as suggested and went to help Morwenna mount. She hesitated and turned to him.

"I do not understand. Why do you have Excalibur, and what else do you have?"

"You will have to trust me, my love. The most important thing is to get you out of here before anyone discovers Myghal's body. I will explain the rest later."

He cupped his hands and held them in front of him beside Morwenna's horse. She gripped her saddle and put her foot in Raoul's hands, stepping up and onto her horse. Raoul called up to her.

"Lead on to the gates. I will be behind you."

Morwenna looked at him uncertainly then steered her horse away. Waestan followed her as Raoul took his reins from Prious who had mounted his horse. He waited for Raoul to mount and they rode side by side behind Waestan. Prious lent toward Raoul and spoke quietly.

"Lord Jowan?"

"Dead, and Daveth. Sadly he interrupted things, but probably just as well. I did not know he was up there. Otherwise he would probably have discovered the bodies before we were away."

"When do you kill the girl?"

"I don't. I will take her to France with me when this is all over."

"The King may not let you."

"Then I will not ask him. Enough now."

Prious looked at Raoul but said nothing. His mind, however, was troubled. What would she do when she discovered that Raoul had killed her father? She will find out eventually. Perhaps that would not be for a while and there were more concerning things to worry about just now.

Morwenna led them through the village and Raoul moved up beside Waestan. They reached the barracks and guards' stables. Morwenna paused and looked over her shoulder at Raoul. He smiled and nodded to her. She was very uneasy but she was not going to forsake her new love.

She kicked her horse on and led them down the steep track to the guardhouse and gates. As she approached the gates two guards appeared through a doorway and stood in the darkness in front of her horse. Morwenna shouted to them.

"Open the gates for my party. We are about my father's business."

"But my Lady, we have no orders regarding anyone leaving the castle. Particularly at this hour."

Raoul recognised the guard as the Officer who had caused their delay entering. He moved up out of the shadows behind Morwenna as she spoke again.

"I am the Lady Morwenna, as you clearly recognise. We have urgent and unexpected reason to leave on my father's behalf. We travel to meet King Mark in Bosvena. Now obey my command and open the gate."

Before either guard could speak again Raoul moved up beside Morwenna.

"Well, well. It's the Officer of the Guard again, although not an Officer now it would seem. No pretty blue sash. I suspect night duty is also the result of holding us up yesterday. I suggest that if you wish to remain a guard at all, you obey the Lady Morwenna's command and open the gates."

The ex-Officer looked up at Raoul with pure hatred in his eyes, but even in the darkness Raoul could see the fear and uncertainty there too. He turned and nodded to the other guard. They walked to the gates and lifted the long locking-bar up and down from its cradle. Propping it against the wall they pulled opened the gates.

Morwenna led them out of the castle to the bottom of the valley opposite. Without looking back she began the steady climb upwards to the village of Tintagel on their left, and the British encampment. They quickly bypassed them both.

Prious moved up and handed the reins of the pack horse to Waestan and led the party back along the path they had travelled only the morning before, back to the round at Goff.

The Fifth Scroll

It was not far to Goff but they walked the horses; it would be a long night. There would be no sleep, at least not out of the saddle. Prious did not think they would be pursued until morning. No-one knew where they were heading. They had told people they were going to King Mark in Bosvena but the only people that might guess where they were actually going were all dead. They could not be tracked in the dark and Prious was not sure who would be there to organise a pursuit after the shock of finding the bodies.

The track was narrow so they rode in single file and hence in silence. Prious was sure there would be plenty to be said when they reached Goff and he was correct. He led them through the entrance to the round and dismounted.

"Raoul, Waestan, fetch our package and bring it here. Come, my Lady, I will help you down."

Morwenna dismounted and stood beside Prious.

"I need to understand what is happening, Brother. At the castle you said Goff was where you had hidden Arthur's armour. You have Excalibur and I assume that other bundle is his Helm. Are we taking it to King Mark?"

Waestan returned before Prious could answer and began to attach the bundle he carried to the pack horse. Raoul returned shortly afterwards. Prious called for everyone's attention.

"We need to determine our path from here."

Raoul spoke before he could say any more.

"There is nothing to decide, Brother. It is here that our paths must separate. I must ride with all haste to Exeter with Father Waestan. We do not know whether Godwine and his army has sailed but we have to cross the ford at Tawton before he can get there or we will be cut off from Exeter. I have to join Sir Breon and drive the Saxons back to their ships and Waestan must reach Sir Baldwin with the news about Gytha and get her back from Bradanreolice."

Morwenna interrupted him.

"But I must come with you, Raoul."

"No, my love, that cannot be. You must go with Brother Prious. He will take you to Tregony and then by boat and road to Winchester. I will meet you there when my work is done and I will seek the King's permission to take you to my home in France. Until then Prious will protect you, will you not, Brother?"

"That I promise."

Morwenna could not hold back her tears. She was now completely bewildered. Raoul continued.

"It is for you, Brother, to dispose of all the baggage."

"That I promise too."

Raoul took Morwenna in his arms and held her to him.

"I am very sorry, my love, but I have duties to perform before we can be together. I will meet you in Winchester, I promise, and if you still wish it, I will take you to France."

"What do mean? Of course I shall still wish it."

"I sincerely hope so. Now I must go. Waestan, mount. We are leaving."

Prious joined Raoul as he turned away from Morwenna. He whispered to Raoul.

"Do you really think the King will let her live?"

"He will if he does not know she is in Winchester until I arrive. Keep her safe."

"What do I tell her?"

"The truth, eventually. I suggest after you leave Cornwall."

Raoul swung himself up onto his saddle.

"Goodbye, my love, farewell Brother. Take good care of her for me."

He turned his horse out of the round, only hesitating a moment for Waestan to follow closely.

Prious put an arm around Morwenna's shoulders.

"You will see him again, I am sure."

"I thought he was a sell-sword, paid by you to protect you, but he was just giving you orders. How can that be so?"

"Because he is no sell-sword. He, my Lady, is Sir Raoul Tyrrell of Radepont, a French nobleman who became a Norman knight. But come, we must leave too. If we ride all night and all of tomorrow we should reach Cornelly and Tregony tomorrow evening. Then we will be quite safe."

He led her to her horse and helped her mount. She was too shocked to argue, which pleased Prious. He was worried she would be enraged and want to go back. It seemed, however, that whatever her beloved told her to do, she would do. He was not sure how he would tell her that Raoul had killed her father and that he would have killed her brother if she had not. Indeed, he would have killed her if he had not fallen in love with her.

+++

Waestan rode alongside Raoul. They trotted the horses for a while then slowed to a walk. They did so throughout the night. Waestan leaned towards Raoul.

"Where are we riding to now, Sir Raoul? I assume I should call you that now."

He only answered the first question.

"Almost due west from Goff, Father. We must keep the moors of Bosvena to our right and we should reach Lannstevan by first light. We will bypass it, again to our right but then we have to cross the River Tamar. The road from Lannstevan to Tawton crosses it at Ponstonel, so that is where we must, hopefully without hindrance."

"I have seen little hinder you, Sir Raoul."

Raoul looked sideways at him.

"You had me worried for a while, Father. There were a few secrets you held back from us."

"I am sorry. I knew Lord Jowan quite well. I find this being on one side and pretending to be on the other a little dishonourable sometimes. It is a shame about Myghal's death. He was a foolish youth but loyal to his family. I suppose it allowed us to escape with everything. Do you think Lord Jowan will ride out in pursuit at dawn?"

"No."

"Surely he will assume we have kidnapped the Lady Morwenna and try to rescue her."

"Lord Jowan is dead."

"Dead! How?"

"I killed him before we left, and Daveth. He got in the way. Father, why do you think I was sent here? Prious was to recover the armour, the sword and any history. I was to kill Lord Jowan, Myghal and Morwenna. King William has ordered all trace of the legend that is Arthur to be cleaned from history. Never should that name be used to threaten Norman rule again."

Raoul kicked his mount into a trot and moved ahead of Waestan. It was a while before Waestan caught up, but even then he stayed behind Raoul until Raoul slowed his horse to a walk again.

"I am sorry, Sir Raoul. I see now how naïve I am in these matters. I am not sure if I had known your intentions whether I would have been willing to help you."

"That, Father, is why we did not tell you."

"But the Lady Morwenna, surely, I mean, you will not her? Nor, indeed, would Prious?"

"I did not intend falling in love with her. If I had not she would also be dead and Prious would have been working some sort of magic to get us out of the castle."

"Yes, I see that now. Brother Prious is plainly more than he appears."

Raoul laughed and smiled at Waestan.

"Brother Prious is a monk who works for Bishop Odo of Bayeux, of whom I am sure you have heard. Anyone who works for Bishop Odo is not just what he appears. A monk, Brother Prious is; just a monk, he is not."

For a while as they rode Waestan felt quite inadequate. He had been naïve. Next he felt angry at being used. Then he felt weak for allowing it to happen, and finally stupid for not seeing what was happening. He remained silent for a while. He did not know whether he should continue speaking to Sir Raoul or not, but dislike his actions as he did, he was fascinated by him.

"How does taking a life make you feel, Sir Raoul? Does it make you feel powerful? Does it excite you?"

Raoul halted his horse for a moment and sighed. Waestan rode past him before he could react and stop his mount. He turned in his saddle to look back at Raoul.

"This is not confession, Father, nor is this a Sunday. Do not let curiosity mix with good works. I am far beyond help. Now ride on."

Raoul kicked his horse into a trot and Waestan followed. When they slowed to a walk again Waestan was back alongside Raoul.

"I am sorry, Sir Raoul. I am a simple priest, and apparently a very naïve one, but one who is trying to understand some of the ways of the crown and the church. Ways that were beyond me until I met Prious and yourself. It was a genuine question."

"Indeed, Father. Well, it is not a question that I have asked myself very often. Perhaps I needed time to think."

He laughed and pointed ahead and to the right.

"A few lights in Lannsteven, and the first glimmer of light in the east. How do I feel when I kill someone? In battle, I am usually too scared to feel anything else. Often I feel relief that I have killed him before he could kill me. I do not kill for pleasure, although sometimes I meet someone it would be a pleasure to kill. No, that is not really true. I kill out of duty, by order of those whom I serve, or to protect those whom I have sworn to protect. It is something you become accustomed to and you stop feeling anything."

"Do you not fear retribution, the wrath of God?"

"Oh, Father, do not talk to me of God. When you have seen what I have seen during and after a battle, no merciful God could allow such carnage, such death and suffering. If God wishes us to fight his Holy Wars, blessed by the Pope under a Papal flag, then he is not against killing."

Raoul stopped speaking. He was aware he was filled with anger, almost shouting.

"I think, Father, for now I would keep your questions to yourself. We have a river to cross and there, I believe, is the track that will take us to Ponstonel."

He kicked his horse on leaving, Waestan to catch up again.

+++

Prious helped Lady Morwenna up into her saddle then mounted his own horse. He led the pack horse out of the round and Morwenna followed. She followed in silence for a long time, deep in thought and full of doubt. Her blind love of Raoul had brought her thus far but she was beginning to become genuinely scared that her love was one-sided and she was being played for a fool.

She knew the paths to Bosvena and they had followed them for a while, but now Prious led them north of the track she knew. She rode up beside him when the track became wide enough.

"Where are we going now, Brother? We seem to have left the road to Bosvena."

"Indeed my Lady. We do not wish to meet King Mark or any envoy of his on their way to Tintagel. We are going to the ford over the Kammel below Nanstallon. From there we will ride back to Tregony by a different path to the one we walked. We will ride around the source of the Fal which will save crossing the river by raft lower down, and I most certainly wish to avoid crossing the bridge at Ponsmeur."

The track narrowed and they rode in silence again until it widened. Prious would look around at her every so often. Morwenna assumed it was to check if she was still following, so when she could she rode up beside him again.

"Fear not, I am still with you, Brother. Where else have I to go?"

"Not back to Tintagel, my Lady, but I would not wish you to have any thoughts of chasing after Sir Raoul."

"He told me to stay with you. You know I would follow him anywhere but he told me to stay with you."

"I will not be concerned then, my Lady."

"Have you known him long?"

"Sir Raoul? I have known him for about a week. In that time I have come to trust him and reluctantly, admire him."

"Reluctantly?"

"He is no man of God, my Lady. He is a professional soldier, a trained and efficient killer, but he is a man of integrity. At this time he is troubled because, for the first time in his life, as I understand it, he is in love, which is why you are here."

"I am not part of the baggage you are to dispose of then?"

Prious laughed and looked across at her.

"No, my Lady. You need to understand that Sir Raoul and I were sent to recover Arthur's armour and Excalibur so that they could not be used by your father and King Mark against King William. Waestan was entrusted by the Archbishop to deliver the armour to your father after Stigand had them stolen from the King William in Winchester. Waestan works secretly for King William so we joined forces. I have to destroy the armour and the sword. King Mark will not join your father and Godwine without it, we are certain, and hence we isolate Godwine."

"Are you not concerned that my father will pursue us to get it back?"

"No, once we recovered it from Goff he would not know where we had taken it. He would be more intent on meeting King Mark and persuading him to still join the rebellion."

Prious was desperately hoping Morwenna would not continue this line of questioning as he was not prepared to tell outright lies. He tried to steer her thoughts back to Raoul.

"My worry, my Lady, is for Raoul."

"For Raoul?" Prious could hear the concern in her voice. "Why are you worried for Raoul?"

"Well, my Lady, I will try to explain. I had a friend once who was a soldier like Sir Raoul. Very similar to him in fact and, thinking about it, maybe that is why I like Sir Raoul. Anyway, he told me once that the only reason he could keep going into battle was that every time he believed he would die. It was the only way he could fight. He was prepared to die. He had nothing to live for and so had nothing to lose. If he lived he was lucky. It was not luck, of course, it was skill. But the point was, because he was prepared to die and had nothing to lose, he could concentrate on killing the enemy. He was not worried about staying alive. He always felt that if he had something to live for he would be afraid to die, be hesitant, and therefore be weakened."

"So are you telling me that if Raoul is killed in the battle to come it will be my fault because he loves me?"

Prious felt bad about what he had said but realised he meant it.

"I do not know, my Lady. I am sure he will fare well. He is a strong man in every sense."

Morwenna rode on for a while. Being in love was not everything she had imagined. She seemed to spend so much time with tears in her eyes. She called to Prious.

"What happened to your soldier friend?"

Prious smiled at her.

"Oh, he is dead. A horse kicked him in the chest one day at his home and hurt him inside somehow. He took a week to die, but die he did. He had nothing to live for!"

"You are a hard man to understand, Brother. You are obviously a very clever man, but sometimes I feel you are playing with me. Treating me like a child."

"Then you have my apologies, my Lady. I do not intend to be demeaning in any way. I am afraid my Breton manner and accent can be misconstrued. I am honoured by your company, and I have promised Sir Raoul I will look after you, and that I will do."

Morwenna just looked at him as she rode beside and slightly behind him. Raoul trusted him so she must keep faith with Raoul and trust him too. There was a hint of dawn's light in the eastern sky. They would be at Nanstallon soon.

+++

Raoul and Waestan crossed the rocky ford at Ponstonel in the early light of dawn. The Tamar had calmed a bit but was still quite high from the recent rains so it was not the easiest of crossings.

The ford was deserted which was a relief to Raoul. He had been worried King Mark might have had a guard of some sort there. It was, after all, a main crossing into Cornwall. They had approached the ford cautiously and once Raoul was sure it was clear they crossed as quickly as they could.

Between the Tamar and Tawton was a strange strip of land. Saxon England ended at Tawton along the banks of the River Taw, as did Devonshire. Cornwall had never been under Saxon rule so had never become a Shire. Cornwall's kingdom ended at the Tamar so this was a lawless strip of land not yet ruled over by England or Cornwall.

Raoul was keen to reach Tawton before nightfall but they could not push their horses too hard. They had ridden them since midnight so they continued to walk and trot into the day. They stopped only for water from streams that they crossed, for them and for their horses. They had no food and no time to hunt.

By noon they had made good progress. They spoke little until they reached the third river they needed to cross. As they waded the horses into the water Waestan called to Raoul.

"What river is this Sir Raoul?"

"I do not know, Father. It is just another we must cross. Ahead of us to the right you can begin to see the edge of the Great Moor, I believe. I have never been there."

"I know it. There is a settlement that the track skirts. It is on a river, on the north of the Great Moor. I will remember its name. Let me think. Ocmundtune, that was it, and then Bellestam. They have small churches. We will be getting close to Tawton when we arrive there."

They crossed to the far bank and rode up the track. It sloped up from the river until it reached a brow which revealed a wide flat grassland with many patches of trees. To their surprise as they rode over the brow they saw three riders blocking the track a short way ahead of them, one leading a pack horse.

Raoul quickly took in as much detail as he could see. Their clothing, hair and weapons told him all he needed to know. They were not wearing chainmail. It would be too heavy to wear when not needed for combat and

115

was, most probably, what was contained in the bundles on their pack horse. To Raoul they were clearly Norman cavalry, scouts almost certainly. He rode slowly towards them. The one in the centre shouted to Raoul.

"Hold there. What would an armed man and a Priest be doing traveling this path?"

"A good question. I might ask the same of three Norman soldiers, cavalrymen I would assume."

"That is easy, we are here by order of our commander, Sir Breon, to see what we might see in these dangerous times and report back to him. You, however, have not answered my question. What might your business be?"

He drew his sword as he said the words in clear emphasis of his meaning. The other two moved forward to either side. Raoul held up a hand.

"No need, no need. I am Sir Raoul Tyrrell on King William's business, and this is Father Waestan of Exeter Cathedral, about the same business. We are traveling to see Sir Baldwin De Redvers at Exeter and then I am to join your commander, Sir Breon. However, if you are this far from Exeter, I must assume that Sir Breon, at least, is not that far away."

The soldier steadied his mount but did not sheathe his sword.

"I know the names of those you claim to be but I have never met either men. You will forgive me but he could be any Priest and, if again, you will forgive me, you do not look like any Norman knight I have met."

"That is the whole point of what I have been doing in Cornwall. Anyway, I am not Norman, I am French and have lived many years in Brittany, so I know your Sir Breon well. Now listen, where is Sir Breon?"

"He is camped at Tawton."

"That at least is very good news. I must reach him as quickly as our mounts can travel. Please take us to him. If we are not who we say we are it will soon be known."

"I would be happier if you would remove your arms whilst we travel."

"Now you know that as a knight I can never agree to that. Dear God man, there are three of you and one of me, but I am no threat to you. We must, however, reach Tawton and Sir Breon urgently, then Waestan can travel on to Exeter."

The soldier sheaved his sword.

"I will ride in front then, you two ride behind me, and these two will ride behind you."

"As you wish, as long as we can continue our journey. I will feel much safer now, in your company. Lead on."

They rode late into the afternoon before Waestan pointed ahead.

"Ocmundtune. He is leading us there. If we cross the river there we will not go through Bellestam. It will probably be quicker. He seems to know where he is going."

"I do hope so. I am almost asleep in the saddle. We had no sleep last night. I am so glad we have an escort and I can relax for a while at least."

They forded the river at Ocmundtune and rode on toward Tawton. Their cavalry escort slowly became less attentive. As they rode they slowly gained in confidence that Sir Raoul and Waestan were who they said they were.

Daylight began to fade into dusk when they met two more Norman cavalrymen. After a brief discussion which neither Raoul nor Waestan could overhear, the two newcomers galloped their mounts eastwards. It was a short while later they saw lights in the distance from the camp at Tawton.

They reached the ford across the Taw. On the opposite bank in the darkness stood a line of thirty horsemen. Every other man held a lantern with a candle lit inside. In front of them was a single rider. He was dressed colourfully. He wore a sword belt and helmet but no mail. It was Sir Breon of Brittany.

Raoul looked at their escort. They had been noticeable more tense as they approached Tawton. If Raoul and Waestan were not who they said they were, they must take some sort of action before reaching Tawton. If they were who they said they were, their escort feared retribution. At first Raoul said nothing. He rode to the bank then leaned across towards the leading cavalryman.

"Thank you for escorting us here. You behaved exactly as I would have done."

"I am sorry, Sir Raoul. I had to be sure."

"Yes, my man. Come Waestan."

He rode down the bank and into the Taw with Waestan behind him. They forded the river and climbed the opposite bank, stopping in front of Sir Breon, who swung a leg over his horse's neck and slid down from the saddle.

Sir Raoul climbed down more slowly and stiffly and turned towards Sir Breon. They embraced warmly. They both began to speak and laughed.

"My apologies, Sir Breon. I have been in that saddle since midnight last night."

"It is so good to see you. I am at your command, you understand. I do hope my men were not too hard on you. If they were, they will be embarrassed now."

"No, no, my friend, they did what was right. Now, this is Father Waestan."

Sir Breon gave a formal nod.

"Yes, I have heard the name. Welcome to my camp."

"Thank you, Sir. I am delighted we have arrived."

Raoul interrupted the pleasantries.

"Now, my dear friend, we have so much to discuss, some more urgent than not, but first a goblet or two of wine and some food would be very welcome. Oh, and anywhere comfortable to sit other than a saddle."

"Indeed, you men, take care of the horses."

Sir Breon threw an arm around Raoul and steered him towards the camp which had been set up within the surrounding mounds of the larger old Roman fort. He led them through the entrance. Sir Raoul sighed.

"I seem to have spent many a night recently inside earth walls built a very long time ago."

"Ah but you will not have been made as welcome as you are here. Come, we have wine, and food ready for you. I anticipated your needs when I heard you were close. I will gather some camp chairs!"

+++

The same dawn light that lit Raoul and Waestan's crossing of the Tamar lighted Prious and Morwenna's crossing of The Kammel. For them too, the crossing was unhindered. They moved quickly away from the ford around the north of Nanstallon hill. They had walked their horses most of the way so Prious was happy to push them a little whilst he was nervous of meeting anyone.

Morwenna had ridden in silence most of the night. She had drifted in and out of sleep as she stared at the rear of the pack horse she followed. The contents of all the bundles it carried began to play on her mind. The early morning sun warmed her a little and when the track widened she rode forward beside Prious.

"Brother Prious, I have to ask you. The bundles on the pack horse. The Armour, Helm and Excalibur I know of. What are in the others? It has been on my mind much of the night."

Prious was not going to lie to her but he was worried about her reaction to the truth.

"They contain the books of your family history, my Lady."

Morwenna halted her horse for a moment. Prious rode on. Her mind heard Myghal's voice warn her father in the Great Hall, and her father's reply, 'we are among friends.' She angrily kicked her horse and rode back up long side him. She turned towards him in her saddle.

"The rest I can perhaps understand, to stop a war, but my family's history I cannot allow. Those books connect us all to our past."

"And that is the problem, my Lady. I have told you, King William has ordered any books or papers that refer to Arthur, King or not, must be destroyed."

"No, I will not let that happen, you cannot do it."

"Then I will not destroy them, I will hide them. I will bury them at my church which only you and I will know about. If you wish to recover them later you may, but the rest I must dispose of."

Morwenna said nothing. Her life had become so complicated and she was finding it difficult to cope. She knew she had a day in the saddle to think all this through. It was only her love for Raoul that held her together. She closed her eyes and thought of him. Her stomach tightened and she gripped the saddle between her thighs. That was all just last evening but seemed so long ago now. She tried to stop thinking about anything but that made it worse for a while.

Morwenna rode up beside Prious again. He wondered what she would be asking this time and he was genuinely surprised at her question.

"Have you ever been in love, Brother, to a woman I mean, ever made love to one?"

Prious laughed and smiled at her.

"I am a monk, my Lady, a man of God."

"I assume you are, although I am beginning to doubt whether it is so, but you have not answered my question."

"Well, my Lady, not that it is any business of yours, but yes, I have. I have not always been a monk."

"So who was she, was she the reason you became a monk?"

Prious looked heavenwards before looking at her and answering.

"You know, my Lady, there really are places where you should not go, and this is one of them. Yes I was your age and so very much in love. She became with child and we were to marry, but then the sickness took her, and our unborn child, of course. I was totally heartbroken and very angry with God for taking her from me. I ran away. I had nothing and began to steal to survive. I was caught by some monks whilst trying to rob them of some of their cider apples. They took me in and I ended up a monk. I always thought I might get back at God from the inside but then I began working for Bishop Odo in Brittany and my life took other paths."

Morwenna stared at him as she rode beside him.

"I see. Thank you, Brother. I am sorry I asked such an indelicate question. I shall think of you differently henceforth."

"Well, you know more about me now than anyone else in England or Cornwall. It should remain our secret."

"It will, Brother, it will."

They rode on in silence until past noon. They were now following the River Fal as it flowed southwards. They stopped briefly to water the horses at a small stream that burbled out of the woods, across the track and into the Fal. They walked leading the horses for a while, mainly to get some feeling back into their legs after such a long time in the saddle. Prious stopped and reached for Morwenna's arm. She stopped and turned to him, a puzzled look on her face.

"My Lady, do you feel able to ride again? I feel we should."

"Yes, Brother, if we must?"

Prious helped Morwenna up into her saddle then climbed onto his mount. The pack horse was tied to his saddle so he took his reins and set off at a trot. When he slowed to a walk Morwenna called to him.

"Is all well, Brother."

"I do not know to be honest. Sometimes I get a feeling something is amiss. Often it is nothing, but too often I sense something is wrong."

Morwenna instinctively looked back over her shoulder. Prious smiled at her.

"No, my Lady, watch the track ahead. If there is anything it is ahead of us, not behind."

They rode on between the hills that rose up on either bank of the Fal until they saw stone cottages appear through the trees on the opposite bank. There was also the sound of raised voices. Prious held his arm out to halt Morwenna and eased his horse forward. The cottages sat in the fork of two rivers.

They had arrived at the cottages below Resugga Castle where Prious had crossed the Fal with Raoul and Waestan by raft. As he drew level with the cottages he could see what appeared to be six of seven soldiers arguing with the two ferryman. Prious knew what he had to do, although the ferrymen would be upset with him. He had overpaid them enormously when crossing so he did not feel too guilty. He handed Morwenna the pack horse's reins.

"Take these, my Lady. Follow me and ride on as soon as you can. I cannot see any bows but that does not mean they have none. Ready?"

Morwenna gave an uneasy grin and nodded.

"Come then."

He kicked his horse into a canter along the path. He was almost at the rope across the river before the soldiers saw them but they could do little except shout.

Prious jumped from his mount. He had drawn his hunting knife from its sheathe on his saddle and ran to the tree that held the rope. He looked briefly across the river and began to saw at the sisal. It was a thick rope and it took some time to cut through it. The soldiers were remonstrating with the ferrymen who were refusing to board their ferry, pointing across at Prious. He was almost through the rope when its own weight, as it hung across the expanse of the river, snapped the rest and the rope snaked away across and into the water. Prious shouted to Morwenna.

"Go now, ride on, ride."

Prious climbed back onto his horse and galloped after Morwenna. She slowed to a walk as the cottages disappeared from sight around the bend in the river.

"Goodness, Brother, this is no track for galloping upon."

"No indeed, but I was worried that might they have bows and be well trained."

"Who were they? Do you know?"

"Cornish soldiers of King Mark. A patrol out looking for trouble. Probably arguing with the ferrymen about paying for crossing."

"Were they looking for us do you think?"

"No, they could not have heard of us and reached here yet. No, they are out collecting weapons and foraging for food. Not that they will need them now. We must move on as quickly as we can. It is not that far now and we must get past the bridge at Ponsmeur. If those soldiers do decide to follow us they will have to cross the other river and ride down the other side of the Fal to Ponsmeur to get across. There is no track on the far side. They would have to travel around the hills opposite, so as long as we travel as fast as we can, they cannot overtake us. Hopefully they will not bother with us anyway."

"Lead on then, Brother. I will follow, as usual."

They reached Ponsmeur without further problems. Prious looked along the far bank to the bridge. There was a group of men standing around its far end. They did not appear to be in any sort of uniform but Ponsmeur had a bad reputation for thieves and robbers. He could not see any horses nearby.

"My Lady, we will trot from here towards the bridge. If those men begin to cross the bridge, gallop your horse and do not stop. Ride at them if needs be, but we should get past the bridge before they can get across."

They trotted towards the bridge. The men took a few moments to see them before two or three began to cross. Prious kicked his mount on, pulling the pack horse after him. Morwenna followed him closely. The men on the bridge stopped. It was obvious to them that the riders would be passed before they could intercept them.

It was not long after that Prious pointed to Krid on the opposite bank.

"We are almost at Tregony, my Lady."

Morwenna smiled broadly at Prious.

"I will not be sad to leave this saddle and rest."

"I cannot promise you much comfort, only a place to sleep."

The light was beginning to fail as they rounded a sweeping bend and saw Tregony hill on the opposite bank. The wooden church of St James stood beside the wharf and cottages were scattered up the hillside close to the track that led up it to the rest of the village at its top.

For Prious, it was the bank on his side of the river that was of prime interest and he was very relieved to see the Rhosmon moored securely to the wharf there. He was confident it would be there but it was good to see it none the less.

"That is our transport to Portsea, my Lady. I am no sailor but I am delighted to see her."

"A sea voyage is a new experience for me, Brother. I hope my stomach is strong enough. Do we sail tonight?"

"No, not tonight. I must take the horses to my church, St Cornelly, on the hill above. My farmer friend will look after them. I will hide your family history there as I promised, then return to the boat. We will sail at first light I expect, unless the tide is a problem."

They rode around the outside of the long bend and stopped beside the Rhosman. The boat looked bigger to Morwenna now she looked down on it.

Prious helped Morwenna get down from her mount and turned toward Edmon who had climbed the bank to greet them.

"Welcome, Brother. Is it just you and the Lady?"

"Yes, my good man. I am very pleased to see you here. This is the Lady Morwenna of Tintagel."

Edmon took Morwenna's hand and bowed to kiss it.

"Welcome to the Rhosmon, my Lady. Let me help you aboard."

He held Morwenna's arm and helped her down the slope of the bank onto the wooded floating wharf, then onto the Rhosmon. He led her forward and settled her on a bench in the bow. He nodded politely and returned to Prious who was untying the bundles containing Arthur's Armour, Helm and Excalibur.

"Edmon. Get your men to put these aboard and find some heavy stones. Place one in the ropes of each bundle to weigh them down. When we sail from here, the first thing we do is drop these over the side in the middle of the river."

"I will get that done for you, Brother."

"Very good. I must take the horses up to my church. I will walk back. It will be dark by then. We have been travelling without a break since midnight last night. The Lady Morwenna will be very hungry, thirsty and tired. Look after her."

"Yes, Brother, but yourself?"

"I will have to wait a bit longer. I have important work."

"We will have a meal ready for you when you return, God speed."

Prious climbed back into his saddle. Edmon handed him the reins of the other two horses and he set off along the track that would take him to St Cornelly.

So much had happened so quickly since he had led Raoul and Waestan on foot along the same track, it seemed a long time ago. He worked it in his mind, it was just four days.

He turned off the main track that followed the valley floor and climbed up the path to the church. It soon came into sight in the gloom. He dismounted and tied the horses to the same rail that the donkey had been tethered to those four days before.

He found the key hidden in the porch beams and unlocked the door. Opening it he saw a small candle burning on the table just inside. His farmer friend, Drew, lit one every evening at dusk and left it to burn out. He must have only just left. There were two large lanterns under the table, each holding a fat candle. Prious opened them on the table and lit them both using the small candle. He hung one in the porch. Drew would see it and come straight to the church and find the horses.

Prious fetched a spade from the store cupboard. The church door was set into its south wall. Turning right out of it he almost immediately turned right again and walked to the middle of the west end outer wall.

He stood with his back against it. Before him was a flat grassed area that then plunged steeply away down to the field below. There were some unmarked paupers' graves along that side of the church so he took just one stride out from the wall and dug a square hole.

He went back into the church and collected a waxed sheet he had used some time before when he had suffered a problem with a leaking roof. He unloaded the four books from the packhorse and wrapped that bundle in the wax sheet. He placed it all into the hole and filled it in, flattening the ground as best he could. The grass would cover it again soon. It looked like a new child's grave.

It had grown quite dark as he worked. He re-entered the church to tidy up and leave everything as he had found it when he heard a noise from outside. One of the horses snorted, another whinnied.

Prious stepped quickly behind the door and waited. A shadow from the porch lantern entered the church first and then Prious was delighted to see Drew walk in.

"Hello Drew, my friend."

His words made Drew jump. He spun round then laughed.

"Brother Prious, you gave me a terrible fright. It is so good to see you. You must come and eat with us."

"Sadly I cannot. If only I could, but I am so glad I have seen you."

Prious put an arm around Drew's shoulders and walked him out of the door.

"Drew, I have to leave and I really do not know when, or even if, I will return. I think coming events may prevent it. I can only thank you for all the help you have been. There are three good horses here. They are yours now. I am afraid I could not return the donkey."

"I cannot accept the horses, Brother. They are far too much. People will think I stole them."

"You can and you will. The saddles and harness go with them. Now, I must get back down the hill."

"You'll be leaving in that boat then. The one on the wharf."

"Yes Drew. In the morning."

"Probably good timing. It has raised some interest, I know. All sorts of whispers about its business."

"Thank you, Drew. Well, it will be gone tomorrow with me aboard it. I must return to Winchester but after that I cannot be sure. Farewell my friend. God be with you."

"And you, Brother, and you. We shall miss you."

Prious turned and walked away, down the path he had ridden up. He hated such farewells.

Food awaited him on the Rhosmon, and a good night's sleep. Morwenna had already fallen asleep, wrapped in blankets in the bow. Prious settled in the stern where he had slept on the voyage from Portsea.

Edmon woke them both with the first of the day's light as his two crewmen untied the Rhosman. They rowed her against the current into midstream where they skilfully turned her. As she swung around, Prious and Morwenna dropped two bundles overboard, Arthur's Armour and his Helm.

Prious could not help himself. He opened the long thin bundle that was Excalibur. The metal glinted in the sunlight. He handed it to Morwenna.

"I expect you know better than I the history of casting weapons into water for one's ancestors. I think it is for you to do."

Morwenna said nothing but took the sword from him. She kissed the cross of blade and guard and threw it over the side. It hit the water flat and seemed to float for a moment on the surface before it sank. Morwenna watched it, surprised at how far down she could see it as it sank before it seemed to melt into nothingness. She began to cry and turned to Prious.

"My father will never forgive me."

+++

Raoul and Waestan ate heartily. They were both very hungry after not eating since the previous evening. The wine Sir Breon provided was surprisingly good too. They sat around a table in Sir Breon's command tent. Waestan leant back in his chair which creaked loudly.

"You eat well on campaign, Sir Breon."

"We came well prepared, Father, and Sir Baldwin will send supplies daily by wagon from Exeter. We did not know how long we might have to wait here for you, but we felt it better to come here than for you to have to reach Exeter. This way we have far more options."

Whilst they were eating, Raoul had told Breon of all that had happened since they arrived in Cornwall. Breon had listened quietly, asking only a few questions. Raoul leant forward.

"We have scouts out I know, and they are vital. The Saxons will have sailed from Dublin by now, I am sure. If the weather and their seamanship are both good, they will arrive at the mouth of the Taw, but they could come ashore anywhere along the north coast if they are blown off course, or, indeed, just go astray. Anywhere west of here is not a problem as they will have to cross the Taw here to move east. I would be more concerned if they landed somewhere east of here along the north Devonshire coast."

"We have scouts east of us too." Sir Breon poured more wine as he spoke. "If they land between the Taw and the North Moor, we will move west through Creedyton and on to Twyfordton. If they land further east along North Moor coast we will need to move quickly through Twyfordton and on to Tonetown, but let us drink to them landing as they planned, at the mouth of the Taw."

Sir Breon raised his glass to his guests who raised theirs in return.

"Thank you, Breon. There is just one other thing to discuss tonight. We must get Father Waestan here to Bradanreolice Island most urgently to meet Gytha Thorkeldottir. I understand she is imprisoned there. I was going to send him from Exeter but now we are here, what do you suggest is the quickest way to get him there?"

Sir Breon thought for a moment before replying.

"I think it will be best to ride to a small port in Somersetshire called Watchmeet, just below Daw's Castle. I can give him an escort of three men. You can get there in a day, day and a half, from here. Pay a local fisherman to take you, they will do anything for a few gold coins. They will call the island Flat Holm there though."

"If that can be arranged then we can have you away in the morning, my friend."

Raoul leant sideways and slapped Waestan on the shoulder.

"You and I, Breon, will ride back across the ford in the morning and study the land. If we are to fight there I do not want any surprises. Now where do Waestan and I sleep?"

"I have had two cots put in my tent, if you do not mind sharing. I will sleep in here at the end there."

"That is kind of you, Breon. I should argue but I am just too tired."

"Come then"

Sir Breon stood and called for his squire who seemed to appear from nowhere.

"Fetch a lantern then take Sir Raoul and Father Waestan to my tent."

The boy left the tent and Raoul and Waestan stood in the doorway and made their final good nights to Sir Breon. The squire returned with a lantern that lit the way to the next tent. It was much smaller than the command tent but a little larger than the other tents that made up the camp.

The squire handed Waestan the lantern and disappeared into the darkness. They entered the tent and Raoul fastened the entrance behind them. The tent was just high enough to stand in the middle. It had a narrow camp cot along each side and a small table between them.

Waestan put the light on the table and lay on the bed, pulling the light woollen blanket over him. He still wore his habit. Raoul unbuckled his belt and hung it with its sword and knives on the tent pole by the entrance. He untied his heavy leather tabard, removed his boots and leather leggings, and sat on the cot. Waestan was lying with his eyes shut so Raoul blew out the candle in the lantern and stretched out on his bed. He pulled his blanket over him. He still wore his linen shirt.

He was on his back looking up into the darkness. He closed his eyes and his mind was immediately full of thoughts, but mostly thoughts of Morwenna. He coughed and tried to clear his head. He was too tired to sleep. It was about the same time that he had lain with Morwenna only the night before.

He could not help but to relive being with her in his mind. Before he was really conscious of it his hand moved to himself and he was very aroused. He moved his hand very gently and soundlessly. He heard Waestan's voice. It was little more than a whisper.

"You must be thinking of your Lady Morwenna. Do not worry about me. I understand."

Raoul was shocked for a moment.

"Yes, I am. How could you tell?"

"I was educated in a monastery, as you know, and I shared a dormitory with seven boys from fourteen years old to eighteen years old. Over five years in a boys' dormitory you learn to hear a man's breathing change. It becomes unmistakeable."

"I heard your breathing change in the woods a few nights ago. I thought a priest was not supposed to do such things."

"Ha, I am a man. When I was younger I tried not to, but then I would dream and it would happen in my sleep. When I confessed the monks said it was wrong but every now and then God gave us a treat. I decided if God treated me it could not be wrong so I would treat myself occasionally."

Raoul laughed quietly.

"So have you ever lain with a woman?"

"No, that I have never done, but I seem to be able to manage without."

"What arouses you then?"

"One thing is the sound of someone else's breathing when aroused."

Raoul suddenly understood his meaning. He had aroused Waestan.

"Oh, I see, well please carry on. Your breathing will not disturb me."

Raoul could hear Waestan. His breathing did change and his cot creaked a little. Raoul found the sounds from Waestan were indeed arousing, as they had been that night in the wood. He fondled himself gently and thoughts of Morwenna flooded back into his mind. Before he really thought about anything he seeded.

As his breathing returned to normal and his heart settled he heard Waestan again. He was panting gently as his cot shook. He caught his breath as he seeded and gave an involuntary groan. After a few moments he spoke.

"Thank you, Raoul. That took me back to the dormitory."

Raoul did not hear him or reply. He was asleep.

Shortly after dawn Sir Breon's squire roused Sir Raoul and Father Waestan.

They had both had a long and deep sleep after their lack of rest the day before.

They dressed and were ushered to Sir Breon's command tent where he had slept. Raoul had dressed in his leathers rather than request some more usual Norman clothing. Sir Breon welcomed them into the tent.

"Ah, Sir Raoul, Father Waestan, come and have some breakfast with me before we start the day."

They sat around the table as they had the night before and helped themselves to cold meats and boiled eggs. Sir Breon broke the silence.

"There is a guard of three men to escort Father Waestan, ready to leave at your order. I have your horses with us Sir Raoul, as I was commanded, and your equipment, mail and uh, proper clothing, but you have no squire with you so mine has readied it all for you, should you require any of it."

"Thank you, Breon. We will get Father Waestan away as soon as he is ready. I brought no squire, I have not needed one since I left England more than a year ago."

"I have a lad that would be perfect for you. He is the brother of my squire. His name is Jory."

"That is very kind, Breon. I am not sure I can do a squire justice at this time, but if he is prepared to spend time in France when all this is over, I will do as I can for him."

"I will have him ready after we have eaten."

They ate heartily, washing it down with ale. Raoul stood as they all finished and turned to the door. He spoke quietly to Waestan.

"Come, Waestan, you must be away. You know what you must do, then meet me at Dorchester. I will see Sir Baldwin in Exeter when all is ended here and then leave for Dorchester. Wait there for me if you arrive first, but I expect I will. One way or the other we will not be welcome there. King William sacked the town on his way to Exeter so welcome or not, they may at least respect us. If I do not survive what happens here and do not arrive after five days, go on to Winchester."

"I am sure I will see you in Dorchester my friend. I hope, Sir Raoul, I can call you that. I will do what we have discussed. God protect you, my son."

Waestan made the sign of the cross and turned to Sir Breon.

"Thank you, Sir, for your hospitality. May God go with you too."

He turned and left them. He mounted the horse that was offered to him and steadied it outside the command tent. He called loudly.

"God be with you all."

He spurred the horse away and joined the three mounted cavalrymen that were waiting for him. They rode at a canter out of the camp.

Sir Breon took another mouthful of ale and faced Sir Raoul.

"Do you trust him? He used to work for Bishop Leofric, and therefore Archbishop Stigand."

"Yes he did, but he changed sides because he believed the future was Norman and he is very ambitious. He wants to be a Bishop one day. He is deeper than he seems. He appears naive but is less so than he pretends. I have to say though, whatever the future, I have begun to like him."

A young boy appeared at the door to the tent and stood looking down at the grass. Sir Breon took Raoul's arm and led him forward.

"Sir Raoul, may I present Jory. Jory, this is your new master, Sir Raoul Tyrrell of Radepont. He is a famous knight and in need of a faithful squire."

Jory dropped to one knee.

"I am yours to command, Sir."

"Stand up, Jory. If you wish to serve me I welcome you. I need you to gather all my possessions that have been brought here from Winchester and place them in whatever tent Sir Breon has given me. First, however, I need a horse, not my courser, my palfrey. Have him saddled and ready as soon as you can."

"Yes, Sir."

Jory turned and ran about his duties. Sir Breon laughed and gripped Raoul's arm.

"He will not let you down, I am sure. His brother has been excellent and Jory has been helping him."

"I am sure you are right. As soon as he is back we will ride out and take a look at the ground. You will have to forgive these leathers. I have been wearing them for days now and they have become comfortable. I will dress like a Norman tomorrow."

"You are the talk of my men already, my friend. Many have heard your name and many have fought with you, but all have heard of your eccentricities."

"I just need them to fight like Normans, Breon, not to like how I look."

"Oh, I think they will do that for you. I do not think you need worry about that."

Jory and his brother arrived at the command tent's entrance with the horses. Raoul and Breon left the tent and mounted them. Raoul beckoned Jory to him.

"Find the horse I rode in on yesterday. Look after him. Once he has recovered from his long journey I will ride him as mine. This palfrey will be yours to ride."

"Yes Sir. Thank you Sir."

Raoul nodded as Sir Breon turned his horse alongside his.

"Do you wish some men to come with us?"

"No. I think you and I should look around together, but if any scout should report back they must ride out and find us."

Sir Breon called some instructions and followed Sir Raoul who rode out of the camp entrance and towards the ford. He caught Sir Raoul as he began to ride down the bank of the Taw and into the ford. The horses waded across and they climbed the bank onto the opposite side. In front of them was a grass flatland that stretched as far as they could see. To their left it rose into the hills of the Great Moor. To their right it tumbled away as woodland northwards towards the sea.

They rode slowly forward leaving the ford behind them. They spent all day riding over the grassland. Sir Raoul was looking for small streams or ditches that might hamper the cavalry but found none near enough to the ford to be a problem.

The ridge along the north side bordered the slope down to the sea and was mainly wooded. A track emerged from the trees some distance from the river. Sir Breon pointed to it as they rode back along the ridge in the afternoon sun.

"That is the top of the main track up the valley from the sea. If Godwine lands in the mouth of the Taw that is the one way up here. Rivers and steep hillsides block any other route. We could defend the track and trap them between us and the sea."

"We could, but I would rather let them up here and fight them on open ground where we can use our cavalry at their best."

"I do agree that would be wisest. Perhaps we should position at least a Conrois this side of the river between the river and here. When the Saxons reach here they will naturally move away to form up further along."

"Indeed. When we know they are coming this way we will do just that. Let us go back now and eat. I could do with some rest after the last few days. I seem to have been walking or riding without eating much for most of the time."

They rode back to the camp and sat on two chairs outside the command tent. A table was brought and some cold food. A jug of wine and goblets followed.

"These men of yours, Breon, are they good?"

"The best, Raoul, truly the best. They are very well trained. The ten Conrois I had with me I have trained myself to the highest level. Many are veterans of Senlac and of many a skirmish since. The other ten Conrois that arrived from Winchester are well spoken of. Many are Familia Regis so will be good."

"Excellent. We have both fought Saxons. If they are well trained, their shield wall can be very effective, even against our best cavalry. If they are supported by good archers, it will be a very hard fight. They will outnumber us three to two at least, but if Prious and I are correct, I do not think King Mark will be joining them, nor the Britons from their camp at Tintagel."

"If the Cornish and the Britons do come, I really think all we could do is to harry them all the way back to Exeter, slow their advance and defend the city until help arrives from the east."

"It will not come to that, I feel sure. Now, let us raise a glass to Father Waestan. May the Lord bless his progress."

"Indeed, Sir Raoul, and ours."

+++

The Rhosmon made good time along the Fal and out into the Carrick. Morwenna was not comfortable on the water but was taken by the beauty of the wooded banks of the Fal.

The sea was a little lumpy in the lively breeze from the south-west and became quite rough as they rounded the end of the Rhos headland. It settled though as they sailed eastwards.

Morwenna watched the coastline as it passed slowly by. Prious moved to her side and put an arm around her shoulders. He gripped some rigging with his other hand to steady himself.

"You look thoughtful, my Lady. Does something worry you?"

"It never really occurred to me before but, if there is a battle, today or tomorrow, my father and Sir Raoul will be fighting on opposite sides. What happens if they meet and have to fight each other?"

Tears ran down her cheeks. Prious decided this was as good a time as any.

"That will not happen, my Lady."

"You cannot know that!"

"My Lady, I have not lied to you, but I have not told you the whole truth."

She turned and looked at him.

"What do you mean?"

"Your father is dead, my Lady."

"No, how can that be? How can you know that?"

"Because he was dead when we left Tintagel."

She tore herself away from him. Edmon saw the sudden movement from the stern where he was steering the Rhosmon but was too far away to know what was being said.

"How could he have been?"

"Because Sir Raoul killed him, which is what he was sent to Tintagel to do."

She took another step backwards, away from him, before her knees gave way and she crumpled to the deck. She was screaming and flailing her arms at Prious as he moved to lift her up. She glared up at him.

"That cannot be true. Why do you tell me such lies?"

One of Edmon's crew came to help Prious. Morwenna struggled fiercely as they took an arm each and half carried half dragged her to the bench in the bow. Prious sat beside her.

"Listen and understand. The King sent us to Tintagel. I was sent to recover Arthur's Armour, Helm and Excalibur. Raoul was sent to kill your father, your brother and yourself."

Morwenna became silent and sat staring at the deck, quivering noticeably.

"He fell in love with you on sight. You killed your brother. Raoul killed your father. He left you in my protection so that I can guard you until he can get back to the King and beg for his leave to take you to France."

Prious could hardly hear her question. She whispered one word.

"Why?"

"Because the King ordered everything and everybody connected with King Arthur destroyed. Your family is Arthur's bloodline."

Morwenna sat on the bench, rocking very slightly and still just staring at the deck. The love of her life had killed her father. She had killed her brother to save Raoul's life, but he would have killed her brother if she had not. He had then used her to get out of the castle. Her whole life was destroyed, her dreams ruined. It was hardly a comfort that he loved her enough not to kill her. He had lain with her, watched her kill her own brother, then gone upstairs and murdered her father.

Prious fetched a blanket from where she had slept and draped it around her shoulders. There was nothing more he could say. She knew the truth now. Whether she would come to terms with it or not he did not know. He felt it best to leave her now with her thoughts, but he would keep a very close eye on her. He did not want her to do anything drastic.

The Sixth Scroll

Waestan had learnt a lot from Prious and Raoul, and he kept the pace up with his escort as he journeyed to Watchmeet. They stopped only to rest their horses and eat when they could. They reached Creedyton before noon and crossed the Creed before following the track to Twyfordton.

The three cavalrymen he had as escort had been instructed to obey Waestan's every command, but they had not expected him to be quite so demanding. They reached Twyfordton in the late afternoon. They had to cross two rivers there before following the track northward that would skirt the North Moor to the old Daw's Castle and Watchmeet below.

His escort were all in favour of resting the night at Twyfordton, but Waestan insisted there was plenty of daylight left and they must move on. They rode until dusk when the road led through a wood.

Waestan called a halt and ordered camp to be made. He was satisfied they had travelled as far as was possible that day. The night passed quickly and he was awake with the dawn. They set out early to complete their journey.

They did not stop at Daws Castle, which stood on the hilltop above the track, but rode down into the small fishing village of Watchmeet. The compact harbour contained eight or ten fishing boats, some bigger than others. It was mid-morning when they arrived and Waestan was surprised to see that many boats in the harbour.

They stopped at the harbour side and Waestan sent two men to enquire after a boat. It appeared that there had been a spell of bad weather that had kept the fishing boats ashore. As the weather settled they had all put to sea, the same good spell of weather that had decided Godwine to set sail from Dublin. They had returned with a good catch and were ready to sail again.

One fisherman agreed to take Waestan to Flat Holm. He knew the waters well and dangerous as they could be, the gold Waestan offered for the passage was enough to temp him.

Waestan went down to the waterside and spoke to the man. He gave him half of the agreed amount in gold coin and boarded the boat. His escort was to wait for his return. They sailed before noon for Flat Holm.

+++

Prious had a bad night's sleep. Morwenna had sat in the bows alone and said nothing to anyone. She would not eat and when night fell Prious was afraid to stop watching her.

Edmon talked with Prious and they agreed that his crewmen that steered the boat through the night would watch her. As it was, she appeared to sleep and awoke with the dawn. Prious began to think she was stronger than he had thought.

Morwenna had shut her mind to most of what she had heard. She realised it must be true but until she could speak to Raoul she closed her mind to it all. Prious approached her as the sun rose in the clear sky.

"How are you, my Lady? What can I get for you?"

"My life back would be a good start."

"I was thinking more of some food or a drink."

She looked up at him and hesitated.

"I need to speak to Raoul. When will I see him?"

"We will sail now towards Portsea. That is not far from Winchester, but it will not be safe for you there. We will sail past Portsea and further inland to Portchester Castle. I have a contact there that has the manor surrounding the old castle. He is called William Mauduit. He was granted the manor by King William after Senlac but he is a sound man I believe. He can keep you safe there until Raoul arrives in Winchester."

"Why am I in danger?"

"Because King William has ordered your death. Even I am in danger for hiding you from him. I will try and keep you safe until Raoul arrives but I work for Bishop Odo, and there is little that he does not learn."

"I feel used and cheated, but I know Raoul loves me. I cannot believe my father is dead, and that Raoul killed him, but until I can talk to Raoul I feel crippled. Do what you must with me."

Prious walked to the stern and spoke to Edmon.

"Bring her food and ale and have your crew keep a close watch on her, as must you and I. It will be a long voyage to Portchester."

+++

Sir Raoul and Sir Breon had eaten well, and had drunk some excellent wine. Not enough to be too much but enough to be enjoyable. Sir Breon slapped the table and laughed.

"It is so good, Raoul my friend, to have you here in England. When you returned to France I thought we might not see you again."

"You might not have. After Senlac I remember you stayed there to clear the area. I moved with the army towards Dover. We needed to secure the port there, but Duke William sent me with some cavalry to take Romney, which was still resisting us. We took it easily enough and then followed him to Dover. That had fallen by the time I reached there and we marched on to Canterbury, which gave up without a fight. From there we marched for London. There was no real resistance and William was crowned King by

Ealdred, the Archbishop of York, on Christmas day. Although Stigand was Archbishop of Canterbury he was still excommunicated at the time and William would not risk the French King saying to the Pope that he had not been properly crowned. But you know all this. I had done my duty to the Pope so I paid homage to King William and returned to France."

Raoul took a long mouthful of wine.

"My brother Sir Walter wanted me to return to Poix and help his son Walter, my nephew, to manage the estates there. Sir Walter is dead now of course, and my nephew is not well I believe. My great nephew, Walter the third will be the new Lord of Poix soon I fear. I understand he and King William's son, William Rufus, are the very best of childhood friends. So I will return to Radepont with my lady if all is well."

There was a noise at the command tent door and an aide entered.

"Forgive me, Sir, a scout has arrived from the mouth of the Taw. As the sun was setting they saw boats approaching the coast. A host of them, fifty at least. He returned to report, the other two of his party will observe their landing and report in the morning."

Sir Breon looked at Sir Raoul who nodded at him. Sir Breon turned to his aide.

"Thank you, have all my commanders told now. We rise at dawn and prepare for battle. Do not dress in mail until you hear from me. I want one Conrois in full mail at dawn on the other side of the ford on the ridge this side of the track. Make it happen."

"Yes Sir, it will be done."

"Bed now then, my friend. Tomorrow will be an interesting day."

"That it will, Sir Breon, that it will. May we both live through it."

Raoul followed Sir Breon to their tents. Whoever had been in the tent next to Sir Breon's had been moved out and Raoul given his tent. A lantern was lit inside and Raoul pulled back the front and stepped inside. All his belongings were laid out neatly and the bed made up. Two chairs stood opposite the bed. Jory had done an excellent job.

Raoul undressed, putting his leathers on a chair. Tomorrow he would dress for battle but he would keep the leathers for France. He had grown to like them. He climbed into bed and was quickly asleep. He was still tired from missing a night's sleep in the saddle.

Jory was with him as the dawn broke, his clothes on a chair by the bed and his leathers gone. Jory helped him dress. He wore a light off-white linen undershirt. His woollen shirt and breaches were both a pale grey. Jory fitted his light leather ankle boots, lacing them comfortably then criss-crossing the laces up to just below his knee. He had been trained well.

"There we are, Sir. Your sword belt is here and I will have your mail and other equipment ready for you. Sir Breon suggests you might like to join him for some breakfast."

Raoul walked to the command tent and stepped through the door. A number of knights jumped to their feet and turned to face him. It took him by surprise for a moment. He had expected Sir Breon to be alone. Breon broke the silence.

"Good morning, Sir Raoul. These are my Conrois leaders, I thought you might like a few words at the start of the day."

"Yes indeed, gentlemen, please, sit again and continue eating whilst I have my fill."

Raoul sat opposite Sir Breon.

"A pleasant surprise for an early morning."

"I did not mean to embarrass you. I thought you would want to meet them all, and it will do well for them to see you."

"Yes indeed. What news from the scouts?"

"There is no activity in the south-west. If King Mark is coming at the head of an army it will not be today, nor tomorrow in time to fight."

"Good, then he will not come at all. What of Godwine?"

"I am expecting a scout back at any moment, but they landed yesterday evening, beaching all their boats. They camped on the shoreline. Very much a temporary camp though. We are expecting them to move early. They sent out scouts, all on foot. They have no horses."

"That is good to know."

"The other interesting thing is they sent two messengers, one to King Mark and the other to Lord Jowen, both on foot of course. We captured them and brought them back here for questioning. They told all very easily. Godwine was expecting to be met at the shore and for Lord Jowan and King Mark to be waiting for him here."

"And if Prious and I had not done our work they probably would have been."

A cavalry man in a full mail hauberk entered the tent.

"Sir Breon, my Conrois is ready to cross the ford and take up position."

Sir Breon looked to Sir Raoul, who spoke in a whisper.

"They are your men for goodness sake. You know our plans, do not keep waiting for me to tell them."

Breon stepped towards his officer.

"Go then, keep this side of the track but display your presence. We need to push the enemy away from us."

"Yes, Sir Breon, it shall be done."

Sir Raoul sat back at the breakfast table. He took a few deep breaths and faced Sir Breon.

"Listen, my dear friend, these are your men and are used to your command. I understand what you are feeling and what you are doing but give your orders to them. We have discussed everything and whilst I know you totally appreciate this is my force to control, I will not confuse anyone as to who is in command. This is your command."

Breon sat back and nodded.

"It is difficult, my old friend. My orders are to obey every order you give, and I will do exactly that. You understand however, how difficult that is in front of my men."

"Exactly, and that is why I say, do not keep looking to me, you know my feelings. Give your orders and keep your authority. Now I had better say something."

Sir Raoul stood and banged the table with a goblet to gather everyone's attention.

"Gentlemen, in the next day or two we will fight this Saxon invasion and I am sure we will drive them back to their boats and away from our shores. We may fight today, it may be tomorrow, but Sir Breon tells me you are the very best cavalry that the Norman army has, and I believe him. So we will fight for our King and we will fight for our honour. We will be out-numbered but we are the better fighters. God save King William."

Everyone in the tent echoed his call.

"God save King William."

A cheer rang out from everyone in the tent. Sir Raoul left and returned to his tent. Jory was waiting for him.

"Now my boy, go to Sir Breon and ask him to join me here as soon as the next scout returns."

Jory was gone in a moment. Raoul was starting to like him. He hoped he could do him justice.

He lay on his bed. He needed to relax. He was angry with Sir Breon. He felt ambushed at breakfast. Sir Breon was right, of course, the men needed to see their leader but he did not feel he had handled it well. He wanted Sir Breon to feel comfortable and for the cavalry to be clear that Sir Breon was their commander, but he also needed them to understand that Sir Breon answered to him. Instead he had probably left them even more confused than before.

There was a rustle at the tent's entrance and he heard Joly's voice.

"Sir, can you please come to the command tent, a scout has returned."

"Joly, come in here."

He sat up on his bed as Joly entered the tent.

"Tell me, boy, did you ask Sir Breon to attend me here when the Scout arrived."

"Yes Sir, but then the scout did arrive and he sent me to fetch you."

Raoul sat up and swung his legs off the bed. He pulled the woollen shirt off his back.

"Untie the laces and get these boots off me, then go and get the leathers I have been wearing."

Jory deftly unlaced his boots and Raoul pulled off his woollen leggings while Jory fetched his leathers.

He pulled on the black leather breeches and tucked his linen shirt into the waistband. He tied the cord that held them around his waist then pulled on the heavy studded leather tabard.

"Reach that brush, lad, and brush out my hair."

Jory picked up the brush and worked on Sir Raoul's hair until it hung over his shoulders and down his back.

"Now no-one will mistake me for an ordinary Norman knight."

"Indeed not, Sir. You look like the professional sell-sword that arrived the other evening. Everyone was talking of you, Sir, how you fought in Brittany and at Senlac. They say you saved Duke William's life in Brittany and turned the tide of the battle at Senlac. They say you are a great warrior."

"Do they, Jory? Well I had better try to prove it then. Come my boy. Stay close, I may need you."

"Yes, Sir, I will."

"Good lad."

Raoul strode purposefully out of his tent and into the command tent. Everyone that had been at breakfast was still there. They all stood as he entered. They all noticed at once that Sir Raoul had changed into his leathers but no-one commented.

"Sit, gentlemen. Sir Breon, is this the scout?"

Raoul pointed at a young cavalryman that stood by their table.

"Yes, Sir Raoul."

"Report, soldier."

"I was just telling Sir Breon, Sir,"

"Well I am here now soldier, tell me."

"Uh, yes Sir, of course. The Saxons are moving up from their camp at the beaches Sir. They would appear to be entirely pedites. They have no horses. They are armed mainly with axes, some swords, short spears and painted wooden shields."

"Did you see bows? Do many carry bows?"

"We saw none, Sir, no bows or quivers of arrows."

Raoul laughed.

"Well done. The bows would be of no use without the arrows."

An uneasy laugh filled the room.

"All things said, that is really good news. They must have been relying on King Mark for cavalry and bowmen. In fact those three hundred or so Britons we saw camped at Tintagel looked to be mainly bowmen. Anything else to report?"

"Only, Sir, that there would appear to be some fifteen hundred Saxons, all carrying their equipment. It will certainly take most of the day to all reach here."

"Thank you then. Well done. Dismissed. Get back to your unit."

"Gentlemen, go back to your Conrois and prepare everything. Do not dress in mail yet but be ready. I will have some special duties for some of you, but otherwise, we will meet here again at noon. Be about it."

There was a moment of hesitation as many eyes looked to Sir Breon for confirmation. He sat looking at his drink on the table in front of him. They all stood and began to leave the tent.

Sir Raoul sat next to Breon and waited until the tent emptied. Raoul beckoned to Jory who was standing beside the doorway. He immediately ran to Raoul's side.

"Go and prepare my courser. I must have some time with him. I haven't ridden him since I left him in Winchester."

"Yes, Sir. Will you need me to ride with you, to carry messages or suchlike?"

Sir Raoul smiled and nodded.

"Yes boy. Saddle your palfrey too."

Jory left the tent with a wide smile on his face.

"Sir Breon, we have been friends for a long time and you are a professional soldier. When I sent you a message to attend my tent when the scout arrived, I did not expect to receive a message summoning me here."

"I apologise, Sir Raoul. I have become used to being in sole command in the field, and my men have a certain sense of loyalty."

"Your men seem more comfortable with the situation than you."

Raoul paused and stood. Sir Breon rose beside him.

"Have your second in command here an hour before noon, and the commander of the men who arrived from Winchester. I have some things to decide. We will discuss them then."

"Yes, Sir Raoul. Understood."

"Good. Now I apologise too. I have been away from the army too long. I meant what I said at breakfast, you must not be afraid to give your men orders, but they do need to understand who is in overall command. So, enough said. I will be back shortly."

Raoul left the command tent and walked down to the enclosure that held the horses. They were all tethered to rails that had been quickly erected in lines across the camp.

Jory had saddled and dressed the courser. The horse raised its nose and shook its head in recognition as it saw Sir Raoul approach. The knight took the horses head in his arms and it pressed its head against his chest.

"Hello big boy. We have work to do together these next couple of days."

Jory watched in amazement at the horse's reaction to Sir Raoul. They had obviously spent a great deal of time together and the horse was devoted to him.

"I will mount, Jory. I may need you to adjust the stirrups."

Jory cupped his hands to help his master mount the tall courser. Once in the saddle Raoul slid his boots into the stirrups. His black calf length boots were slightly wider than the laced ankle boots he usually wore but they fitted into the stirrups easily.

"They are perfect, Jory. Nothing to do. Mount up."

Jory jumped up onto the palfrey.

"Comfortable boy?"

Yes, Sir, very."

"Good. Stirrups are our biggest advantage. They are why Norman cavalry are the best there is. We can do so much more in the saddle. Come boy."

Sir Raoul led the way through the camp to the entrance. Everywhere men were sharpening swords and lances and polishing mail, but all stopped and looked up as Sir Raoul rode past them. Jory glowed with pride as he followed his new master.

They left the gates and crossed the ford. As they reached the top of the bank on the far side they could see a Conrois over to their right riding in a column two abreast along the edge of the woods. As they almost reached the track from the shore they all turned left into an almost perfect line abreast and trotted across open grass.

Their commander saw and recognised Sir Raoul from a distance. He halted his men and expertly wheeled them left. He walked the line towards Sir Raoul who was now trotting towards them. He halted them again and rode to their centre and greeted Sir Raoul.

"Welcome, Sir. Would you like to drill the men?"

"No, no, that was very impressively done. You are one of Sir Breon's Conrois?"

"Indeed, Sir Raoul. I am Geroux Decanne, Sir, at your service. I was at Senlac, Sir, and I rode with you to take Romney, although I did not lead a Conrois then. You would not have known me."

"They were all good men with me at Romney. Well, Geroux Decanne, keep up the good work. Do not engage the Saxons, just show your presence. I want them to form up west of the track. The further the better within sight. The first should appear about noon. I will send another Conrois to relieve you shortly after noon. Your men will have worn mail for long enough by then. Get them back and rest."

"Thank you, Sir, and may I say, on behalf of all my men, it is a privilege to be under your command."

Sir Raoul laughed.

"Say that after the fight. Good luck."

Raoul wheeled his courser away and rode around the end of their line and further away from the river. Joly beamed with delight as he followed.

They soon reached a slight rise in the ground that ran across their path, parallel to the river and almost a mile from it. Raoul reigned in and waved Joly up beside him.

"What do you think, Joly? Why do I stop here?"

"High ground, Sir. Not much but something."

"Well done, my boy, exactly. If these Saxon Princes are any sort of fighters they will form a shield wall along this slight ridge. They will wait here for us to attack them, I am sure. They will know we have cavalry but they will not know we have only cavalry. If they did, and had time to prepare, they could dig ditches in front of here to break up a charge, but they will not have the time nor the equipment. Good, so what is cavalry's biggest problem on the battlefield?"

Jory hardly hesitated.

"Archers, Sir. More for the horses than for the knights."

"Correct, and they would appear to have no archers. Fifteen hundred men Joly, all pedites, and Saxons always use a shield wall. What does that tell us?"

This time Joly did hesitate.

"I have spent all my time with cavalry men, Sir, I am not sure what you are thinking."

"What I am thinking, my boy, is that a Saxon shield wall is usually three men deep, and almost certainly with cavalry on the field. Three deep might just stop cavalry if the Saxons have enough long spears, which from what the scout said this morning, they are not carrying. Even so, a shield wall three deep can put off all but the very best trained horses. How are you with numbers, boy?"

"Not good, Sir."

"There are fifteen hundred enemy. If they form a three deep shield wall, how many men in each rank?"

"I can do that, Sir, five hundred."

"Yes Joly, my boy, five hundred men wide, standing shoulder to shoulder with overlapping shields. Look along the length of this rise boy, from the trees over there to the moorland over there. How wide is that?"

"I cannot guess, Sir, but much more than five hundred men wide."

"Yes, yes, yes. Room around each flank, and plenty of it. We will make a commander of you yet, Joly. Let us hope these Saxons are true to form and do as we expect. Come, boy, we have a meeting shortly."

They rode back at a canter, crossed the ford and entered the camp. It was still bustling with activity. Sir Raoul halted outside the command tent and slid down from his courser. He patted its neck and talked into its ear. It nodded its head and snorted.

Raoul turned and handed the reins to Jory who was still in his saddle.

"Take care of them then come and attend me here."

"I will, Sir."

Raoul nodded and entered the tent. It was empty except for two stewards who were filling some wine jugs and placing goblets on the central table.

Raoul called one of them to him.

"Fetch Sir Breon for me, with haste."

"Yes, Sir Raoul."

Raoul sat down and poured some wine for himself. It was a deep red but appeared black as he looked down into the pewter goblet. He took a sip and lent back in his chair. The blue and white striped walls of the tent flapped in the breeze.

He took a bigger mouthful and swilled it around his mouth. His mouth was dry but so was the wine. He was not sure whether he felt better before or after it. Sir Breon entered the tent.

"Ah, you are back. I will send for the others."

He turned back to the entrance and shouted some orders to some men outside. As he came back in Raoul spoke.

"Is this the command tent?"

"Well, of course."

"So who was in command when I returned?"

Sir Breon went to say something then hesitated.

"Say no more, I understand what you are saying."

There was a noise in the entrance and two knights entered. Sir Raoul stood and Sir Breon followed. The knights were dressed in full colours and fully armed but without mail. They immediately approached Sir Raoul, stood to attention and slapped their right arms across their chests in salute, then turned and did the same to Sir Breon.

"Pray introduce us, Sir Breon."

"This is Sir Geffers of Toulouse. He has been with me in Exeter. This is Sir Villiers Margeau who joined me from Winchester."

"I am very pleased to meet you both. Please all sit."

Both men sat opposite Sir Raoul and Sir Breon.

Sir Raoul summoned a steward.

"Wine for us all please."

As the steward poured wine for them all, refilling Raoul's goblet, Sir Villiers leant forward.

"Sir Raoul, I fought with you at Senlac. I was in the Conrois supporting the Duke himself, and rode with him to support you when you held the stream with your Bretons. Your men saved the day. It is an honour to meet you, Sir."

Raoul paused very deliberately then raised his goblet.

"The honour is mine, the Duke led a fine Conrois that day. Only half of you lived through it I remember."

"Indeed, Sir, it was a very long day."

"And you, Sir Geffers, have you seen much action?"

"No, Sir. I came to England less than a year ago but was in charge of training cavalry at home in Normandy. I rode with King William to take Exeter, and we sacked Dorchester on the way, but sieges are my only experience."

Raoul took a mouthful of wine. He was determined to appear totally confident about what he wanted.

"Firstly, equipment. Sir Breon, we have plenty of weapon wagons with us."

"Yes, Sir Raoul, the normal support for our numbers."

"I am thinking particularly of spears and lances."

"As I said, Sir Raoul, the normal support for a force this size."

"Do we have five hundred lances?"

"With what the men carry and in the wagons I am sure we do."

"Good, then have them gathered. Spears, we have five hundred and more, surely."

"Yes, certainly. Almost every man carries one and we have many in the wagons."

"Good, now, how exactly are we made up? Sir Geffers, your numbers?"

"I have a few over five hundred men, Sir Raoul. Ten full Conrois of fifty men and half a Conrois of twenty five or so, scouts."

"I see. Well send a Conrois, fully briefed, out to replace the one that has been on duty on the other side of the ford since early this morning, as soon as I finish the noon briefing. Next, select two Conrois and send them west to the far end of the open land before us. Fully equipped with spears, they will stay hidden until the fighting starts then approach the Saxons from the rear and await orders. Their main objective is to dissuade the Saxons from moving further west today. If they attempt to do so, they must do all they can to slow or stop them. Otherwise, stay out of sight and do not engage."

Raoul paused and took a mouthful of wine. He leant forward over the table. Sir Geffers and Sir Villiers did the same. Sir Breon was sat back in his chair.

"Your scouts, Sir Geffers. I want two or three groups sent west to the Tamar at least. One group must watch the crossing at Ponstonel and other crossings as where I met your scouts. I do not want to be surprised by any force from Cornwall. I am certain none will come but we must not be surprised."

They were interrupted by a messenger from the Conrois on the far side of the ford. The first Saxons were emerging from the woods along the track. They had seen the Conrois and were forming a shield wall and moving away to the west as more men arrived.

Raoul felt the tension in the tent increase. Suddenly it was getting very real. He deliberately took another mouthful of wine and calmly continued. He noticed Jory appear at the entrance.

"I am convinced the Saxons will move a little to the west and form up along the slight ridge across the grassland. By the time they all make the climb from the shore it will almost be dark. I do not want them to know we are all cavalry. Sir Geffers, I need a Conrois to disperse and light fires along the top of the bank on the far side of the ford. I need them to look like the edge of a camp of infantry to the Saxons."

"Yes, Sir Raoul, that can easily be done."

"Good man. I am sure the Saxons will make a temporary camp and form up in the morning. They do not like to fight at night, but that Conrois of yours, Sir Geffers, must watch them all night. Move scouts up close to them. I want no surprises in the night."

Sir Geffers nodded as Raoul then added his final instructions to him.

"In the morning then, I need two Conrois with spears on the right and the rest on the left. Sir Breon will be on the right and I will be on the left with you. I want one Conrois assigned to me personally. Geroux Decanne's will be perfect. All understood."

"Yes, Sir Raoul. We will be ready."

Raoul turned to Sir Villiers.

"You have ten Conrois too, Sir Villiers?"

"I do Sir, at your command."

"Fully trained with the couched lance?"

"Yes indeed, Sir."

"Then your role is simple. When the Saxons have formed their shield wall, you will ford the river and form up ten Conrois wide for a full charge with couched lances."

Sir Villiers sat upright in his chair and smiled proudly.

"Yes Sir, our honour Sir."

"Do I need four hundred and ninety nine apples, Sir Villiers?"

Sir Villiers laughed and smiled warmly.

"Indeed not, Sir, but we will ride as if we held one between the shoulders of every pair of horses along the line abreast, Sir, that I promise you. The men will be proud to serve you, Sir."

"Then that is all for now. I am going to rest for a while. Make ready, full mail and mounted at dawn. I want every man in the saddle and fully armed as the sun rises."

Sir Raoul stood and raised his goblet.

"To our victory tomorrow."

The others stood and echoed his toast.

Sir Raoul turned and left the tent with Jory shadowing him. He entered his tent and unbuckled his sword belt. Jory took it from him and laid it against a chair. Sir Raoul undid the ties on his leather tabard and Jory helped him remove it.

Sir Raoul sat on the edge of his cot bed and swung his legs up, lying back slowly. Jory sat on the chair opposite.

"Is there anything you need, Sir?"

"Just make sure I have plenty of water then wake me at dusk if I should fall asleep."

"Yes, Sir, I will, but may I just ask you something, Sir."

Sir Raoul lifted himself back up onto his elbows.

"Yes, of course, my boy."

"I just wish to learn, Sir. Tomorrow, Sir, why cannot we just split our force and charge the shield wall from both sides?"

"A very good question, my boy, and one that shows you are thinking. It is simply this. The Saxons do not know we do not have any pedites and that we are entirely milites, cavalry. They will form up as a shield wall expecting an attack on foot and assuming the cavalry they have seen to date are small mobile detachments which they can cope with as needed. If they knew they were facing a thousand cavalry they would form their shield wall in a circle three men deep instead of a line. Once in a tight shield circle they would be very difficult to break and they could probably hold a tight circle all day long. If we can make them form a straight wall before they realise we are all cavalry they will not have the discipline nor time to form a circle quickly enough. The Saxons are brave fighters, Jory, very brave, but their big weakness is they lack discipline. You will see tomorrow. Now, let me rest."

"Thank you, Sir. I will rest outside."

"Then get some more blankets and rest inside the entrance there."

"Thank you, Sir, I will check the horses then return."

Sir Raoul lay back and closed his eyes.

+++

Waestan did not enjoy the passage to Flat Holm. The estuary of the River Severn was a volatile stretch of water with the biggest tidal race known to sailors. Even with favourable weather the waters were not kind to them.

The wind, however, stayed in the south-west and blew them naturally towards the island, and as darkness fell they gently bumped against the wharf at Flat Holm.

Waestan gave the fisherman another gold coin, as much as he might earn fishing in a month, and instructed him to wait for him. There would be more when he took him back.

There was a small hamlet behind the wharf. Waestan approached the first cottage and rapped on the door. An old man opened it and looked at him for a few moments. He was framed in the doorway which was dimly lit by the candles within.

"What can I do for you Father?"

"I have come to see the Lady Gytha who I know to be on this island. Can you take me to her?"

"She is in the manor house, Father. It is not far, nothing is on this small island, but beyond my reach at my age. I will call my son."

Waestan was surprised as the door slammed shut in his face. He had not expected that. He was about to knock again when the door opened. A younger man stood on the threshold. He was in his late forties or early fifties but a lot younger than the first occupant.

"You want to go to the manor?"

Waestan was taken a little aback.

"Yes, good Sir. I have business with the Lady Gytha."

"Whose business would that be, Father?"

"God's business. I am cleric to Bishop Leofric and an envoy of Archbishop Stigand."

"Indeed, Father. Now that is difficult. You see the Lady Gytha is a prisoner here of King William, and all on this Island are sworn to his banner."

"And all are God's people and subject to the Pope's will. I understand your dilemma good Sir. I give you my word I am here only to talk to The Lady Gytha and nothing else."

There was a moment's silence. Somebody spoke in the cottage but Waestan could not hear what was said. The man stepped out of the cottage doorway.

"Follow me, Father."

He led Waestan up a path that climbed into the heart of the island. A large stone building appeared out of the darkness. All of its windows seemed lit.

"Make yourself known, Father."

"Thank you, my son."

Waestan smiled to himself. He need not have bothered to say anything. The man was gone before he could have heard him.

Waestan walked to the manor house door. It had a brass knocker which Waestan gripped and banged loudly. It took a few moments before the door opened and a young man greeted him.

"Oh, I am sorry, Father, how can I help you?"

"I am an emissary of Archbishop Stigand and cleric to Bishop Leofric, here to speak with the Lady Gytha."

There was some commotion within the house. The young man turned away before facing Waestan again.

"You are aware, Father, that Gytha Thorkeldottir is here as a prisoner of King William."

"I am, my son, but she is also a child of Christ, as are we all, and in that capacity I am charged to speak with her. I have no will to remove her from your custody."

"Wait, Father."

The door closed briefly then reopened.

"This way, Father, we will take you to her."

Waestan entered and followed the young man through the poorly lit old building. It was not well maintained and was no more than a large farmhouse. Waestan was led through the ground floor and upstairs to a suite of rooms where Gytha was held. A young handmaiden led him into a large room where Gytha sat comfortably before a wide fireplace that crackled as it burnt its fresh logs. The candles around the room gave little light.

Waestan knelt before her and took her hand. He kissed it.

"Your Majesty, I am honoured to meet you."

"It is a while since anyone has called me that, Father, what is it you wish from me?"

"I can see you have lost none of your wisdom, your Majesty."

Gytha laughed and reached for a goblet of wine on the table beside her. She drank deeply and turned back to Waestan.

"Why are you here, Father? I am told you are here on business from Archbishop Stigand and my old friend Bishop Leofric."

"Indeed, my Lady. We have met before but you would not remember me. I am cleric and secretary to Bishop Leofric. I was in your presence several times in Exeter."

"Indeed you were, Father. I am very good at faces. Names I am the worst at, and as bad at where I have seen someone, but faces, yes. I remember you."

"Then you know I am here in good faith, my lady, with much news."

"Now that is something I have craved for many a day now, Father. This is a desolate island for an old woman. What news have you?"

Waestan was prepared to lie as he must to gain her trust. He remembered Prious saying that the best way to lie was to tell as much truth as you could, and to tell people what they wanted to hear.

"Your grandsons, Godwine and Edmund, have landed in the mouth of the Taw and marched up the valley to Tawton. They were met there by King Mark with the army of Cornwall and by Lord Jowen of Tintagel with his Britons. Jointly they have become King Arthur's army of rebellion in the south-west. Soon every other Saxon across England will flock to their banner."

"Yes, yes, just as Bishop Leofric predicted, and Archbishop Stigand was so right to support us. So why are you here? Just to tell me this."

"No, my Lady, not just to tell you this. They march upon Exeter which will fall to them swiftly I am sure."

"I am sure too. Exeter was good to me, the people there were always with us."

"Yes, indeed, but both Godwine and Stigand said I must come to you now for news that will change everything, and then armed with this news, I must return to Exeter and meet them there. Once your grandsons have taken Exeter they will have a base to release you from here."

"I see. Why do they not take Exeter and then release me. I can join them there with my news."

"That I cannot answer, only that in such matters of war and state, days can count and fate can play terrible tricks. I can only plead, my Lady, that Archbishop Stigand and Bishop Leofric have charged me with this task and I would not wish to fail them."

Gytha sat still for a while. She gestured to the two maids that were in the room and they left hurriedly. She turned to Waestan and paused before speaking.

What she told him took him aback. He found it hard to believe, but she explained what had happened and gave Waestan details of names and places to follow up in Winchester.

There was a moment's silence before Waestan could speak. It was difficult to absorb and he was determined to remember all the details he was told.

"My Lady that indeed is the most momentous news. Your grandsons will be astounded and delighted I am sure. I will return immediately to them, and I am certain it will only be days before they are able to bring about your release."

"Thank you, Father. God bless your journey."

"And may God bless you, my Lady."

Waestan rose and left the room. What he had just heard still seemed unreal. He was ushered out of the manor house and he found his way in the darkness down to the wharf where the fishing boat awaited him.

He stepped aboard and looked around. The crew were sleeping but the fisherman he had been negotiating with rose and went to him.

"Welcome back, Father. I have laid some blankets in the stern for you."

"Thank you. When can we sail?"

The old fisherman laughed.

"In the morning with the light, Father. The tide will be in our favour then. If we leave now and fight the tide we will not be back sooner than if we leave at dawn and ride it. Have patience and rest."

Waestan reluctantly settled in the stern and tried to sleep as his mind raced. Gytha's words would not leave him. He wondered if he should travel straight to Exeter when they got back to Watchmeet, but Sir Raoul had instructed him to meet him in Dorchester. There may have been a reason in his mind, but he was certain he could not possibly have predicted what he now knew.

Sleep finally came but it took a long time, and dawn then seemed to come all too quickly.

+++

The Rhosmon had sailed eastwards all the previous day. The wind had been light but had blown from the south-west and helped their passage. The sea had been lively but the swell had followed them. It would lift the Rhosmon's stern and they would ride the wave until it overtook them and they dropped stern downwards into its trough. The next wave would lift their stern again and push them along.

Prious became bored and watched the shore. They had passed the Dodman by dusk. They left the close shore and passed Rame Head in the night. By dawn Edmon pointed ashore in the early light.

"There, Brother, you can just see Start point. We could reach Portchester by nightfall if the wind remains favourable but I will not promise it. At worst, and perhaps most likely, we will have to stand off Wight overnight and sail in with tomorrow's dawn light. There is a double tide at Portsea so we should have plenty of water."

"Let us hope for her Lady's sake we can reach there tonight. She is most unhappy."

"You will keep her happy, Brother. I am sure of it."

"I wish I had your confidence in me, Edmon. She has had too many shocks and surprises for one so young."

"That is as maybe, Brother, but you have God's touch. She has total faith in you. It is obvious to the likes of me."

"If that is true my friend, let us hope it sustains a little longer."

Prious walked towards the bow where Morwenna was stirring.

+++

Raoul had fallen asleep for a short while. Jory woke him as the evening came on.

"A meal is ready Sir, in the command tent, when you are ready."

"Thank you, Jory."

Sir Raoul sat up and swung his legs off his camp cot.

"Pass me my tabard and my sword belt."

Jory helped him dress.

"Is everything ready for me for the morning?"

"Oh yes, Sir, and in the very best of order. I have to say, Sir, I have had so much help from other squires. They all want to say they did something for you. Your mail has never shone so."

Sir Raoul smiled and clapped Jory on the shoulder.

"Do not get too used to such an easy life, my boy. It may not last."

He ducked out of his tent and walked the short distance around to the front of the command tent. As he entered every man in there jumped to their feet.

"Good evening, gentlemen. Let us enjoy some food and wine together and then all get an early night. Tomorrow will be a hard day, made all the harder by a late night."

He sat opposite Sir Breon and reached for a goblet of wine.

"To a victorious day tomorrow. I assume the Saxons are behaving themselves?"

Sir Breon laughed and raised his goblet.

"Just as you predicted, Sir Raoul. They are camped just beyond the rise. They sent some small patrols forward who we quickly turned back. The men camped along the far bank seem to have convinced them they face a combined force of pedites and milites. To tomorrow's victory."

Every man raised his goblet and joined the toast. They all ate well before Sir Raoul stood and the tent fell silent.

"Get to your beds, gentlemen. Tomorrow we can drink late when our enemy is defeated. I will see you at dawn."

His commanders cheered him as he left the tent. Jory appeared from nowhere and followed him back into his tent and tied the flaps shut. He helped Raoul undress and settle on his bed.

"Goodnight boy. Do not let me oversleep."

"I will not, Sir. Before I blow out the lamp, Sir, is there anything else I can do for you?"

Raoul lifted his head and looked at Jory in the dim light.

"No, I do not think so, thank you, my boy. What could I need now?"

"Forgive me, Sir, I have not served you long. Many of the knights you lead require, um, comfort from their squires, especially on the eve of battle."

Raoul was shocked for a moment, but of course Jory was right, many Norman knights did require some physical comfort from their squires, eve of battle or not.

"Thank you, my boy, but no. I am a Frenchman not a Norman. We have different habits. Settle down and sleep."

Raoul lay back and closed his eyes. His mind needed to rest, but he fell asleep hoping Jory had not taken his refusal as some sort of insult or personal rejection.

The Seventh Scroll

Jory roused Sir Raoul before the dawn. The camp was awake. The squires had a system when the first to awake at what seemed the first signs of dawn awoke those around them and so all the camp came to life together.

Sir Raoul sat up and took a moment to gather his thoughts. This would be a day that shaped the rest of his life. Jory was wide awake and full of energy.

"Come Sir, I assume you wish to wear your leathers beneath your mail."

"Correct my boy. We must maintain the image."

"It is all here Sir. Let us get you dressed."

Sir Raoul dressed in his leathers and then Jory helped him add his mail. It was very heavy. It was easy to move in but weighty to wear. He strapped his sword belt around the mail. He knew that would cause comment amongst his knights, and clapped Jory on the shoulders before him.

"Thank you, my boy. Is my courser ready and dressed?"

"Oh yes, Sir, and he has never looked better."

"Good lad. Thank you for all you have done. I had better go to the command tent. In truth, I am not that hungry, but I suppose I ought to eat something. Bring my mount to the tent. I will need him shortly."

"Yes, Sir, he will be there when you need him."

"Fine. Have my helm, shield and spear with him."

"Of course, Sir. All will be ready for you."

"I am sure it will."

Raoul left his tent and went to the command tent. His commanders were gathering. He helped himself to plate of cold meat and warm bread. It was a little early for wine but an early goblet lifted the spirits.

Everyone was in full mail. Most had a ventail hanging over their chest. Many had a coif hanging like a hood behind their heads.

Sir Breon approached him.

"Sir Raoul, I think we are all here."

"So it would seem, my friend."

Sir Raoul banged the table with his goblet and called everyone to order.

"Gentlemen, you all have your orders. Sir Geffers' men, we have two Conrois beyond the enemy lines. Three Conrois on the right flanks, four Conrois on the left, and one with me wherever I may be. Sir Villiers, your ten Conrois have the opportunity to make your names live in history with a classic couched lance charge. We all know the plan but we all need to use our initiative as the day progresses. This should be ended by noon, but we may be still fighting late in the day. I know I can trust you all. God be with us all."

"God be with us."

The call rang inside the tent. Sir Raoul shouted above the noise.

"To horse, gentlemen, to horse."

He looked across the tent and called loudly.

"Geroux Decanne, to me."

Geroux swiftly crossed the tent to him.

"Yes, Sir Raoul, my Conrois is yours."

"Stay close to me Geroux. We must fill any gaps through the day. Are you with me?"

"We are honoured to be at your side, Sir."

"Let us be away then."

Jory was waiting outside the tent. He was holding Raoul's courser who was lively. He could feel the tension. Jory helped Raoul up into his saddle and checked his stirrups. Raoul pulled his coif over his head, tucking his hair away inside. Jory passed him his helmet which fitted comfortably over his coif. Raoul lifted his ventail and tied it to his helmet. Jory lifted his shield and Raoul took the straps, hanging them over his right shoulder with the shield down his left, over his sword and his left leg. He held his reins in his left hand and reached for his spear with his right. He breathed deeply then nodded to Jory, who released his reins.

He turned his courser away to the right. He used the reins but mainly his horse moved steered by his knees and legs against his sides. They had trained together for years. Sir Raoul looked to his right as he rode to the camp entrance and Geroux Decanne was at his shoulder. They crossed the ford and rode up the other side.

The sun was rising as Sir Raoul rode towards the moorland to their left. Geroux and his Conrois fell in with him. Four other Conrois followed them towards the enemy.

The Saxons were also ready with the dawn. They formed up in a line three deep. It was the way they always fought. As the sun rose and the light grew they looked to the east. The sun was in their eyes and it was hard to see clearly.

Godwine and Edmund were in the centre of their wall. They looked for the expected Norman foot soldiers. There was activity along the river bank in the distance but it was hard to see what the movement was. They were conscious though of cavalry movement wide on each flank.

Godwine and Edmund were angry and becoming more and more nervous. They were confident enough in their shield wall but were angry that the Cornish army had not yet arrived. They had sent more scouts and messengers west the night before but had still heard no news. They were relying on the Cornish for some cavalry, but apart from pure numbers, the

Cornish were to provide archers too. There was still hope they would arrive before the day was done.

The light grew into daylight and still there was no sign of Norman pedites. Godwine began to worry, but before he could come to any conclusions one hundred Norman cavalry charged in from his right.

They rode across the front of his shield wall. Their kite shaped shields were towards the Saxons and as the leading riders reached half way along the Saxon wall they threw their short spears into the Saxon line. The Saxons took many casualties and their line instinctively moved forward to strike at the horses and men in front of them.

The Norman cavalry immediately swung to their right and rode away from the Saxon line. Many of the Saxons broke away from their wall with a cheer, running forward after the Normans.

Godwine screamed at them to stand but such lack of discipline was a weakness of the Saxons. Before they realised what was happening another hundred horsemen charged in from their left, cutting down every man that had left the Saxon shield wall.

Enraged by seeing their comrades slaughtered in front of them, more Saxons ran forward from their line. The Normans wheeled away again and another two Conrois charged in from the right, riding over and killing the Saxons who had left their wall.

They too swung away from Saxons. All these Conrois rode back towards the river then turned outwards and back along the flanks from where they had charged. There was one Conrois unbloodied on the Norman right and Sir Raoul and Geroux's Conrois on the left.

Sir Raoul surveyed the field in front of the Saxon shield wall. He was on their right flank looking along their line. They had lost some men to the spears of the first charge and at least as many each time their line had broken. There were many bodies on the grass in front of them.

It looked to Sir Raoul that his cavalry had hardly lost a man, a handful at the most, pulled from their horses. He was sure they could do the same again but he did not want too many bodies on the field in front of their shield wall in case they troubled some of the horses that had to ride over them.

He looked to his right. Whilst this had been happening, Sir Villiers had formed up his ten Conrois in line abreast along the river bank and rode them up onto the top. It was a formidable sight. Five hundred cavalry with long lances, each held under their right arms and against their chests. Five hundred horses shoulder to shoulder in a tight line.

Sir Raoul looked to his left. The two Conrois he had sent to the far west were in line abreast in the distance walking towards them. He heard the sound of hooves to the right as Sir Villiers' men rode forward at a walk then began to trot.

He shouted to Geroux.

"This is going to take some timing. We must not let them circle."

He waved a signal to the Conrois opposite them and charged forward. His Conrois were with him in an instant. The Saxon shield wall could see Sir Villiers' men begin their charge towards them. Godwine was screaming orders, trying to make his line fold back at each end and move into a circle, but it was not something they had trained for and his men were confused.

Sir Raoul led his Conrois behind the shield wall. The Saxons in the third row tried to turn to defend themselves but they were also trying to face their front. Sir Villiers' line was now closing at a canter.

The Conrois on the far flank followed Sir Raoul's lead and charged in behind the far end of the shield wall and the Saxons were in turmoil. Some broke from the rear rank to attack the Normans behind them, but now Sir Villiers' charge was at a full gallop and approaching fast. Sir Raoul stood in his stirrups and screamed.

"Away, away."

The Normans behind the shield wall broke away moments before Sir Villiers five hundred horses bore down on the Saxon's weakened line.

If the shield wall had been complete and solid they might have stood some chance, but they were broken in places and confused. The sight of five hundred lances and five hundred heavy horses riding at them at speed was too much.

Most broke and turned to run before the charge hit them. Some stood their ground but their wall had no strength and no depth to deter the Norman horses. They burst through the Saxons and it became a rout.

As Sir Raoul turned back towards the Saxons he was joined by the two Conrois from the west, keen to join the fight. He led the four Conrois back into the melee. The Saxons were fighting as individuals, unarmoured on foot against cavalry in full mail. The Normans did have many wounded and a few killed, but the Saxons were driven into the woods along the north ridge and back towards the sea.

Sir Raoul tried to rally his men. He shouted loudly but was not heard nor often heeded when he was.

"To me, to me, they are beaten, let them go."

Many did return to him but many had a blood lust and were intent on killing as many Saxons as they could between there and the sea. Sir Raoul rode slowly back to their camp. His courser picked his way through the Saxon dead. A few Normans lay among them. He had less than half those who had left the camp with him. They would find out later, but he felt they had lost no more than a hundred men, if that many. The rest were in the woods and along the track to the sea.

He was very happy to have won the day with such relative ease. It was not yet even noon, but he was tired of all the killing. He knew that if King

William were there the King would be pursuing the Saxons down to the sea trying to kill every single one. Raoul could hear him.

"Every one that lives can come back and fight us again."

He was right, of course, but Raoul was surprised at how he felt, he had just had enough killing for one day. For the first time he had ridden into battle with thoughts of Morwenna in his mind. For the first time he had a reason to live through the day. If this was love it would be the end of his life as a soldier.

He led those that were with him back across the ford and into the camp. Jory was there to meet him outside the command tent. He took his helmet and shield. His spear was in a Saxon on the field. His ventail had fallen across his chest and he pushed his coif back off his head. His hair tumbled free onto his shoulders and he shook his head.

Jory was holding his courser's bridle and Sir Raoul slid down out of his saddle.

"Thank you, boy. Well done."

He turned and held his courser's nose. He kissed it slapped his neck.

"Thank you, my dear friend."

The horse tossed his head and pushed his nose into his chest. Raoul hugged it then turned to Jory.

"Look after him, boy. He has done all I asked of him. Then come to my tent."

Raoul walked quickly to his tent and removed his mail. It would have been much easier if he had waited for Jory to return and help him but he wanted to be free of it.

Jory returned to his tent before he expected.

"That was quick. Is he properly rubbed down?"

"Oh yes, Sir. There are many knights who have not yet returned and many squires wanting to help with your courser."

"I see, well deal with my mail. I will be in the command tent."

Sir Raoul walked slowly to the front of the command tent. Knights and cavalrymen were entering the camp a few at a time.

He entered and sat a central table. There was a jug of wine and four pewter goblets laid out on it. He filled one and drank deeply then looked around the tables. There were just a few others sitting around. They were nearly all sitting alone.

A knight at the table next to him glanced at him and suddenly jumped up and raised his goblet.

"Sir Raoul, forgive me. I did not see it was you. Congratulations on a great victory."

Everyone in the tent stood and joined the toast. Every man had been lost in his own thoughts and had not seen him enter.

"As you were, everyone. Thank you for all you did this day."

Raoul just wanted some time to settle himself, as did every man there. They sat in silence as slowly their numbers and the noise grew.

The next to arrive were as the first and sat quietly and drank to calm themselves, but soon others arrived still full of blood lust enjoying every moment of their victory. They drank and spoke loudly before any of them noticed Sir Raoul sitting in their midst. In fact, it was not until Sir Breon entered the tent and joined him that many realised he was there.

Sir Breon joined him and filled a goblet with wine.

"Gentlemen all, to our leader today, Sir Raoul Tyrrell."

The tent fell silent for a moment then everyone joined the toast.

"Sir Raoul Tyrrell."

Raoul felt he must say something. He rose from his seat and filled his goblet.

"Gentlemen, I have to thank you all for your courage and support this day. This command belongs to my dear friend Sir Breon of Brittany, and it is his name that will be remembered after this day, but it has been my privilege to serve with you through this fight. Long live King William."

"Long live King William."

Everyone raised their goblets and echoed his toast. Raoul sat back down and drank more wine. It was the middle of the afternoon so he left the tent and walked past his own tent towards where the horses were all tethered.

His horses were all in the front line. His courser looked magnificent. The squires had brushed him well. Beside him was Myghal's horse that he had ridden from Tintagel, and beside him his much-loved palfrey that he had given to Jory.

Raoul spent a while with each of them, talking to them and patting them, hugging their heads. It settled them and it settled him. Jory appeared beside him.

"Is all well, Sir Raoul?"

Raoul looked down at him and smiled.

"Yes, my Boy. You have done well. What age are you?"

"Almost sixteen, Sir, and the proudest squire in this camp."

"Indeed, well listen boy, I have never had a squire before because I never felt I needed one. If you wish to remain as my squire, I cannot promise it will always be like this, in fact I may never fight again."

"What we have done today, Sir, will live with me forever. I would love to continue to serve you and to learn from you."

Raoul laughed and put a hand on Jory's shoulder.

"Do you speak French, Jory?"

"No Sir, I do not."

"Well, if you wish to stay with me that may be the first thing you learn from me."

Jory beamed at him. He quivered with excitement.

"Does that mean I may serve you, Sir?"

"So it would seem, my boy, so it would seem."

Jory dropped to one knee and grabbed his hand. He kissed it and looked up at him.

"I swear, Sir Raoul, I will never let you down."

Raoul laughed and pulled him to his feet.

"I am certain you will not, my boy. Now fetch me some food to my tent. I will eat there before I return to the command tent. I think the evening's celebrations may last much of the night."

+++

Waestan was awake as the fishing boat sailed from Flat Holm shortly after dawn. The wind was brisk and the tide was almost fully in and turning. The estuary was relatively quiet. The wind was blowing from the south-west and was following the tide in but as the tide turned it began to blow against the flow.

The fisherman knew the waters well and they sailed along the Welsh coast, using the wind to his best advantage. He knew exactly where he wished to change tack. They actually sailed some distance past Watchmeet before he swung their bows around and sailed a steady easterly course straight towards his home port.

The receding tide perfectly countered the wind and they sailed comfortably across the estuary and into Watchmeet harbour. It was almost mid-afternoon before they tied up against the wharf.

Waestan stepped ashore and paid the fisherman the rest of what he had promised him for a safe return. There was no sign of his escort. He walked along the harbour and noticed the village inn. A large picture of a ram swung outside the door. Waestan entered and looked around the small room. His escort were sitting in one corner, mugs of cider in front of them. Waestan approached them.

"To horse gentlemen, we can travel far before nightfall."

The three cavalrymen were taken completely by surprise. They looked at him blankly before one of them spoke.

"But Father, we were not expecting you yet. Surely it would be better to wait until tomorrow morning?"

"Get off your arses and ready our horses. We leave as soon as you pay your way. Move yourselves."

His three guards reluctantly stood and finished their mugs of cider. They paid the landlord for what they had consumed and left the inn. Waestan ordered a mug of cider and awaited their return. His timing was almost perfect. He had almost finished his cider as the guards returned.

"Ah, there you are my children. I thought I had lost you. Come, we must away. If we ride hard for the rest of today's light we may reach Tonetown, where I have heard there are some fine inns."

He left the inn with them and mounted his horse. He had ridden it from Tintagel and they were getting to know each other well. They rode out of Watchmeet and followed the track towards Tonetown. There was some good daylight left and the horses were well rested so Waestan kept up a good pace.

They were short of Tonetown when the light began to fade. Waestan halted them and they rode a short way from the track and found a clearing close by. They settled for the night. The cavalrymen were not happy but there was no choice. They had thought their duty would be a good rest. They would avoid fighting the Saxons and not have to risk their lives in battle, but this priest was unexpectedly pushing them hard.

They all slept around the edge of the clearing. Nothing disturbed them until Waestan awoke them all with the dawn.

"Mount up, gentlemen. We will stop and eat in Tonetown. There will be an inn there. Then we ride on for Ileminstre where we will find an inn for tonight."

Waestan mounted his horse and led them back to the track. The thought of an inn at the end of the day was some encouragement.

+++

Sir Raoul left his tent just before dusk and entered the command tent. The tent became silent then everyone inside began to clap and cheer. Raoul saluted them and made his way to the centre of the tent. He stopped and held up a hand. The noise quickly abated and Raoul spoke loudly.

"Gentlemen, my gratitude to you all for your loyal service. Let us celebrate our victory."

Again the tent filled with cheers as Raoul sat down opposite Sir Breon.

"You look well, my friend. How did you fare today?"

"Very well, Sir Raoul. Your tactics were perfect. A few Saxons reached their boats and left our shores, but only a few."

"What of Godwine and Edmund?"

"Nobody has yet reported their deaths. I think they may have escaped us."

"That is a pity. It means they are still a potential threat."

"Perhaps so, but I feel after today's defeat they will not invade again."

Raoul poured some wine and took a large mouthful.

"That is probably so, Sir Breon. After last year's defeat and now this, I doubt they will hurry back."

"You have won a great victory, Sir Raoul. Your name will be remembered for many years."

"No, Sir Breon. I was not here. Brother Prious, Father Waestan and I were never here. Bishop Odo will write the history and we will not be part of it. In the years to come they will talk of the time when Sir Breon and his thousand knights sent the Saxon invaders back into the sea. Why you were here waiting for them no one will know. Now let us just drink to the future. Where is Sir Villiers and Sir Geffers, and my friend Geroux Decanne?"

"Sir Villiers is over there."

Sir Breon called to him and waved him over.

"I have not seen Sir Geffers yet. He pursued the Saxons back down to the sea. He is not back yet. Do you wish me to summon Decanne? He is not a knight."

"Well he should be. He is an excellent leader. His Conrois is a credit to him and to you. Have him made a knight, I insist."

Sir Breon spoke urgently to a waiter who crossed the tent and found Geroux. He was led to the table. Sir Raoul spoke in a loud voice.

"Ah, Geroux, come and sit with me. It was my pleasure to ride with your Conrois today. You must thank them all for me. Did you lose many men?"

Geroux was uncomfortable with Sir Breon and Sir Villiers at the table. He stood as he replied.

"We lost six men, Sir Raoul, once their line was broken, but we despatched very many more."

"Good man. Now sit here with me."

Geroux moved around the table and sat in the empty chair next to Raoul.

He was very conscious of jealous eyes staring at him.

Wine and food was distributed around the tables as they all swopped stories of the day and of the past. After some time Raoul remembered King William's words to him after their victory in Brittany. He could hear him speaking to him.

"The victory is won, boy, and the celebrations well joined. Now is the time for the leader to leave and let his men relax without his presence."

Sir Raoul stood and banged the table for silence. Voices died slowly.

"Today has been a great victory. Your victory. I thank you all. It has been my privilege to fight with you. Tomorrow I will leave you for Exeter and Winchester. Farewell every one of you, I am thankful to you all."

Every man cheered as Raoul walked through them and left the tent. Jory appeared beside him.

"Is everything ready to leave early tomorrow, boy."

"Yes, Sir. All is packed and can be quickly loaded as required in the morning."

They arrived at Raoul's tent and Jory held back the entrance flaps. Raoul ducked in and Jory followed. Two candles burned in lanterns, one near the entrance and one on the table by the head of Raoul's cot.

Jory helped him undress. He removed his boots and his leathers then his linen shirt and leggings. He sat naked on the edge of his cot.

"It was hot under that leather and mail. I will need some clean linen in the morning."

"I have it ready for you, Sir. I thought you would."

"Well done, boy. Now get a good sleep. We have many miles to travel these next few days."

Raoul lay back on his bunk. He stared up at the ridge of the tent. Jory settled across the entrance.

Raoul thought back through the morning. So many men had died. Most were Saxons but they were still people, many with families and loved ones. Morwenna filled his mind. This love thing would be the end of his soldiering if he let it.

His mind filled with memories of his evening with her in Tintagel. He felt himself becoming aroused and unconsciously his hand moved. He gripped himself gently and rolled his fingers. He heard a movement. For that moment he had forgotten about Jory. He was suddenly so embarrassed. His hand let go of himself and he opened his eyes. Jory was kneeling beside the bed. He was naked too.

"Allow me, Sir. No knight should do it for himself, and certainly not one such as yourself. You have a squire now, Sir. It is my duty to please you."

Raoul was speechless and for once at a loss. He knew this would be happening in almost every tent in the camp, this night especially, but he had never had a squire and never experienced it. He did not wish to upset Jory so he said nothing and closed his eyes, lifting his hands behind his head.

Jory took him in his hands and began to caress him gently. Raoul realised how aroused he was. He thought he would have lost his stiffness. He tried to concentrate his thoughts on Morwenna but Jory's hands kept bringing them back to himself.

Often in his life a woman had held him and tried to bring him to seed, some successfully, others not. He had never had any man do it to him accept himself. As Jory moved his hands, gripping him like he would a sword hilt and moving rhythmically Raoul could feel his seed building. A man knew what a man needed.

Raoul opened his eyes. He had drunk a lot of wine and it was slowing his responses. He looked down the cot. Jory was kneeling on his right. He held and was working on his master with his right hand, but Raoul could see Jory was fully aroused and he gripped himself in his left hand and was rubbing himself in time.

It was suddenly all too much for Raoul. He felt his seed build inside him and he caught his breath as he spurted across his stomach. Jory slowed his hand but did not stop completely, encouraging every drop out of his master. Raoul spoke.

"Now you, boy. Finish yourself."

Jory looked at him and hesitated.

"But, Sir…"

"Do it."

Jory knelt upright and changed to his right hand. It only took moments for him to seed in powerful young spurts across Raoul where their seeds mixed.

Jory was panting and sat back on his knees.

"Now, boy, get my old leggings there and clean us up."

Raoul lay back, his mind totally confused. He was used to living with Normans but not to living a Norman life. Every Norman knight had a squire whose duties were clear. Most Norman noblemen, including the King himself, had a bedfellow, a favoured friend who slept with him when they were away from their wives. In fact many Norman nobles only slept with their wives to prolong their blood line, preferring the company of their bedfellows.

Raoul knew it was not his way of life. He had done what he had just done because he had not wished to belittle Jory in any way, and not to let him feel unwanted or inadequate. It was not Jory's fault, just what was expected of almost every squire in the camp that night.

Jory wiped Raoul's stomach.

"Enough, boy. It will dry. Get some sleep now. We will be away to Exeter early in the morning."

"Yes, Sir, and thank you Sir. Thank you very much. I now, really am, your squire."

Raoul did not answer. He shut his eyes and after a long day, much wine and a new experience. With thoughts of Morwenna he was quickly asleep.

+++

Waestan breakfasted with his guards in Tonetown before they set out for Ileminstre. They were further from Tonetown than he had thought so it was a very late breakfast. They rode until mid-afternoon on what was an uneventful journey through some beautiful countryside. Ileminstre was, however, less distance than he had thought and they reached it with much of the day left. As they reached the edge of the town Waestan turned in his saddle.

"I am sorry to tell you gentlemen that it is far too early to end our journey for the day."

He could see the annoyance in their faces.

"We will ride on to Crucaern and stop there overnight. I am sure there will be an inn to be found. I will stand you a meal and a flagon of cider each and somewhere to sleep for the night in return for your patience. Tomorrow you may return to Sir Breon. I will ride on alone to Dorchester. From what I understand, Norman cavalry may not be welcome there."

The men glanced at each other before one spoke.

"We have been there, Father. We rode from Winchester with King William to take Exeter, but Dorchester too had refused to pay its taxes in full. They were disrespectful when we arrived so King William ordered the centre of the town to be burned and for us to enjoy their women. We did both. It was a great day."

"I am sure you found it so. God help them. Did many die?"

"Only those who resisted, Father. The King ordered it so. Many men fought us and died, a few women who resisted too much and some children who got in the way of our enjoyment."

Waestan looked at them for a moment. He was going to say something but then thought better of it. These men had done as ordered. He turned away and rode on. He did not really care if they followed him or not.

As the sun went down they rode into Crucaern. There was indeed an inn in the centre of the town. Waestan tied his horse outside and entered the inn. There were a few men at the tables but it was ill lit by too few candles and it was difficult to see anything.

It went quiet as he entered. They did not see a priest in there often. He was approached by the innkeeper.

"What can I do for you, Father?"

"I am travelling with three soldiers. I need beds for the night and food and drink for us all, and I need our horses looked after. I will pay you in advance in silver coin."

"Norman soldiers, Father?"

"Yes, is that a problem to you?"

"Not to me, Father, especially if you have silver coin, but it may be to some of my other customers who have, or had, relatives in Dorchester."

"I see. I do not wish to cause you any difficulty."

"No difficulty, Father. I have one attic room that you can have. I am afraid your soldiers will have to sleep in the stables, but I have a side room here where you can eat and drink."

"Good. Food for four then, four flagon jugs of cider and let me know how much."

"Come this way, Father. There is a door to the outside through here. It will save your men walking through the inn."

"Lead on, but I need our horses to be well looked after, fed and watered."

"My son will do that, Father. He is a good lad with horses."

The four men ate well and enjoyed their cider. It was slightly cloudy and potent. The cavalrymen questioned Waestan about Sir Raoul. They had only caught a glimpse of him before they had been despatched with Waestan and were keen to hear about him.

Waestan spoke highly of him, telling of his killing the thieves that had tried to stop them reaching Tintagel. They were duly impressed by it all. The one who always had something to say asked Waestan a question.

"Why does he look like he does and yet is still so highly regarded? He does not look like a knight. He looks more like a sell-sword. His hair, his leathers, he is no Norman."

"No he is not. He is a Frenchman who joined the cavalry of Duke William in Normandy five or six years ago. He trained as a cavalryman and fought in Brittany where he earned his spurs and became a knight for fighting back to back with Duke William. He stayed with the Duke's army and came to England. His eldest brother, Sir Walter Tyrrell, Lord of Poix, opened your assault on the right at Senlac with his men of Poix, and Sir Raoul rallied the Bretons on your left and held the stream when you might have lost that battle before noon. The King has much to thank the Tyrrells for."

The men were enthralled. Waestan finished his cider. The others had too.

"Come then, I will take you to the stables and check on the horses with you. I may see you in the morning, I may not, but I suggest you leave early and make your way to Exeter."

They left by the side door, where Waestan would return, and walked along the side of the inn to the stable. Waestan was suddenly aware there were men blocking their way. Looking quickly around he realised they were caught in a semi-circle of about a dozen men. They were all armed with pitch forks and clubs. Waestan held out an arm as his guard drew their swords.

"What is this, my sons? This is no time for violence."

One of the men stepped forward.

"We have no argument with you, Father, but these men are Normans, and cavalry too from what we see and hear."

"What of it, my son."

"We all had relatives in Dorchester. Norman cavalry are not welcome here."

Waestan had learnt from Sir Raoul. Confidence was the key. He stepped forward to face the man.

"Now, my son, think carefully before you take this further. You have three trained soldiers here, swords drawn and ready to fight you. You might kill one, perhaps two. If you are really lucky perhaps all three, but how many of you will they kill, and for what purpose. Sir Breon of Brittany will be returning to Winchester soon with a thousand Norman cavalry. If they hear that Crucaern has risen against the Normans they will come this bit further north and Crucaern will cease to exist. You are a lot smaller than Dorchester. Think of your wives, your daughters and your children. If you wish to condemn them then continue, otherwise, be away to your homes."

He stared the man directly in the eyes.

"I might also add that as I am a man of God, our Lord would be very upset with anyone who hurt me."

The man took a step backward.

"Be sure they are gone with the dawn, we do not want them here."

"A very wise decision, my son. Be gone, all of you."

They all turned slowly and walked away. Waestan stood without moving and watched them go. He heard a voice behind him.

"Thank you, Father. You saved us all."

"You check the horses now, get some rest and leave early before they change their minds. Thank you for your company thus far. Be gone before the dawn."

"We will, Father, thank you."

Waestan returned quickly to the side door and ducked back into the inn. The innkeeper was clearing their table.

He looked a little surprised.

"Is all well, Father? I thought I heard voices."

"You did, my son, and if I thought you knew anything of it I would be very upset."

"No, no, Father, I would do nothing to upset a good paying customer like yourself."

"Perhaps I paid you too soon, my son. Now, I will away to my room, but first you will provide me with another mug of your cider for my trouble, for which you will not charge me, of course."

Waestan watched the innkeeper pour a mugful from a cask which stood in a row of others against the wall.

"Thank you, my host. I will see you with the first light. I have had enough excitement for this night."

Waestan climbed the stairs to the small attic room which was his for the night. He put his mug of cider on the small table beside his pallet bed and undressed himself. His heart was still beating hard in his chest. He was quite proud of himself. He had learnt a lot from Raoul.

He lay back on his bed and was asleep before he had finished his cider. It did not concern him when he awoke with the dawn. He had not paid for it.

+++

Raoul dressed himself. Jory had laid out leggings and a shirt beside his leathers. He ate what Jory had brought him in his tent, seated on the small chair that his clothes had been on. He wanted to leave early and quietly. He had said his farewells in the command tent the evening before.

He buckled his sword belt around his waist and checked his fighting knives. He looked around the tent that had been home for the last few nights. He could see nothing that had been left behind so he left the tent as the sun began to rise.

The camp felt alive somehow but he saw no-one as he walked to the horses. Jory had them ready for him. He helped Sir Raoul into the saddle of his courser and mounted the palfrey. He held the reins of Myghal's horse which was packed with Sir Raoul's mail and their other belongings.

"Come then, my boy. Exeter awaits us."

As he rode slowly towards the camp entrance the whole camp seemed to come to life. Knights and cavalrymen burst out of their tents across the entire camp and surged towards the entrance, forming a roadway many deep on each side for Sir Raoul and his very proud squire.

Every man was cheering and clapping. Sir Raoul held his right arm across his chest in salute as he rode between them. He was almost overcome by it all. He had not expected anything like this, nor indeed had he wanted it.

As he approached the entrance he noticed three men on horseback, Sir Breon, Sir Villiers and Sir Geffers, line abreast. He looked down to his right. Geroux Decanne was standing amongst his men who were clapping and cheering enthusiastically. Sir Raoul halted his courser and beckoned Geroux to him.

Geroux stepped forward out of the crowd and walked to Sir Raoul. Raoul lent down to his side and held out a hand which Geroux clasped.

"Your men were magnificent yesterday, all down to your leadership and training. Thanks, my friend."

He sat back upright on his courser and saluted. Geroux returned the salute, arm across his chest. Raoul rode the last few yards to the gate smiling to himself. That would upset a few.

At the gate he did not stop but saluted the mounted men and kicked his horse into a trot turning to his left along the river then left again around the corner of the camp. Jory was behind him leading the pack horse.

Raoul reached the old roman road that led straight to Exeter. It was a gradual downhill slope from the edge of the moorland to the sea at the mouth of the Exe. He slowed to a walk and waved Jory up beside him.

"Did you know that was planned, boy?"

"Yes, Sir, but I only found out this morning. It was planned after we retired last night. They made me promise not to tell you."

"Did they? Well remember this, you are my squire and your total loyalty is to me now. No secrets, you understand?"

"Yes, Sir. I understand."

"Good lad. I want to be in Exeter as soon as we can be without pushing the horses too hard."

He kicked his horse into a trot. Jory followed his lead. It was not too long however before he slowed to a walk again and Jory rode up beside him.

"May I ask you a question, Sir?"

Raoul looked sideways at him and smiled. He liked the boy's enquiring mind.

"Of course, lad, what troubles you?"

"Nothing troubles me, Sir. I am just interested. As we left the camp you stopped and spoke to Geroux Decanne, but then at the gate you rode out and saluted but did not stop to speak. Will those at the gate not take that badly?"

"I hope so, Jory, I hope so. You have Norman blood, of course, so this will be hard for you to understand. I am not Norman nor of noble blood. I earned my spurs in battle, and much of that involves luck and God's favour. I have had much of both. Most of the Conrois under Sir Breon were led by Norman knights. Many of them noblemen who have never fought or proved themselves until yesterday. They lead their Conrois because of who they were born, good leaders or bad. Geroux is a cavalryman who has risen through the ranks, and his Conrois is the better for it. He has no noble blood and has earned his position on merit. Frankly, my boy, he reminds me of me. He is a professional soldier who has overcome his lack of nobility. I did it to annoy those at the gate. Very childish of me really."

"But you are of noble blood, Sir. You are a Tyrrell of Poix."

"Not to the Norman army, Jory. My eldest brother became Lord of Poix on my father's death. When he died earlier this year, my nephew inherited the title. He may still be Lord of Poix if he still lives, but if not he has a son who now is. I was the fourth son of my father and would inherit nothing, which is why I left home to make my own fortune, but ended up as a common Norman cavalryman. Besides, the Lords of Poix are the hereditary standard bearers to the King of France, who at this time has no love for Normandy."

"Why is that, Sir?"

"Because the Duke of Normandy paid homage to the King of France. When William the Bastard of Normandy conquered Brittany then England, The French King claimed he should be King of England because Duke William was his vassal. They went to the Pope for a ruling. As the Pope had blessed William's invasion, making it a holy crusade, and as William then promised him more gold, the Pope sided with King William."

"Thank you, Sir. I never knew such things happened."

"Many do not, Jory, and are probably the better for it. Now let us ride for a while, I need some peace."

"Of course, Sir, thank you."

They rode on in silence. Raoul's mind was filled with thoughts of Morwenna. He could only think of seeing her again soon, holding her and lying with her. He had lain with many woman since he had joined the cavalry almost seven years ago. Some he had paid for when he was younger. Once he became a knight many were keen to lie with him in the hope that he would fall for them and take them with him, especially in Brittany. None of them had meant anything but an evening's pleasure. He could not understand why he felt this way about a woman he hardly knew. All he did know was he wanted to be with her now.

Prious should be in Portsea by now. He hoped his new friend would take good care of her until he arrived.

+++

The weather had been fair and the Rhosman had stood off the Needles all night, away from the tidal race there. As dawn broke they turned with the tide in towards the shore. Edmon pointed their bow towards Portsea and the brisk breeze carried them inshore.

The waters narrowed and they sailed passed Portsea where they had docked so often. The narrow entrance widened out into a large inland harbour. They sailed on until they saw a large castle ruin appear before them. This was the old stone walls of the Roman fortress of Porchester.

They sailed up to a large wooden wharf and tied up to it. Prious and Morwenna gathered their belongings before Prious gestured to Edmon to join him.

"I cannot thank you enough, Edmon for your services to me."

"You are most welcome, Brother. Bishop Odo was more than generous, as you know, for our services. It was a lot easier than shipping cargos around the coast."

"Then I would ask another service for which I will pay, now, in advance if you will."

"What is it you wish, Brother? If you are as generous as your Bishop I will be only too happy to serve you."

"I need you to wait here for me, or at Portsea, if that is easier. I will pay you now but again you must wait for up to fourteen days for my return. If I do not arrive by then you may leave, but if I do return, I will pay you more to take me to France."

"I will do that for you, Brother, but I would prefer if we could wait in Portsea. We have been away with you for some time now and the um, facilities in Portsea for the crew, are more complete there."

Prious smiled and found his purse. It held many gold pieces. After a brief exchange with Edmon he paid him and replaced his purse.

"Farewell Edmon. I hope we will see you shortly. God be with you."

"I am sure you will, Brother. God be with you too."

Prious took Morwenna up the path from the wharf that led around the castle walls to the entrance. The wide gap in the wall had no gate. It was obvious where large wooden gates had once stood but there were none there now.

As they entered the castle they could see how big it had once been, but now in its centre, was a large manor house from where the whole area was administered. They walked towards the manor house doors which opened as they approached. A steward greeted them.

"Good day Brother, ma'am. How can I help you? What is your business here this day?"

Prious smiled and faced him.

"I will tell you, my son. My name is Brother Prious and this is the Lady Morwenna. I come to visit your master, William de Mauduit, Lord of this Manor who knows of me by way of my Bishop, Bishop Odo, half-brother to King William. Pray inform him immediately of our arrival."

The steward hesitated then replied.

"Please then enter and wait a short time while I find my Lord and bring him to you. We did not expect such illustrious company unannounced."

"That is understood, but please make haste."

Prious smiled and turned to Morwenna.

"Come, my child. We must enter and introduce ourselves. We should be safe here."

They followed the steward through the doors and entered a lavish and large hallway. There were many doors leading off it and a large staircase that led up into the upper floors.

The steward disappeared behind the staircase but it was not long before William de Mauduit himself appeared on the stairs and descended them to greet his guests.

"Welcome to Porchester, both of you. You must be Brother Prious and this, the charming Lady Morwenna. Come through here and sit down. We will call for some refreshment and discuss your business here."

He led them into a furnished hall where a large fire burned. The walls were hung with tapestries of hunting scenes and a semi-circle of padded chairs faced the fire.

"We always heat this room, even in weather like this. It can still be cold if you are sitting. So now, Brother, please be seated. I am keen to know what business you have here. I take it you arrived on the boat that is just leaving our wharf?"

"Indeed, my Lord." Prious was quickly interrupted.

"No, no, Brother. I am merely Lord of this Manor, a Liege Lord, no more. I am no Peer of the realm."

"Forgive me, my Liege, especially for surprising you with this visit, unannounced. I carry out special services for Bishop Odo, of whom I am sure you are aware, half-brother to our King William. In his service we are given the names of a number of people across the country that we are assured we can trust if our needs be in the service of our King."

Prious paused as two servants entered with wine and some soft cakes. They placed their plates, jugs and goblets on the tables before the chairs and left the room. Morwenna sat silently as Prious continued.

"I have been in Cornwall on a special mission with someone who I believe you know well, Sir Raoul Tyrrell."

"Indeed I do. We fought together at Senlac, but he was already a famous knight having fought valiantly with Duke William, as he was then, in Brittany."

"As you did at Senlac, and as a result I believe, you were granted the lands and the manor here at Porchester."

"Yes, Brother, that is so. We have the manor house here within the outer castle walls, but I have promised King William that given time to earn our wealth here, we will rebuild a castle here in his name that he will be proud of."

"I am sure you will my Liege, but I have been in Cornwall with Sir Raoul. As we speak I believe he will by now have put down a rebellion there, and defeated an invasion of Saxons from Ireland."

"I, of course, have heard nothing of such until now, but it sounds something that Sir Raoul would be about."

Prious laughed.

"Yes, you obviously know him, my Liege. I, however had other tasks which have been completed, and I have returned ahead of Sir Raoul by sea. I have with me the Lady Morwenna, daughter of the late Lord Jowen, who was Lord of Tintagel in Cornwall. He was one of the rebels there."

"I know little of Cornwall. Kernow, or Little Wales as I have heard it called. Not part of England."

"Not yet, no, but I do not believe it will be long before it is. The King's other half-brother, Robert, the Count de Mortain, looks upon it favourably."

"Ah yes, I am sure he would. An ambitious man, that Robert."

"So, my Liege, I need a favour of you. I have brought the Lady Morwenna with me as a favour to Sir Raoul. She is um, favoured by him, and he wishes to take her with him to France, when he returns shortly. Quite frankly, she is in danger from the King's men until Sir Raoul can return from Cornwall by land and plead with the King for her life. It is difficult I know, but can I entrust her to you until Sir Raoul can arrive here to collect her."

"I can do that, Brother. I will look after her here, but I cannot shield her from the King's men if they come for her."

"Of course, but they should not. They will not know she is here until Sir Raoul returns. I, however, must return to Winchester to report to Bishop Odo and meet Sir Raoul."

"God speed then, Brother. You may leave the Lady Morwenna in our care."

"My final need is a horse. I would pay you for one, my Liege."

"No, indeed, Brother, I will lend you one. We have many fine horses here. Now drink and eat and I will have one readied for you."

William stood and summoned a steward. He ordered a horse made ready for Prious. Morwenna took Prious' hands.

"Thank you, Brother. Whatever happens now I owe you for everything."

"I am sure you will be safe here, My Lady, until both Sir Raoul and I can come back to collect you. God bless you, my Lady."

Prious kissed her hand and left the room with William.

+++

Sir Raoul and Jory entered Exeter by the South Gate. The soldiers on guard there seemed to be expecting them. As soon as they announced themselves one disappeared towards the castle. The officer of the guard at the gate offered to lead them to Rougemount and Sir Baldwin De Redvers.

They were led into the Bailey and were greeted by an honour guard who stood rigidly as they dismounted.

Their officer slapped his arm across his chest in salute and addressed Sir Raoul.

"I bid you welcome, Sir Raoul, on behalf of the garrison of Exeter, and also offer congratulations on your victory at Tawton. If you would follow me, Sir."

"Thank you, but please, first, be sure to look after my squire and my horses."

"They will be offered the best accommodation we have, Sir Raoul."

"Good. Be sure they are."

He was led up the steps into the large wooden Mott and ushered into the main hall where Sir Baldwin was awaiting him. He jumped to his feet as he saw Sir Raoul enter.

"Sir Raoul, welcome, welcome, and congratulations on your victory at Tawton. Simple effective tactics I hear, and a classic couched lance charge. Wonderful."

"Thank you, my Lord Sheriff. The twenty Conrois under my command were all excellent men. It was their victory really."

"You are too modest, Sir Raoul. Sir Breon sent two messengers to me immediately after the fight with a full briefing. I was given all the detail."

"So it would seem, my Lord, but it will be remembered as Sir Breon's victory. I am, of course, not here. I do the King's will as an agent of Bishop Odo. I doubt history will ever know why Sir Breon was waiting for the Saxons at Tawton ford, only that he was and that his force defeated them."

"I hear you did not pursue the Saxons back to their ships."

"Indeed not, my Lord Sheriff. You have been very well briefed. They were truly beaten, routed almost. We had killed more than half of them and lost very few ourselves. I returned to camp but many chased them to the sea despite my orders."

"But the Princes Godwine and Edmund escaped."

"So I am told, although I am sure not all the Saxon bodies have been examined yet. Do not forget the two Conrois I had positioned to the west returned to join the battle. They wanted to be part of it and I will not fault them for that, but in the unlikely case that King Mark of Cornwall did bring his army east we would have been wide open if every one of us was chasing Saxons through the woodland and tracks to the sea."

"I did not wish to diminish your achievements, Sir Raoul, believe me. There was, however, one or two other matters that were concerning me."

Sir Raoul found it impossible to keep annoyance out of his voice.

"I am sure you did not, my Lord. What might these matters be?"

"Father Waestan is one. I believe you despatched him to Flat Holm. What was that concerning?"

"You know Father Waestan, my Lord. You recruited him. He was in Winchester seeing Archbishop Stigand for Bishop Leofric when I arrived there with Brother Prious. Stigand sent him to Cornwall with Arthur's armour, not knowing, of course, that he had been turned. Luckily he decided to go by sea and took passage on the boat that was to take Brother Prious and me. The detail does not matter, but he was central to us recovering the armour, taking the sword Excalibur and my killing Lord Jowan and his son. With what we learned in Tintagel, we sent him to Flat Holm to question the Lady Gytha there. You will understand, of course, she knows him only as Bishop Leofric's secretary, and loyal to their cause."

"What was he hoping to learn?"

"We do not know. He is there to see what she may tell him, given he will be telling her that her grandsons invaded successfully and were marching on Exeter with King Mark of Cornwall."

"I see. Well that may be connected with the other matter. We intercepted a Friar called Erste travelling with messages for Godwine from Archbishop Stigand. He told us all he knew but it was what he did not know that was intriguing. He said that when they took Exeter they would uncover a secret that would change everything, but he did not know where this would come from. Given what we do know all we could think of was that if he took Exeter he would try to move north and free his grandmother from Flat Holm. Where are you meeting Waestan?"

Sir Raoul hesitated. He could not understand why he felt as he did. He had probably spent too much time in Prious' company, but quite suddenly he trusted nobody but himself. His simple soldier's life had become much more complicated in ways he had never knew existed. He answered Sir Baldwin.

"I told him I would be here for one night then leave for Winchester. If he discovered anything significant, he should return here and report to you, then follow me to Winchester. If he discovered nothing, then he should go straight back to Winchester. We might meet on the road but he would more likely take a more northerly route."

"I see. Well you will remain here the rest of the day then and dine with me tonight?"

"Most certainly, Lord Sheriff. I would be grateful if you would make my squire and horses as comfortable as possible."

"Of course. We have a room prepared for you and hot water should you wish it. Do you require fresh clothes?"

Raoul smiled.

"Thank you, Lord Sheriff, perhaps a fresh shirt for the morning, but otherwise I have become accustomed to my attire. It is more me I feel."

Sir Baldwin clapped loudly and two stewards entered the hall. He beckoned to one.

"Take Sir Raoul to his room. Make sure he has everything he requires, everything. Then call him in good time to join me for some wine before we dine later."

The steward bowed and turned to Sir Raoul.

"Pray follow me, Sir"

He led Raoul to a room on the far side of the Mott. It was quite spacious and a fire was burning in the hearth. A bath tub stood before it half filled with warm water and a large pan was on a stand by the fire.

"Would you like to bathe, Sir Raoul? I will pour hot water into your tub should you wish it."

"Why not, my man. Who knows when I may next have the chance? Is there time?"

"Oh, indeed, Sir."

Raoul began to remove his sword belt and leather tabard. He felt relaxed yet uneasy at the same time. He wished life were simple again.

+++

Prious rode towards Winchester. He was not in a hurry, indeed he really was not looking forward to arriving. When he did he would have to see Bishop Odo and tell him of his travels from leaving Winchester until to his return. Quite how he could explain events between Sir Raoul and Morwenna he was not sure. He could only tell the truth. Bishop Odo was too astute to fall for any falsehoods, and it was very dangerous to lie to him because he probably already knew the truth of what you were going to tell him.

The day passed slowly. Prious rode into Bishop's Waltham. The village stood outside the Manor of the same name. It had been granted very many years before to the Bishop of Winchester, and was therefore now owned by Archbishop Stigand, who despite his promise to the Pope, in return for release from his fifth excommunication, he had still not relinquished.

It was a pleasant village and at its centre was a fine old inn, of which Prious was very well aware. He dismounted outside the inn and a stable boy ran too him.

"Can I look after your horse, Brother?"

"You may, my lad. Rub him down, feed and water him, and have him ready in an hour, or perhaps a little more."

Prious entered the inn and looked around. A few tables were occupied, but most were empty. It was only noon if that. Prious sat at a table in the middle of the room and looked around him. The only other customers were much older than him and seemed disturbed by a monk in their presence.

The innkeeper came to his table.

"What can I get you Brother? We have some hot broth and fresh bread if you wish to eat."

"Yes, that would be excellent, and wine. Have you some good wine? I feel like some good wine."

"I can do that for you, Brother. Are you travelling to Winchester?"

"Indeed I am, on the King's business, and that of Bishop Odo. I would be grateful therefore of your best service."

"That you shall have, Brother, I assure you."

The innkeeper scurried away and Prious smiled inwardly. That would set some hares running in Archbishop Stigand's own home village.

Prious enjoyed his food and particularly the excellent French wine he was served. He ate slowly and drank more than was wise at mid-day, but his mood was such that he might have drunk more.

He paid the innkeeper and walked outside into the afternoon sun. The lad had his horse waiting, looking well brushed and refreshed. He overpaid the lad and mounted his horse. He rode slowly out of the village towards Winchester. He was certain news of his coming would be there before him, both to Odo and Stigand.

He reached the edge of Winchester in the late afternoon. His head was heavy with his mid-day wine and he could not face an evening of having to think too clearly. There was a pleasant looking inn on the edge of the city. He dismounted and sighed. A quiet night was called for, another glass of wine or two, then he could face what was to come tomorrow.

+++

When Waestan left the inn at Crucaern shortly after dawn, his guards had already left the town. He mounted his horse and took the track to Dorchester. It was an easy day's ride but he wanted to get there and find an inn near the centre of the town where Sir Raoul would find him easily. Having experienced their welcome in Crucaern he was wary of their welcome in Dorchester. He was Saxon, a priest from Exeter, but he would need to pave the way for Sir Raoul.

He rode steadily all day, stopping only briefly around noon, and arrived in Dorchester in the late afternoon. The edge of the town seemed quite normal, but as he rode into the centre the damage and destruction became very apparent.

The middle of the town had been burnt to the ground and was still being cleared. Some buildings were already being rebuilt and some were as yet untouched. Waestan assumed their owners were dead. In the middle of it all stood an inn, almost untouched except for smoke damage. The Normans had left it unharmed for their own use.

He halted and dismounted outside the inn. He tied his horse to a rail as no lad had approached him. He untied his pack and entered. It was empty except for three or four young girls in their late teens and a man in his late forties or early fifties who rose to greet him.

"Hello Father, can I be of service?"

"I hope so. Are you the innkeeper?"

"That I am, Father. I keep what remains of it."

"I see. Do you have two rooms I can have for tonight, and possibly tomorrow?"

"Indeed I do, Father. One is for you, I assume, and the other?"

"I am to wait here for a friend and travelling companion who I hope may arrive today, if not tomorrow, but I will pay for the room for tonight whether or not he arrives."

"Very well, Father, if you so wish."

"Yes, well, I am Father Waestan, a Saxon and cleric to Bishop Leofric of Exeter."

"I have heard of Bishop Leofric, and as a Saxon you are welcome here. Who are you expecting to join you?"

"I am awaiting a close friend of mine, a knight."

"I will have no Norman in this inn, and indeed should it be learnt there was a Norman knight staying here I would not be responsible for his safety."

"I would expect no more, but this knight is not Norman, he is French, Sir Raoul Tyrrell of Radepont. He is no more Norman than I am. You will know when you see him. He looks like no Norman you will have ever seen."

Waestan prayed Sir Raoul would still be wearing his leathers and had not cut his hair. The innkeeper smiled at him.

"As you are a Saxon man of God I accept your word, Father. I will try to spread the knowledge so there are no misunderstandings."

"Thank you, my son. Now I have a tired horse outside. Do you have a stable and a lad that can look after him?"

"Yes, Father. I will instruct my lad. We only offer service these days when I know which of our guests are welcome."

"Excellent. Take me to my room then and I will rest a while before this evening and a meal. If my companion should arrive, call me at once, of course."

"Follow me then Father, your room is this way."

+++

Raoul was woken from an afternoon sleep by a knocking at the door of his room. He had bathed, which was a pleasant and rare luxury on his travels. He sat up on his bed and swung his legs around to the floor. He was half dressed in leggings, leather over wool, but had no shirt or tabard. He called out.

"Yes. Come in."

The door opened and a young lad in livery opened the door.

"My Lord Baldwin invites you to join him, Sir, for wine before dinner is served."

"Thank you, boy. Tell him I am on my way."

The boy bowed and backed out of the door. Raoul was looking forward to a relaxed evening and a good meal but was also aware one had to be very careful what one said in such company.

He dressed quickly in a clean shirt and his heavy leather tabard. He fastened his sword belt around it with his two fighting knives and opened the door. Another young liveried lad stood outside the door.

"If you would care to follow me Sir Raoul, I will take you to my Lord, the Sheriff."

"Pray lead on, my boy."

It was not far across the wooden castle Mott. Raoul was sure he would have remembered his way back to the hall, but it was nice to be led. Sir Baldwin rose from his chair beside the fireplace as Raoul was shown in. A large table was laid slightly away from the fire but the boy led Raoul around it to where Sir Baldwin stood. The boy bowed and moved away.

"Good evening Sir Raoul. Are you well rested?"

"I am indeed, my Lord Sheriff, both clean and rested."

Sir Baldwin laughed and poured Raoul a large goblet of wine.

"I hope this will be to your taste, Sir Raoul. It is some I have had imported from the east of France, the Rhone Valley. I am sure you know of it."

"I do indeed, my Lord, but rarely have I drunk it. Your health."

Raoul took a mouthful and rolled it around his tongue.

"Mmm, very good, my Lord. I have been told much of the Cote de Rhone, north of Avignon, but have never travelled there myself."

"Nor I, Sir Raoul, but its wines have always been a favourite of mine."

Throughout the evening and the excellent meal that they were served, their conversation was polite small talk and not at all contentious. Sir Raoul felt at ease but did not let the wine dull his mind.

As the food was cleared away Sir Baldwin poured more wine and leant forward at the table.

"Tell me, Sir Raoul. What happens next?"

Immediately Raoul was alert. He felt his heart beating in his chest.

"Well, as I told you earlier, the first thing is that I must leave early tomorrow for Winchester and report to Bishop Odo and then the King, if he wishes."

"Oh, I am sure he will, after your success at Tawton, but after that, what is in your mind."

"That will depend on what the King or Bishop Odo might have in mind for me, but if there is nothing immediate, I will return home to Radepont in France."

"That would be a loss to the King, I am sure. There are many challenges ahead for him. Unrest in the north will be his next issue, I feel sure."

Raoul was now becoming very uncomfortable. Sir Baldwin was starting to gently question him hoping the wine would relax him enough to tell him something of interest.

"You know far more of such things than I, my Lord. I am a soldier and no more. I am not one for affairs of state and do not pretend to understand such things."

Raoul lent back in his chair before he spoke again.

"My Lord, I cannot thank you enough for your hospitality tonight. I must ask you to excuse me now if I retire. I wish to travel as far as possible tomorrow so I wish to leave with the dawn. It has been a pleasure to meet you, my Lord. We may meet again, we may not, but I am in your debt."

Sir Baldwin stood with him and clasped his arm.

"It has been my pleasure to meet you, Sir Raoul. I wish you a safe onward journey. I will have your Squire and horses made ready for first light."

"Thank you, my Lord. I am most thankful."

As Raoul left the hall a boy bowed and led him back to his room. Raoul thanked him and entered his bedroom. He could feel his body relax as the tensions of the evening drained from him. He undressed and lay on his bed. Sleep took him almost before his head touched his pillow.

He slept well and awoke desperate to fill the pot behind the screen in the corner. He walked across the room and did just that. As he moved out from behind the screen he heard a knocking on his door.

"Yes, I hear you. What do you want?"

"It is shortly before dawn, Sir. I was told you wished to be roused to leave at dawn."

"Thank you, I am awake. I will be ready shortly."

"Thank you, Sir."

Raoul sat on the edge of his bed for a while and settled his thoughts. He would like to reach Dorchester this day but he had to be realistic. It was too far, he could not do it. He had made it clear he wished to reach Winchester with all speed so he needed to keep up the pretence and leave early.

He dressed and left his room. A steward was waiting outside and led him towards the Mott gate. Just inside the gate a room had a table laid with bread and meats. Just inside the door were some saddlebags. Raoul took one and filled it with both. There was also some jugs of wine with large cork stoppers. He took two and squeezed them into another saddlebag.

He hung them over his shoulder and left the castle Mott, descending the steps down to the bailey where Jory was standing with their three horses. That day Jory had his courser loaded with their packs and he added the saddlebags of food and wine.

Raoul mounted the horse from Tintagel and Jory mounted his palfrey. Apart from the normal guards there was no-one there to wish them farewell, so Sir Raoul led Jory towards the castle gates and out into the city. He took the path to the east gate and they left the city riding towards the rising sun.

They rode steadily all that day. They rested around noon and ate well. Jory had gathered some food in Exeter too, but the wine was a special extra. They rode on through the afternoon and until the sun began to become low in the sky behind them.

Raoul was sure they were beyond half way to Dorchester but well short. They had followed the coastal road, skirting the coast but south of the most commonly used easterly road. They arrived at a small coastal town of Cernemude with dusk. There was a small inn there and Raoul decided to stay there rather than camp in the open. The locals were welcoming enough and they were comfortable until they left early the next morning. Raoul was determined to make good time that day to Dorchester.

+++

Morwenna was at a loss how to feel. In the last few days her security had been totally with Brother Prious. She had never felt completely secure but Prious seemed to have her best interests at heart. What she was sure of was that Prious was loyal to Sir Raoul so she felt secure in his company. Now he had left her here with William Mauduit who she did not know at all and she was afraid.

He showed her to a suite of rooms at the rear of the manor which were more than comfortable and she settled into them during the morning. A steward brought her some food around mid-day and she rested through the afternoon. In the evening she was summoned to a family meal. William and his wife were there with their two sons and daughter and she actually enjoyed her evening meal with them.

As the meal came to an end she excused herself and returned to her rooms. She pulled the shutters across the windows and sat in the candle light beside the fire. It was warm enough but she was desperately lonely.

She thought of her father and her brother. Her chest filled with emotion and she burst into tears, lonely mournful tears. She had not really comprehended their loss whilst traveling, and the boat had been so uncomfortable she had been too busy trying not to be sick. She stood shakily and ran to the bed. She threw herself on it and curled up, knees under her chin. She always did that as a child when upset or frightened.

She tried to calm herself by thinking what Raoul would say if he could see her now. He would hold her and cuddle her. Another wave of tears hit her.

She heard a gentle knocking on her bedroom door and a voice. It was William's wife.

"Are you well, my dear? Can I get you anything?"

Morwenna steadied herself and took a breath before replying.

"Yes, I am well, thank you, and no, I have everything I need, thank you again."

"Good, but if you do think of anything, please come and find me. Even if you just want some company and to talk for a while."

"I will, thank you."

She knew she should have opened the door and let her in but she could not face that now. The tears had stopped though, at least for a while. She closed her eyes and thought of Raoul and the wonderful evening she had spent with him. Sleep took her before the tears could begin again.

The Eighth Scroll

Prious woke early but was in no hurry to rise. He had not slept well for the last few hours. He had fallen asleep easily enough after a good meal and more wine, but he had woken after four or five hours as he guessed and had to get out of bed and use the pot in the corner.

He climbed back into the bed and lay on his side. He knew what was coming. His mind filled with the past few days' events and how he was going to tell Bishop Odo of them. Odo had so many sources of information. He knew so much anyway that lying to him was very dangerous. At least Odo had very little intelligence from Cornwall but Prious could not be sure how little.

Odo had a large pigeon loft and it was surprising sometimes how quickly he heard things. He certainly received messages that way from Exeter but Prious was not aware that he had a contact in Cornwall. Prious was sure he would know if Odo did because Odo would surely have told him, so he could contact Odo urgently if he had ever needed to. That, however, was Bishop Odo's strength. He could not be sure.

No matter how Prious tried, his thoughts would not let him sleep and the dawn light was just rising when he finally fell asleep again. He did not sleep for long so now he just lay on his back as the light grew to full daylight and he heard movement within the inn.

He had decided the simple truth was all he could tell. His real dilemma was what he said about Morwenna, but he could only try to delay. If the Bishop or the King decided to act before Raoul himself got back to Winchester he did not know what he could do.

Finally he rose and dressed. He wet his face in the basin by the window and opened the shutter, but the window looked out of the rear of the inn and the house next door was almost touchable. There was little to look at.

He gathered his few possessions into his pack and tied them ready for his horse and carried them down to a fine breakfast with a pleasant ale that the inn brewed themselves beside the stables. He arranged with the innkeeper to have his horse prepared and brought to the front of the inn and paid for his food and drink. He had paid for the bed the evening before when he arrived.

He thanked the innkeeper and left by the front doors. A lad held his horse and four Familia Regis cavalry men formed an arc behind them. The one with a sash threw his right arm across his chest in salute.

"Good morning, Brother Prious is it?"

"Indeed it is. Why do you ask?"

"We were sent to welcome you back to Winchester and to escort you safely to the castle where His Grace the Bishop Odo is looking forward to greeting you."

Prious laughed out loud and mounted his horse.

"That is very kind of his Grace. I was on my way to see him."

"It is not my business Brother, but I rather gather he had hoped to greet you last evening."

Prious laughed again. He could see the cavalry men each looked concerned.

"My friends, this life sends us challenges, all of which I enjoy, but I also enjoy a chance to catch one's breath between them. Now lead on, I shall enjoy your company and hopefully now I will not get lost in the centre of Winchester. I would hate to arrive in the Cathedral grounds whilst trying to reach the castle."

He laughed out loud again, but rather felt his humour was missed by his escort.

+++

Raoul and Jory were awake and away early the next morning. They rode hard all day. They passed many small towns and villages but did not stop. Raoul was determined to reach Dorchester as soon as the horses could manage. He was determined to meet Waestan who he was sure was there by then.

They rode into the edges of Dorchester in the late afternoon. It was quiet and all seemed normal until they entered the middle of the town. The devastation was profound. Raoul looked around him and wondered at the wanton destruction, by fire mainly. He had fought many battles, but they were all soldier to soldier, set piece fights. What he saw around him that afternoon was more than he had imagined. Jory looked around awestruck.

"This is unforgivable Jory. Whilst we are here you are French and my squire. Understand?"

"Yes, Sir. Normans did all of this?"

"They did, my boy. I can only imagine the loss of life of townsmen, their women and children that went with it. Done by many of the men we fought with at Tawton I know, but I am afraid it sickens me."

As they reached the centre of the town a large inn became obvious, well preserved amongst the destruction around it.

"I will lay money we will find Waestan there. See the horses settled when we arrive and I will find you lodging inside. I do not wish any misunderstandings. If the townsfolk think we are Norman we will have a problem."

They rode up to the front of the inn. A young lad approached them.

"Greetings. Would you be Sir Raoul Tyrrell de Radepont, French knight and companion of Father Waestan of Exeter?"

"I would be, my lad, what of it?"

"I am instructed to welcome you, Sir Raoul, to show you in and to give your horses and squire the very best of attention. Father Waestan arrived yesterday and awaits within."

Raoul dismounted and gave his reins to the lad. He looked up at Jory.

"Help the lad with the horses then bring our gear inside, yours too. You deserve a decent bed tonight."

He turned away and entered the inn. Waestan was sitting on the far side of the room in a bow window with a mug of cider before him. He leapt to his feet as he saw Raoul.

Many others looked up as Raoul entered. The innkeeper was talking and drinking with some local townsmen, and a number of young working girls sat with them. Raoul was a new sight to them all. He wore his black studded leathers with his sword belt and knives at his waist. His long dark hair hung over his shoulders. He was unlike any Norman knight they had seen. He must be French. They had never seen a French knight.

Waestan walked quickly towards him and embraced him.

"I am so pleased to see you, Raoul. I was not even sure you had survived any battle. What happened?"

"Get me some wine and a mug of cider for my squire and I will tell you all, but first I will sit on anything else but a saddle."

He made his way to the window table and sat opposite where he had seen Waestan sitting. Waestan spoke to the innkeeper then returned to the table.

"So tell me, my friend, what happened."

Raoul told Waestan of everything that had happened since Waestan had left Tawton. He described the battle they had fought and how he was disappointed at the Normans' behaviour when he ordered them to let the Saxons leave. They were soundly defeated and he was disappointed by the bloodlust that had ruled most of them.

Waestan could do nothing but sympathise. What he had seen and experienced crossing Somerset had upset him, and once he had arrived the day before and spent a night and a day in Dorchester he was ashamed to have any connection to the Normans.

The innkeeper had brought some very good red wine and a mug of cider as Jory entered the inn and walked to their table. Raoul pushed the cider mug towards him.

"Take that, my boy, and find yourself somewhere to sit whilst we discuss the business we have."

"Thank you, Sir."

"Now, Waestan, my friend, where does one piss in here."

"Through that door on the right of the bar. There is a latrine dug along the wall out there."

Raoul went to the door and relieved himself outside. He returned and went to the innkeeper.

"I need your assistance, and will pay handsomely for it."

"Certainly, Sir. How can I be of service?"

"Well firstly, I need an extra room for my squire, Jory. He has served me well and I owe him a good night."

"I can do that, Sir, we are not full."

"Indeed, but most importantly, I want one of these pretty young ladies to look after him tonight, all night. Most importantly though, I do not want him to know I am paying for her services. She is to have him believe she is attracted to him and just a local girl. Do you understand me?"

"Yes, Sir, I do, and it shall be done. What of yourself, Sir, do you desire company this night?"

"No, I do not. I have much to discuss with the Father and have travelled too far for anything but sleep. Do you need payment now?"

"No, Sir, the morning will do well."

"Very well. Thank you, and more drinks for our table, and the boy."

Raoul returned to Waestan.

"So now, my dear friend, you have heard of my doings, what of yours?"

Waestan looked at Raoul and sat back in his chair. He looked up at the ceiling beams and sighed. After a moment he sat forward as if he had suddenly come to a decision.

"I went to Flat Holm and saw the Lady Gytha. She is old and frail but very sound of mind. I told her that her grandsons had invaded and met King Mark of Cornwall and were marching on Exeter. I told her they had sent me to her for the news they had instructed me to ask of her. At first she insisted she would tell her grandsons when they came for her and she was returned to Exeter. I told her that in all such matters time could be of the essence and eventually she told me."

Waestan paused and Raoul's first reaction was to press Waestan, but some instinct made him hold back and wait. Waestan continued.

"I have lived with this knowledge now for a few days and nights and have not slept much because of it. I have seen so much of what Norman rule can be, our inevitable future or not. Then I meet you again, someone who I have learned to trust, and you tell me of Norman bloodlust on the battlefield. I have to say I have thought long about whether I should tell anyone of what I know. To be completely honest I am still in some doubt. However, you have become my friend, and I have come to trust you in such matters, so I will tell you and it will up to you what we do with the knowledge. I only wish Prious was here also."

Again Waestan sat back, almost inviting Raoul to say something.

"Father, I am not sure of my own feelings towards the Normans either. I have served and fought for King William, I have been knighted by him, and I have done all he has asked of me except that I have spared the life of Morwenna. I have yet to plead with him and Bishop Odo for her life. I too am uncertain of my loyalties, but all I can promise you is to try to do God's will and remain true to what I feel is just and right."

"That is why I have decided not to hide it from you, my friend."

The innkeeper arrived at the table with more wine and cider. Raoul thanked him but was almost shaking with anticipation.

"Father, you were saying."

Waestan stared at the table top in front of Raoul, then looked up at him.

"King Harold is still alive and is hidden under the King's nose in Winchester."

There was a moment of silence whilst Raoul absorbed what he had heard.

"Alive, you say, but how?"

"According to Gytha, he was badly wounded, losing an eye to archers and sustaining a second chest wound. He was carried from the field and his brothers fought on until they were killed. After the battle they could not find Harold's body and Lady Edith, his wife, was brought to Senlac by Duke William to try to identify him. She identified a body whose face was mutilated beyond recognition, saying she knew it was Harold by marks on his body only she would know of. The body was eventually buried as King Harold, but it was some other poor knight."

Raoul stared at Waestan, his mind racing. Surely this could not be true.

"So why, Father, do his grandson's not know this?"

"I asked Gytha the same question. She said if anyone knew it would finally become known and the search for King Harold would become so intense he would eventually be found and killed."

"That I am sure is true. So where is he?"

"He is in the home of an old Moorish healer in the centre of Winchester, in the shadow of the Cathedral. He was seriously wounded and is still not fully recovered from his injuries."

"Who else knows the truth?"

"Only the Lady Gytha and I know where he is. Not even Edith Swan's-neck knows that. The only people who know he is alive is Gytha, Edith, you, me and Archbishop Stigand, although he believes him to be hidden in London."

They sat in silence for many minutes. Raoul's mind was alive and Waestan was worried about having told him. Eventually Waestan broke the silence.

"What do you think we should do?"

"Nothing for now except return to Winchester and think. If we tell the King or Odo, Harold will be killed without doubt. They cannot have the defeated King of England alive to be a figurehead for rebellion. If he returns to health and remains in England it can only lead to civil war and to more killing."

"My thoughts exactly. I keep wondering what Prious would say."

Raoul smiled and saw the monk in his mind.

"I will tell you what he would say. He would say that we do not need to decide yet. He would say to leave the decision until it needs to be taken. The best decisions are made with all the knowledge available, so if a decision is not immediately needed, wait and see what more knowledge comes to you."

Waestan laughed and took a mouthful of cider.

"Yes, indeed, I can hear him saying exactly that. Thank you, my friend, I might now sleep tonight."

"Good, then let us decide one thing only here and now. We must keep this a solemn secret between us both, until we again discuss what we should do, hopefully with Prious also. Agreed?"

"Most definitely, my friend. Most definitely."

"Excellent, then let us eat, Father, and eat well, then to bed and an early start for Winchester. Prious will probably be there by now and I must join him. It will take us two long days in the saddle to reach there, I believe, and my fear is how long Prious can protect Morwenna before I can get there to protect her."

+++

Prious smiled to himself as his escort of four Royal Guards, true Familia Regis, set off at a trot. He very deliberately walked his horse behind them. They soon stopped waited for him. Their leader rode back to Prious and spoke.

"Brother, the Bishop wishes to see you urgently, we must make haste."

"His Grace will have to wait until I arrive. I will travel in my own time, hopefully in your company. When we are close to the castle I will find an inn where I can take a room and stable my horse. From there, we will walk to the castle and I will be delighted to report to His Grace the Bishop. I have much news for him but none that needs to be delivered in haste."

The Guardsman stared at him. He could not believe what he had just heard. To him, Bishop Odo's instructions were sacrosanct. He could not believe someone could ignore them this way.

"Then I can only ask you, Brother, that when you meet His Grace, you explain that we did all we could without physically accosting you, to bring you to him in haste."

"Do not be concerned, my man, I will tell him."

The Guard turned his horse away and walked into the city. Two guards dropped back behind Prious and two led the way. They almost reached the castle by mid-day, and Prious saw the inn he had in mind. It was well known and had a large sign with a painted Stag's Head above the door.

Prious reined in outside. He dismounted and looked for a stable boy. A young lad ran towards him.

"Can I help you, Father?"

"If you belong to this inn, indeed you can, but it is Brother. I am a monk not a priest."

"I am sorry Brother, but yes, I belong to the inn."

"Excellent, then take my horse and look after him well. Bring my pack inside whilst I take a room and enjoy some lunch."

He gave the boy a coin and turned towards the guards.

"I am going to enjoy some food, will you join me."

They looked at each other before their leader spoke.

"We cannot possibly, Brother, as you well know. Two of us will wait here whilst I and one other will report to His Grace, who will be very unhappy."

"Well tell him from me that if it is so urgent that we speak, join me here and I will buy him his luncheon."

The guard looked at him incredulously and turned his mount away towards the castle.

Prious knew he was building up problems but he was hoping that if the Bishop was really angry with him, Odo's normal sharp mind might be blunted a little.

He entered the inn and found the landlord. He took a room for at least two nights and perhaps more. The innkeeper was delighted and promised he would have rooms if his companions should arrive in the next few days.

Prious ordered some food and a large goblet of wine. Too much wine was a problem, but one large glass calmed the nerves and sharpened the mind, and he would need both that afternoon.

+++

Morwenna lay staring at the ceiling as the daylight grew in her room. She had slept better than she could have hoped, but having woken to the dawn chorus she could not sleep again.

Her mind was fixed on Raoul. Her stomach was tight and tingled when she thought of their time together, her breasts felt every movement against the linen of her nightdress. If Prious was correct he might arrive late tomorrow or the day after. It was not that long after all. The thought of Raoul holding her consumed her and she gripped her stomach with her hands.

She heard a gentle knocking at her door. The door opened and a young maid quietly entered the bedroom. In the half-light the maid saw Morwenna sit upright in her bed.

"Oh Ma'am, please forgive me. I thought you were still asleep. I have come to make up the fire for you and to put some water on to warm. I can come back if you wish."

"No, no, please do so. Thank you."

Morwenna lay back. Her thoughts of Raoul would remain just thoughts. Her hand went between her thighs and she was very wet. Her fingers lingered for a moment but she heard the maid at the fireplace and the spell was broken again. She suddenly saw her friend Elowen in her mind, standing beside her. She laughed as she spoke to her.

"Come on, Morwenna, enjoy yourself, be yourself."

Morwenna sat up and smiled. She would miss Elowen.

"Excuse me Ma'am. The fire will build now and warm the water, should you wish some warm water to wash. My Lady Jenifer has asked me to call you when breakfast is ready."

"Thank you, yes, please call me when it is time."

Morwenna rose slowly and used the warm water to wash herself. She was still very unhappy but there was nothing she could do. She had thought of leaving the household and trying to reach Winchester by herself but she was alone and had no money. She might miss Raoul and be worse off.

She dressed herself and sat on a chair near the window, looking out at the water. It was not as spectacular as the Cornish cliffs but somehow the water was soothing. There was a knocking at the door and the maid entered.

"Excuse me Ma'am, the lady Jenifer invites you to join her for breakfast."

"Thank you. One moment and I will be with you."

Morwenna gathered herself and her thoughts. The Lady Jenifer? She had not heard her name the night before but she had seemed pleasant enough, and she had come to her room last evening to see that she was well.

She followed the maid from the bedroom and down the stairs to the hall. As she entered she saw the Lady Jenifer, as she now knew her, seated at a large table with breakfast food spread before her. There was no sign of her husband William or her sons, or indeed, her daughter. Her hostess stood as she saw Morwenna enter the hall and turned towards her.

"Oh, my dear, welcome. Come and sit down and join me. You must be hungry now. Come, come."

She settled Morwenna in a chair beside her at the table.

"Please, choose what you would enjoy and fill your platter."

"Thank you, my Lady, I will."

Morwenna looked at the spread before her. The Lady Jenifer already had a platter filled with food and Morwenna could not but think there was enough laid on the table to feed the household for luncheon too. She took some cooked meat and a cold egg. She paused then added a little cheese and some fresh bread.

"Good girl. Now enjoy your breakfast. The menfolk are out hunting and my daughter Steren has not risen yet, but in truth, there is not much here to rise early for."

Morwenna smiled and began to eat as Lady Jenifer started to talk to her.

"Well, my dear, I hear you have travelled from Cornwall. I know nothing of it. Is it a nice place to live?"

Morwenna spoke between mouthfuls.

"Oh yes, my Lady. Cornwall is a small Kingdom, surrounded on three sides by sea and the fourth side is bounded by the river Tamar for the most part, that separates us from Devon, but there is some land between the Tamar and the end of Devon which no-one really knows who has claim to. That piece of land and Cornwall, or Kernow as the locals would call it, have never been part of England. Many know it as Little Wales, or West Wales. The Cornish language is Celtic and close to Breton or Welsh, even Gaelic."

"It is so good to learn about this land. I have only been here just over a year. The good King William gave these lands to my husband for his loyal service at Senlac and before, not as a soldier but more as a planner and administrator."

"I am sure that is a very important role to a King."

"So how was your journey, my dear? It was a long way surely?"

"Indeed, my Lady. We travelled by horse from my home at Tintagel, on the north coast, down to the south coast at Tregony, and then by boat for three days and two nights to here. I am not a good sailor so it was not a pleasant trip."

Morwenna felt her strength ebbing. She paused and poured a small glass of wine. She took a large swallow and a mouthful of bread to follow.

"And what of your family, my dear?"

Morwenna stopped eating and sat rigidly at the table. Tears appeared in her eyes, she could not help herself.

"Forgive me, my Lady, I have no family. Not anymore."

Lady Jenifer took Morwenna's hand across the table and gripped it gently.

"I am so sorry, my dear, I did not know."

Morwenna was too naïve to realise that the Lady Jenifer was questioning her, searching for anything she did not know about.

Morwenna let the tears subside a little.

"I lost my mother, my elder sister and youngest brother to fever. The last few years have just been my father, my brother and me. Until a few days ago."

Tears took her again. Lady Jenifer squeezed her hand.

"Take your time, my dear. You are obviously still very upset. It might help to tell me about it."

"Oh, my Lady, I am sorry. You see my father and brother got caught up in a rebellion against King William by King Harold's sons and King Mark of Cornwall. They were to use the legend of my family ancestor Arthur. They had his sword and armour. It all seems so stupid now."

"No, no, my dear. It is so difficult for us women when our men get involved in such things. Please, carry on."

"Well, from what I understand from Prious, he was sent with Sir Raoul Tyrrell to our home by King William. Prious was to recover the armour and Excalibur and destroy them, and any records of Arthur."

Morwenna stopped and tried to breathe between sobs. She was staring at the table. She looked up at Lady Jenifer.

"I am so sorry, this is very difficult for me."

Jenifer squeezed her hand again.

"I do understand. Here, have another mouthful of wine. There is no haste."

Morwenna did as she was told and tried to smile.

"Thank you, my Lady. It is difficult because Sir Raoul was sent to kill my father, my brother and myself."

"Oh, my goodness, that is awful, but you are still alive."

"For what it is worth, yes I am. You see we fell in love. It really was love at first sight, or so I still believe, but then, my brother found us, Sir Raoul and I, in bed together, and attacked him. Raoul was unarmed and my brother was going to kill him. I hit my brother with a metal candlestick and killed him. I did not mean to, but I could not let him kill Sir Raoul."

She sat in silence, her wet eyes glazed. This time no tears came. She shuddered and spoke again.

"Sir Raoul made me get ready to leave and went to get Prious, which he did, but he also went upstairs and killed my father and our steward. I did not know, of course. I helped us escape the castle and Prious brought me here, telling me the truth on the way. Sir Raoul went to fight the Saxons. I do not even know if he is still alive. He promised to come to Winchester to beg the King for my life and to take me to his home in France."

Lady Jenifer released Morwenna's hand and leant back in her chair.

"Oh, my dear, dear girl. I do hope he loves you as much as you do him."

"I know he does, I know he does."

Jenifer stood and turned towards the doorway.

"Eat some more and have more wine. You need to get your strength back. I will return shortly."

If she could repeat all she had heard to her eldest son and get him away by noon, Bishop Odo would hear it all late that evening or early tomorrow morning at the latest. It sounded to her that this Sir Raoul had just used Morwenna, but then if that were so, why had he not just killed her once they were out of the castle? She could not help thinking the poor girl would not have long to live anyway. If King William had ordered Morwenna dead, she had never heard of him changing his mind about anything, let alone anything such as this.

+++

Raoul awoke at first feeling refreshed. He had slept well and deeply. He had not realised how tired he had become after the relentless pressure of recent days. He had been on edge since he left Winchester with Prious. It seemed so long ago but was actually less than two weeks.

Reality returned to him. The weight of the recent knowledge he had gained fell back upon his shoulders. King Harold Godwinson was still alive. The consequences were enormous. Next his mind flashed to Morwenna. He felt a wave of guilt that he had not thought of her first. She had hardly been out of his mind since he left Tintagel.

He looked slowly around the room and felt a cold feeling of foreboding. Whatever happened next, he must reach Winchester and see Bishop Odo and the King. They would have to listen to him. He had done all else they had asked of him and given them a great victory over the rebels and the invasion in the south-west.

He found himself sitting up in his bed. He rose and washed the sleep from his face. A quick breakfast and a quick departure for Winchester. Jory should be up and have the horses ready. Raoul almost regretted his gift to him, which he would never admit. This would test his loyalty.

When Raoul descended the stairs and entered the inn, Waestan was sitting in their window seats awaiting him.

"Good Morning, Sir Raoul, I have ordered us some breakfast and some saddlebags of cold food. If I read your mood from last evening, I feel we may be traveling with minimum stops to Winchester."

Raoul laughed and joined him at the table.

"My dear Father, you read me perfectly. Yes we will eat well and then stop only briefly tonight. I wish to reach Winchester with every haste. Have you seen Jory?"

"Not to speak to, no, but he is about. I am sure he will have the horses ready."

As Waestan spoke the inn door opened and Jory entered. He approached the table and bowed to Sir Raoul.

"Sir, the horses are ready when you are. They are packed and I have loaded food and water for both ourselves and the horses."

"Good lad. We will eat and join you. Make sure our packs are loaded too."

"I will Sir, have no fear."

"Oh I have none, my boy. Did you have a good night?"

The way Sir Raoul asked made Jory wary. There was a look in his eyes that Jory had not seen before, and if he had to guess, it was mischief.

"I actually had a wonderful night, Sir. Good food, good cider and good company."

"I am delighted to hear it, my boy. We will join you shortly."

Jory nodded and left the inn. He had had a wonderful night and little sleep. The young lady involved had been too good to be true. She stayed with him all night and had been more accommodating than he could have possibly hoped. He had imagined for a short while it was his personal charm, but that would have been too perfect. When Sir Raoul had asked him, the look in his eyes told him it had been his doing, and he felt all the more loyal to him for it.

It was not a long wait before Sir Raoul and Father Waestan joined him. They had paid for their rooms and their food and drink, and were ready for the journey ahead.

"I apologise now, my friends, we have a long journey, and I intend to travel as fast as our horses and ourselves can do so. We should reach Winchester by tomorrow evening if all goes well. Let us away."

He led Waestan and Jory out of the town at a trot. Jory led Raoul's courser loaded with their packs. They were all determined to reach Winchester as soon as was possible.

+++

Prious could delay no longer. He stood from the table and walked towards the innkeeper. He handed him a coin.

"Take this. It will more than cover my wine and meal. Just in case I do not return as planned."

He smiled broadly at the innkeeper who thanked him with a puzzled look on his face. Prious paused.

"Oh, I have every intention of returning, and you have my horse, of course, but my employer may have other ideas."

Prious walked out of the doorway and into the narrow street outside. Two guards were standing beside their horses and quickly mounted as they saw him.

"Lead on my friends, I will walk behind you."

One guard walked his horse away but the second gestured to Prious to follow the first and fell in behind him. The inn was almost at the castle gates and they arrived in moments. The gates were open and the other two guards were mounted in the Bailey and waiting for them.

Their leader dismounted and called to Prious.

"Follow me Brother, His Grace awaits you."

He led Prious up the steps and into the wooden keep on the Mott. Prious recognised the door from his last visit with Raoul. The Guard knocked and waited. After a short pause they heard the Bishop's voice.

"Enter."

The guard opened the door.

"Brother Prious, Your Grace."

Prious entered the room. There was a fire lit and the room looked the same as before except that now it had a chair behind a heavy writing desk where Bishop Odo sat reading a parchment. There was no other chair so Prious stood patiently before the desk. He could not imagine that Raoul would arrive before evening the next day, so the longer everything took the better. After a few moments Odo put down the document and looked up at Prious.

"Well, Brother Prious, have you stopped playing children's games."

"If you have, Your Grace."

Odo thumped the table with his fist and stood up leaning across the table at Prious.

"I am your Bishop and half-brother to the King of England. I play with people's lives doing his bidding, and for now, Brother Prious, playing with you has ceased being fun."

"My apologies, Your Grace, but I returned from Cornwall to report that I have carried out all the King's wishes. I did not believe there was anything that needed to be so urgently reported."

"It is not for you to judge what is urgent. So tell me of your journey and of your success."

"I will gladly, Your Grace, but I would ask that after all that has happened and with a long story to tell, would Your Grace kindly allow me to sit to tell it?"

Bishop Odo sat back down and stared at Prious. He was trying to see through Prious. He was hoping to assess what Prious was attempting to achieve. The monk had always been loyal to him. He was always intelligent and did an excellent job, so why did he seem so determined to upset him? Perhaps this trip had changed him.

Odo picked up and rang a small hand bell on the desk. A guard opened the door.

"Bring a chair for Brother Prious."

"Yes, Your Grace."

The guard almost hesitated as he left the room, leaving the door open. He was gone for a very few moments before he returned with an armed dining chair. He re-entered the room and placed it opposite Bishop Odo at the table. He glanced at Prious with a look of disbelief and left the room. Whatever this monk had done to upset the Bishop, Odo had respect for him.

The two men looked at each other across the table. As their eyes met, Prious spoke.

"Your Grace, before I begin, do you have any news of Sir Raoul. As we parted he was leaving for Exeter expecting to fight the Saxon Princes. Have you heard anything?"

Bishop Odo sat and looked at Prious. His own mind was racing. Somehow Prious challenged his intellect in a way he was not used to. He calmed his temper and tried to relax himself.

"I have had news by pigeon from Exeter. Sir Raoul won a great victory at North Tawton against the Saxons with Sir Breon. I have no details. The Saxon Princes escaped and some blame for that may lie with Sir Raoul for not following up his victory, but I do not have enough evidence to judge one way or the other. He is alive and on his way east to report."

That at least was good news to Prious, until then he had no idea for certain whether his friend was alive or dead.

"Thank you, Your Grace. Let me then report."

Prious had thought of little else but this moment since he had left Cornwall. He told Odo the whole story. He told him of killing the guards on the boat, of their planning with Father Waestan and the journey to Tintagel. He was sure Odo would have some intelligence and if he lied he would be immediately under suspicion.

He told of their time in Tintagel. He explained how Sir Raoul had got involved with Morwenna and how her love for him had led to their escape after Raoul had killed Myghal and Lord Jowan. Now, of course, came the difficult part.

He explained that Sir Raoul had become fond of Morwenna having used her to help them escape and so committed himself to beg the King and Bishop Odo to spare her life. In return he would take her to France. He had, of course, to admit to bringing her and leaving her in Portsea. He omitted to say Porchester. He should have known that was a mistake. Everything else was true, and he had carried out his mission completely and successfully. The armour, sword and family history were destroyed, and at the bottom of the Fal at Tregony.

"Well Brother, it would seem you carried out your King's wishes. It would appear that Sir Raoul has done everything as instructed, and more at North Tawton, except kill the girl. Has he gone soft?"

"No, Your Grace, not exactly. In every other way he has served you well, and it is fair to say that without his support, and personal bravery, I would never have completed my task."

"What of this Priest, Waestan? What is your opinion of him? He is traveling now with Sir Raoul having visited the Lady Gytha at Flat Holm. He is a tricky one, that priest. He was a church man, one of Bishop Leofric's circle and he has been seen with Archbishop Stigand. Sir Baldwin de

Redvers swears he has changed sides and is our man now, and indeed, your account would suggest he is our man, and yet even you had doubts at times."

"Overall, Your Grace, I see him as an ambitious cleric who sees King William and the Norman dynasty as the future. He is Saxon, of course, and therefore always under suspicion."

"A fair assessment, Brother. I will have to see what he reports from Lady Gytha. The problem is he will need to report to Archbishop Stigand too, if we are to maintain his position of being our eyes and ears within Stigand's circle. Should I hear that he tells Stigand anything he does not tell us, or indeed, anything he does tell us, I will have him killed. As for Sir Raoul, he has been such a loyal servant and friend to the King in the past, I cannot believe he has put us in this position. I will talk to the King tomorrow. I am sure he will not let the girl live. There is no point to anything we are doing about this Arthur figure if any of his bloodline continue to live. As for Sir Raoul himself, it is up to him if he wishes to make himself a problem. No one is bigger than the Realm."

Prious stood and leant forward, taking Bishop Odo's hand and kissing his ring.

"Thank you, Your Grace. It has been my pleasure to serve you, and I thank the good Lord that I could do all you asked of me."

"So you keep reminding me. Stay close, Brother Prious. I may need your services again shortly."

"I will, Your Grace. Your guards know the inn close by where I have a bed."

Prious left the room. The guard outside led him to the oak doors of the Keep. Just before he reached them Prious held the guard's arm. He pressed a gold coin into the guard's hand.

"Now listen, my son. I am staying at the inn just along from the castle gates. What time does your duty end?"

"Midnight, Brother."

"Then at one minute past midnight you will visit me in the inn and tell me whoever His Grace sees between now and then. If you fail to come or tell His Grace of our arrangement, it will not be gold you feel in your palm but cold steel in your throat. Understand?"

"I do, Brother, I do. I prefer the gold in my hand. I will see you after midnight."

"See that you do."

Prious walked down the steps to the base of the Mott and across the Bailey to the castle gates. It was quite late in the afternoon when he returned to the inn. It would be a long evening until midnight.

+++

The Lady Jenifer did not return before Morwenna had eaten enough and had waited as long as her patience allowed. She took a variety of cold food and wrapped it in a large napkin. It would be perfect around midday.

She returned to her bedroom to find the maid had made her bed and was putting more logs on the fire.

She spun around and stood as Morwenna entered the room.

"Oh, pardon me, my Lady. I will leave you in peace."

"No, no, please. Wait before I drop all this."

Morwenna placed the napkin on the table exposing all the food it held.

"Oh, my Lady, I would have brought you some luncheon."

Morwenna laughed.

"I was not going to risk going hungry when there was so much food there. The menfolk are out hunting and the young Lady still sleeping, I understand."

"Perhaps that is so my Lady."

"Now listen, sit yourself down here beside me. What is your name, my dear?"

"I am Evette, my lady."

"You are not a Saxon girl then."

"No, my Lady, I served the family in Normandy and they brought me here when they were granted these lands. It was better for them to bring their own household who knew Norman ways, than to train local girls once here."

"I can see why, perhaps, that is so."

Evette looked into the fire for a moment then looked back at Morwenna.

"The rest of the family were in the back of the house at breakfast this morning. I think the Lady Jenifer wished to speak with you alone. I believe the eldest boy, Gregan, is leaving for Winchester."

Morwenna sat silently and tried to think. It was no good, she could not cope with intrigue and plotting, but she was frightened.

"Sit with me and tell me about yourself, Evette. Where were you born?"

The two girls spoke for most of the afternoon. Evette was concerned she would be missed but Morwenna insisted she should stay. If questioned, she should say that the Lady had demanded she stay. By the late afternoon the girls had got to know much about each other. Evette insisted she must go as her duty was almost over.

Morwenna begged her to return for the evening, after dinner, if there was to be one. As it was, a meal was sent up to her room as dusk fell. Morwenna ate alone and sat back near the fire until there was a soft knocking at the door. Evette entered quietly and at Morwenna's invitation, joined her in a chair near the fire.

They talked until late. Morwenna told her about her home and mostly about Sir Raoul and about her evening with him. Evette had dreamt of a knight coming and falling in love with her. Morwenna's story was every young girl's dream, except, of course, for the death of her father and her brother.

"Tell me, Evette, what is your first duty in the morning?"

"On rising, my Lady, I would come to your room to make up the fire."

"Then stay here with me. Sleep with me here and keep me company."

"That would not be proper, my Lady. I should never have stayed this long."

"Nonsense, who will notice?"

"Oh, my Lady, I would love to but..."

"No buts. If anyone asks I insisted. I order you to stay!"

Morwenna laughed and Evette joined her.

They both undressed and climbed into Morwenna's bed. They cuddled each other and talked until they slept. It was almost childhood innocence. They both slept dreaming of Sir Raoul. Morwenna had described him so well.

+++

Raoul pushed them hard all day. They stopped and slowed only for the horses and to relieve themselves. They ate in the saddle. Raoul and Waestan had packed some cold food but it was unnecessary, Jory had packed plenty and left it easily accessible as they rode. Dusk fell before they turned off the track to the left and into some woods. Raoul led them through the trees away from the track. When they reached a small stream, he led them to the right until they reached a shaded clearing.

"We'll stop here. We'll light a fire and sleep under the trees. It looks like it might rain."

It was the first words Raoul had spoken for hours, or any of them in fact. Jory jumped down and tied his two horses to a tree branch.

"I will light a fire. I have brought some dry kindling but we will need to collect some wood to burn through the night. Waestan swung his leg over his horse's neck and slid from his saddle.

"I will do that."

He tethered his horse and wandered into the trees, relieved himself and began to gather loose wood from the ground.

Raoul dismounted and settled his horse. Jory would feed and water the horses when the fire was lit. Raoul was troubled and concerned, but he could tell Waestan was not himself either. They needed to talk. He joined Waestan in collecting some wood.

They returned to the clearing and dropped the wood beside Jory who had used his flint to light the kindling and start the fire.

"When that is lit see to the horses, make sure we have enough wood and find us all some food."

"I will Sir. You and Father Waestan just sit here by the fire and I will see to everything."

Raoul looked at young Jory. They were getting used to each other and Raoul was beginning to understand he did not need to instruct Jory anymore unless he needed anything out of the ordinary. It upset Jory to be told to do what he felt was his normal duty. He put a hand on Jory's shoulder.

"I am sorry, my boy, just carry on. You know what needs doing better than I."

Jory nodded and smiled warmly.

Raoul took his blanket from his horse and spread it under the edge of the trees close to the fire. Waestan was already settled there and spoke as Raoul sat beside him.

"We need to talk."

"Indeed, Father. I have felt your discomfort grow through the day. I was not sure whether it was the pace of our travel or if something was troubling you."

"Oh, the travelling is no problem to me. I have become used to that since we met. No, it is the burden of the secret we carry and my fear of reaching Winchester."

"Fear? A strong word, Father. What exactly worries you?"

"It has been on my mind all day, every moment of it. I thought I wanted status, to be a Bishop one day, perhaps, to be part of those that rule our country, but meeting you and Brother Prious has made me see what so much of it is about. I simply cannot cope with the intrigue, the plotting, it is not as I imagined."

"I am just a soldier, Father. I do what I am ordered."

"You are far more, a knight and a clever mind, and a leader of men. No, you see I just do not think I can cope with arriving in Winchester. I will have to see Archbishop Stigand and Bishop Odo, but who do I see first, and what do I tell them. If either discover I have not told them everything or that I have told anything to the other, I will be killed. Knowing what we know I could well be killed by either for knowing too much. If I tell them nothing and later either of them questions Gytha, and then learns that she told me, I am dead too."

Raoul smiled at Waestan.

"Father, I understand your dilemma, but I am not the one to help you with it. Brother Prious is the one to guide you in such matters. We will see him tomorrow evening, before we see anyone else. We will enter Winchester quietly and find him before anyone else knows we are back."

"But there is more, my friend. I have always felt the Normans are the future and that they will rule for very many years to come, and I still do, but I have seen the other side of them. The death and killing they seem to spread."

"It is war, Father, conquest and putting down rebellion."

"No, it is more. Senseless, most of it, and enjoyable to them. I do not wish to be part of it, but as a Saxon, I realise the futility of trying to fight them. I am completely lost as to what I should do."

They sat in silence for a few moments as Jory began to water and feed the horses. Raoul built up the fire a little then sat back down.

"Well as I say, Father, Brother Prious is the one we must talk to, but I promise you this. I will not be staying in England. I am going back to my home in France with Morwenna. You are welcome to join me in Radepont. Now where is that boy with our food?"

Waestan looked away. His eyes were filled with tears he did not wish his friend to see.

+++

To Prious it had seemed the longest evening of his life. He sat in the inn with wine and enjoyed some excellent food. A home-cooked lamb stew with some vegetables which he thoroughly enjoyed.

As the evening carried on some local musicians arrived and a sing-along began. It made the time pass a little quicker but midnight seemed to never arrive. Eventually the Guard he was expecting entered the inn and looked around until he saw Prious at his table in the corner. He wound his way across the crowded bar and sat next to Prious, who had a jug of wine and a goblet ready for him. The guard poured himself some wine, took a mouthful and spoke.

"Good evening, Brother."

"Good evening, my man. What news have you?"

"Little, Brother, but it might mean something to you."

"Then pray tell me."

"The only visitor His Grace received was a young man from Porchester, Gregan, the son of William Mauduit. I could not hear what he reported but the Bishop thanked him and called for me. He ordered me to arrange for him to see the King at breakfast and to summon two Knights to be ready to see him for duties immediately after on his return from seeing the King. Otherwise, Brother, there is nothing to report."

"That is enough, my son."

He handed the guard another gold coin.

"Be gone now. This meeting never happened."

"Indeed not, Brother. For both our sakes."

Prious nodded as the guard left his table. He would be amazed if someone at the inn did not know him or the guard and report their meeting in the morning. In the meantime he must stay a step ahead.

Brother Prious woke just before dawn and rose immediately. Washing and dressing as quickly as he could, he packed his bundle and went down for the early breakfast he had ordered the night before. He ate well but did not delay. He could see Raoul and Waestan in his mind doing the same and leaving their camp wherever they had stopped, which indeed they were, but he had never met Jory and did not know of the great advantage he was to them.

Prious paid his account and spoke to the innkeeper.

"I may well be back tonight, I do not know, but if you are asked, I am still in my room. You will discover I have gone if you are sent to fetch me."

"I understand Brother. God Bless you."

"I think I may need his blessing this day. Thank you my son."

Prious left the inn and mounted his horse. It was just becoming light as he rode out of Winchester. The streets were clear and deserted but were slowly coming to life. He could see no uniformed guards but that did not mean necessarily mean he had left unseen.

He had decided to ride westward to meet Raoul and Waestan. He was sure they would be traveling east as fast as they could because Raoul would have Morwenna on his mind. He was also sure, therefore, that they would be taking the shortest route along the coast road. They had no reason to believe they should hide their progress.

As Prious left Winchester he saw the road ahead had two tents, one on each side of the road, a troop of some six or eight palace guards between them, stopping all those along the road. He had little time to think, but decided leaving Winchester was not a problem immediately. Arriving back would be. He must reach Raoul and divert him south to Porchester and Morwenna.

As he reached the road block a sergeant of the guard stood before him and halted his horse.

"What is your business on this road, Brother?"

"What right have you to ask me, my son?"

"I ask as a palace guard under the orders of the Bishop Odo."

"Well, I am about the King's business, so pray stand aside and let me pass."

"The King's business is the Bishop's business."

"Not so, my son. All the Bishop's business is the King's business, but not all the King's business is Bishop Odo's. Now stand aside and let me pass, or prepare to suffer the wrath of your King."

Prious stared at the sergeant and settled his horse as it stepped backwards.

"Pass on then, Brother. I will report your passing."

"Please do, my son."

Prious kicked his horse on along the track. Odo would hear of his departure but not for some hours, and he would have to think about it. Was there perhaps some business of the King's he did not know about? One thing Prious did know for certain, however, was that his life as he knew it was over. If he could reach Raoul in time he could divert him to Porchester. There had been no point in him going there. He could not have protected Morwenna against two determined knights, even if he had tried to run with her. He had to tell Raoul and send him. He must ride towards them until he found a suitable place to wait where he could not miss them.

+++

Bishop Odo also rose with the dawn. He was attended by two boys who washed and dressed him before bringing him some breakfast. He would eat shortly with the King but food would not then be in the front of his mind.

He left his rooms and walked to the Great Hall where he found King William with William Fitz Osbern. They were just beginning their breakfast.

"Ah, Your Grace, come and join us. You wished to see me I believe."

"Indeed Sire, if this is a good time?"

"Of course it is, sit down. Ah, and here is Robert. Good morning my brother, join us too. It is not often I have both my brothers at breakfast."

Robert, Count de Mortain, sat with them at the table and acknowledged Odo and Osbern. Odo he could stomach, as a half-brother he had some family loyalty, but he loathed Fitz Osbern, bedfellow of his other half-brother, the King.

"Well, Bishop, you asked to see me. What is your business?"

Odo was annoyed. He had hoped to catch the King alone. If he had, he might have persuaded him to have some leniency in the matter, but with Osbern and Robert there he would have to be seen to be strong.

"It is concerning Sir Raoul Tyrrell and the daughter of Lord Jowen of Tintagel. Sir Raoul has killed Lord Jowen and his son as you ordered, Sire, but my man Brother Prious brought the daughter, the Lady Morwenna, back with him and I heard late last night, has left her with William Mauduit in Porchester. His son brought me the news."

"Mauduit, yes, I granted him those lands after Senlac."

"Indeed Sire, and loyal to you again, he has reported events to you."

"So what is this Prious and Sir Raoul up to?"

"Well Sire, as you are aware, Sir Raoul has given you a victory over the rebellion and invasion in the south west. As we ordered, you will remember, Sire. He killed the rebel Lord Jowan and his son but he is on his way to us, Sire, to plead for the life of the daughter. He wishes to take her home with him to France."

King William looked around the table then back at Odo.

"What is wrong with the man? He carries out his other orders, wins a great victory, and then goes all soft over a woman. No, Odo, have her killed. What is the point in all the trouble we are going to in order to stamp out any history and the blood line of this Arthur, if we let her live. No, have her killed."

"Yes Sire, I will arrange it immediately."

"Then think what we should do with Sir Raoul. He has been a loyal servant and I owe him my life, but we cannot have someone choosing which of my orders to obey."

The King lent across the table and took Robert's arm.

"You have always had an interest in this Little Wales, or Cornwall is it, have you not, my brother?"

"Indeed Sire, I have."

"Then I shall make you Earl of Cornwall."

"Thank you, brother. I had rather hoped to be Duke of Cornwall. It is ruled by a King, Sire, King Mark."

The King grinned at him.

"Then take Little Wales for England. Dethrone this King Mark, subdue and control it, and I will make Cornwall a Duchy."

"Thank you, Sire, I will."

"Good, now Odo, be away. Get rid of this girl and find me Sir Raoul and this monk of yours."

"I will, Sire."

Odo left the hall and returned to his office. He sat at the table and rang his bell. A guard appeared at his door.

"Fetch me Sir Piers Gavonne and Sir Paulo Sorella. Tell them to come with all speed. They should be in the refectory awaiting my summons. Oh, and summon Gregan Mauduit too. Make haste."

He sat back and looked up at the ceiling. He was annoyed now. He had opened the door for his half-brother Robert to make a move on the south-west. Robert knew only too well the tin that was found there, and some gold and silver as well.

His thoughts were interrupted by a loud knock on the door. It opened and the Guard entered.

"Your Grace, Sir Piers, Sir Paulo and Gregan Mauduit."

"Send them in."

The guard stood back into the doorway and the two knights strode in, standing opposite his desk. Gregan Mauduit entered and stood respectfully behind them.

Sir Piers spoke first.

"Good morning, Your Grace. Sir Paulo and I are here to do your bidding."

"Indeed, Sir Piers, you are. Step forward young man."

Gregan Mauduit moved between the two knights and stood before Bishop Odo.

"You do your family proud my boy, and you must tell your father so. Your King thanks you, and your family, for your loyal service."

"Thank you, Your Grace, I will tell them so."

"Good lad. Your next task is to guide these two knights to your home in Porchester with all speed. God bless your journey. Now leave us whilst I instruct them."

"Thank you, Your Grace, I am your servant."

He bowed and left the room.

"Now, Sir Piers and Sir Paulo. Your King requires you to follow this young man back to his home with all speed. When you reach there you will find with them a young girl named The Lady Morwenna of Tintagel. You will kill her. There is no mercy nor respect to be shown. She is an enemy of the Throne whilst she lives. Do you understand your orders?"

Sir Piers answered.

"We do, Your Grace. Your instruction is most clear."

"Then be away. Treat the boy well, he is a loyal servant of the King, as is his father and his family. Treat them well but do your duty."

"We will, Your Grace."

The knights turned and left the room. There was another knock at his door. The guard entered.

"Your Grace, there is a report from the road block on the west road."

"A rider reports a monk leaving Winchester early this morning on the King's business. The guard knows him as the Brother Prious, Your Grace."

"Thank you, leave me."

Again, Odo leant back in his chair and looked aloft. Prious, riding west. Probably to meet Sir Raoul, but this was worrying. No Norman knew more about Cornwall than Prious. On the King's business? Did Robert or the King have a hand in this? Odo was uncertain and did not like the feeling.

+++

Prious rode along the west road for a little over two hours in his estimation until he came to a roadside inn. A double sided picture of a lamb's fleece swung above the door. He had seen it before on his travels and he decided this was where he would wait for his friends.

He was worried that if he kept riding west he might miss them. They might turn off the track for some reason and he might miss them. At his most optimistic guess of their progress they would not be here yet, but they could be close. On the other hand, it could be well into the afternoon before they reached there. The inn stood beside a bridge near Romsey, which he had just ridden through. The bridge crossed the river Test and seemed the ideal place to wait. Unless they took a more southerly path and less direct path, they would have to cross the river here. Given the urgency of their journey he was confident they would be on this road.

He dismounted and sat outside the inn. A young man came out and greeted him. Prious ordered a jug of wine and a jug of ale and two mugs, and asked that his horse be fed and watered.

It was a dry day. The sky had threatened rain both that day and the day before. It had not done so thus far but was very warm and humid. He quietly thanked the good Lord above and smiled at the young man as his drinks arrived.

"Is there anything else I can get you, Brother?"

"No, my son, but if I am still here after noon, a meal will be in order."

"Certainly, Brother. I will see your horse is attended to."

Prious poured some ale and took a long drink, then poured some wine into the other goblet. He did not often drink ale but he was thirsty. The wine, however, was surprisingly good, perhaps because they were so close to the south coast and easy access to France.

Noon came and passed. The young man brought a platter of bread and cold meats.

"I am sure you will enjoy these, Brother."

"Thank you. I am hoping to greet my guests soon. If you see anyone join me at the table here, please attend us."

"I will, Brother."

Prious finished his food and was going to order some more wine when he saw movement on the bridge. Three horsemen with four horses. He stood immediately. He could not miss Sir Raoul. Even at a distance, his hair and leathers were instantly recognisable. Once he saw Sir Raoul, Waestan became obvious. He did not know the third rider. He looked young and was leading Sir Raoul's Courser which carried their pack.

He waved and called to his friends as they approached the inn.

"What has kept you? I have been waiting hours for you."

Raoul reigned in and looked at the inn. He had been watching the road ahead but knew the voice the moment he heard it.

"Prious. What are you doing here? It is wonderful to see you. Waestan, look who we have found."

Both men turned towards the inn and dismounted with much slapping of shoulders and happy greetings. Jory held the horses as Raoul and Waestan joined Prious at his table.

"Oh, Brother, you do not know Jory. He is my squire and has rapidly become indispensable."

"Good day, my son. You are lucky to be attached to such a noble knight."

Jory replied confidently.

"Good day, Brother. I have heard so much about you and have been looking forward to meeting you, and I am, indeed, lucky."

Jory nodded a bow and turned to Raoul.

"I will see to the horses, Sir, then return to you all."

A cheeky grin spread on his face.

"And before you ask, Sir, cider would be wonderful if they have some."

He led the horses away behind the inn. Waestan laughed quietly.

"Actually, Raoul, cider would be nice."

Prious waved to the young man who had just come out of the inn doorway.

"I will deal with all that, are you hungry?"

"No, thank you, Brother. We have eaten in the saddle. I was trying to make what speed we could to Winchester to see you, and then I must see the King. We have much to discuss first though, but I would do so in haste. Oh, wine for me."

"Two more jugs of the wine please my son. Do you have cider?"

"Indeed we do, Brother. It arrives from Somerset by cart each week. It is…."

"Yes, yes, Two jugs of that then and goblets."

The young man left hurriedly. Prious looked at Raoul.

"It is so good to see you, my friend. There is so much serious business to be said. If your squire returns can we speak in front of him?"

"I have complete faith in him. He is a loyal lad."

"Good, oh, our drinks."

The young man from the inn placed a tray of goblets and jugs on the table.

"These two are the wine, these two the cider."

"Thank you my son. Add it all on my account."

"I will, Brother, thank you."

Raoul reached for a jug of wine and filled a goblet.

"Thank you, Brother. Now, who shall begin?"

"You and Waestan should begin and tell me all your news."

Prious felt a little guilty but he was sure as soon as he told them his news, Raoul would be away to Porchester.

Raoul spoke briefly of their journey and the battle at Tawton. He told of Waestan leaving for Flat Holme and suggested Waestan continued their story. Jory returned and Waestan waited whilst Jory took a goblet and a jug of cider. He sat with them but back from the table, slightly behind Raoul.

Waestan told of his visit to Flat Holme and Lady Gytha. He told of his deception and came to the key to his visit. He paused and looked at Raoul.

"Do you wish to tell Prious, or shall I?"

"It is your secret, Father, you tell him."

"Tell me what?"

Prious could not wait any longer.

"Well, Brother, the fact is that King Harold is alive and still recovering from his wounds received at Senlac. Only Gytha and Archbishop Stigand know that he is alive. Stigand believes he is in London, but in fact he is in Winchester and has been since Senlac."

Prious leant forward and almost hissed his question.

"Where in Winchester?"

"Almost in the shadow of the Cathedral at the home of a Moorish healer called Al Herad. Do you know of him?"

"I do, Father, I do. He is a well-known healer. Many monied people turn to him when all else fails. He holds many secrets of Moorish medicines, herbs and spices, and often heals those who have lost all hope. Others think of him as a warlock, a sorcerer, but he continues to survive because those who doubt him might one day need him. He was brought back to Winchester by a wounded Norman from a campaign in Andalusia."

"Well, Gytha says King Harold has been hidden there for almost two years now. He was taken from the battlefield at Senlac with great secrecy. There was much ado about King Harold's body. No-one could identify it after the supposed death as so many bodies were unrecognisable. King William made Harold's wife Edith Swan's-neck travel to Senlac and identify his body from marks on him that only his wife would know. Only the Good Lord knows who she identified as Harold, but it was not him. He was gravely wounded, most assumed fatally, but this Moor saved him."

Prious sat silently for a few moments.

"I cannot imagine any more important news. This rebellion was not to be just against Norman rule, but to put the Saxon King Harold back on the throne. A much more powerful cause."

Raoul reached across the table and placed a hand on Waestan's arm.

"Now tell Prious what you told me last night."

Waestan looked up at Prious. He could not speak for a moment, but then it all spilled out. His concerns, his doubts, his true inner feelings, he told all in a totally truthful and obviously sincere way.

Raoul looked straight at Prious.

"To be honest, Brother. I feel something similar. Once I have seen the King I will simply return to France and be done with Normandy."

Prious sat back from the table and rubbed his brow. He sat forward again and spoke.

"Dear God, help us all. I too have a serious problem. I have lied to Bishop Odo, or not told him the whole truth concerning Morwenna. I have been found out and risked his wrath and my life further by coming to warn you. Forgive me Raoul, but I had to hear your news first. I left Morwenna with William Mauduit in Porchester. He is an honourable man with a respectable Norman family. Late last night, Mauduit's eldest son arrived in Winchester to tell Odo that Morwenna is at his home in Porchester. I believe this morning, two knights have been dispatched to kill her. There was nothing I could do to stop it. I thought if I came west to find you, you Raoul could go south from here straight to Porchester and might get there in time."

Raoul was visibly shaking.

"Jory, get our horses. Now!"

Jory leapt to his feet and ran behind the inn.

"I do not know what to say, Brother, for good or ill. I must be away. Farewell both of you. I just hope to God above I can reach Morwenna in time."

"Listen, Raoul. Edmon is waiting for us in Portsea. When you leave Porchester meet us there. He is waiting to take us all to France. God speed, my dear friend."

Raoul could not speak. A mixture of concern for Morwenna, anger at Prious, and an inner dread, silenced him. He ran to meet Jory as he brought their three horses to the front of the inn.

He mounted swiftly. He found some words.

"We will ride west to Romsey. There is a track south from there I am sure. All being well we will see you in Portsea. Pray to your God, both of you, that I get there in time."

Raoul and Jory rode out of sight, Jory behind Raoul and leading his courser as a packhorse.

Waestan took a long mouthful of cider and sat back in his chair.

"Well that all happened a little fast."

"I am sorry, Father. I knew once I had told Raoul he would be gone, but I had to know what you had learned first. I just hope it is not too late. I fear it may be."

"So what do we do, Brother? Raoul was certain you would know what was best. You know Normans better than any of us."

"That may be true, but do not forget I am a Breton, a Celt. I am closer to the Cornish, Gaels or Welsh than the Normans. Sometimes I think that it may be their greatest strength. Here I am a Celt, Raoul a Frenchman and you a Saxon, all working for their ends. They see themselves as a superior race, Viking strongmen. I for one have had enough."

Prious lifted his goblet and drank it. He emptied his jug of wine into it then reached for Raoul's jug and filled it again from there. He looked at Waestan and took a large mouthful.

"So again, what do we do now, Brother? Do we follow Raoul south and meet him in Portsea?"

"I fear I owe Raoul more than that. We dare not tell anyone of our secret, if we do it will mean our certain death from one side or the other. If the Normans get wind of it, they will take the Kingdom apart stone by stone until they find Harold and they will kill him. To them he is dead already.

No, we have one option, and that is to go to King Harold and take him with us out of England before anyone else uncovers our secret."

Prious smiled at Waestan.

"What say you, Father? It is your secret after all."

Waestan lifted his eyes from his goblet and stared into Prious' face.

"Raoul said you would know what to do. How do we go about it?"

"It could not be easier really. We simply get back into Winchester, unseen. Go to the healer, talk Harold into coming with us, and leave Winchester, again unseen, for Portsea."

He looked into Waestan's eyes.

"It is that straight forward."

"In that case, Brother, I think I need another jug of cider before we leave."

+++

Gregan Mauduit proudly led Sir Piers Gavonne and Sir Paulo Sorella out of Winchester on the south road. Bishop Odo's words were fresh in his mind and he could still picture him saying them.

It was barely an hour since they had left the Bishop. The two knights had gathered their weapons and their horses hastily. They took little else with them. They discussed their mission briefly and decided they would only be away for one night and back the next day. Their task seemed easy enough and the Bishop's words were clear. "They need show no respect." It seemed they might get some pleasure from their task.

They rode all day without a break. Gregan was certain they would arrive in good time for an evening meal if nothing untoward happened, and indeed the sun was only low in the western sky when they rode into Porchester Castle.

+++

Prious and Waestan rode through Romsey and took the main Winchester road. Prious knew where the road block was that morning and they were well short of that. If it was there in connection with them they were looking for Raoul and Waestan's return. They knew he had left Winchester and had probably met his friends, warning them they would be arrested when they reached the capital. There was a chance Odo would have lifted the block, or he might have set up blocks on the side lanes in case they left the main road. Prious turned his head towards Waestan who was riding beside him and a little behind him.

"We will turn off the main road here and head due east until we meet the main road south of Winchester and ride in from there."

205

"As you advise Brother."

"Well, this is one of those situations where I could out-think myself and over complicate things. I could end up trying to be too clever. No, instinct tells me to keep it simple."

"Very good. I am all for a simple life."

Prious saw the large smile on Waestan's face and laughed with him.

"Me too, Father, me too."

They followed farm tracks and crossed rough ground keeping the sinking sun at their backs until they reached Winchester's south road. Prious turned north towards the city and called to Waestan.

"A large part of me says we should just go south now to Portsea. Are you sure you want to do this bit with me?"

"Oh yes, I'll come with you. I would just get into trouble without you, get lost or some such. Anyway you need my luck and sharp brain, and, of course, my persuasive tongue."

Prious nodded.

"That I do. Come then and feel lucky."

They rode into Winchester as the sun was getting very low and the light was fading. Prious led them through the side streets of the capital, away from the castle and around the cathedral. He knew where he was going. There was an inn where he stayed many times when he had not wished it to be known he was in Winchester. They dismounted behind the inn and a young boy ran to welcome them and look after their horses. Prious gave him two coins.

"One for each horse my boy. Do you remember me?"

"Yes Brother, you are not here and your horses are always ready."

"Good lad. Take care of them. They have travelled far today."

They entered the rear of the inn but did not enter the public room. The innkeeper saw them and came to greet them.

"Hello Brother. It has been a while."

"It has my friend. Now listen, firstly take this."

Prious handed him three gold coins. It was a great deal of money.

"Do you wish to buy the inn, Brother?"

Prious smiled at him.

"No my friend. Your boy has our horses. Find me another which I hope we will need. Ready a room for the Father and I for tonight which we may not need however. We may need to leave sooner than I would like, so the extra horse is urgent."

"I will arrange all that Brother, but still I do not need all of this."

"When I leave here I will not be back, my friend. Look on it as a thank you for all the times you have helped me in the past, and then forget you ever knew me."

Prious turned away and led Waestan out before the innkeeper could say more.

"This way, Father."

He walked quickly away with Waestan close behind.

+++

Sir Raoul and Jory stopped by a stream and dismounted to rest the horses. Jory had begged his master to stop. They had pushed the horses hard all day and now the light was failing. Raoul knew Jory was right. They all needed to rest but he was so desperately worried now. In his heart he knew they were too late.

"Eat something, Sir, please. We have a little left. You may need your strength."

"Thank you, boy. You must forgive me but my mind is elsewhere."

"Of course, Sir. We will get there quicker by stopping. We can ride on soon."

"Yes indeed. I am just so angry we went astray. I was not thinking clearly enough. We went too far south before turning east. We have wasted so much time. If anything has happened to Morwenna before we get there I will never forgive myself."

Jory was going to say something but thought better of it.

The Ninth Scroll

Gregan Mauduit rode up to the manor house inside the castle walls and dismounted. He rang a large bell in the doorway and returned to his horse.

"Welcome to Porchester Castle, Sir Knights. Pray dismount and we will join my family."

As he spoke two young stable lads ran around from behind the house in answer to the bell and waited to take the horses. Gregan handed one his reins.

Sir Piers Gavonne dismounted slowly and somewhat clumsily. He was in some discomfort. As they had ridden through the afternoon he could not get his mind away from their task ahead. Their instruction to show no mercy or respect meant they could use this girl before they killed her, and he intended to. The more he had thought ahead, the more aroused he had become, to the point where as they entered the castle gates, with the movement of his horse and the tightness of his leggings, he almost seeded where he sat.

When he dismounted his tabard hung low enough to hide his embarrassment, but his arousal did not fade. As Gregan led them inside, Sir Paulo spoke.

"Are you ready for this, Piers?"

"More than ready. I am going to enjoy it."

"Do not forget there are two of us here."

"There will be plenty of time, my friend, it is just that if I do not go first I will probably seed in my leggings."

Paulo laughed.

"I might have the same problem."

They entered the sizable library off the main hallway. The rest of the Mauduit family were seated around the fireplace and the large table was laid with food. They had been delaying eating in the hope that Gregan might return in time to join them.

As the doors opened they all looked around and saw the two knights who followed Gregan into the large room. His father jumped to his feet to welcome his unexpected guests.

"Welcome, good Sirs. I am William Mauduit, Lord of this manor. This is my wife, the Lady Jenifer, and my youngest son and daughter. Gregan, pray introduce our guests."

"Yes, father. This is Sir Piers Gavonne and this is Sir Paulo Sorella. I have led them here at the King's command, given to me by His Grace the Bishop Odo. He also commanded me to pass on his gratitude for your loyal service in sending me to him with news of the Lady Morwenna. The King is most grateful to you also."

"Wonderful, some wine gentlemen?"

He poured two goblets of red wine and handed one to each knight.

"Are you here to escort the Lady to Winchester?"

Sir Piers answered.

"No, my Lord. We will conclude our business with her here."

A terrible realisation began to dawn in his mind. He looked round anxiously at his wife. She looked away quickly. She too had the same thought, and it was her fault. She had pressed that they should inform the King to ingratiate themselves to him, but she had never dreamed that what she now feared might be the outcome.

William tried to make conversation as they drank their wine.

"Sir Paulo, that sounds of Italian origin. Am I right?"

"Indeed you are, Lord William. When the Pope gave his blessing and a papal flag to Duke William, now our King, I and many others rode to join him on his holy conquest to invade England, and I have remained here with him since. Sir Piers, however, is of true Norman stock."

Piers finished his wine and subconsciously pulled his tabard down. If anything, the wine had just made things worse.

"Where do we find this girl?"

"She is in her room, upstairs. Gregan will show you where. Then Gregan, come straight back down here, immediately."

"Yes, father."

Gregan led the two knights out of the room and up the stairs. He showed them the doors to Morwenna's bedroom. Sir Paulo put a hand on his shoulder and turned him around.

"Do as your father said, boy."

Downstairs, Lady Jenifer looked up at Lord William.

"Surely they will not hurt her?"

"They are here to kill her woman. We should have just let things be until Prious got back, and not meddled in affairs which we knew nothing about."

Gregan re-entered the room. He looked at his parents then sat by the table. The light was fading in the room. It was time to light the candles.

Upstairs Sir Piers opened the bedroom door and walked in. Sir Paulo followed and closed the door behind him. One girl was sitting on the end of the bed in her nightdress. Another was clothed and placing logs on the fire.

Morwenna jumped up off the bed and shouted.

"What are you doing in my room?"

Piers walked towards her.

"You would be the Lady Morwenna then?"

Evette turned to run and help Morwenna but Sir Paulo caught her arm and pulled her to him.

"Just you watch with me, girl, and you need not be hurt."

He held her from behind, his arms pinning hers to her sides, his hands gripping and fondling her breasts.

Morwenna's immediate anger turned to fear. She stepped back but the bed was behind her. Sir Piers grabbed her throat with his left hand and almost lifted her off the floor. His right hand went to the laces of his codpiece which he pulled open.

Morwenna was now panic stricken. Where was her Sir Raoul? In the stories her mother told her years before, he would burst in now and save her.

Sir Piers threw here backwards onto the bed. He lifted her nightdress, kneeling on the bed between her legs as she struggled beneath him. He punched her face and grabbed her arms, pinning her back.

Morwenna was stunned and lay still. He entered her roughly, and for her, painfully. Her mind screamed for Raoul, then she screamed aloud.

Sir Piers had been anticipating this moment all day, and for him, that was what it was, a moment. He was so aroused that after only a few thrusts he seeded into her. As he did, he caught his breath and his hands slipped from her arms. His whole weight came down onto her body but her arms were free. Her hands went to his face. She gouged her nails down his cheeks, drawing blood. Sir Piers pushed himself back off her, slapping her hard. His hand went to his waist, drawing his fighting knife.

"You bloody she-cat. Now feel my claws."

He drove the knife into her side between her ribs and twisted the blade. He wrenched it out of her. Briefly, blood flowed from the wound but then she made a loud gurgling sound and a streak of blood ran from her mouth as her eyes glazed. They stared unseeing at the ceiling.

Sir Piers stood before the wash basin and wiped his cheeks.

"The damn bitch!"

Sir Paulo had become aroused watching Sir Piers and had been pressing himself against Evette.

"Well thank you, my friend. I have never been one for fucking the dead!"

"Then fuck the live one. She's only a servant."

This time Evette screamed as Sir Paulo bent her forwards over the table they were standing beside. He held her neck in one hand and opened his leggings with the other. He raised her skirt and tore away the little she had beneath. He kicked her feet apart and entered her from behind.

"Just enjoy it and I might let you live."

Evette sobbed as he thrust into her. He took some time to seed. When he did he grunted and shuddered.

Sir Piers had walked to the door and opened it.

"Now kill her and follow me downstairs. I need some more of that wine and some food."

He walked out of the room as Sir Paulo stepped back from the table. He wiped himself in the back of Evette's skirt and fastened his codpiece in his leggings. He pulled down the front of his tabard as Evette stood up and turned to him.

"Are you going to kill me now, like poor Morwenna?"

"I should, but I think I will let you live. Perhaps you will have my child to remind you of me, your Latin lover."

He laughed and left the room, following Sir Piers downstairs for the wine and food which he hungered for.

+++

Prious knew where he was leading Waestan. It was not far from the inn but Prious stayed off the main street just north of the cathedral. He still had to pull Waestan into a side alley when he saw three Royal Guardsmen walking towards them. They were laughing loudly and had obviously been drinking but Prious did not want to risk being recognised despite how unlikely.

They arrived at a large wooden door at the entrance of an old four storey wooden house. The alley was narrow and the bay windows on each side seemed to almost touch above them.

A small sliding hatch in the door opened and a woman looked out at them. For a moment Waestan thought she was a nun, but then he realised she was a Moorish woman with a black scarf over her head and a black mask over her mouth and nose. Just her eyes were visible. Her voice was low.

"What is it you wish?"

Prious answered her.

"We have come to see Al Herad on urgent business."

"He only holds meeting during the day, so be gone."

She slid the hatch shut. Prious banged on the door but nothing happened. He raised his hands and slid the hatch back from the outside. He called in a loud whisper.

"Tell Al Herad that if he wishes his royal guest to live he must see us now."

They waited a few moments longer before they heard bolts draw back. The woman opened the door and stepped back.

"Enter."

They did so and she closed and bolted the door behind them.

"Your names?"

"Brother Prious and Father Waestan."

"You are Christian priests?"

"Father Waestan is a priest, I am a monk, but we are both men of the Christian Church."

She looked them up and down.

"You carry no weapons."

It was a statement, not a question.

"Follow."

She led them up a floor on the wide wooden stairs and into a large room towards the back of the house. A Moorish man dressed all in black rose to meet them.

"Come, sit with me and tell me your business."

"The Father and I have come to talk to you and your royal guest."

"So, you believe I have a royal guest. I am not sure how you have come to that conclusion."

Waestan was tired and not in the mood for clever word games.

"Because the Lady Gytha directed me here."

Al Herad's eyes seemed to flash as he heard her name.

"I see, and where did you meet her?"

"On Flat Holm Island where she is held, a prisoner of King William."

Prious interrupted Waestan.

"Listen, we will tell you all but it has been a very long day for us both already and I really do not wish to do this twice. Please summon King Harold here and we will explain all."

Al Herad sat looking at them for what seemed an age. He leant forward and rang a little bell on the table beside him. The door opened and the lady that had showed them in stood in the doorway.

"Fetch Harold, and tell him we have important guests."

She left, shutting the door behind her. After another silence Al Herad spoke.

"You do understand that if I choose not to trust you, I cannot allow you leave here alive."

Prious smiled. Waestan looked at Prious, whose voice was steady.

"I assumed you would be in a position to do so, but we came anyway and unarmed. We are not fighting men and simply here to warn you and help if we can."

He was interrupted by the door opening. A man stood in the doorway. Prious was not sure what he expected but the man certainly did not look like a King. He was quite tall but very thin, not the warrior build King Harold had once been. His hair was long and unkempt and his clothes very plain. The right side of his face was badly scarred and his left arm seemed to hang limply at his side as he moved into the room. Prious knew Harold to be forty-five or forty-six years old, a good age for any man, but this man looked even older and moved slowly and stiffly.

"Good evening gentlemen. You had better explain who you are and how you happen to be here. Indeed, why you are here."

"Hopefully to be of service, Sire. I am not sure how I should address you."

"That will do."

The old King sat carefully next to Al Herad. He was conscious of Prious and Waestan watching him closely.

"I do not move as well as I did. My Moorish friend here has healed my wounds but I will never be anything like the man I was. I should not be alive but for his skills. He cannot, however, work miracles. Now who are you and how did you discover I was alive and here."

"My name is Brother Prious. For many years until recent days I have been an agent of Bishop Odo. I am a Breton, a monk, and have been active mainly in Cornwall. This is Father Waestan. He is a priest and a Saxon and was Clerk and assistant to Bishop Leofric of Exeter until the Bishop's arrest. As such, he carried out many tasks for both Bishop Leofric and Archbishop Stigand. After Leofric's arrest he was turned by Baldwin De Redvers and worked for Bishop Odo too. A difficult position to be in, working for Stigand and Odo."

Harold grunted a half laugh but showed no smile. The left side of his face did not move easily.

"We were sent to Cornwall, me by Bishop Odo and Father Waestan by Archbishop Stigand so we travelled together. We were under the protection a knight in disguise as a sell-sword, Sir Raoul Tyrrell."

"I know him. I am sure that was his name. A young Frenchman, cavalry man. He saved Duke William's life in the battle against the Bretons. I was there, fighting with the Duke. Four or five years ago now. The Duke knighted him after the battle. He fought against me at Senlac, as did his eldest brother, Sir Walter."

"That is the man, Sire. We were involved in gathering knowledge of rebellion in the west involving your sons and King Mark of Cornwall. Everyone involved in the rebellion seemed to believe there was a secret that would change everything, and that would be learnt by all in time. They all said that only your mother, the Lady Gytha, and perhaps Archbishop Stigand, were party to it."

"Yes, my boys are coming to put me back on the throne."

"I'm afraid I have to tell you, Sire, that your sons have been driven back into the sea. King Mark failed to join them and they were met by a thousand Norman cavalry in Devon."

"Are they alive?"

"It is our belief that they are, Sire, back in Dublin by now I am sure, but they will not be coming again, Sire, not after the defeat they suffered. Father Waestan was sent to see your mother on Flat Holm to find out this secret. He was easily able to trick her into telling him you were here and it is only a matter of time before someone else finds out. We are supposed to be reporting this to Bishop Odo as we speak."

"So, we are back to my first question. Why are you here?"

Prious looked at Waestan. He had to tell the truth.

"Well Sire, Sir Raoul is out of favour with King William. He was ordered to kill all the family of Lord Jowan of Tintagel, a conspirator in the rebellion, but he fell in love with the daughter and would not kill her. He also led the Norman cavalry that defeated your sons' forces at Tawton, but once he had routed them, he did not order the survivors killed, hence allowing your sons and many others to flee the battleground, reach their boats and escape. He is now trying to save the girl's life on the south coast having delivered Father Waestan and his secret to me."

Prious was aware of Harold's stare. The old man's eyes seemed to look inside him.

"I helped Sir Raoul to hide the girl and did not tell Bishop Odo of her, and so I have fallen from favour with him. Father Waestan has simply had enough of Norman violence and the intrigue he has experienced. He does not wish to be questioned by Stigand or Odo and possibly be forced or even tortured into revealing that you are alive and hidden here in Winchester. We have a ship waiting for us in Portsea where we are to meet Sir Raoul. We are to sail with him to his home in France. So we are here to offer you passage with us to France. Your cause is lost and it is only a matter of time, perhaps little time, before you are discovered and killed. You will get no mercy from the Normans. As far as they are concerned you are already dead and must remain so."

A silence filled the room. Nobody moved or spoke until Harold sat back in his chair.

"I do not know why I trust you, Brother Prious, but I believe you. I can see that you, Father Waestan, are caught up in something way beyond your experience. When do you leave?"

"As soon as we all reach Portsea. We would leave Winchester now."

"Al Herad has protected me here for almost two years. What think you, my friend?"

"I will hide you here for as long as you wish to remain, but I do believe that every day now the risk of your discovery becomes greater. I too trust these men. They come here unarmed to talk with us. If they are not genuine then they are very brave indeed or very, very stupid. I do not believe Brother Prious to be stupid and I do not believe Father Waestan to be very brave, other than through ignorance. This may well be a heaven sent opportunity to leave the country, given your sons are not coming for you, whichever God has sent it."

Harold stood shakily and looked around the room.

"I think it is time to change things. I will come with you. Can you organise me a horse Herad? I will gather up a small pack and a large purse. If I think about this for too long I might change my mind."

Al Herad left the room for few moments leading Harold out. Prious and Waestan looked at each other but said nothing. Neither could have imagined Harold would have agreed so easily.

Al Herad returned to the room.

"Harold will be ready soon. You have horses I assume?"

"A few moments away."

"I suggest you get them and return. Harold will be ready. You were wise to tell the truth. I have my sources of information. Not all of what you told us was unknown to me. I would not tell Harold but I can do no more for him, and I also believe the longer he is here now endangers both him and my family. Thank you, for good or evil. May your God walk with you."

Prious followed Waestan from the room. He turned back to Al Herad.

"And yours with you."

They did not take long to walk back to the inn. The lad had their horses ready and they thanked the innkeeper. Prious took his arm.

"Thank you again. We will not meet again I am sure. If anyone asks we are upstairs asleep, and if anyone asks tomorrow we left early for London."

"Indeed you did, Brother, and thank you for your custom and your kindness."

Prious nodded and the innkeeper helped him mount his horse. Prious led Waestan back to Al Herad's house and kicked the door twice. The large door opened inwards and Harold rode out, a large hooded cloak over his head and shoulders.

Prious led them south and out of Winchester. Three men on horseback at that time of the late evening was unusual but not too uncommon. They cleared the capital and rode on into the night.

+++

As Sir Raoul and Jory rode towards the old walls of Porchester Castle, Raoul's mind was in turmoil. He still held a little hope that they were in time but deep inside he knew the worst. It was probably about an hour before midnight. They had ridden through the dusk and followed the track in the half light from a bright crescent moon, which threw dark moon shadows despite its small size in the sky.

They reached the open gate in the walls. It had been very many years since it had last been able to close. They stopped in the opening and Raoul studied the large manor house that had been built within the walls. Some windows were lit from within. On ground level to the left of the doorway, four large windows were shuttered but clearly lit from behind. On the two upper levels some light showed in a few windows.

Raoul led Jory towards the large doors of the house and stopped outside, sliding down from his saddle and handing Jory his reins.

"Wait here for me boy. If I do not come back out, ride on to Portsea and tell Prious."

"Yes, Sir, and Sir."

Raoul turned back towards Jory.

"I am here if you need me Sir, for good or bad."

Raoul looked up at Jory and just nodded. His stomach felt knotted.

He walked to the doors and opened one wide. He did not bang on the doors nor ring the large bell, he entered the hallway. It was dimly lit with few candles. He looked around in the gloom. There was almost no furniture that he could see, just a small table near the door and a rack of old weapons against the right hand wall, mainly old spears.

Ahead of him, a large staircase led upwards. There was a passage with a door each side of it. A movement caught his eye on the stairs and he saw the shape of a young woman sitting on the top step. For a moment his heart leapt until he looked harder and he could see it was not Morwenna.

He could hear voices from behind the big double doors into the room on his left. They were loud and raucous. He walked forward and up the stairs. Evette watched him walk towards her. His black leathers gave him an eerie look in the dark and his weapons gleamed in the candlelight. She suddenly thought she should be afraid, but with what had happened that evening she realised she did not care. He stopped in front of her.

"Do you know the Lady Morwenna? Is she here?"

She looked up at him with sad eyes. His face was in shadow from his long hair that hung forward as he looked down at her.

"You are Sir Raoul. She told me of you. You are just as she described. She knew you would come."

He grabbed her shoulders.

"Where is she? Is she well?"

There was a desperation in his voice. She stood quickly, breaking his grip, and turned down the passage to the right of the top stair. She reached a doorway where she stopped and stood aside. Raoul was behind her. She looked up at his face as tears ran down her cheeks. He pushed passed her into the bedroom.

The candles gave little light and the fire had died back but he saw her immediately on the bed. He moved towards her, and as he saw her lifeless eyes staring at the ceiling, he sank to his knees beside the bed and let out a wail of despair that brought Evette into the room. She ran up behind him and held his shoulders as he sobbed helplessly.

She felt him tense as his sorrow turned to bitter anger. Anger at himself and anger at whoever had done this.

Morwenna was lying with her feet just over the end of the bed, her feet wide apart, her nightdress above her waist. There was some blood beside her on the bed from the fatal wound in her side, but Raoul could see that her death had at least been quick. The blade had punctured her heart which had stopped pumping blood out of her.

Raoul gently put his hands under her arms and lifted her up the bed so that her head rested on the pillow. He shut her eyes and kissed her forehead. He moved her legs and feet together and pulled her nightdress down her body, covering them. He took her hands and laid them on her chest. He could see blood on her fingers. She had marked her attacker. He felt a moment of weakness and he lay beside her on the bed, but then as the anger returned, he sat upright.

All this time Evette had been standing beside the bed, crying. She spoke.

"I am sorry. I should have done that."

"No. That was for me to do. I should have got here earlier and it would not have been necessary. What happened?"

"Two knights arrived with Gregan just before sunset. They burst in here. I was with her. One attacked her. He leapt on her and raped her. She scratched his cheeks and he killed her. The other one raped me because she was dead. He did not kill me. The other one told him to. I will make him regret letting me live. Part of me wishes he had killed me."

"I will kill them both. Where did they go?"

"Nowhere. They are in the library downstairs. They will be very drunk by now I expect."

"Who else is in there?"

"Lord and Lady Mauduit and Gregan. The two younger ones were sent to bed earlier."

"How is the room laid out?"

"Through the doors there is an open area, about eight paces, to the table. Between the table and the fireplace are some comfortable chairs, but I suspect they are all still sitting at the table."

"You have a choice to make. You can stay here and remain here after this, or you can come down with me now and go outside to my squire. You can leave with him, with or without me."

He did not wait for an answer. He stood from the bed, kissed Morwenna on the cheek and left the room. Evette hurried after him.

Raoul waited outside the door and steadied himself. He could sense Evette behind him but did not look around. He tried to clear his mind a little. He knew that to fight now, whilst so consumed with anger and grief, was a very dangerous thing to do, but neither would it allow him to wait.

He drew his short fighting knife from his belt and held it point down close to his right thigh where it would not be immediately obvious. If he moved fast and was lucky, he would reduce the odds against him.

With his left hand he opened one door and marched in leaving it open behind him. He walked quickly towards the table. He was lucky. The knight with scratches on his cheeks was sitting sideways on to him on the left. There was nobody in the chairs with their backs to the doors.

Raoul crossed the space from door to the table almost before anyone realised someone had entered the room. The knight he walked towards began to turn towards him as he approached. Before anybody could move or speak. Raoul's hand struck forward and plunged the knife into the side of the knight's neck with such force that its blade point appeared on the other side. He wrenched it forward and it split the knight's throat open.

Sir Piers Gavonne's hands grabbed his throat as if to try and stop the blood that sprayed across the table. He tried to rise from his chair but life left him with all the blood and he pitched forwards onto the table.

Raoul stepped back swopping knives and drawing his sword.

"Who's next?"

It was the first time he had looked properly around the table. He assumed it was William Mauduit that sat on the end of the table beyond the dead night. Next to him around the table was the other knight, then the Lady of the house and to Raoul's immediate right, a boy of sixteen or seventeen.

The two men stood, pushing back their chairs. The knight drawing the sword from his side. He had obviously drunk a lot but surprise, fear, and the death of his friend sobered his blood rapidly. William Mauduit found his voice first.

"Who in God's name are you that walks into my home and kills one of my guests?"

Raoul knew he would have to fight the knight but was not sure about the Mauduits, who were not armed that he could see.

"I, my Lord, am Sir Raoul Tyrrell. I am a French knight who loved the Lady Morwenna. This guest of yours, this slab of dead flesh, raped and killed her. Your other guest, given my Morwenna was dead, apparently only likes live meat, so he raped your maid, Evette."

"I, Sir, am Sir Paulo Sorella. My friend Sir Piers and I were sent here to kill the Lady Morwenna by order of Bishop Odo. She was an enemy of the King."

"She was a young woman, she was no one's enemy save by an accident of birth, and the King did not order you to rape her, or the maid."

"Bishop Odo said that as an enemy of the King, we were not show her any respect."

Raoul had heard enough. He smashed his sword down across the table.

"I am going to kill you, Sir Paulo. Whether anyone else needs to die depends on whether any of you stand in my way."

He moved around the table and Lord William jumped back out of his path. Sir Paulo wisely wanted room to fight and quickly passed Jenifer and Gregan, backing into the open space between the table and the door, facing Sir Raoul the whole time.

Raoul followed him into the open room. He was fighting his favourite way, with sword and long fighting knife. Sir Paulo drew his long knife also.

Raoul swung his sword from above his right shoulder. Sir Paulo parried across his body but jumped back at the same time. He knew about sword play. He too was well trained in the art. They exchanged a number of blows. Raoul was listening for sounds from behind. The Mauduits were not armed but Sir Piers had been. Lord William or Gregan could draw one of his weapons if they dared to.

For the first time in many years Raoul felt a flash of self-doubt. Sir Paulo was very good. Raoul lunged at him and he again jumped back towards the door but this time he stopped suddenly and took a half step forward, an expression of astonishment on his face. He looked downward to see a spear point protruding from his chest.

Raoul stepped back as Sir Paulo's knees gave way. He knelt upright for a moment as life left him then pitched forward to the wooden floor. The speared point hit the wood first, but instead of being pushed back into him it turned him onto his right side.

Behind him in the doorway stood Evette. She had not gone outside as Raoul had told her to do, but seeing the door left open she stood back in the hallway to see what was happening.

She saw Sir Piers die and Sir Paulo rise from his chair and stand to fight Sir Raoul with his back to the door. She saw her chance for her personal revenge and a rage swept over her. She turned and took a spear from the rack on the wall. It was as long as she was tall but not too heavy. She held it level with the ground and stepped into the doorway.

Sir Paulo was fighting with his back to her, two or three steps in front of her. She ran at him, the spear aimed at the middle of his back, but at that very moment he jumped back towards her. Evette almost let go of the shaft as the spear struck. With her movement forward and his backward jump, the spear stuck home harder than she could have managed.

She walked to the body and kicked it as hard as she could in the groin. Sir Paulo could feel nothing but it made her feel much better. She screamed at the body.

"You bastard."

Raoul stepped forward and gripped her shoulder.

"Come, you have done more than enough."

Raoul turned to the table and walked towards the Mauduits. None of them had moved. They had stayed still and watched. They were not a fighting family.

"Sit down, all of you."

Jenifer began to speak.

"Sir, this is all my fault, but I never thought it would lead to this."

Lord William interrupted her with a shout. Jumping to his feet he sounded as if he meant it.

"Shut up you stupid bitch. What in God's name did you think would happened when you get involved in things that do not concern you?"

"Enough. Sit down and listen."

Raoul hung his sword and knife back at his side.

"Part of me says I should kill you all for your part in Morwenna's death. Brother Prious did not ask much of you, but there has been enough killing for now. I am going to leave you alive but heed me well. I want you to bury Lady Morwenna in your chapel grave yard and tend the grave well. I want you to throw the bodies of these two knights into the water to feed the fish. If I return and find Morwenna's grave unattended, or these knights buried near her, I will kill you all."

He almost spat the last few words. He turned around and took Evette by her hand, leading her out of the building.

Jory was still in his saddle. He had been so tempted to try to help his master but knew he must do as instructed. As Raoul appeared at the door his first feeling was of relief, not only had Raoul survived but he was leading a woman out. Jory had never seen Morwenna.

Raoul led the girl to Jory's horse and lifted her up behind his squire.

"This, Jory, is Evette. She is coming with us."

He said no more as he took his reins from Jory and mounted himself. He rode to the gates and stopped, but did not look back. As Jory drew alongside he kicked his horse on.

Raoul rode by instinct. It was a few hours ride to Portsea harbour, and although it was now after midnight, he never thought to stop and rest. He led them a little north until he met the track eastwards. He rode on until he met the main track from Winchester to Portsea and turned south.

He was very tired, both physically and emotionally. He refused to think of anything. His mind felt numb, incapable of coping with all that had happened. He was so full of anger, despair and guilt that he had stopped feeling anything.

Jory became more and more concerned as they rode through the darkness. Raoul was silent and did not seem to even acknowledge their presence. Evette hung on to his waist and seemed to be asleep until she spoke quietly in his ear.

"He seems very troubled."

"He blames himself for being too late to save the Lady Morwenna. I hope when he has time to think about it he will realise there was nothing he could have done differently. He is a great knight. I am privileged to serve him."

"Then I will serve him too. He has given me my freedom. Morwenna told me a lot about him."

Raoul slowed his horse and stopped. There were some lights ahead. Jory rode up beside him.

"That is Portsea ahead. I think we should ride on to the dockside and find the Rhosmon while I can. I need to rest soon."

"We can stop for a while, Sir. I still have a little food."

"No, boy. If I stop now we may never reach the harbour. I will sleep on the boat."

They rode on through Portsea to the dockside. They found the Rhosmon at the far end of the wharf and dismounted. Jory tethered the three horses to a mooring rope as Raoul looked over the boat. The dawn was beginning as he stepped onto the gangplank.

He saw movement in the stern. The crewman who had been on watch had seen them arrive was rousing Edmon, his captain. It was a little earlier than he would normally have woken, but not much, and he was quickly on his feet to welcome Raoul aboard.

"Sir Raoul, it is so good to see you. Are you well?"

"We have been awake and travelling mostly, since dawn yesterday. I need to sleep. My squire, Jory will talk to you. He needs to sleep too."

Raoul walked past him to the stern and lay down. He had not even unbuckled his weapons. Sleep overwhelmed him.

Edmon stepped across onto the wharf and approached Jory and Evette.

"You must be Jory?"

"Yes, Sir, and this is Evette."

"Welcome, both of you. May I ask, where is the Lady Morwenna?"

"She is dead, Sir. Murdered at the King's command by two knights before we could reach her. Needless to say, both knights are dead."

"The poor girl. She was as beautiful as she was innocent of this world. We will care for the horses and unpack them, but have you any idea of Sir Raoul's intentions."

"As I understand it, Sir, Brother Prious and Father Waestan will probably arrive later today from Winchester, tomorrow at the latest, and then we sail for France."

"What of the horses? We could manage these three, but no more. It will take us most of the morning to get them aboard."

"These are the three that matter, the courser the most. The horses that the others arrive on can stay, if they arrive."

"Good, leave it all to us. You must both rest. Eat first if you wish. There will be some hot porridge soon."

"Thank you, no. Evette and I ate in the saddle, but please, promise to waken me if Sir Raoul awakes before I do. He needs taking care of."

"I promise, now get some sleep.

+++

Prious and Waestan rode through the night with Harold behind them. Their horses had at least been fed and watered that evening and had some rest. Harold's they had assumed was at least fresh.

By dawn they had reached the small priory at Southwick. It was newly founded but Prious knew the Prior from many years before. They were welcomed and well catered for. Nobody questioned their business but the monks fed them well and looked after the horses whilst they ate. Prious said their farewells and they rode on after a little over an hour. Prious knew their visit would be reported to Bishop Odo but it would be far too late for him to do anything about it.

They reached Portsea by mid-morning and found the Rhosmon on the far end of the wharf. As they arrived Edmon had two of Raoul's horses on deck forward of the mast and the third was in the air, hanging in a sling as they craned him aboard. They dismounted and watched as the horse was gently lowered to the deck. Edmon came to greet them.

"Prious, Waestan, it is so good to see you again, and welcome to your companion."

Prious replied.

"It is good to see you, my friend. We will introduce our guest later when we are at sea, later this afternoon I hope. I see Sir Raoul's horses are aboard."

"Yes, Brother. He arrived early this morning with his squire and a young lady."

"Morwenna?"

For a moment their hearts rose.

"No, Brother. They are all asleep. Raoul, his squire, Jory, and a young Norman girl, Evette. Sir Raoul was not himself, very distressed."

"Indeed, I can imagine. How soon can we sail."

"Quite soon, the tide is rising, but I can take no more horses."

"I can see that. Waestan, I suggest you take the horses to the church and leave them there. Say nothing, of course. Odo will hear of it tomorrow. Just say they are travellers' gifts to the church. The priest here may recognise you but do not be drawn into conversation. If he presses you tell him you are returning to Cornwall."

Waestan nodded and led the horses back up the wharf towards the church.

"Come aboard and rest. You must have been traveling all night too. I am sure you can make yourselves comfortable without disturbing the others."

The noise and movement did disturb the others. Sir Raoul awoke slowly, opening his eyes to see Prious standing near the mast. He stood shakily on stiff and aching legs but felt better than when he had laid down. He called out.

"Brother Prious, my dear friend, you are here. Will you introduce me to your companion?"

Prious turned and smiled broadly.

"Raoul. I am so glad to see you. Of course, Sir Raoul Tyrrell, this is our guest, Harold."

The old man looked at him and nodded. Raoul saw the badly scarred face and limp arm. He would not have recognised the man if he did not know who he was. He realised Jory had risen and come to stand beside his master.

"We have met before. We fought together against Conan in Brittany. We spoke after the battle when I was knighted. Do you remember Harold?"

"I do. It seems so very long ago now. Now I see your face I remember you."

Prious took Raoul's shoulder.

"I was very sorry to hear about Lady Morwenna. I did not believe the Mauduits would betray her."

Raoul turned away and put his arm across Jory's shoulders as if Prious had said nothing.

"This, Brother, is my squire, Jory. You met briefly at the inn."

Jory bowed to Prious.

"Indeed. Bless you, my son. Your master is very dear to me."

Raoul looked about the deck.

"Where is Waestan?"

"He took the horses to the church."

"Why did you not just leave them on the wharf? They would have been looked after. Why risk taking them to the church."

Prious looked around himself as if looking for support.

"It seemed the right thing to do."

Raoul called to Edmon.

"Get the boat ready to cast off. Sails up and everything ready to go. I will fetch Waestan. I feel very uncomfortable. We sail then for Le Havre and the mouth of the Seine. Arm yourself Jory and follow me. Prious, stay here with Harold. We sail the moment I return."

Prious gripped Raoul's forearms.

"Give Waestan a few more moments and then we will sail, with or without him. His secret is not important once we have left with Harold."

Raoul looked into Prious' eyes.

"I cannot do that Brother. He is our friend."

Prious stood back and nodded. Whilst what he had suggested was the wisest option, he was embarrassed he had said it.

Raoul left the boat with Jory at his heels. Jory wore a short sword Raoul had given him to practice with.

Waestan was in the dockside church. He was sitting in a front row pew with his hands tied behind his back and blood running from his nose and a cut lip.

Remembering his last visit he had led the horses to the stables behind the church and tied them to a rail. He could not see anyone in the stable so he walked around to the church and entered through the open doors. He saw the priest that he had met before.

As the priest turned towards him Waestan heard a noise beside him. Just inside to the left of the church doors, near the baptismal font, stood four Cathedral Guard. They had just happened to have arrived on a mission for Archbishop Stigand that morning and had come to see the priest, who called down the church aisle.

"Father Waestan, how nice to see you again. Did your trip go well?"

Before Waestan knew what had happened the four guards had surrounded him, grabbing his arms. Their Sergeant spoke.

"Well now, that is a name we know. Bring him forward away from the doors."

The other three guards manhandled Waestan up the aisle. The priest stopped them.

"What in God's name are you doing? This is Father Waestan, he works for the Archbishop."

"Ha, he used to. As we were leaving Winchester there was a general order from His Excellency, that Father Waestan was to be arrested on sight with anyone travelling with him. Tie his hands behind him."

"But Sergeant."

The priest tried to stop it but was ignored. The sergeant moved in front of Waestan and punched him hard in the stomach.

"Now then, my treacherous friend, where are your travelling companions?"

Before Waestan could answer the sergeant punched him again, in the face this time. Blood ran from Waestan's nose. He tried to speak.

"I have no travelling companions. I work for Archbishop Stigand. Something is very wrong."

"Indeed it is Father."

The sergeant punched his face again, cutting his lip. Waestan tried to fall but the guards were holding him. They pushed him back into the front pew. The priest began to argue with the guards.

"Is this really necessary? This is a house of God. I will not allow such violence in my church."

Whilst the arguing continued, Raoul and Jory arrived at the church doors and saw what was happening. Raoul pulled Jory aside, out of sight, and whispered to him.

"I need your help, my boy. It is time for you to earn your spurs. Go in there and try to break them up. Do anything to split the guards up, and do not get hurt."

Jory grinned. This was his chance to prove himself. He ran into the church and straight up the centre aisle. The guards heard his footsteps and turned towards him. As he came closer he called out loudly.

"Do not worry, Father Waestan, I will fetch help."

The sergeant shouted to his men.

"Take him, quickly."

The two guards holding Waestan moved towards Jory who ran between the pews and chairs to the side aisle away from them. They chased him as Jory twisted and turned through benches, chairs and pews.

Sir Raoul walked rapidly into the church and up the aisle, his fighting knife drawn and hidden by his arm. He spoke as he approached the sergeant, who looked at Sir Raoul and began to draw his sword.

"No, no. Something is very wrong here. Father Waestan is on important business."

Waestan knew what was going to happen but did nothing except shout at the sergeant who instinctively looked towards him.

"You see, I told you."

It gave Sir Raoul time to step in close and plunge his knife into the sergeant's stomach. He ripped the blade upwards and pushed the dead man away. He jumped at the second guard who too was drawing his sword, bustling him over and driving his knife into his throat.

The two guards that had been chasing Jory had moved into the central aisle with swords drawn and walked slowly towards Sir Raoul and Waestan.

The priest had watched in horror. He stepped forward.

"Not in my church. Not in my church."

Waestan had to do something.

"Come away, Father. Do not get in the way."

The priest moved beside Waestan.

"What is happening?"

"Sir Raoul was evening the odds a little whilst he had surprise on his side. Now it is only two to one instead of four. Now the mind games."

Raoul faced the two guards and began to talk to them as he drew his sword.

"You do not have to die here today. You can leave here now and live, or you can stay and die."

The two men hesitated. One held back a little but the other stepped forward and swung his sword at Raoul who parried the blow with his fighting knife and slashed his sword into the guard's side. The guard grabbed the wound and sank to his knees, blood pumping through his fingers.

"I did warn you."

Raoul brought his sword down across the guard's neck, almost taking his head off. As the body fell sideways the last guard who had held back, turned to run from the church, but Jory was behind him, his short sword drawn. The man ran into it before he saw it. It struck upwards below his breastbone killing him instantly. Jory was twisted sideways by the man's weight and nearly fell with him. Jory's sword was torn from his hand. He stood over the body and heard Raoul's voice.

"Well done, boy. Your first kill in my service. Now retrieve your sword and cut Father Waestan's bonds."

Jory rolled the body of his victim and pulled his sword from its chest. He realised he was shaking. He felt a mixture of pride and horror, of power and shame, all at one time, but pride was winning. He wiped the blade in the guard's tabard and moved to cut Waestan free.

The priest stared at Sir Raoul.

"You, Sir, are of the devil."

"That I may be, but I am alive. Now in your stables are three fine horses. Sell them and use the money to help the poor. I do not think they will worry if the devil sent them food."

Raoul turned away from the priest.

"Father Waestan, my friend, can you walk?"

"I can manage, thank you. Lots of me hurts but I am well enough."

Raoul turned back to the priest.

"A wise devil would end your life now, so no one would know what happened here. Make up any story you like but promise me you will not mention Father Waestan's name. Promise me."

The priest stared at Raoul's face, trying to read his eyes.

"I promise. God forgive you, my son."

"It is a little late for that, Father, but believe me, if I hear you have broken your promise, I will return and seek you out. Remember that, a devil's promise. Come my friends."

Raoul led them out of the church and back along the dock to the Rhosmon. They boarded quickly and Edmon and his crew cast off. They sailed slowly out of Portsea and headed on a course across the water to France. Prious approached Raoul.

"Was Waestan in difficulty?"

"Let us just say that I do not think any of us will be able to return to England in what is left of our lifetimes. Next time just leave the horses on the dockside. Now, please, I just need some sleep."

Raoul settled in the stern as Prious helped Waestan.

"Are you in much pain, Father?"

"Only when I speak."

"Oh, I see. I will leave you in peace then. Was there much trouble?"

"Four dead cathedral guards. Three for Raoul and young Jory's first, all in the church. Raoul is going soft though. He did not kill the priest who saw it all."

Prious nodded and looked for somewhere to sit. The boat was quite crowded with the three horses in the bows, but luckily the weather was kind. They should not be at sea too long.

+++

The Rhosmon sailed through the rest of the day and into the night. Edmon stood high on the stern leaning against steering oar, holding the boat on long tack towards the French coast. . The wind was light but blew steadily and with the calm seas they had made good progress.

A large candle burned in a lantern hanging high on the mast, but it gave little light. Most of the light came from the moon which was getting larger every night. There was hardly a cloud in the night sky and both the moon and the stars were bright.

Everyone had slept at first, except for Edmon, but he had been aware that Harold had woken early and walked up to the bows. The old King stopped and talked to the horses who appreciated the company, then he stood in the bows looking ahead and up into the heavens.

Prious woke next. He stood and waved a hand at Edmon but did not call out for fear of waking anyone else. He saw Harold's outline in the bows and walked to join him.

"Good morning, Harold."

The old King turned to greet him.

"Ah, good morning Brother. The sea air suits me, it seems to fill my chest better, and that helps to clear the mind."

"Indeed Sire. Have you had any thoughts as to what you will do next?"

"Only thoughts, Brother. When we reach Radepont I will decide for certain, but I think I will travel on to Saxony and see if I can raise any support there. If there is none I shall not be too upset. I will never be well enough to fight again. I hate to admit it but my sons are useless, all of them, so I cannot rely on them. It may be time for me to quietly live out any life I have left to me, alone somewhere. What are you planning?"

"I think like you, we will get to Radepont and discus it there. I want to record what has happened so someone has a true account. The Normans have a habit of rewriting their history to suit themselves. I will take some time at Radepont and write up my diaries whilst it is all still fresh in my mind. Perhaps a few people will get to read the truth."

The sun began to rise in the east and they began to see the horizon darken and become ragged. It was the coast of France in the far distance.

As the light increased others began to awaken and start to stretch their legs and move about. Only Sir Raoul stayed prone in the stern. If he was awake he did not want to be. Evette tried to tidy up the blankets into a pile with little real success. With everybody standing in the stern of the boat it seemed very full.

Edmon swung the steering oar towards him and came across the wind more changing to a more south westerly course. Prious looked up at him and Edmon called down.

"I think we are a little too far east for Le Havre. I think in another hour or two we will be in the mouth of the Seine."

"What then?"

"We will see where the tide is. It should still be going out so we may be best to anchor off Le Havre for a while until it starts to come in. The Seine meanders terribly right up past Rouen. With the tide running out we will hardly make any progress upstream against it. Once it stops and turns we can come in on the flood and I will try to reach Rouen before it turns again. That is where I will land you. There is a wharf there where we can get the horses off."

"That will be fine. Thank you."

He turned to see Raoul sitting up. Evette had some ale for him, but he did not smile once while Prious watched them. Jory fussed about too, almost looking upset by all the attention Raoul was getting from Evette.

Waestan was still and sore. His nose felt bruised and his cut lip hurt. No matter how careful he was he kept opening the cut, but he was actually in good spirits.

It was indeed nearly two hours before they anchored off Le Havre. Edmon strongly advised against going ashore. The soldiers in Rouen were much less inquisitive than those in Le Havre.

The crew had raised a blanket as a curtain across part of the stern so everyone had some privacy, for which Evette was especially grateful. Jory cleared the deck behind the horses and made sure they were fed and watered.

Eventually the crew raised the anchor and they sailed into the Seine. Edmon made everybody stay right up in the bows or sit down in the stern. The river swept in large bends in a general direction east of south towards Rouen and then on down to Paris. For every mile they travelled south however they sailed five or six times the distance around the bends. The boat was hard to handle but the crew knew what they were doing. They did not know the river well at all though. Edmon had sailed up to Rouen once, some years before.

Prious and Waestan stood in the bow. With all the twists and turns Prious preferred to be well away from the swinging beam on the mainsail. They had experienced bends in a river sailing up the Fal but they were tighter and the tidal flow was less strong.

"How are you feeling, Father?"

Prious was staring ahead up the river as he asked.

"You mean bodily or mentally?"

"Both really."

"Bits of me hurt, and do not make me smile, but I am alive, which is much better than those four guards in the church. They were not kind men but Raoul showed no mercy, even before he really knew what was happening. I am worried about our friend."

"In what way?"

"Well, we have both seen what he can do. He is a killer when he needs to be. He walked in and killed two men before they even realised they were in a fight. Then it was only two to one. I realise now he had sent Jory in to split the four of them up. Then he started the mind games. It worked on one. One he killed, the other turned to run and ran straight into Jory's sword. Raoul will turn that boy into a killer if the lad lives long enough."

"We have both seen Raoul do that sort of thing before. Why was this different?"

"Maybe it was not. Perhaps it was my imagination, knowing now what he has been through, but it really did seem as if he just did not care if he lived or died."

They stood in silence for a while, watching the river banks.

"I will talk to him when I can get him alone. I am not sure if he has ever cared. He told me once, you might have been there, that the only way he can be a soldier is to assume he is going to be killed fighting, that way, every time he survives he is winning. One day, he knows, his luck will run out."

Waestan nodded gently.

"Otherwise I feel, well, confused. I just need a little time. One day I am in Devonshire, happily working in Exeter Cathedral for Bishop Leofric. The next day I am working for Sir Baldwin de Redvers and the King. The next day I am in Winchester, working for Archbishop Stigand, or am I working for Bishop Odo. Then I am in Cornwall mixed up in spying and killing. Then I am deceitfully extracting information from an old lady. Before I know it I am smuggling a deposed King, who is supposed to be dead, out of the country to France where it is assumed I must make a new life. It may just take a day or two for me to come to terms with it all."

Prious clapped a hand on Waestan's back. He could not help but laugh.

"Oh dear, my poor friend. Put like that I can see your point, but do not tell me you have not enjoyed it all, felt alive."

"Perhaps so, at times, but I have had enough, as we have discussed. No, a quiet life in France for a while will suit me nicely."

They talked quietly in the bows until Rouen came into sight.

+++

The wharf at Rouen was busy. The Rhosman was lucky to find a berth there, but having done so, it took some time to find a winch to lift the horses off her deck.

Rouen had been the first capital of Normandy. It had grown up as a city on the Seine's eastern side. Originally the east bank of the Seine was supposed to have remained as French but Normandy had spread east and the border between Normandy and Picardie had become blurred. Even Vexin, just north of Paris had been absorbed into Normandy, which was why Sir Raoul's family home had moved from Archere and Tirel-sur-Seine to Poix in Picardie.

Duke William, however, was not fond of Rouen. It held bad memories of his childhood and when he came to power he moved his capital to Caen, further west. The people of Rouen never really forgave him for downgrading their city and it weakened their allegiance to him.

Sir Raoul was insistent that everyone stayed aboard whilst the horses were unloaded and they could leave for Radepont. They would have to walk and share time on horseback.

Raoul went ashore to see the commander of the docks. He was pleased to find it was still an old friend he had known since childhood. They exchanged greetings and Raoul explained that they had left England speedily after he had upset King William over a woman. They drank some wine together before Raoul made his farewells having cleared their way south and the Rhosmon's release from port.

They made their farewells to Edmon and the ship's crew. Edmon had worked for Prious for over a month now and had been well paid for it. They parted with genuine gratitude on both sides.

Harold and Evette rode and the others walked as they left Rouen on the road south to Paris. It ran almost due south, cutting off one of the Seine's last huge twists and re-joining the river just before the Andelle flowed into it. A strong wooden bridge crossed the Andelle there but Raoul led his fellow travellers eastwards along the north bank before they could cross it. They had made good progress that day and Sir Raoul suggested they camp for the night at the edge of the forest that grew up to the Andelle's bank.

The weather looked as if it might rain through the night, and although they were not many hours from his home, Raoul felt it best to bed down comfortably before darkness and any rain.

Prious tried to catch Raoul alone. He wanted to talk to him, but Raoul managed to stay close to Evette and Joly, which was easy for him as they both seemed to compete for his attention.

Between them all they built up a good fire with plenty of spare wood and settled for the night. They were an odd company but they slept well and were all awake with the dawn.

They breakfasted on the food they had left that they had carried from Rouen and began their journey along the bank of the Andelle. The track was little used and flooded on occasion. Progress was slow and the hills rose on both sides of the valley. It was early afternoon when the bank they followed widened into a flat grassy area and a small chateau appeared before them. It stood beside the tree covered slope on one side and the Andelle across the grass on the other.

The track they had been following swung sharply to their right where it crossed the Andelle over an old wooden bridge. A smaller track led straight on towards the building.

As they approached the chateau they could see a small spring that bubbled up into a pond of clear water. From the pond a narrow stream, that a man could step over, crossed the grassy field and flowed into the Andelle.

They stopped in front of the chateau and the main doors opened outwards. An old man and woman appeared and rushed to welcome Raoul. He turned to the others who were dismounting and gathered at the foot of the steps that led up to the doors.

"Fellow travellers, these are my friends and housekeepers, Jean and Ellen. They will be looking after our welfare. They care for my home whilst I am away, which is often a lot. Come in, please. Jory, if you would help Jean with the horses then join us."

They entered the hallway. It was not lavish but comfortable. Ellen brought wine for everyone.

"The house is not large, although, as you can see, there is much space around it to enlarge it over time. For tonight, Harold and Evette will have a bedroom each to themselves, Prious and Waestan I must ask to share, and Jory can sleep in my room."

They drank and talked for a while. Much had been discussed on the journey from Rouen but nothing had been decided exactly. Jean and Jory returned from seeing to the horses and Raoul banged his goblet on the table.

"Jean and Ellen will show you to your rooms. Please settle yourselves in and do as you wish until dinner. I know Ellen will do us proud. We will talk this evening and have a restful night. Tomorrow we all begin a new life, so this evening we will drink to the old and welcome the new."

Raoul turned away quickly and left the hall by a door behind the staircase. Jean and Ellen led the others up the stairs to their respective rooms. Jory began to bring the few of Raoul's belongings from the horses into his room. It was mainly his mail and spare weapons. There was very little in the way of clothing.

Jory left the house to see if he could find Sir Raoul. He was sure he had left the house for some peace and quiet but he was worried about his master. He left the front of the house and walked towards the river. It was some sixty or seventy paces from the edge of the building to the bank of the river over uncut grass. Jory could make out the track of someone who had walked across the field leaving a trail of flattened grass.

There were trees growing along the river bank. They were spread every ten to fifteen paces. Jory followed the trail, turning upstream. A short way along he saw Sir Raoul. He was sitting on a wooden bench between the trees and looking out over the river. He approached slowly and quietly then broke the silence.

"Is all well, Sir?"

Raoul looked around quickly and smiled.

"Hello, my boy. Come and sit down."

Jory joined his master on the bench.

"I have put all your things in the room, Sir, and the horses are tended to."

"Good lad. I should have said something before but I have had too much on my mind."

Sir Raoul stretched out an arm and put a hand on Jory's shoulder.

"You have a decision to make, my boy, which will shape your future."

"What decision is that, Sir?"

"Well, tomorrow, or the next day at the latest, I will make my way east to my family home in Poix. It is not far, but I am going to say my farewells to any of my family that are there. I will take Harold with me and start him on his trip to Saxony. From Poix I will go south to Rome. There are many Normans in the south, all fighting for the Pope against the Moors. I will join them. You need to decide if you wish to come with me. I would welcome you with me but will happily release you if you wish to return to England."

"There is no decision for me to make, I will come with you. I will serve you and learn to become a knight."

"Believe me, my boy, I am delighted to hear that."

"Could I ask one thing, Sir?"

"Of course, what troubles you?"

"Will Evette be coming with us?"

Raoul laughed out loud.

"Oh, my boy, I am sorry, indeed not. No she has her freedom now, but she is free to remain here or return to England. I will not take her to war with us."

Raoul stood up and walked around the bench, standing behind it with his hands on Jory's shoulders.

"No, my lad. Where we are going is a man's world. We may live or we may die, but there will be no more women in my life. Come, boy, we will walk upstream a little. I want to remember the chateau from the east as the sun goes down behind it, then we will enjoy some wine and a good meal."

Jory had never felt so happy.

+++

They all gathered in the dining room as the sun finally sank and the glow from the candles and a large log fire made the room warm and inviting. Ellen had been cooking a range of meats and vegetables and Jean had opened some of the best wines they had to let them breathe and now poured them for everybody.

Prious stood next to Raoul and spoke quietly.

"You seem a little happier, my friend."

"Do I? I at least know what I am going to do now, and will tell you all shortly. You can all decide what you would like to do overnight."

"I am not sure what to expect."

"I hope you will be happy. I think you have had enough of the life you have been leading. Whilst you have been very good at the games you have been playing, I think there comes a time when you have ridden your luck enough."

Prious looked at Raoul and smiled.

"You may be correct. I do not know for certain."

Raoul called across the room.

"Waestan, come here."

The priest left Evette and walked towards Raoul.

"How are you recovering? I do not want you getting into any more trouble when I am not around to get you out of it."

Waestan paused and tried not to smile.

"I think people will stop bothering me. They will have heard what happens to people that do."

"I have a job for you Father. I will explain later."

Ellen began to bring in hot food platters and place them on the large central table. Raoul's voice filled the room.

"Come my friends, be seated. Bring your goblets. The night begins."

They sat around the table and made small talk whilst they ate and drank. It was the first evening in a number of weeks that they all felt relaxed and relatively secure. When they had all finished eating and their platters were cleared from the table, Raoul banged the table with his goblet. He leant forward as the others fell silent but he did not stand.

"My friends, it is time to tell you what I propose."

He paused and looked around the table. He had everyone's attention.

"Tomorrow I will leave with Jory and Harold for Poix, my family home. I will see Harold on the road east and north for Saxony where he will make his own destiny. Whist I am in Poix I will have drawn up a document handing over control of this chateau to Brother Prious, along with an annual allowance from my personal fortune, which is considerable and is housed in Poix. This allowance is for the upkeep of the building and the food and lodging for Brother Prious, Father Waestan and Evette for as long as they may wish to remain here. It will also ensure that Jean and Ellen have employment here for the rest of their lives. There will be a considerable surplus each year which Brother Prious may use as he sees fit on charitable causes among the poor of this area. Father Waestan, you, in return, will administer the estate and you should find there is much income from the estate which I have been very lazy about collecting. I wish this chateau to become a charitable place of God, and it will be for you to find your successors to continue the good works beyond your lifetimes."

There was silence as Raoul paused, but everyone's eyes were on him.

"I need you, Prious and Waestan, to consider whether you wish to do this for me and for the poor in this region. I would also like to think that you might gather around you other men of God to support your works. When all is settled in Poix I will leave for Rome. I am going to join the Pope's forces to fight the Moor's. Soldiering is the only life I know and I can do it well. I will teach Jory to be a better knight than I if I can stay alive long enough. Now fill your goblets and we will drink to the future."

Jory jumped to his feet and picked up a jug of wine. He walked to the table head and filled Raoul's goblet. Raoul drank deeply and stood himself.

"I will leave you all now to think on it and talk together. I need some fresh air before bed. Jory, I leave you to see everybody has all they require to drink. See Jean if you need more."

Raoul left the room and there was quiet for a while before Waestan spoke.

"I always wanted to administer an estate. I can make us money and you, Prious, can give it away."

Evette left the room and climbed the stairs. Harold stood and laughed.

"Sometimes people fall on their feet. Enjoy the rest of your evening."

He too left the room. Prious pushed back his chair.

"I take it you wish to do this then, Father?"

"Why, do you not?"

"No, no, I would not say that. I think we could make a good job of it. No, my concern is Sir Raoul and if he is doing all this for the right reasons. I need to talk to him first."

Waestan picked up his goblet.

"He is a grown man, he knows what he is doing. He is a trained killer. Believe me, I was in that church in Portsea. How could such a man settle down to a quiet life? He has to find a war to fight."

Waestan was suddenly aware of Jory staring at him.

"I am sorry, boy, but what I say is true."

"He has not been the same, Father, not since we left Porchester. I did not see it all, I was outside, but Evette has told me all that happened, first to Morwenna and herself, and then when Sir Raoul arrived. He killed the knight that raped and killed Morwenna, tore his throat out, but Evette killed the one who raped her before Sir Raoul could."

Prious interrupted them.

"What both of you say is true, but I want to speak with him. There is more I need to understand before I agree. Do you know where he is, Jory?"

"Not for certain, Brother, but I found him earlier by the river. It seemed to be a place he might go often. Walk to the river, turn upstream, and a few trees up there is a wooden bench on the bank. He could be there."

"I will go and look. Keep Father Waestan company, I will be back shortly."

Prious left by the front door and followed Jory's directions. The moon was bright between the broken cloud and he could see well. As he approached the bench he saw Raoul was indeed sitting there, looking out over the water. Raoul looked around as he heard Prious walking towards him.

"Good evening Brother. Have you had enough wine?"

"Too much, probably, if the truth were known. This must be a favourite place of yours."

"It is, Brother. When I found this place, what, four years ago or so, I stood here early one evening. The water eddies just beyond that tree and I watched the fish taking flies off the surface. It made me think about life. One moment a fly touched the water, purely by chance, just there, at that time, the next moment a fish rose and took him. The fly was dead, the fish was fed. Why was that fly there at that exact time and place? There must have been a hundred things happened before that could have meant the fly was somewhere else and would have lived. It is like a battle. You have to be so lucky to survive. I had this bench put here and I often come here to think."

"I see. Of all your decisions, are you sure this one you have made is the right one?"

"I believe so. You see, the fly was unlucky, the wrong place at the wrong time, but the fish was there because he knew flies sometimes come near the surface there. He was in the right place at the right time, but it was not luck, or if it was he made his own luck."

"I just wish to be sure you are leaving for the right reason, not just as a reaction to losing a loved one."

Sir Raoul looked at Prious, and Prious was shocked by the cold look in Raoul's eyes.

"A loved one? I have thought a lot about that since Morwenna's death. How in God's name could I have been in love with her? I hardly knew the girl. We had met once, lain together once. I killed her father, caused her to kill her brother, used her to get us out of the castle. No, I could not have loved her. She was a beautiful and attractive young woman and I led her away from her home, not to happiness but to her death. If I had not lost our way, or travelled faster, if something had delayed her killers on the way from Winchester, there are so many things that might have meant she was still alive. I have hardly slept since finding her dead without trying to change something, to make time go backwards, but she is still lying there on the bed, raped and murdered, dead."

"It must have been terrible to see her there, it will take time to get over, time to let the image fade."

"That is the worst part, Brother. The image in my mind. When I found her she was half on the bed. Her nightdress was ripped down at the front and her breasts were showing. It was also pulled up to her waist. She was naked below her waist, legs wide apart, just as she had been when her killer stood and left her. I can see every detail in my mind now."

"It is a terrible memory to have."

Prious realised Raoul now had tears pouring down his cheeks. He hadn't seen them at first in the dark.

"Oh, you bloody stupid monk. You do not understand, how could you understand? I am aroused by it. Every time I see her there I feel myself harden, I can feel it now, and I hate myself for it, and worse still, nothing else seems to arouse me anymore."

"Raoul I, I do not know what to say. What can I say?"

"There is nothing to say. You know it all now. I hate myself more than you can imagine, so I will go and fight for the Pope and be a fish until one day some Moor makes me a fly and has me for breakfast. So I need you to stay here and do good works with the fortune I have collected in Brittany and England and try to buy me some favour with your God, if he exists. I will need it I fear."

Raoul stood, moved around the seat and walked towards the house, leaving Prious sitting alone on the bench. Prious was trying to decide what to do, wishing he had found the right words, but it was too late now.

Raoul still felt his arousal under his leathers as he walked across the grass. He could not go back into the house like this. He turned into the stables and in the darkness he loosened his codpiece and took himself in hand. It was not long before his seed spurted over the straw at his feet and he leant against the wooden wall, putting himself away and regaining his breath. His mind was now in turmoil. Part of him felt at the height of his self-loathing, but for part of him it was the best moment of his day.

He walked back around to the front of the house and went straight up to his room. Prious had passed him whilst he was in the stable and was already with Waestan and Jory in the dining room.

Waestan was first to speak as Prious entered the room and poured himself a goblet of wine.

"Did you find him?"

"I did, and we spoke at some length."

Waestan and Jory both looked at Prious but he said no more.

"So have you come to any decision or conclusion?"

Waestan could not contain his impatience.

"I will stay here and we will make this place a house of God."

"I am delighted, Brother. What did Raoul say to convince you?"

"Our friend, Sir Raoul, is determined on a course that I have no will to deny him. Go with him, Jory, and serve him well. His mind is troubled but only he can mend it. He came back before me, so I suggest Jory, you go to him and see if he needs you."

"Yes, Brother, I will, and thank you for your concern for him. I will not let him down."

Jory left the room. Waestan and Prious sat alone near the fire. The candles were dwindling and room grew darker. They had both replenished their goblets.

"You are unhappy, Brother. There is no denying. What did he say that troubles you so?"

"He spoke of love, Father, or lack of it, but that was just hiding the truth. He spoke of chance, even fate, of luck in life. His mind is very confused, but he is determined to seek his destiny as a soldier. He goes to fight for the Pope, God's voice in Christendom, yet he questions our God's very existence. We will do as he wishes, Waestan and perhaps we can save his soul. Now, as we are sharing a room, I suggest we retire together whilst this fine wine allows us to walk unaided."

Raoul had climbed the stairs to his room. He did not wish to talk anymore. He entered his bedroom and closed the door. He assumed Jory would join him once Prious had returned and he realised his master had also.

He hesitated as he heard a noise behind him. He spun around. Evette stood beside the bed lit by the warm light of the fire and the few candles that still burned. She was completely naked.

"I have been waiting for you, Sir."

"Get some clothes on, Evette, and go to your room."

"No, Sir, listen, I owe you my freedom, but now you cast me off. I wish to replace Morwenna in your heart and in your bed."

"Dear God, Evette, get dressed and leave me."

The door opened behind him and Jory entered the room. His eyes first just saw Raoul's back but then he saw Evette haloed in the light from the fire. She looked very enticing to him.

"I am sorry, Sir, I am intruding."

"No you are not, Jory. Evette was just leaving."

They both saw the tears on Evette's face.

"I am sorry, Sir, I did not realise I am so unattractive to you."

"You are not unattractive, my child, not at all. I just do not wish to be attracted to anybody just now. Jory, find her clothes and take her to her room. Stay with her and comfort her if you will."

Evette picked her nightdress up from the end of the bed and pulled it over her head. Jory opened the door and led her out.

Raoul walked to the bed and lay out on it. He had not undressed, just lay on the covers. He shut his eyes and Morwenna was there, on the bed before his eyes. He sat up and shouted.

"Dear God help me!"

He laid back again as Jory re-entered the room.

"Did you call, Sir? I thought I heard you call."

"No, boy, I did not. Is that poor stupid girl in bed?"

"Yes, Sir, she is."

"Perhaps you should be with her, my boy. Give her what she needs."

"It is not me she lusts after, more is the pity. Let me help you undress, Sir."

"No, just leave me boy. Make yourself comfortable and sleep."

"Are you sure you are comfortable, Sir, you do not need anything more from me?"

"No, Jory, nothing. Now please, just leave me."

"Yes, Sir. Sleep well."

"And you, boy, and you."

+++

Jory woke early and left the room quietly. Raoul was awake and heard him go but remained where he was.

Jean and Ellen were up early too, preparing breakfast for all in the dawn's new light. Ellen gave Jory a warm smile.

"You are down early, young Sir. Are you hungry? There is hot oats and milk in the pot and eggs and salmon to follow if you are."

"Thank you, that sounds wonderful. I have a day's travel ahead and a full stomach is always a help."

"I have some cold food packed for you to carry with you."

"Thank you again. As soon as I have eaten I will take it and ready the horses."

"You are welcome, young Sir, but you must promise my husband and I one thing. Look after the master for us. He has been so good to us. We realise he is sorely troubled but he is a good kind man to many."

"That is an easy promise to make."

Harold entered the room and grunted a greeting to Jory whilst he sat opposite him. Jory replied.

"Good day, Sire, you are awake early."

"An old man like me needs little sleep. I do little enough to tire myself and have done little but rest for the last two years."

Ellen brought them each a bowl of hot oats and milk. Harold looked up at her.

"Thank you, lady. Do you have any honey? I used to have oats with honey on top."

"I will find you some."

Jory and Harold ate together in silence. Ellen brought some honey then some whipped egg and thin sliced salmon.

Jory finished and left the dining room just before Prious and Waestan arrived. They entered together and greeted Harold who rose from the table as they sat.

"Excuse me Brother, Father, I will take a short walk before we leave. I will be in the saddle all day."

They enjoyed a hearty breakfast. Ellen brought in a fresh jug of cider.

Waestan laughed as he saw it.

"Thank you, Ellen. I could get used to this."

"Likely you will, Father, likely you will."

"Ellen, tell me, does anyone ever swim in that spring pool at the front of the house, or does anyone ever drink the water?"

"Not swim, Father. Travellers will sometimes leave the track and collect fresh water from the stream."

Prious looked up from his food.

"What makes you ask such a thing?"

"Just an idea I have. We should let it be known that the spring has healing qualities, that bathing in it and drinking it can cure all types of illness. I will bless the spring formally of course and we can charge people to use it. It will not be long before somebody gets well after using the water and we will have our first miracle. Our income will rise with the spring's reputation."

"You have a very cynical mind sometimes, Father."

"Inventive, Brother, inventive."

The door opened and Raoul entered.

"Good day, Brother Prious, Father Waestan."

They chorused a greeting as Raoul sat at the table head. Ellen entered from the kitchens.

"Ah, good morning, Ellen. Just egg and salmon for me please."

"Yes, Sir Raoul, of course."

She wiped a tear from her cheek as she spoke.

"None of that now, Ellen. I am relying on you and Jean to look after these two. They will not be as easy as me, I am sure."

Raoul smiled at his friends.

"Where is everybody?"

Waestan answered.

"Jory is readying the horses, I believe, and Jean is probably helping him. Harold is taking a short walk. We three are here, but Evette we have not seen."

Ellen came back in with Raoul's food.

"Thank you, Ellen. When you have a moment, would you kindly go to Evette's room and ask her to join us?"

"Yes, Sir, I will do that now."

Ellen left by the hall door. Raoul had not eaten much when she re-entered the room. She had a worried look on her face.

"Sir Raoul, she is not in her room, Sir. Her bed is disturbed but does not look slept in. Shall we search the house, Sir?"

Raoul sat back from the table and sighed.

"No, thank you, Ellen. If she is in the house she will appear when she is ready. If not, she has left during the night. She is free to go and do as she pleases."

Ellen went back into the kitchen. Prious lent forward as he spoke.

"I presume she is upset you are not taking her with you."

Raoul shook his head slowly.

"No, Brother, more than that I am afraid. After I left you last night she was waiting for me in my room."

"She wanted to persuade you to stay?"

Raoul laughed.

"In a sense. She was naked. She wanted to replace Morwenna, in my life and in my bed. After our conversation you can imagine I was not at all receptive. I sent her back to her room, Jory took her."

"I see, so you think she has gone?"

"I fear so, yes. If she has gone back, the way we came, so be it. If she has tried to be clever and gone east so we overtake her, then there is more disappointment for her ahead. A problem I do not wish. Enough, it is time I departed. I am not one for long goodbyes. I will fetch the others and see you at the front shortly."

He stood and left the room. He took a door to the rear of the staircase and went to the stables through the back of the building.

Jory and Jean had just finished readying the horses. They had saddled one of their spare horses for Harold. It was healthy enough but was of little use to the chateau. Raoul's courser carried their pack, although there was little of it. The weight was Raoul's chainmail and shield. They had little provisions or other equipment as they would gather all they needed for the journey south at Poix.

"Thank you Jean. Look after Ellen for me, and help those men of God to settle."

Raoul laughed as he said it.

"I will, Sir. God speed you on you journey, and thank you for our security."

"Come, boy. Mount up."

Jean helped Sir Raoul up into his saddle then walked quickly through the house. He collected Ellen on the way and found Prious and Waestan already on the front steps of the chateau.

Harold was with them too, having returned from his walk.

Raoul and Jory rode around the side of the chateau and stopped in front of the steps. Jean helped Harold mount and stood back beside Ellen.

"No farewell speeches. God bless us all."

Raoul turned his mount and rode down the track past the spring. Reaching the main track he led Jory and Harold left and over the old wooden bridge across the Andelle. He turned left again past the chateau on the far side of the river, eastwards towards Poix.

They had all called their farewells as Raoul, Jory and Harold turned away and watched them cross the river until they disappeared from sight behind the chateau. Ellen was crying as Jean led her inside.

A movement at an upstairs window caught Prious' eye. Evette stood watching the departure.

Prious and Waestan remained on the chateau steps. Waestan turned to Prious.

"Will we ever see him again, Brother? I shall miss him."

"No. He will not return. He has gone to seek his death but I fear he may take a long time to find it. In the meantime happiness has left him. I just hope the boy survives him."

"I think he will. He is a bright lad."

"That he is, Father. Come now, you have a pond to bless."

Epilogue

Penny and I got out of the car and quietly closed the doors. I opened the back and we each took a spade. I closed the rear door and we climbed the steps up to St Cornelly church, closing the wrought iron gate behind us. With the doors in front of us I led Penny to the left and around the corner to the west end wall. It was strange to think that what we had been reading about Brother Prious and the church had all happened almost one thousand years before.

I should have asked permission, of course, but I knew it would be refused, and I simply could not wait to look. There was very little chance of anything surviving all that time buried behind the church but it was worth a try.

Prious had said a pace out from the wall, which would be under the grass just beyond the edge wall. I was going to stand with my back to the middle of the wall and take a pace away when realisation hit me.

"I'm sorry Penny, I'm a bloody fool. We are wasting our time."

"What's the problem?"

"Now I am standing here it is blinding obvious to me but I just had not thought. A couple of hundred years after Prious' time here they doubled the size of the church. With the slope at this west end, they built out at the other end. All they added this end. was the bell tower, but it wasn't here when Prious buried the books. If anything remained it must have been destroyed when they dug the foundations of the tower. One pace from the old wall line would be just at the edge of the tower and now under that concrete surround. I'm sorry I've wasted our time."

"No worries, my love. I could do with a couple of days break here in Cornwall."

"Come on then, we'll head on into Portscatho and get some sleep. The cottage shouldn't be too cold."

We walked back down to the car and replaced the spades in the back. We climbed in the front and I reversed back then drove up the lane. Turning right we dropped down the hill to Tregony bridge. As we crossed it Penny laughed.

"Maybe we should be digging over there. Excalibur and the armour are under there somewhere."

"Indeed they are. When I write this up, and if anybody believes the truth, perhaps one day we'll see people with metal detectors walking those fields."

"You're going to write it up then?"

"I think so. To me the most interesting thing is that it explains why the whole King Arthur thing is all spoken legend. There is no recorded proof anywhere. King William, through Bishop Odo, had any evidence of the real Arthur destroyed, and of course the family connection fascinates me.

"What do you think happened to Sir Raoul?"

"I don't know. It would appear he went to fight in Sicily, but according to Prious he left for Poix in the mid-summer of ten sixty-eight. The monk told me he left in ten seventy. Perhaps he took King Harold all the way to Saxony, perhaps he just delayed in Poix on family business, perhaps he returned to Radepont for a while. That will have to be my next line of research, and perhaps another story."